This is a work of fiction. Similarities to real people, places, or events are entirely coincidental.

THE UN-QUEEN

First edition. June 1, 2019.

Copyright © 2019 Fiona West.

ISBN: 978-1-7328774-5-0

Written by Fiona West.

To my parents: Your sickeningly sweet relationship is the best. Thank you for being my cheerleaders and my inspiration. I love you both!

SETTING THE STAGE...

ONCE UPON A TIME, ABELIA, princess of the queendom of Brevspor, and Edward, prince of the kingdom of Orangiers, signed a marriage contract at the tender age of twelve. Having been best friends since they met, their wise parents saw that it would be futile to try to keep them apart. It didn't much matter anyway; neither of them were slated to inherit the throne in their respective countries. But as in so many fairy tales, tragedy struck, and everything changed for our princess when her four older sisters perished in a tragic fire. Now the heir apparent, her heart was broken, her health damaged, but none took her pleas for help seriously. So at the age of sixteen, Abbie fled the only home she'd ever known, the only land she'd ever known, changed her last name and forged a new life in Gardenia, on the other side of the continent. (You can read this story for free in The Streetdwellers.)

But she wasn't the only one whose fairy tale had taken a sharp left turn. Edward's older brother Lincoln attempted a coup, which Edward foiled by accident, putting him also in line for the throne at age 21. Lincoln mounted forces in another country to fight back, and Edward believed he needed the political influence of his betrothed behind him to win. He sent emissaries to find Abbie, and they took her on a wild journey across the Unveiled, an "uncivilized" part of the continent where magic is uncontrolled and unpredictable, where she made friends and enemies in equal measure.

But Abbie's fears over fulfilling their contract were due to her health, not her handsome prince: having finally been diagnosed with lupus, she believes that her chronic illness is incompatible with the stress of a royal life. After looking over their contract, she finds a loophole: it never says she has to be queen. Because they were both in line to ascend in their countries, the marriage contract was left intentionally vague about what role each person would play for the other. So they decide to marry, but that Abbie will play no part politically, hence the derogatory nickname that becomes the title of this book: The Un-Queen.

Let's find out what our lovers are up to now, shall we?

CHAPTER ONE

141 days to the wedding

ABBIE WAS JUST WASHING up the dishes when there was a knock at the door. That is to say, she was sitting on the couch, snacking, her e-reader propped up on her knees, her hair in a bun, wearing yoga pants and a sweatshirt, thinking that she should be doing the dishes, when there was a knock at the door. Abbie checked her watch; 3:02 p.m. That couldn't be Parker. His security had come by around 9 a.m. to sweep her apartment for bugs, bombs, and terrorists, much to her amusement. They even checked the magic powering her fridge, which was apparently making a "suspicious noise." She made them coffee. They said he'd pick her up at 7:00 for dinner.

Therefore, when someone knocked at 3:02, she ignored them.

The knock came again.

"Go away!" she yelled through a mouthful of popcorn.

"Are you certain? I've come all this way, and I really thought we were past this stage in our relationship," came a muffled, accented voice from the other side of the door.

She was off the couch and throwing the door open in record time. Parker stood there, scowling.

"Abs, you didn't check the peephole. You've got to look before you just let anyone in. I could've been a murderer. A very well-dressed murderer."

The ex-princess dragged him into her apartment by his tie, wagging her eyebrows at his security to make them snicker before she slammed the door. "Oh, hush. I'd know your pomposity anywhere; I could smell it wafting in from the hallway."

Parker mockingly sniffed an armpit, then grimaced. "You're right. How long has this been going on?"

"Since the day we met. You asked me if I would care to 'take a turn around the grounds' with you. You were seven. Why haven't you kissed me yet?"

Grinning, Parker moved into her space, their noses touching, backing her into the wall. "I was politely waiting for you to finish speaking."

"You shouldn't wait for that, it could take forever," she said.

"Well, good news, then; we've got forever."

Abbie slid her arms up over his shoulders. "Say that again."

"We've got forev—" She cut him off, pulling him closer with both arms, kissing him hard.

He pulled back playfully. "Did you miss me?"

Abbie shook her head, leaning in for another hard kiss.

"Not even the tiniest bit?"

She shook her head again, grinning.

Parker sighed. "You're such a liar."

"I know. I have to keep you from getting a swollen head with everyone kissing your royal backside all the time. Did you miss me?"

"I gladly admit that I did. But only every minute of every hour of every day we've been apart, which is 20 days, 480 hours, or 23,800 minutes."

"Pathetic."

"Ouch."

"Buck up, Your Majesty." Using his title reminded Abbie who exactly was pressed up against her, and she paled. She wasn't ready for him to see her apartment . . . This was not the first impression she'd intended at all. He was turned away from the worst of it, but he could see into the kitchen if he turned his head . . .

He brought his mouth closer to her ear and lowered his voice. "You went tense. Are you concerned that I'm looking at the mess?"

She raised an eyebrow even though he couldn't see it. "Stop reading my brain."

"Stop making it so obvious. Also, anyone who shows up four hours early has to realize the place may not be ready for company. Also, I couldn't care less. I'm here to see you, not your apartment." True to his word, Parker did not look around, but Abbie didn't feel better. She still knew it was there.

"Just go out for ten minutes—fifteen, tops—and I'll take care of the worst of it." She shoved him toward the door, but Parker dug in his heels.

"Oh, I'm not leaving. I just got here!"

"You gonna fight me?" She pushed him again, and he laughed and adopted a lower stance so she couldn't tip him over.

"Oh no, I'm not as foolish as I look. I'd never fight you."

"Good."

"Additionally, I don't have to."

Abbie crossed her arms. "Why is that?"

"Because of that." He pointed over her shoulder, and when she turned to look, he slipped past her and into the living room, flopping down on the couch, its denim slipcover shifting at the corners.

"Hey!"

"I'm disappointed, darling. That's the oldest trick in the book. Your siblings clearly didn't prepare you adequately for a life in politics."

She came around the couch cautiously as he surveyed the place.

"Where's this mess, then?"

"Ha ha."

"I'm not joking, actually. Does this embarrass you? I didn't realize you were a neat freak."

Abbie's face reddened. "You can't be serious. Look: dishes in the sink, clean laundry still unfolded in the basket, shoes under the couch, my bed unmade . . ." The flicker of interest in his eyes at the mention of her bed wasn't lost on Abbie, but she decided not to mention it. "Popcorn on the floor."

Parker helped himself to a handful out of the bowl. "Abs, this is nothing. The dishes are clearly from your lunch; you did the ones from breakfast. Fold while we catch up, and I can survey this bed situation later." He winked, and she allowed her lips to hook into a half smile. "This popcorn is very good; what's on it?"

Abbie sat down next to him, one leg curled under her. It felt odd to be so alone with him; they'd always had Rubald and Rutha as a buffer. He didn't seem uncomfortable in the least, and she wondered how he managed it. More practice managing his royal emotions, maybe.

"Avocado oil and sea salt."

"I must mention it to my cooking staff."

"Dude, you can make your own popcorn."

"On second thought, perhaps I will." His attention shifted to her e-reader. "You were reading?"

She nodded. "Not a romance, sorry."

"More's the pity. Though it would explain why you attacked me in the entryway . . . so unladylike."

Abbie grinned.

"So what *are* you reading?" he asked.

"Work stuff. Government standards for reclaiming food waste for livestock." Abbie pulled the laundry basket toward her and subtly pushed the clean underwear to the bottom as she pulled out a Brevspor Bengals T-shirt to fold.

Parker made a face. "That's what you're reading on a Saturday? Shouldn't you be doing something fun?"

"I was saving my fun for when *you* got here."

"Why didn't you say so?" Parker tossed his popcorn over his shoulder and launched himself at her, Abbie shrieking with laughter as he mauled her, covering her neck with loud kisses. There was a knock at the door, and they paused.

"Everything okay in there?" It was Dean, Parker's lead security.

"Yes, thank you," Abbie called, her laughter returning. "Everything's fine!"

"You're supposed to be protecting me, not her!" Parker called over the sofa.

"We like her better!"

"And who can blame them?" he murmured, his eyes still teasing as his lips went back to her neck, and Abbie let out a happy sigh as he laid her back on the couch. "I missed you, darling."

"I missed you, too, hon," Abbie said, the blood quickly leaving her brain in favor of parts farther south, parts that were apparently very pleased to be in Parker's presence again.

"I knew it."

"Shut up."

CHAPTER TWO

ABBIE BROUGHT HIS FACE up to hers and melded their mouths together. His deep groan made her sternum vibrate, and she giggled, cringing a little inwardly at how silly she sounded. Is this what love did to people? He'd been here less than ten minutes, and they were already horizontal . . . not that she minded. When they'd been kissing for a while, he stopped caring whether he was crushing her, releasing his full weight, pressing her into the cushions. She wouldn't have minded if she could breathe. Maybe if they moved to her bed, they could lie side by side . . . Good Woz, where did that thought come from?

He noticed her wonky breathing and sat up, pulling her with him, pushing the loose bits of her hair away from her face.

"Sorry, I forgot you need oxygen."

"Quite all right," Abbie said, imitating his accent. "Where are you taking me tonight?"

"This is your town; what's your favorite place?"

Abbie didn't hesitate. "Martissant's, hands down." She salivated at the thought of their six-mushroom risotto.

"Then I guess it's good that I called Lauren three weeks ago and asked her what your favorite was so I could get us a reservation."

"And when you say reservation, you mean that you bought the place out for the night for security reasons?"

"That's correct, yes." He pulled out his phone, glanced at the screen, then put it away.

She reached for a pair of capris in the laundry basket, glancing up at him. "You can take a call if you need to."

He glared at her reproachfully. "I'm not wasting our precious time together on work."

"But king work isn't regular work. I realize that," she said as she smoothed out the creases. "I don't want nations to perish because we were making out."

He cleared his throat. "Abs, look at me, and hear this as I intend it." She put down her folding, and Parker reached for her hand. "The rest of the world can take care of itself for a little while. Right now, it's you and me. This weekend, I am available to no one else."

"Not a full weekend," she countered, and he nodded.

"No, not a full weekend, but it's the best I could do. You're on my calendar now most weekends, and the next person who 'adjusts' your time gets fired."

Abbie smiled; she didn't mind him defending them to his staff one bit. "I got you something."

Parker looked confused as she pulled her laptop out from under the couch and powered it up. "Are you showing me a picture of it?"

"No, impatient pants, just hold on." Abbie scowled at the screen. She could feel Parker still gazing at her, and she tried not to squirm under his open regard. "Ah! Here we go." She turned the screen and plunked it onto the coffee table in front of him.

"What's this? Football?"

She nodded. "To distract you while I shower. I got a paid subscription."

He scowled. "You didn't have to do that."

"Why wouldn't I? You're going to be here more often, so now we can watch those dudes run up and down the field together."

He seemed to be holding back a smile. "It's a pitch, not a field."

"See?" She gesticulated toward the screen as she stood. "I have so much to learn."

He looked at her with skepticism. "Can you afford this?"

"Normal people just say thank you."

"Don't do that. I'm quite serious—can you afford this? I'd gladly repay you for it."

Her hands went to her hips as if drawn by a magnetic force, and she narrowed her gaze. "I'm not allowed to get you presents?"

Parker looked like he could sense the noose dangling in front of him. "No"—he shook his head slowly—"no, I didn't say that."

"Damn straight you didn't. I know I'm yours, but you're mine, too. I can skip a few meals if needed."

"Abbie, you are *not*—"

"I'm kidding! I'm kidding," she said, hands up, as she crossed to her bedroom door, pulling off her sweatshirt, revealing the cotton camisole she wore underneath.

"Where are you going?" There was an edge to his voice.

"I said I'm going to shower. I'll just be a minute; watch the football."

Parker muttered something under his breath, and Abbie crossed her arms.

"Sorry, I didn't catch that."

"I said it'll have to be the best match ever played to effectively distract me from the fact that you're naked in the next room."

Abbie grinned and blew him a kiss as she closed her bedroom door.

TRUE TO HER WORD, ABBIE didn't take long; she scrunched her curls with a light gel and let it hang down her back, applied lipstick, and slipped into her outfit. It was a faux wrap dress with tiny white polka dots on a dark-blue fabric and large creamy plumeria printed over the top. Mrs. Braun had sent some things with her when she left, knowing she'd be doing a few public appearances. It had been surprisingly hard to leave her . . . much harder than leaving Kurt, who had not called, written, texted, emailed or chirped her since their father's death. Jackass.

Excited to see his reaction, Abbie threw open her bedroom door . . . to silence. He'd passed out, shoes kicked off, football still playing. Abbie tiptoed over and made sure he was just asleep and not having a medical emergency. She was the one with the health issues, not him, but she still felt better when she heard him snoring softly. Abbie gently shook his shoulder.

"Parker. Parker, honey, I'm ready. Let's go eat." Her fiancé did not stir. Abbie sighed. He was going to be mad if she let him sleep, but what was she supposed to do, douse him with water? He clearly needed the rest.

Grabbing the quilt from her bed, she covered him up and kissed his head. Abbie retrieved her phone and e-reader from the coffee table and turned off the match. Slipping off her heels, she padded across the tiny apartment and opened the front door.

"I'm ordering Imaharan food; you guys want anything?"

The two security guards exchanged a glance. "We were under the impression that you two were going out; the carriage is ready for you."

Abbie held back a sneer. She was sick of carriages, but public trains were a security nightmare, walking was too dangerous for Parker, and cars were impossible inside the Veil. Someday, when they came out with a clean motorized alternative that didn't give everyone in the city asthma, she'd be first in line to get one.

"Unfortunately, His Majesty finds himself royally exhausted and hath sadly lost consciousness upon the royal sofa whilst his beloved doth make herself ready."

Dean sighed and shook his head, pulling out his phone.

"Do you have some thoughts about that, Dean?"

He straightened. "No, ma'am. Here's an approved list of restaurants . . . How would you like to be addressed?"

"Ms. Anderson is fine here."

"Very good, Ms. Anderson. We like tu-fut duck and New Year's chicken with extra rice."

Waldo leaned over and whispered something, and Dean nodded.

"And your fiancé likes broken egg soup and the kitchen sink with noodles. There should be an account set up to pay for it under Crawford. We'll send someone to oversee the preparation."

Abbie nodded and started back inside, then turned.

"You can't drink on duty, can you?"

They shook their heads, grimacing.

"Well, when you're done, there's cold beer in my fridge. I can't drink it, so you'll have to help me out."

She went back into her still apartment, crossed to her bedroom, and called in their order. Her disappointment rang loud in the quiet room. She understood; she understood completely. But she and Parker still had so little time together. She wasn't supposed to quit her job until Tenth Month. Maybe she should move to Orangiers now. Then it wouldn't just be the odd weekend here and there. She didn't have the money to go back and forth much, and she just didn't feel right about letting Parker pay for her travel, not yet. Honestly, that was going to be tough even after they were married.

Should I change? Nah. He can still enjoy the fashion effort whenever he wakes up. Abbie curled up in bed, lost in thought. She could see him through the door and tried to read, but found herself just staring at his face; such a handsome face. The last few weeks had been rough. He'd barely had time to call her; a few times, she'd already been asleep when he'd found a moment. Based on their emails, she knew he was only getting five or six hours of sleep a night. It made sense that he passed out every time he slowed down enough to rest.

The delivery gal's quiet knock startled her, and she hurried to answer the door. She handed out bowls and forks to Dean and Waldo as they passed the rest of the food inside. Though they were always polite and appropriate with her, she would not want to meet either of them in a dark alley under any circumstances. Something lurked just behind their smiles that told her they were not to be trifled with, even without taking into account their giant biceps. She was glad to be on the same side.

Abbie put their food in the fridge and started back to her bedroom, then stopped. *How often is he here, in the flesh?* Carefully, she crawled over him and squeezed herself between Parker and the back of the couch. She curled up next to him, her head on his chest, her arm across his middle. His was so deliciously flat compared to hers. He sighed and she smiled, inhaling his gingery scent mixed with hers from the quilt. *Is this what our quarters will smell like? No, our house will probably smell boring, like lemons and lavender, because some well-meaning housekeeper will clean everything within an inch of its life five times a day.*

Yes, a rough few weeks. The fallout from their engagement announcement had been swift; legal experts, parliament, and the palace advisors had all objected, despite the support of the general population being at 70 percent. Rohnhart had been right; it was a shitstorm. And it was far from over. Just this week, a sixth lawsuit had been filed against her by the Ravensdale Monarchy Preservation Society. As Orangiersians, they weren't allowed to sue Parker, the reigning monarch, but they could sue her six ways from Sunday, and so they were, claiming she and Parker were twisting the language of the contract and that she was obligated to play the part of queen. She couldn't see how the two of them were going to resolve it all in six months' time.

Yet as she lay there, listening to his heart beating and his steady breathing, feeling his body pressed against hers, she felt for the first time in weeks that it was going to be okay. That they were going to be okay, together. Her apartment was often quiet, but at that moment, it felt peaceful, too. Tears of gratitude welled up, but she blinked them back, closed her eyes, and fell asleep.

CHAPTER THREE

PARKER'S BUZZING PHONE woke him. He tried to lift his hips to reach into his back pocket for it and found that there was an auburn-haired woman in a fantastic blue dress asleep on his chest impeding the movement.

Wait. Abbie . . . date night. Fermented fish guts.

She stirred. Her hair smelled like eucalyptus and peppermint. He wrapped his arms around her and squeezed.

"Before I kill you for not waking me so I could take you out for a proper date, did you have a nice nap?"

"For your information, I tried to wake you. It didn't take."

"What time is it?"

"8:15."

"Let's go."

"What? No, it's too late now."

"I paid for the whole night. Let's go."

Abbie sighed. "Parker . . ."

"On your feet, woman. Let's go!" At this, she raised an eyebrow, and he grinned. "Does it help matters if I say you look ravishing, and by that, I mean that I would like to ravish you slowly in that dress in about six months' time?"

Abbie's cheeks flushed. "That's a very ambiguous statement; what definition of *ravish* are we using? Will you be carrying me off by force? Are you planning to rob me?"

"No, darling, the other definition; enrapture, fill with intense delight. Though I'm willing to employ one of the oth-

17

ers—not the worst one—if you don't get off the couch and put your pretty shoes on." She turned to look squarely into his eyes, and he could see her genuine confusion.

"Why is this so important to you?"

"Because I'm not here when you need me! I can't hear about your day, I can't touch you, I can't . . ." He'd underestimated how frustrating this was going to be. Not the physical part; that was just as awful as he'd anticipated. But the emotional part, the heart part. After wanting to be with her so deeply for years, he'd thought getting to spend time together twice a month was a step forward, but it was like drinking salt water; the more he drank, the thirstier he became.

"I just want to do something special for you. I want to make you feel treasured when I'm here. Because most days, I know I'm letting you down."

Her mouth dropped open. "Edward, you did not just say that. You take that back right now."

He shook his head, afraid to meet her gaze.

She stood up. "Now you listen to me, future husband of mine, because I'm only going to say this once, and then we're going to go eat ridiculously expensive food: *you are not letting me down.* You've got the toughest job on the continent; no one knows that better than I do. I know you're doing your best—"

"It isn't sufficient. Not for you."

Her voice went low, code lethal. "Do not interrupt me." Her stare leveled him, and he hoped to Woz she'd bring it to another context in the near future.

"Make no mistake, Your Majesty; I am no wilting flower, no lonesome puppy lying by the door, waiting for you to walk through it. I have a life and I'm living it. That doesn't mean I don't miss you . . ." Her voice cracked, and he could see how the emotion bothered her, that she wanted her words to carry weight and not manipulate him with tears. "I do miss you. But I'm okay. I love hearing from you, but I understand when you're too busy. As you may recall, I haven't called you every day, either." She crossed her arms.

"Are you finished?" He worked to keep his face serious. "Because I don't want to find out what happens if I interrupt you again . . ."

"You'd regret it."

"I believe you." He paused. "But I still want to be there for you."

"You are, hon. You will be." She reached out a hand. "Let's go."

DINNER WAS AMAZING. Lauren had chosen the restaurant well—an intimate place, a historic stone building covered in vines. Since the sun was down, they ate outside on the patio, which was lit up by candles that covered the unused tables. She got some kind of rice dish after confirming that there was no gluten in it, and he got a steak, which they cooked to a perfect medium-rare. Parker thought the chef seemed a little disappointed that he wasn't able to show off for them with something more complex, and that suspicion was confirmed when their waiter brought out several dishes they hadn't ordered: duck foie gras with peaches, crème fraîche, oats, and pecans; chilled garden zucchini soup that tasted as fresh as spring; some kind of salad he was happy to let Abbie monopolize, since it had goat cheese.

They talked about nothing. She told him stories about work, interpersonal conflicts, and he tried to commit the names of the main characters to memory. He told her about his new staff, legislation they were working on, his video game conquests, and the antics his best friends James, Saint, and Simonson reported back as they searched for his brother Lincoln to arrest him for treason (most recently, a hot sauce eating contest which had had disastrous consequences). If being away from her was like holding his breath, this was like hyperventilating, in the best way possible. He hated to have to tell her what he'd decided. As she finished her mango sorbet, he leaned forward.

"I have to tell you two things I don't want to tell you."

She set down her spoon and patted her mouth with her napkin. "Shoot."

"Do you want the good news first or the bad news?"

"Always the bad news first."

"I'm assigning you a security detail."

She didn't miss a beat. "Here's five reasons why that's a terrible idea."

He massaged his temples. "Abs..."

She started ticking off her fingers. "One: I'll lose any anonymity I have right now. Two: they'll impede me at work. Three: there's nowhere for them to stay at my apartment. Four: I just *really* don't—"

"We've gotten more death threats."

He heard her breathing stop momentarily, and his stomach dropped.

"How many more?" she asked, her voice even.

"Six."

"Which makes a total of . . ."

"Twelve."

"Twelve unique threats? Or could there be several by the same people?"

"You're grasping, darling . . ."

She reached across the table and took his hand, and he could've sworn she was attempting to bat her eyelashes.

"Woz preserve me. Abelia, you're getting a detail. You don't have to like it. Attempt to evade them if you want, but they've both been thoroughly warned about you, including the incident with the nightstallions."

"That was an outlier."

"If only."

She withdrew her hand, her forehead crinkling, eyes aflame. He rated this one at the top of her most adorable looks: *Very annoyed, but trying not to take it out on Parker, who is probably right even though I don't want to admit it.*

She crossed her arms. "What's the good news?"

"My mother and sisters want to help plan our wedding."

Her eyes rolled so hard, he feared she'd strain a muscle. Her head drifted down to rest on the table, and her voice was muffled.

"I told you to *start with the bad news*, hon."

"Look, they know you haven't got much family and few friends . . . they're trying to be nice."

"They're Orangie women. They won't understand."

He sipped his wine. "What is it they won't understand?"

She righted herself. "In Brevspor, the groom plans the wedding as a tribute to his bride; he plans everything. He picks her dress. He designs the decorations. He picks the menu of all her favorite foods. And traditionally, her friends and family then grade him on how well he knows her, and by extension, how well the marriage will go. Obviously, you don't have time or capacity to do that. In Orangiers and most other patriarchal societies, young girls dream of planning and executing this day. Beyond the chocolate fountain, I really couldn't care less what kind of flowers I'm holding, what I'm wearing, what we eat, or who attends. So the idea of planning this event with my future in-laws, who have much more emotionally invested in the event, sounds horrible. Horrible." She leaned forward. "Horrible."

"They'll be here on Friday night to do a preliminary planning session and pick a color palette. I suggest you purchase some magazines."

She scowled. "Speaking of unpleasantries . . ." Abbie reached into her purse as the waiter took her blue porcelain dessert bowl away. She produced a long white envelope and laid it on the table between them. Parker suspected what was in it but decided to play dumb.

"What's this?"

Abbie smiled like a cat with a canary. "My first debt repayment."

He removed his napkin from his lap. "Strange, I don't recall any circumstances under which you owe me anything."

"You paid off my college loans."

"As your future spouse"—he nodded—"yes, I did."

"But I didn't want that favor."

"I understand that, but—"

"So now I am, as they say, returning the favor."

Parker cocked his head. "I don't think that's the correct use of that expression . . ."

"I know it's not."

He leaned forward. "You said your first debt repayment . . . Are there more coming?"

She shifted in her seat, and her eyes betrayed her uncertainty. "As long as I have employment."

"Are you planning on seeking employment in Orangiers? If so, you'll need a work permit . . ."

Her eyes narrowed. "Are you threatening to deny my work permit?"

His eyes narrowed right back at her. "That depends. Are you going to pick up that envelope and put it back in your bank account, where it belongs?"

"No, because it belongs in yours," she growled.

He crossed his arms, sitting back from the table. "Well, I don't accept that."

"Well, then I guess our waiter is going to get one Jersey of a tip." Abbie rose, smiling spitefully, and gathered her coat and purse from the waiting attendant. "Are you coming?"

Uh-oh. She really isn't going to pick it up. She's going to leave that pile of money sitting there . . . How much could it be, though? A few hundred dollars? Still, it's not like it's from the royal coffers; this is her money. She's worked hard for it, and now she's just throwing it away . . . Well, that's her prerogative, I suppose. I don't have to prevent all her mistakes . . . That seems like it could be a full-time job.

"Abelia, you're a prideful, ridiculous woman, and I love you." The young king stood, stretched, and took his own coat from the attendant. Strolling over to her, he offered her his arm with a smile and watched a mild panic settle over her features. She kept her head held high until they reached the front door, where she whirled on him.

"Parker! How can you just leave that sitting on the table? I can't believe you didn't—"

Someone behind them cleared his throat, and they turned to see their coat attendant.

"Sorry to interrupt, ma'am, but I think you left this on the table . . ."

Abbie swallowed hard and bit out an insincere thank you to the attendant as she accepted the envelope and stuffed it into her purse. As they ascended the steps to the carriage, she stabbed a finger into Parker's chest.

"This is *not* over."

No, Parker thought, *it is assuredly not over . . . but round one goes to me.* His feeling of smug success was short-lived, however, when he discovered that she had zero interest in making out on the way home and did not invite him into her apartment when he walked her up, forcing him to say goodbye in front of his security.

"Are we still on for breakfast?"

She glared at him. "Yes."

"Shall we meet here?"

She continued to glare at him. "Yes."

"What time?"

She kept right on glaring at him. "Seven is fine."

"Okay, well, sleep well, darling." He leaned forward and she took a quick step back.

"Good night, Edward." She extended her right hand and waited.

A handshake? Really? He didn't want to laugh and seem like he was gloating or delighting in her obvious displeasure, but he couldn't help letting a little chuckle slip out. He gave her the warmest smile he could manage, holding her gaze, and shook her hand firmly. He turned and fled down the stairs, before she could see how hurt he actually was.

CHAPTER FOUR

140 days to the wedding

THE NEXT MORNING AT 6:20, Abbie was standing in line at Pain Céleste, her favorite bakery. She'd set her alarm for 6:45, planning to start the coffee, throw on clothes, and be ready by seven. Guilt, however, had other plans and had woken her at five thirty to talk over her decisions of the previous evening. It had been childish not to kiss him good night; she'd ruined the end of their date. Of course, they were going to disagree sometimes . . . but it was wrong of her to punish him for seeing things differently. In retrospect, she felt she should've talked the issue through rationally, not tried to strong-arm him. Of course, he was also wrong, but that was another issue, maybe.

Abbie ordered a gluten-free apple oatmeal muffin for her and a maple bourbon bar, a blueberry bear claw, and a red velvet cake doughnut for Parker, figuring he could always share with his security if he didn't like all of those. There were still a lot of his likes and dislikes she didn't know . . . and a lot of things he didn't know about her.

Grabbing the box, Abbie checked her phone for the time and noticed a familiar face over her shoulder at a corner table. It was only six thirty; what was Dean doing here? Did that mean Parker was here? She turned and acknowledged him with a subtle nod. He returned it, and when she walked toward the door, he followed a moment later, his coffee in hand. He followed her for two blocks down Cedar Street, and when she turned onto Plumeria, she stopped to let him catch up, noting the surprise on his face.

"What are you doing here?" She tried to keep her voice friendly.

"I think you already know the answer to that question, Ms. Anderson. Didn't expect to see you up so early, though, after such a late night."

"Me either." She lifted the box slightly as they walked. "Apology doughnuts."

The middle-aged man nodded. "I've been there."

"Are you married?"

"I was." He sipped from his travel mug. "Didn't buy enough doughnuts, I guess."

"I'm sorry."

"It's okay." They turned onto her street and he eyed a runner passing them.

"So, do I have a code name?"

Dean chuckled. "Yes, but I don't think I should tell you what it is."

"Is it the Harpy?" He shook his head. "The Falcon? The Fox? The Clown Fish?" He laughed. "Fine, then tell me his code name. I want to gloat."

"My lips are sealed."

"Don't worry, I'll unseal them."

"Should I be worried, ma'am?"

"Yes, you should. Uh-oh." Parker's carriage was already out front. "See you later." He held the door for her, and she hurried up three flights of stairs.

Parker looked relieved when he saw her coming. "There you are; we tried to call, but it went to voicemail."

"Sorry, it must still be on 'disturb me and die' mode. I thought I'd beat you here." She kept her momentum going up the stairs and bumped into the waiting king. "Hold this," she said, fishing in her bag for her keys.

"No need." Waldo opened the front door for her, grimacing. "Ma'am, no offense, but your security is quite lax. I picked this in less than three minutes."

"No doughnut for you, Waldo." She went inside and Parker followed, hanging back.

"We do need to talk about the security situation, Abs."

"Hush. Come in and sit down. You're just grumpy because you thought I was MIA and your blood sugar is low."

He crossed his arms. "I already ate."

"I thought this was a breakfast date?"

"I get up at five."

"Oh." Abbie looked around, frustrated. "Well, I got doughnuts. You don't have to have any." She put down the doughnuts on the counter and hung up her purse. "Look, I know you're mad at me."

His posture did not get less defensive. "Not angry, per se . . ." She crossed the kitchen to where he was still standing by the front door. She put her arms around him, his crossed arms still between them.

"I know you're mad at me," she whispered. "I'm sorry about last night. I didn't handle that correctly."

"We agree on that much."

"How can I make it up to you?"

His shoulders dropped half an inch. "I have a few ideas."

"Oh?" She pressed a soft kiss to his lips.

"You could move to a safer building."

She shook her head, kissing him again. "I like my building. It's approved by the government."

"Not my government. And I'm sure it's fine for teenage runaways and failed day traders who don't have twelve death threats against them . . ."

Abbie's phone plinked and she pulled it out. "It's Davis. He wants to know why there's 'two weird dudes' outside my apartment again today." She turned it so he could see. "And Mrs. Beaverton caught me this morning on her way to church and asked me the same thing." She put the phone away. "You can't tell me all neighbors have that level of concern for each other."

"No, but you don't need that if you have biometric entry and windows with bulletproof glass." He paused, looking at her lips, and Abbie smiled at him. "What did you tell them?"

"I told them Uncle Ed was visiting, of course."

She rubbed his biceps, grinning at him, but he didn't crack.

"Come on, hon. I'm sorry, okay? I'm sorry. I got you a blueberry bear claw . . ."

"What's a bear claw?"

She darted to the box. "It's a fried pastry with a light glaze. See?"

He peered inside. "Blueberry, huh?"

"Yes, blueberry. Or if you don't like that, I also got red velvet and maple bourbon."

"Nothing else with fruit?"

She swallowed hard, masking her disappointment. "Yes, I also got an apple muffin. You can have that." She passed the box to him. "Do you want some almond milk with it? I don't have cow's milk."

"Certainly. Thank you." She poured herself some coffee and brought both drinks over with her to the table. "This is pretty good," he said, peering at the pastry, "but it tastes a little . . . different."

"Does it? Hmm." *That would be the gluten-free factor,* she thought. *Try as Celeste might, delicious as it was, the muffin never let you forget that it wasn't made with wheat.* She hid behind her coffee cup and intended to steer the conversation in another direction when her stomach growled loudly. His confused expression cleared, and he set the muffin down on the table.

"Abelia."

"Yes?"

"Am I consuming your breakfast?"

"What? No. Of course not."

"What did you have for breakfast, then?"

"I had a muffin on the walk back."

He ignored her lie. "Why did you give me the one thing you could eat?"

She sighed. "Because they were apology doughnuts and you wouldn't accept them, which meant . . ."

"That I didn't accept your apology?"

She nodded, gripping her mug. He stood up, nodding, wiping his hands on a cloth napkin from a basket on the table. Walking into the kitchen, he opened cabinets and peered into the shelves until he found what he was looking for: a deep saucepan. He filled it with water and set it on the front burner, its green flame springing to life from his match.

"What are you doing?"

"I'm making you breakfast."

"Oh, I really don't need anything."

"Nonsense." He pulled the eggs out of the fridge. "And in the future, even if I'm upset with you, please don't give away your food. It's not as if you have a myriad of options. I won't have you sacrificing your health for the sake of peace between us." She let him add a splash of vinegar to the pan before she came up behind him and wrapped her arms around his middle. He put a hand over hers.

"Darling, I don't mind disagreements; however, I do mind being shut out for having a differing opinion. I don't like being manipulated."

"Okay. I'm sorry."

"Okay."

She let go as he moved to get two teacups and watched with fascination as he cracked an egg into each one and dumped them into the spinning water together. "Forgive me, Parker; what the Jersey are you making me?"

He scowled good-naturedly. "I'm making eggs."

". . . hard-boiled eggs?"

"No, poached eggs. Have you never tried them?"

"I guess not . . ."

He grinned at her. "My mother always made them when the staff were on holiday. I think it was the only breakfast food she knew how to cook besides cold cereal and milk."

"Well, your future wife can do better."

"My future wife's the man. So to speak."

"So to speak."

Abbie leaned back against the counter, watching him. "What else can you cook?"

"Cheese toasties."

"What's that?"

"You melt cheese between two pieces of bread in a pan with butter."

"Oh, a grilled cheese. Ever had it with a dill pickle?"

"Woz preserve me." The timer went off, and he took the eggs out with a slotted spoon and put them on a plate. Abbie felt he looked inordinately proud of himself given that he'd put eggs in hot water, but she appreciated the effort nonetheless.

"Thanks. What else?"

"What else can I cook?"

"Yes. What culinary delights do I have to look forward to when the staff are on holiday?"

He snickered as they sat back at the table. "Let's see. Does heating soup from a can count for anything?"

She chuckled, shaking her head as she took her first bite and reached for the salt.

"Then that's it. Poached eggs and cheese toasties will have to do."

"We can survive on that. Oh, and I've got lunch covered today. I ordered Imaharan food last night when you were doing your dead guy impression."

His eyes lit up. "Kitchen sink?" She nodded. Parker pumped his fist in triumph, and it was very un-king-like, which made Abbie love him all the more. "It's better the next day, anyway."

"Waldo told me you liked it."

"Woz bless that man." He took another bite of the muffin. "I have to be airborne by three, by the way."

Abbie nodded slowly, pulling her lips to one side, not looking up from her plate.

"We've still got seven hours, though."

"Right."

"Don't get morose on me."

"I'm not."

"Abbie . . ." He tipped his head down to try and make eye contact with her, but she couldn't quite meet his gaze.

"I'm really not."

"You can't even look at me!"

"I have to pee." Abbie shot to her feet and her chair fell over. Parker jumped up and blocked her way to her bedroom, and by extension, the bathroom.

"Oh no, you don't. I'm onto this ploy."

"Excuse me," she muttered, tossing her hair. "I need to get through."

"No, darling, I'm the one who needs to get through, to you. I apologize, I should not have said that; it's perfectly natural to be sad that I'm leaving. Will you forgive me?"

Abbie opened her mouth to say again that she was fine, but no words came out. She allowed herself to be gathered into Parker's strong embrace.

"I'm not crying."

"I know you're not." He smoothed her hair as she rested her head on his chest, her tears wetting his shirt.

"I'm a badass, independent woman."

"You are, you're a total badass." Hearing Parker repeat her cursing made her smile.

"I don't need you here. I can totally take care of myself."

"You're a total doyenne."

She lifted her head to look into his eyes. "What's that?"

"An expert in your field."

"Oh, yes, I'm a total doyenne."

"I know, that's why I said so." He held her for a few more moments before she broke away, brushing away her tears.

"I did actually need to pee. But thank you for the hug and the apology. When I get back, do you want to watch football and make out during the commercials?"

He seemed to consider this. "Am I correct in thinking that making out is snogging?"

She nodded.

"In that case, absolutely."

CHAPTER FIVE

SHE DECIDED NOT TO go to the airfield, opting for a private goodbye at her apartment and an afternoon of cleaning and moping. She did not read for work. She left the football match on and took a nap. She ate her leftovers from Martissant's on the couch for dinner, then walked to the grocery store. Dean followed her there and back.

"Ma'am, I strongly urge you to consider the king's request for you to move," he said as they trudged back up the stairs. "We could help you find more suitable lodging, have you packed and out of here in a matter of hours. You own very few belongings." She held her tongue until she'd unlocked the door and let them both inside.

"I appreciate your concern, but I'm fine here." She began putting away the groceries.

"Right. I'll take my leave, then." He put his bags down on the counter for her.

"Dean, I'm a normal person, not a royal. You don't have to 'take your leave.' You just see yourself out."

"Just so you're aware, your new security personnel will arrive tomorrow morning."

"What?" Abbie looked up from putting romaine in the crisper. "The way you've been trailing after me all weekend, I assumed you were my new security."

"No, ma'am. His Majesty has other plans. However, I trust you'll be coming to Orangiers in the near future?"

She held up her fingers as she put the eggs away. "Two weeks. I'll see you then. Beer for the road?"

Looking around as if he were being watched, he flicked his head up, and she tossed him a bottle. He put his fingers to his lips, and she winked at him. The security officer closed her front door behind himself, then called, "Do up the locks, please."

Rolling her eyes, Abbie crossed to the front door and threw the bolt.

"And the chain," the muffled voice prompted.

Abbie obliged him, then headed for the bathroom to brush her teeth. Passing through her bedroom, she stopped in surprise. There were now three beds in her bedroom, a newly assembled set of bunk beds blocking the window of the tiny room. She pulled out her phone and dialed.

"Hello, darling."

"Don't 'darling' me. Why are there more beds in my house? You did this while I was at the store?"

"Those are for your security; we discussed this." Abbie could hear other people in the background and papers shuffling and water glasses being filled. He was in a meeting. She was interrupting. *Good.*

"Uh, no, *darling*, we absolutely did not discuss me sharing my bedroom with strangers, however vetted they might be by Dean or whoever."

"Don't worry about it. Wait until you meet them to pass judgment."

"Can't. Don't want to. They can sleep on the sofa."

"Both of them? That'd be cozy."

"We did it the other day."

"Yes, and it was very cozy . . . pleasantly cozy, but cozy nonetheless."

"They can take turns. I don't need two here at once, anyway. This place is barely big enough for two people who like each other, and I sure as Jersey don't want them in my private space."

"I promise they will respect your space."

"No."

"Forty-eight hours."

Abbie shot air out of her nose. "No."

"Twenty-four hours."

"If I had tools right now, the beds would already be gone. I bet Davis has a friend at his party who would disassemble them for me for ten bucks. Hey, Davis?"

"Hang on; all right, give me a minute here." She heard him exiting the room, walking down the hall. "Okay, I'm back. I hear you that it's a tight fit."

"You can say that again."

"I hear you that it's a tight fit." He paused. "Just trying to make you laugh."

Abbie said nothing.

"Look, it's late. I can't have them removed tonight. It would look suspicious. Who moves bunk beds at eight thirty at night?"

"People who work!" She was yelling now. "And putting three people in my apartment violates my lease! If they see two more people living here, I'm going to be in big trouble!"

"Okay. I'll move one bunk out and we'll let them hot bunk. Deal?" She heard him yawn and remembered it was three hours later there.

"Fine! Why are you still in meetings?" Still yelling.

"Abbie?" His voice was soft, sleepy. "I miss you . . ."

"I miss you, too!" she shouted. "Now shut it down and go to bed!"

ABBIE WAS IN THE CARRIAGE the next morning before she realized that the new security guys had never shown up. Well, she couldn't be expected to wait around all morning; they'd just have to meet this evening. Her opinion of them was dropping by the minute, however. Abbie walked into work and had just started the coffee maker in her office when she heard a knock. A young woman with white-blonde hair and a deep tan was standing there. She didn't look like she spent a lot of time underground; her skin alone gave her away as a new hire.

"Can I help you?" Abbie asked, feigning indifference as a power move.

"Yes, Ms. Anderson. I'm your new assistant, Georgina Addington. I go by Georgie."

Abbie shook her head, eyes on her paperwork. "I don't have use for an assistant; my schedule is uncomplicated. I answer my own phone, and I use the secretarial pool when I need something typed or do it myself."

"I'm not that type of assistant, ma'am."

A wave of understanding washed over Abbie, and she closed her eyes. "Come in and close the door, please." She motioned for the young woman to sit, looking her over. "How, pray tell, did he swing this?"

"Our mutual friend wields considerable influence, even here." Georgie, if that was her real name, sounded Gardenian, not Orangiersian. Abbie figured checking on her credentials wasn't unreasonable if she was putting her life in this woman's hands.

"Where are you from?"

The woman gave her a knowing smile. "I'm from Gardenia, of course. Just like you, ma'am." Abbie had worked hard to soften her accent in Common Tongue when she'd lived on the street. It was nice to see the woman committing to the role. "I'll be with you during the day, see you home, and then Tezza Macias, your new roommate, will take the night shift."

"He knows me too well," she muttered.

"Pardon?"

Abbie lifted her head and glared at Georgie since Parker wasn't available to glare at. "Our mutual friend. He knows me too well. He knows I'm much more likely to obey a woman than a man."

"I can hardly blame you, ma'am. Rest assured that I may not have the physical stature of Dean and Waldo, but I'm an expert in martial arts, threat detection, and enchanted shielding. I can and will protect you."

Abbie waved a hand at her flippantly. "Were I in any danger, that would be a great comfort."

Georgie's polite exterior slipped. "Why do you believe you're not? I've seen the death threats, ma'am."

"Let's talk about this another time," Abbie said, glancing at the closed door. "Where's your office?"

"Right across the hall. If you wouldn't mind leaving your door open, it would be helpful to me. Also, feel free to give me actual secretarial work to do. Much like going to bed with a bad lover, I can only fake it for so long."

Abbie smirked. The rest of the morning went by quickly; she was still behind from her trip across the Veil and wrapping up her father's affairs, so she had plenty to do at work. Abbie expected to feel watched, but every time she looked up, Georgie appeared to be as busy as she was. Parker texted her around lunchtime.

Parker: So?

Abbie: So . . . what?

Parker: So how do you find Georgie? She learned that accent just for this assignment.

Abbie: Am I supposed to be impressed by that?

Abbie: Because I kind of am.

Parker: I suspected as much. #kinging

Abbie: Stop gloating. How's your day going?

Parker: Busy. Love you.

Abbie: Love you, too, hon.

⚬⚬⚬

IF GEORGIE WAS THE light, Tezza was the dark. She gave Abbie a professional handshake, but her expression was closed. She was dressed entirely in black form-fitting clothing. Her dark hair was twisted into a high bun, but it was obviously quite long when unfurled. Her stance was wide, her hands clasped behind her back, as though Abbie were a military officer inspecting her.

"Where are you from?"

"Op'Ho'Lonia."

"Oh, really? I've never been there. What's it like?"

"Humid."

They stared at each other while Abbie tried to think of more questions. Her brain was tired after a long day.

"Have you eaten dinner?"

"Yes."

"Is there anything I should get for you, so you're more comfortable here?"

"No."

She tried to think of a question that would garner more than a one-word response.

"How much experience do you have in this line of work?"

Tezza crossed her arms. "Plenty."

Abbie gave up. "Okay, great, well, welcome aboard, so to speak. Let me know if there's any issues during the night, I'm just . . . hanging out . . . here."

Boy, this gal was unnerving. Tezza nodded once, then turned and disappeared into the bedroom while Abbie cooked dinner and ate. She somehow anticipated when Abbie was ready to go to bed and came out with a book in hand, not looking up. She set the tome on the couch as she moved to the front door.

"In for the night?" she asked.

Abbie nodded cautiously. Tezza turned her back again, and Abbie heard her mutter an incantation, then heard the locks click over, though she hadn't touched them.

"Whoa." Abbie came over to the door and tried the dead bolt. It wouldn't budge. "You spelled my door to a certain opener?"

Tezza nodded.

Abbie crossed her arms. "What if I need to get out in the night? What if there's a fire or I have a hankering for pizza?"

"Why would you be leaving without your security?" Tezza sat on the couch and picked up her book again. True to his word, Parker had the bunk beds removed while she was at work. There was now a high-end futon in her room, which actually fit the space quite nicely.

Abbie: Tezza is . . . intense.

Parker: Indeed. We thought she was a better fit for the night shift than the day shift.

Abbie: Yes, I can see how she might frighten people.

Abbie: Thank you for the futon. It fits better.

Parker: You're welcome.

Abbie: We'll have to break it in with some "snogging" on your next visit.

Parker: Putting that on the agenda in ink . . . can't change your mind now.

Abbie: Why would I want to? You're an excellent kisser.

Parker: Are you busy?

Abbie: Just about to go to bed . . .

The phone rang, and she answered.

"This seemed better done in person," he started. "I know you were supposed to come on the ninth . . ."

"Uh-oh."

"I know, I'm so sorry. It was unavoidable, darling. Can we bump it out a week?"

"I guess so. But you'll still come here the next weekend?"

"Well, actually . . ."

"Uh-oh," she sighed.

"No, just listen. I've been called to a summit the week after in Imahara, the week of the nineteenth. Would you like to meet me there?"

"Meet you?"

"You could stay at my rental—in your own room, of course. And you'd save money, flying a shorter distance." He would think that, of course, having never booked nonrefundable commercial blimp tickets, which she had already purchased for Orangiers. She might be able to transfer them for a fee . . . *More money down the drain. Relationships are more expensive than I realized.* She swallowed most of her objections and another sip of water. "What's the summit regarding?"

"Ah, yes, I thought that might be of interest to you as well. It's on human rights, pressing all continental countries to sign an accord on human rights, both inside and outside the Veil."

"Intriguing. If I agree, would I actually get to see you? Or would you be in meetings the whole time?"

"It's Wednesday night to Saturday breakfast, so we'd still have most of the weekend for sightseeing and whatnot. And we'd have a bit more freedom to wander, take a ride, maybe."

Abbie grinned. "That sounds like more fun than sitting in my apartment."

He paused. "And I hesitate to mention it, but there is a formal ball Friday night. It might be a good chance for you to learn more about human trafficking informally, make some connections. If you'd like to accompany me, I'd be pleased to have you. I promise I'd get you to bed at a decent hour."

She pulled the covers up higher, her heart warmed that he'd thought of trying to help her develop that side of her interests. "I'll think about Friday night, but the rest of it sounds like a good idea."

"Good. It's a date."

"Good." She yawned. "Okay, that's all I've got."

"Me too. Glad you're happy with your security. See? You can trust me."

She muttered something unintelligible as she sank down into the pillow, unable to keep her eyes open.

"Sorry, I didn't catch that . . . Abs? Are you still there?" she heard him say, but his voice was far away, and then she was out.

CHAPTER SIX

134 days to the wedding

QUEEN LILY'S AIDE BERNICE texted Abbie the Wednesday before Parker's family was set to arrive to help with the planning; they would be staying downtown at the Regency Hotel, and Abbie was to meet them at 6:00 p.m. for dinner in Her Majesty's suite. In addition to Lily, Rhododendron, Ginger, and Dahlia would be along as well; they'd decided to leave Forsythia behind this time. The attaché confirmed the dinner date again on Thursday, and by Friday morning, Abbie was pretty tired of this chick. Georgie and Tezza switched when she ran home to shower and change into something more appropriate for meeting Parker's mom. She applied some makeup and tried to get her hair to all curl in the same direction. She'd met Lily before, of course, but they hadn't spent one-on-one time together. Abbie felt her own personality was less abrasive in large groups; she mostly kept her mouth shut, nodded a lot. But it didn't matter, really, whether Lily liked her or not; the contract was signed. She'd obviously approved of the match at one point.

Abbie climbed into the carriage and Georgie came after her.

"Excited?"

"Nope," Abbie admitted ruefully. "Distract me?"

"Okay!" Good old Georgie. She'd only been around a few days, but the girl was up for anything. "What do you want to talk about?"

"I'm curious about your magical abilities . . . How does one become a non-technical magic user? Like, I know you have a bond with the magic . . ."

"Yes, that's right. Inside the Veil, magic is kind of like a horse that's been domesticated. It's familiar with what you want, willing to be saddled, used to being bridled. It still needs to be brushed, watered, fed, paid attention . . . but it's more or less available if you let it get to know you, get comfortable with you."

"What's special about the Veil, exactly?"

"The Veil creates a special environment that meets some of the magic's requirements without need for human interaction all the time. It's a network of generators that create connections between zones of magic so it can interact with itself. Magic is geographical, and the idea of meeting magic from other zones is highly interesting to it. Them?" She cocked her head for a moment, then shook it. "I never know what pronoun to use for magic. It feels plural to me, but it's technically one entity."

"How does that make the lights come on, though?"

"We basically convinced it to bond with objects instead of people or other zones. The objects have components created with magic, so that puts a false positive on them. People think tech users have it easy, but actually, creating that bond, those components, isn't that simple. It takes a lot of time to create something physical through magic."

"You weren't interested in that?"

She shook her head. "It's like how some people can't look at animals in zoos. I prefer my magic wild."

"What does it feel like, when it comes?"

Georgie looked thoughtful. "It's hard to describe. For me, it feels like a buzzing in my ears, like a mosquito . . . You might not be aware of it at first, but if you feel it long enough, you start to recognize when it's bidding for your attention. Others say it's more like a tingle or a warm light on their face or a tap on the shoulder by an invisible hand. Tezza says hers is like a liquid pooling around her ankles."

"Wow," Abbie said. "All right, you've sold me. When do we start?"

She was rewarded with a huge smile as Addington shook her head. "His Majesty was clear during our orientation that we were not to instruct you in developing magical ability."

Overprotective know-it-all, she grumped internally. "What's it like outside the Veil?"

"Very different. It's more like a puppy at the beach. You want it to retrieve a stick for you, but all it wants to do is chase the seagulls, eat your lunch leftovers and sniff after hermit crabs. Much tougher to get its attention. Unveiled magic usually wants something before it'll bond with you."

"Wants something? Like what?"

"The puppy analogy works well for a reason—it might want to play with your stuff, if you have something it wants, or just be entertained. Sometimes it wants to mess around in your head, find out new things; most people aren't crazy about that." She paused, looking down. "But at times, it's more like a lion. A lion that sometimes acknowledges you as its keeper . . . and sometimes sees you as prey."

"Has it ever tried to eat you?" Abbie whispered.

Georgie laughed. "No, of course not. I'm a professional. That's why we do extensive training. But there have been a few times when it wasn't interested in company and I left it alone."

Abbie nodded, relieved. "Of course."

"Veil history is fascinating. I wrote my thesis on it. It started out with this one community, Jumonville in Gardenia, that was just trying to protect itself from beasts. Then one little girl, Milly Fullerton, noticed that their fire in the hearth hadn't gone out in days. Her parents both thought the other one had been stoking it. The magic had been keeping the logs intact."

"I mean, is there anything you can't do?"

Georgie shrugged one shoulder. "VT has only been around for about a hundred years. There's a lot we still don't know. Most of our applications are practical . . . but it's been theorized that much more is possible. There are some superusers, obviously, like the Warlord of Gratha and the Duchess of Gripewater, but they're not real open to revealing their methods. Oh, we're here."

ABBIE'S HANDS WERE shaking as she approached the hotel suite. Lily and Rhodie were both always so polished, so professionally royal; never a chipped nail, never a hair out of place. There is a type of nonverbal conversation that happens when two women size each other up physically, and Abbie always felt like she was stuttering. *I can do this. Parker loves*

me; they'll love me, too. And if they don't, they can take a flying leap off the nearest—

The doors swung open, and Lily's aide stood there, smiling.

"Good, you found us. Come in."

She stepped into the suite, trying to feign confidence, and was immediately mobbed by the sixteen-year-old twins.

"You're finally here!" This was Dahlia . . . she thought.

"What took you so long?" This was Ginger . . . she was pretty sure.

Abbie tried to hug them back, but they were pinning her arms against her sides in their exuberance. All she could do was issue a surprised laugh.

"Sorry, I don't get off until five, and then I had to run home and shower. You would not want to be hugging me if I hadn't."

They released her and shared a giggle in stereo. Still nervous, Abbie glanced over their shoulders to see if Lily approved of this strong display of affection and found her smiling broadly, serene as always. Rhodie's posture, however, was less open, nor did she rise to embrace Abbie when Lily did. Lily placed a kiss on each cheek and then held her tightly, and against her will, Abbie's heart glowed.

"Welcome back, dear. It's so good to have you with us again. I'm sorry I didn't attend your father's memorial; I had been ill and I was unable to travel. But our thoughts were with you."

"Thank you, Your Majesty. I appreciate that."

"Oh please, feel free to call me something more informal. You're family now."

"Almost." Abbie grimaced, thinking of the lawsuits.

"Oh, don't worry about those legal issues, dear. Edward and his government will sort it out soon enough."

She smiled. "I hope so." Abbie moved to Rhodie and kissed her hello.

"How are you, Your Highness?"

"I'm very well, thank you. And you?"

"I'm well."

Rhodie was watching her expectantly, sizing her up, and Abbie felt the color creeping into her face. She grasped for something to ask about.

"How's your research going? Parker said you've been spending a lot of time in the lab."

"It's going fine. My grant will be completed in a few months, and then I hope to do another expedition."

"Oh, really? Where to?"

"I'm uncertain what the locale will be. Perhaps to Trella. The plant species there are heavily undocumented." Her turn of phrase made Abbie imagine trees being hassled by angry customs officials about their missing paperwork, but she kept a straight face.

"Daughter, I should think you'd be happy to have another scientific mind to converse with." It was subtle, but Abbie was pretty sure Lily was chiding Rhodie for not being more friendly. But she understood Rhodie's hesitation; she'd broken Parker's heart in Gratha. She still had some penance to do for that.

"Oh," Abbie said, shaking her head, "Rhodie's on an entirely different plane. I'm just a glorified trash collector."

"I'm sure there are health implications to what you do," Rhodie said.

She said the words "what you do," Abbie thought, with a certain intonation she couldn't quite place. *Disdain? Haughtiness? No . . . apathy. Well, I've never backed down from a challenge.*

"Well, there are greater health implications when I don't do it, but yes, we're trying to keep Gardenia sustainable. I think we've made some strides in the last few years."

"Mmm." Rhodie sipped her water.

Lily sat down on the couch, so Abbie followed and sat beside her. Ginger and Dahlia bookended them. Rhodie stayed in her high wingback chair, but pivoted to remain part of the conversation.

"Abelia"—Lily squeezed her hand—"thank you for allowing us to participate in the planning. We're all excited to put together a beautiful ceremony for you two."

"Oh, well . . . I'm glad for the help," she lied. "I don't have any idea how to do this." *That part is true, at least.*

Lily motioned to her attaché, who brought forward a giant scrapbook. "The twins and I have been busy collecting ideas." Abbie forced herself to breathe in and out slowly, stifling the giant sigh she wanted to heave as Lily opened the book across their laps. "We've put together some color palette ideas for you . . ."

What started as annoyance was giving way to anxiety, and Abbie tried to stay focused on Lily's words. *Just keep your polite pants on, pick the first one, and then you can eat and go home. Colors, eat, home. Colors, eat, home.*

The queen cleared her throat. "This first one is plum and emerald. Easy to find flowers this color that time of year, and not too Christmas-y."

Abbie was opening her mouth to say that it looked great when Dahlia interrupted. "I don't like this one. It's going to make Edward look too red, don't you think, Abbie?"

"You liked it when we put it in the book, weirdo." Ginger rolled her eyes at her sister.

"What color tuxedo would you pair with that? Parker will blend right into black!"

Lily interjected, "I'm sure Edward will want to wear his military uniform."

"But then they'll both be wearing white," Dahlia said. "Isn't that strange?"

"Well, I can wear another color," Abbie said, and the girls stared at her. Rhodie coughed, and Abbie wondered if she was covering a laugh.

"We appreciate your flexibility, but in this case, dear, there are some cultural implications to the color of a woman's wedding dress . . . ," Lily said gently.

Abbie lifted an eyebrow. "What kind of implications?"

The Orangie women looked at each other, baffled. *What am I missing here? It's just a dress, right?*

"You must wear white," Rhodie said, finally, a smile playing at the corners of her lips. "Just trust us. Edward will want you in white."

"Maybe we should wait until he's here to voice opinions," Abbie said, hoping she could leave sooner.

"No, no," the three on the couch chorused.

Lily laid a hand on hers again. "We are more than capable of advising you on his preferences. We promise to run all the salient details by him before anything's set in stone."

"Okay," Abbie said, forcing a smile, pressing her shoulders back so they couldn't slump. *I can do this. I can do this. I can do this . . . I think.*

"I liked this one better," Dahlia said, skipping ahead a few pages. "Rustic winter. Deep brown and light green remind me of a winter wood. So romantic."

"Okay," Abbie said, nodding, "that looks—"

"How's she supposed to do a bouquet, then? Think about it. There's no floral colors in it."

"She could have a white bouquet," Lily mused. "That would look lovely in the snow, especially with her deep-red hair."

"Are you going to wear it up or down?" Dahlia brushed Abbie's hair off her shoulder.

"I don't—"

"But the photos will be washed out if there's too much white and black in them . . ."

Abbie rolled her lips between her teeth to keep from yelling, and she noticed Rhodie, her shoulders shaking slightly, silently laughing. Her eyes held sympathy, and Abbie grinned a little.

"Abelia, would you like a glass of wine?"

"Oh, I wish I could, but I'm on methotrexate."

"How about a mocktail, then?"

"Sure," Abbie said, standing with Rhodie, withdrawing to the corner of the room as the twins continued to argue and the queen attempted to mollify them. Rhodie rooted around until she found a lime and a zester.

"You look as miserable as I'd feel in your place."

"Do I? I am trying . . ."

"I can see that. Far more than some other Brevsporan women I've met, who would have charged in here without regard for anyone else. I didn't think you'd last five minutes under the influence of their antics." She put pineapple, ice, and coconut milk into the blender. "Of course, it doesn't negate how you've treated my brother in the past . . ." The noise of the blender gave Abbie time to form a response.

"No, it doesn't. I sincerely wish it did."

"Mmm." Rhodie gave her another appraising look, this time more than surface-deep, and handed her a virgin piña colada. Abbie took a sip.

"Ooh, that's tasty. Does it have sugar in it?"

Rhodie shook her head. "I wouldn't dare; it's agave. I was subjected at length to a presentation about your illness and what types of foods I wasn't allowed to offer you. I don't wish to be put in the remedial class by His Highness."

Abbie laughed, and Rhodie gave her a small tight-lipped smile.

"I wonder why he didn't mention the methotrexate," Rhodie said.

"He doesn't know. He's been asking to go to the doctor with me; I'm sure he'll add it to the presentation after that. He's very . . . vigilant."

Rhodie's smile widened. "Aren't you happy about that?"

Abbie shrugged. "It's meant with affection. Misplaced, perhaps, but . . ."

"Genuine."

Abbie nodded. "Definitely genuine." She sighed. "Shall we?"

"It's your party." Rhodie wandered back to her wingback chair, and Abbie made her way to the couch, clutching her drink like a security blanket. She waited until the royals looked up at her.

"I have an idea. Why don't each of you pick a favorite palette, and then I'll choose from those three?"

Ginger pursed her lips. "No, no, you have to see all of them. If Dahlia wasn't skipping around so much . . ."

Abbie sat back down and patiently went through the velvet rose palette, the gilded winter, the amethyst and lavender, the dark romance, none of which appealed to her. After much debate regarding its appropriateness for a morning wedding (which Edward insisted on, apparently), she settled on a palette called "winter jewel," which consisted of a midnight blue reminiscent of the Brevsporan blue of her flag, a pale green, and a ruby red.

During a dinner of garlic roasted pork, asparagus, and potatoes, her phone rang, and she excused herself and stepped out into the hall.

"Hello?"

"Hello, beautiful."

She snorted. "No sweet talk. You owe me for this, Broward."

"How much?"

"Big time."

"Unbearable, is it?"

"Almost. And this was the easy part. Do you know how picky I am about dresses?"

"It'll all be worth it."

"Let's elope. I bet Pap's ordained; he'd do it just to see us finally make out."

Parker paused. "I can't tell if you're joking."

"You're tempted. Don't deny it."

"No, I'm not. My mum would never speak to me again."

Abbie snorted. "What kind of excuse is that? I don't speak to my 'mum.'"

"Your mum's dead!"

"And my life is better for it."

His tone softened. "Come on, Abs. Give them a chance. You've forgotten what a family can give you. Maybe it's a good reminder, before we start our own . . . right?"

She huffed. "Maybe."

"Are they giving you a hard time?"

"No. Well, Rhodie a little, but I deserve it."

She heard him go into full "me man, me protect woman" mode. "What did she say?"

"Nothing, hon. Never mind."

His anger was rising. "No, not 'never mind.' I told her to be nice to you. What did she say?"

"Just . . . don't worry about it, Parker . . ."

"Put her on the phone."

Abbie sighed. "She's angry that I broke your heart."

"Oh." He paused. "I see."

"Do you still want to talk to her?"

"I suppose not."

"Does it help if I say again how sorry I am?"

He sighed. "That's behind us."

"It's not behind her. But she did make me a piña colada, so that was nice."

"See? Nice. My family is nice. A tad overprotective, but mostly nice."

"I did put it back together again, didn't I? Your heart?"

"Yes, you did. Just give her time, and she'll see that."

"Before I forget again, I have two doctor's appointments next Wednesday, so . . ."

"Oh? With whom?"

"Dr. Honaker, my rheumatologist, and Dr. Lowery, my nephrologist."

"Should I be there for that?"

"I don't know. Should you?"

"Let me rephrase that," he said, and she heard him shift the phone to his other ear. "I would like to be there for that. I will clear my schedule. But I can only come for the appointments. I already have other things booked the next day."

"Okay. I'm sorry I didn't let you know sooner."

He laughed. "No, you're not."

"No, I'm not. I was hoping you'd be busy. Why am I telling you this?" She sighed. "I should go back inside."

"All right, darling. I miss you."

"I miss you, too—wait!" She yelled the last word.

He hadn't hung up yet. "What?"

"Why do I have to wear a white wedding dress?"

He chuckled. "It's symbolic of your virginal purity."

"Well, that's fertilizer. Now I want a color."

"Of course you do."

CHAPTER SEVEN

132 days to the wedding

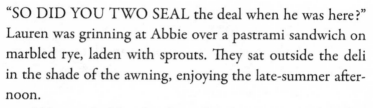

"SO DID YOU TWO SEAL the deal when he was here?" Lauren was grinning at Abbie over a pastrami sandwich on marbled rye, laden with sprouts. They sat outside the deli in the shade of the awning, enjoying the late-summer afternoon.

Abbie cocked her head, confused. "We can't finish the contract until the lawsuits—"

Lauren tsked at her. "Not that deal, girl—the other deal. The deal where you both take your clothes off and you go to town on his man parts."

Abbie choked on her lentil soup and reached for the napkin in her lap to cover her cough, glancing around to see who'd heard them. No one was staring.

"Laur, how can you just say stuff like that in public?"

She grinned again. "No one's listening. They're all too self-absorbed or have headphones on. It's the age of magic hegemonization, girl, the magic of the Veil at our fingertips. It's a good time to be alive." She sipped her ice water, the condensation dripping. "Answer the question. Mama needs details."

"No details available, sorry. Status unchanged. He intends to wait until we're married."

"That's very chivalrous of him. I bet he'd change his mind if you showed up at his front door wearing nothing but a trench coat."

"You are clearly unacquainted with his herculean levels of self-control; the man is a machine. He doesn't do anything he doesn't feel is right, and in his mind, that would dishonor me and dishonor his family name. He'd probably just chuckle and send me home. Also, your plan would be a little awkward considering there's three layers of security between him and his front door."

"Huh." She swallowed. "Oh! Naked selfies. See? These problems are totally surmountable."

"I'm fine with it, actually." Abbie stared down at her soup like she was truly having a conversation with the bowl instead of her best friend.

"Oh?"

"Yup."

"Huh." Lauren was giving her the "I don't believe you for a hot second" stare, and Abbie knew she needed to distract her, or there would be a lot more questions she didn't want to answer.

"How's your new guy? What's his name, Shane?"

Lauren nodded, grimacing. "His name is Shane. He's . . . unremarkable."

"Oh?"

"Yes. He's fine. Not great, not wonderful, just . . . fine. He likes to cook, he likes taking me to bed, and he takes out the trash. He therefore serves to supply some of my more urgent needs."

Abbie scratched her head. "Are you sure you're not Brevsporan? You'd fit right in there, and the men would be more into it."

"My license to practice law isn't valid there." Lauren leaned forward. "So back to my original line of questioning . . ."

Abbie rolled her eyes. "Fine, Counselor . . ."

"Why are you fine with waiting? Don't you want him?"

Abbie forced herself not to squirm in the metal chair, trying not to think about the feel of his warm, strong hands on her hips, his tantalizing kisses on her neck. She scowled at her friend. "Of course I do!"

Lauren held up her hands. "Look, I had to ask; most political marriages aren't all that warm and cozy, if I understand correctly. But I thought you guys had something more . . ."

"No, we do," Abbie said quickly, "we definitely do. Of course I . . ." Abbie dropped her voice to a whisper. "Of course I want him."

"And he's shown interest in you that way?"

Abbie snorted. "It's pretty much twenty-four seven interest. If his looks get any hotter, he's gonna set off the smoke detectors in my building. Even the ones without batteries."

"So I say again: Why are you fine with waiting?"

"I don't know, it's just . . ." Abbie felt her face warming under her friend's persistent scrutiny. "It's just going to be weird to go from barely anything to everything. I vacillate between wanting to do it right now and wanting to put it off indefinitely. I feel like I'm expected to throw some switch and go from sweet blushing bride to hot bedroom babe. I don't even know if I have that switch."

Lauren threw her napkin onto the table, signaling her readiness to get down and dirty with the details. "I'll tell you anything you want to know."

Abbie shook her head. "It's not a matter of knowing things; I know things . . . some things . . . about what to expect . . . It's just weird. I can't explain it." She paused. "It's more about being seen than doing it wrong. I'm sure I can learn technique; I don't know if I can learn . . . the rest of it."

"There's nowhere to hide," Lauren said, looking over Abbie's shoulder toward Dempsey Park.

Abbie dropped her spoon into her empty bowl with a clatter. "Exactly. As you know, I'm selective about the truth. Naked is about as far from lies as you can get."

"Have you told him about . . . what happened in the alley with Tracker?"

Abbie considered the question; she was at the point now where she didn't think about it every week anymore. A rival from Ward's group of teenagers had caught her alone on the street and tried to force himself on her. If her dog hadn't intervened, it would've been a different story.

"No, I haven't. I don't think I need to. I don't think that's where it comes from. This is all me; I'm just too uptight, too much of a control freak. I feel this need to protect, to keep my real self to myself, and he wants me to share. I don't know if I can. But he'd never push me into anything I didn't want in bed. If anything, he's too nice, too polite."

"That's what they want you to think. You'll keep thinking that right up until he pulls the fuzzy pink handcuffs out of his nightstand."

Abbie burst out laughing, startling a sleeping dog under the table next to them. *Man, I'm going to miss her so much.*

"Are you going to come visit me?"

"Aww. Of course I'm going to come visit you. Mom, too. I assume your new digs have guest rooms."

"Wow, I've never heard historic Bluffton Castle referred to as 'digs' before . . . but yes, we've got plenty of space. And I'll come back to visit, too. I promise."

"You'd better. Though I can't offer anything better than my couch . . ."

"Oh, don't worry about that. He's got plenty of money. He'll rent me something *secure*, I'm sure." Abbie rolled her eyes.

"Don't you mean, '*We've* got plenty of money'?"

"It doesn't feel like mine."

"You're too independent for your own good, Abs. Relax. Let him pay for stuff. He wants to take good care of you. That's nice. Better than cheap-ass Shane, wanting to split everything down the middle"—she leaned forward—"including the cost of the contraceptives." The look she gave Abbie over the rims of her glasses made Abbie snicker.

"At least that's one thing I don't have to worry about."

Lauren's face betrayed her surprise. "You guys are going to start trying for kids right away?"

Abbie nodded. "We don't really have a choice. My lupus may prevent kids anyway. We need all the chances we can get."

"That just seems . . . quick."

"I haven't had time to think about it, honestly. One problem at a time. Did I tell you he wants me to move?"

"To Orangiers? Now?"

She shook her head. "Just somewhere safer around here. He doesn't approve of my apartment."

"Praise Woz Almighty. I'm liking this guy more and more."

"Oh, don't start."

"I've been telling you that place is a fertilizer field since you moved in. Besides your hot neighbor, there's no benefit to that place."

"Here's why you're wrong: One, it's cheap as Jersey. Two, I have other nice neighbors who look out for me. Three, it's mine. It's where I found myself again. I have history there. And frankly, I just can't go through any more changes right now."

"Why, what other changes are happening?"

Abbie grunted. "You didn't notice?"

Lauren looked around. "What?"

"My security detail, Georgie."

"Girl, you got a bodyguard?" Lauren's voice was low and her eyes were alight. "Why have I not been properly introduced to this fine individual?" She immediately started fluffing her hair, wiping her face for crumbs, checking her teeth in her black phone screen. Abbie grinned inwardly.

"But you're with Shane . . ."

"Shane? Shane who? I will throw Shane out on his backside tonight for a hot bodyguard."

Lauren was used to Abbie messing with her; she probably wouldn't be too mad that she let her assumption go uncorrected. "Blonde, about five foot eight, built. Drinking a chai, red shirt."

Her friend was looking all around and finally noticed Georgie, who smiled at her and waved. Lauren waved back shyly.

"A lady?" she said through clenched teeth. "You couldn't have told me it was a *lady* bodyguard?"

Abbie snickered. "I'm not sorry."

"What does she do?"

"Follow me around. Pretend to do secretarial tasks at work. Read while I hang out at home. Frankly, it's been downright boring. I told Parker I don't need them, but he's a man, so . . ."

"Girl, I get it." Lauren rubbed her hands together in anticipation. "Okay, let's see these letters, and then I gotta get back to work."

Abbie dug into her bag for her mail, then dumped it onto the table in a pile.

"What's this?"

"Oh, that." Abbie snatched the letter back from Lauren and stuffed it into her bag.

"Yes, that. What was that? It wasn't a legal document . . ."

Abbie glared at her. "No, it wasn't, nosy. My brother's government wants me to come on as an advisor. They clearly don't understand my relationship with him. He won't even call me back since I left Brevspor."

Lauren pulled her hair back. "Have you tried texting him?"

"Yes. And email. Nothing."

"Hmm. Weird. What does he want, smoke signals?"

Abbie sighed. "I wish I knew."

"He's pretty young, isn't he?"

She nodded, sitting back. "Eighteen. And he needs to get married. Soon."

"Wow."

Abbie tipped her head back and forth. "It's not that unusual in Brevspor. Unusual for a man, maybe. But not for a woman. The legal age is sixteen. But most women put off marriage until they can support a husband."

Lauren giggled. "I'd love to see you with a pack of subservient men trailing after you."

"One's plenty, thank you. And I'm the one who walks a step behind." She tapped the other papers on the table, and Lauren obligingly picked them up and began to read.

"Hmm. We're going to have to find you a solicitor in Orangiers to deal with some of this stuff. I can write you a request for a postponement until you're headed there next—which is when?"

"This weekend."

"That's probably okay, but we'll check anyway. And for your actual court date, a weekend won't do; it's got to be during the week."

"More missed work. Great."

"The fact that they haven't formed a class action says a lot. They're hoping you'll give up; they want to drown you in court dates, paperwork, lawyers' fees . . . They don't need to organize; they've got the money to fight you."

"Well, it's working."

Lauren gave her a sympathetic look. "Hang in there, hon. It'll all be worth it." She kept her eyes on the paperwork. "Have you thought about mediation?"

Abbie shook her head. "I don't want to put this in the hands of one person."

"It wouldn't be," Lauren said absentmindedly, still reading while she talked. "That's arbitration, this is mediation. It's nonbinding, but you need someone who's impartial. That would be the tough part."

"Well, that sounds promising. I'll put some thought into it."

"Can I take these with me?"

Abbie shrugged. "Sure. I guess I'll start fires with something else."

Lauren's gaze narrowed. "Stop posturing. You don't even have a fireplace." She slid the papers into her leather briefcase. "You'll get my bill in the mail. He can afford it."

Abbie grinned. "Yes, he can."

CHAPTER EIGHT

130 days to the wedding

PARKER LED THE WAY into the doctor's office, feeling unaccountably nervous.

"Abbie. Nice to see you again."

"You too," Abbie replied, shaking Dr. Honaker's slim khaki hand. The petite, black-haired woman motioned for them to sit.

"And this must be your fiancé . . ."

"Yes; Dr. Honaker, this is Edward."

"Nice to meet you, Edward." She gave him a slight bow.

"And you, Doctor. A pleasure." He suppressed a smile. Someone must have advised her not to try to shake his hand, thereby avoiding the awkward moment they'd already had with her nephrologist a few minutes earlier.

"How are you feeling, Abbie?"

"Pretty good."

"You're sleeping well?"

"Mostly."

"What are you taking when you don't?"

"Valerian. And I'm on magnesium all the time."

"Remind me of the dosage?"

Abbie tapped through several screens on her phone. "It's magnesium citrate, two hundred milligrams."

"That's not very much, really. We could up that if you'd like."

"No, it messed with my digestion last time; this is the most I can handle."

"Okay. And you're eating well?"

"Most of the time."

"Do you wake up feeling rested?"

"Sometimes."

"What percentage of the time?"

"About half."

She only feels rested half the time, and she's nagging me to get more sleep? I've got to stop calling her so late at night. I'm probably keeping her up.

"Is it safe to assume your Raynaud's isn't bothering you this time of year?"

Abbie nodded.

"Any complaints regarding your digestion?"

She glanced at him so fleetingly, Edward wasn't sure she'd actually done it.

"Yes, sometimes things are running too fast."

"Hmm. Any idea what's triggering it?"

"I'm not sure. We'd talked about cutting out night-shades, but I didn't know if that could affect my digestion, or ..."

Dr. Honaker shook her head curtly. "No, that has to do with inflammation, it shouldn't be affecting that. Could there be a hidden source of gluten in your diet? Soy sauce, salad dressings?"

Abbie made a note in her phone, then looked up. "No, I make my own dressings, and I use tamari."

"Cross-contamination from another source? Are you still living alone?"

"No, I recently got a roommate . . . and now that I think about it, that's about when the problems started up again, actually."

"My guess is that she's using your cutting boards, knives, and dishes. Have a talk with her, explain the issue; she'll probably be understanding."

Something to mention to my own cooking staff, Parker thought.

"Oh yes, she's very understanding; I'll talk to her about it."

And if she's not, he thought, *I'll fire her.*

"Still avoiding alcohol?"

Parker cleared his throat. "May I ask a question?"

The doctor looked at him expectantly.

"Why does she have to avoid alcohol?"

"It doesn't play well with the methotrexate she's on."

"Oh, I see. I apologize for the interruption."

"Don't be sorry." The doctor's face was relaxed, friendly. "It's good to understand your partner's condition. You can be a better support to her that way."

Like not obliviously ordering a glass of wine when we're at a restaurant together, as I did last time I was in Gardenia? Did that bother her? Why didn't I notice she wasn't drinking?

"How's the joint pain?"

Abbie's knee was bouncing. "Pretty bad." That was news to him, and based on Dr. Honaker's expression, it was news to her as well.

"How long has it been pretty bad?"

"A few weeks. I've been under more stress lately."

"Uh-huh. The gluten may also factor into it, in your case. And what are you taking for it?"

"Nothing."

Dr. Honaker put down her pen and sat forward in her chair. "Abbie, we've discussed this."

Abbie twisted her rings and didn't make eye contact. "Yes."

The doctor's tone was gentle, but firm. "There's no reason for you to suffer. Why didn't you take anything for it?"

"Acetaminophen doesn't work. Ibuprofen does, but I'm not supposed to take that, my nephrologist said. I can't take it daily."

"I know you favor nonprescription remedies . . . Have you considered massage?"

"No. I don't want strangers touching me like that."

"It wouldn't have to be a stranger. Perhaps your partner could offer some relief, if he's up for it, or a close friend."

Calling me her partner makes it sound like we play tennis together; she's my future wife, for heaven's sake.

"Yes, of course," he said. He kept all the flirting inside, but Abbie still caught something in his tone that made her hold his gaze for a long moment.

"What about moist heat for your pain?"

"I take showers. They help a little. Baths work better, but I don't have a tub."

"I thought you were going to a health club for their hot tub?" Dr. Honaker asked.

"I was. It got too expensive, and then I got a weird skin thing that I attribute to the facility's lack of cleanliness . . ."

"Have you tried meditating for the pain?"

Abbie snorted.

"I'll take that as a no . . ." Dr. Honaker smiled down at the paperwork. "Don't underestimate what the brain can do for the body, given the opportunity." She looked up again. "Are you avoiding sun exposure?"

"Rigorously."

"How often are you exercising?"

"Once a week or so . . ."

"Let's up that to three times a week, please, consistently. Daily would be better, but let's work toward that slowly. It doesn't have to be strenuous; just get out and move. It will help keep your inflammation down . . ."

"Okay."

"There's a new medication that's just come out; I'd like to put you on it. I think it'll control your inflammation better, so you won't need pain medication. But there's not a lot of research on this particular drug yet, so I want you to stay in contact with me regarding your flares."

"Okay, that sounds like a good idea." Abbie nodded.

"And you'll communicate with me?"

"Yes, I will. I promise."

Parker really wanted to believe that she was going to keep her word. *No matter; I'll keep her on the straight and narrow. My spies are in place.*

"How many days until you get married?"

"One hundred and thirty," Parker answered without a pause, and Abbie's lips were quivering like she was trying not to grin at him like a starry-eyed teenager for knowing it off the top of his head.

"Will you be living in the area?"

"No, I'm moving to Orangiers," Abbie replied.

"Please let us know where you plan to transfer your care, so we know where to send your files and medical history. I would hate for you to lose the good progress we've made." Dr. Honaker paged through Abbie's file. "Well, as usual, my last request is that you—"

Abbie shot to her feet. "Take care of myself? Yes, I will, thank you, Doctor."

Her eagerness to cut off the end of the doctor's sentence set off warning bells in Parker's head. "Pardon me. I didn't quite catch what the doctor was saying..."

Dr. Honaker smiled at him, both of them ignoring Abbie's minor panic. "I always ask her to give up coffee."

He turned toward Abbie, trying to control his reaction. "You're not supposed to drink coffee?"

Abbie's gaze darted around the room, and she shrugged one shoulder, then crossed her arms defensively. "Studies differ on whether it actually makes a difference. Coffee keeps me on my feet. I'd rather be awake at 3 p.m. And I'm monitoring my iron levels."

"As it happens," the doctor continued to Parker, "it was only one study that differed, and it was a very small sample set. The rest of the studies firmly recommend against it."

"How fascinating. Well, thank you so much for your time, Doctor. May I have your card in case I'd like to follow up with more questions?"

"Certainly." She pulled one out of a cluttered desk drawer and handed it to him.

Walking back out of the downtown clinic into the bright sunshine, he instinctively pulled her into the shade until the carriage pulled up. There were so many dangers for her; he never wanted to be a source of pain or illness, but it felt almost impossible not to be. *I should try harder not to fight with her, not to stress her out.*

"Well?" she said as they climbed into the carriage.

"Well, what?" He pivoted toward her in his seat.

"Well, was that helpful?"

"Yes, very." He couldn't process everything he'd heard . . . It all felt remote, suspended in his mind, like a speckled night sky he couldn't organize yet into constellations. "I can't believe—" He tried to catch himself before he said something stupid.

Her shoulders visibly tensed. "What can't you believe?"

"Never mind."

"Nope, too late."

He dipped his head to look at her over the top of his glasses. "The coffee. She seemed quite adamant, Abs."

She huffed a sigh. "She and I disagree on the coffee."

"Clearly."

He reached for her hand. "I didn't know you were hurting so often."

"Every day." Her tone was flat, not bitter, just resigned.

"Why don't you tell me, when I ask how you are?"

"Why would I?"

He shook his head. "I don't understand your question . . ."

She squeezed his hand. "It's a constant, right? So what good does it do to let it ruin your day, too?"

"Can I ask you about it? Should I?"

"Sometimes, I guess. I don't know. Not all the time. That's tedious for both of us."

He lifted her chin so that he could look into her eyes. "Knowing how you're feeling is not tedious for me. I love you."

"I love you, too." She pushed his hand away gently and looked out the small window. "But this is all new for you now. Wait until it's every day, every hour, every meal."

"I'm up for it."

"I sure hope so," she sighed.

CHAPTER NINE

123 days to the wedding

A WEEK LATER, ABBIE was brushing her teeth to get ready for bed when her phone plinked.

Parker: How was your day?

Abbie: Fine. Yours?

Parker: What did you do?

Abbie: Oh, you know. Went to work. Worked. Lunch. Worked. Came home.

Parker: Nothing significant?

Abbie: Nope. You?

She'd no sooner hit "Send" than her phone rang, and she quickly spit and answered. It hadn't been that long since she'd seen him, but they were only a few days away from her first visit to Orangiers since his coronation, and then the next weekend after next, they'd be in Imahara together. She was getting excited.

"Too tired to text?"

"Just wanted to hear your voice." He spoke quietly, no teasing in his voice.

"You okay?"

"Yes."

"You still working?"

"No."

"You watching something?"

"No."

"I think I got more information out of Tezza in our first conversation." He didn't laugh. They sat in silence, made twice as awkward by the lack of body language and physical presence. Abbie sat on the edge of her bed, rubbing the binding of her quilt.

"Tell me about your day."

"Classified."

"Oh." Abbie rubbed her forehead instead.

"Tell me about yours."

"It was fine. Bernard is falling right into my hands with this Tate land business. It won't be long before he gets what's coming to him. He's the guy who shoved me, you remember." She sipped the water by her bed. "Georgie is a good fit for the secretarial job; she's just the type. She was none too happy that he was screaming at me again, but she positioned herself nicely to intervene if necessary and let me handle it. I appreciated that."

"Mmm." He didn't sound distracted, but he didn't sound like himself. Abbie decided to keep rambling, hoping to provoke him into a debate, ease him out of whatever crap day he'd had, whether he'd admit it or not.

"Though I think the others are suspicious of her, because she's too tan. Environmentalists tend to be anti-sun. Which is funny, because they're more likely to get out and enjoy nature. I think they're just better about hats and sunblock and all that. They realize the long-term effects of sun damage, though that knowledge doesn't seem to affect other health professions. I mean, seriously, most of the nurses I know smoke tobacco. It's bizarre, don't you think?" She paused. No response. "Parker?"

"Yes?"

She kept every trace of sarcasm out of her voice. "Do you need a hug?"

He said nothing.

"Honey, what happened?"

"They should've waited for backup. They should've waited."

"Who?" She waited, but he said nothing . . . then she realized who he meant. "Did something happen to your friends?"

"Saint, Simonson and James, they cornered Lincoln at a hideout in Heartwood Forest somewhere. His sentries got a shot off on James."

Abbie was trembling. Edward had been friends with these men for years; all his school stories involved at least one of them. She hadn't even met Arron James yet; he wasn't allowed to die.

"What kind of weapon?"

"Crossbow. To the chest. Non-magical."

She sucked in breath. It could've been a lot worse, but it could've been better placed, too.

"Oh Woz. Is he going to be okay?"

"Not sure yet. They medevaced him to Briggin; he's in surgery now." He sighed. "I'm not supposed to be telling you this."

That pissed her off. "Who am I going to tell?"

"I don't know, darling."

"Now I know you need a hug." She paused. "Do you want me to come? I could call in sick tomorrow."

"No, it's okay."

"But he's one of your best friends, hon. If Lauren were dying, I'd want you here."

"No, it's fine. I'll know more tomorrow."

"Where are Saint and Simonson?"

"In Briggin. They had to fall back when James was hit. We didn't get Lincoln. It was the right thing to do."

"Why don't you go, too? To Briggin?"

She heard him exhale a shaky breath. "The security situation would be a nightmare. Plus, it could draw Lincoln to the hospital if I'm there, and that's the last thing they need. A king running around in everyone's way, everyone falling all over themselves to accommodate me instead of focusing on Arron's care. Plus, you wouldn't be able to come this weekend."

"It wouldn't be like that. You don't have to be at the hospital all the time; rent a house like you did for Dad's funeral. Go in shifts. Isn't it a military hospital in Briggin? I'm sure they're used to hosting self-important generals and such. You're no worse than them."

"No better, you mean."

"No, I said what I meant. You should go. Go be with your friends. Imagine how encouraged he'll be to wake up from surgery and see you there. Not all healing is physical; he did this for you. He needs to know that you care about what happened. And the rest of your military forces would be bolstered as well."

"What about your visit?"

"I'm going to see you in Imahara. I'll come for the thing on Friday, too."

He paused. "You make some valid points."

"I know."

"Perhaps I should just let you run things."

"Hard pass."

"I guess I should go pack."

"Okay, hon. I love you."

"I love you, too. I miss you . . . I miss you very much."

"I know, hon. Get some sleep, too, okay? Let the staff pack for you."

"Okay. Good night."

"Good night."

Abbie pressed the phone to her chest over her heart, tears sliding down her cheeks, and for the first time in her life, she wished she knew how to pray.

PARKER WAS WALKING out to the blimp at sunrise when he heard high-heeled footsteps behind him and turned to look. In the blossoming light of early day, he squinted to see who it was, and all his staff stopped to look as well.

"It's the First Daughter, sir," said Dean.

"Rhodie? What's she doing here?"

He stood still, like he'd been taught, and let her advance toward his position rather than meeting her halfway. Rules like that chafed against both his practical side and his people-pleasing side. He told himself it was just impolite to make her walk the whole distance, but it wasn't so. He stood nevertheless, waiting for her, and he could see now that she was dressed to travel, pulling her own suitcase behind her over the rough landing field, still somehow a picture of elegance.

"I'm coming with you."

Parker kissed his sister on one cheek, then eyed her warily. "Why?"

"Because I'm a doctor, and Arron needs all the help he can get."

"No, you can't step on their toes just because you're royal. They're not Orangiersian, Dr. Broward; your medical license here means nothing there."

She lifted her chin, and he knew he was about to get a lecture.

"My work has been published in Attaamy as well, and my expeditions and collaborations are well known there. Dr. Pasqual and I have been in communication already; I don't think they'll have any problem accepting a competent doctor's help."

"Well, you still need *my* permission to come. And I'm not giving it without a reason." He lifted an eyebrow, then added, "A real reason."

She turned on her trademark charm. "You don't think that's a bit nosy, little brother?"

Parker widened his stance and crossed his arms, unmoved. It was too early to be playing games, and he couldn't find a smile in his sleep-deprived, quietly terrified state.

Her lips twitched, and he couldn't tell if she was holding back tears or a smile. "He's my friend, too, Parker. I want to be there when he wakes up. I . . . I need to be there. I need to see that he's okay." In a rare moment of embarrassment, her voice had dropped to a whisper in the presence of his staff, most of whom had politely drifted away or turned their attention to their phones. Only Dean and Waldo remained nearby. Parker saw the sincerity in her eyes; she actually did need this. Was there more going on between her and his friend than he'd realized? Now he felt bad for giving James grief about his weakness for Rhodie; he'd considered it an insignificant crush.

He said nothing, but nodded. Parker turned and led the way onto the air stairs, leaving her to trail a step behind, but he still heard the long, quiet sigh of relief she breathed out. His phone plinked.

Abbie: Boarding?

Parker: Yes.

Abbie: Okay. Text when you land, please.

Oh dear, Parker thought. *She has her polite pants on . . . She must be really worried. Letting others run things has never been one of her strong suits . . .* He was only boarding this flight because of her pushing. He wouldn't be surprised if she showed up in Briggin, if she had the money. But because of that dumb debt repayment, he was pretty sure she was broke. He still needed to work on that. He'd recognized her handwriting on the insured envelope she'd mailed him earlier in the week, and he'd had them stamp it "Return to sender." *Round two to me.*

Parker: I will. Go back to sleep.

Abbie: And let me know how James is doing when you get there.

Parker: Yes, I will.

Abbie: Who did you take with you?

Parker: Abs . . .

Abbie: Can't sleep.

Parker: Core staff, security, Rhodie. Isn't it like 3 a.m. there?

Abbie: Yes. Rhodie?

Parker: She asked to come along at the last moment.

Abbie: Good, I'm glad. She'll be a good support to you. You should have people who care about you there with you. I wish I could be.

Parker: I know, darling. Taking off; talk soon.

Abbie: Okay.

It was a white lie, he told himself. He was allowed to use his phone in transit, but she needed to try to sleep or she'd be wiped at work today. He wondered how the stress of this was going to affect her health, if it would trigger a flare, how bad it would be. At least her security was there to check in with him. He didn't have to worry that she was hiding anything for once.

He read over new legislation he'd been asked to endorse, noting possible loopholes, discrepancies, weaknesses. Rhodie sat across from him, staring out the window, her own reading lying forgotten in her lap, and he followed her gaze: Tupelo Crossing. The earth still bore the signs of the battle he'd fought there just a few months before, brown circles of grass from their tents, deep gouges scratched into the earth from the cannons that had missed. Truth be told, his soul looked much the same way. Video games were one thing; war was another, and he wasn't cut out for it. He carried those fifty casualties like they were marked upon his flesh.

He hoped desperately that he wouldn't have to add Arron's name to that list.

CHAPTER TEN

122 days to the wedding

PARKER AND RHODIE ARRIVED at the hospital about an hour later. Just the smell of the disinfectant in the tile hallways made him wish he'd paid for Abbie to come; he hated hospitals. Whenever he had lunch with Rhodie, they always met elsewhere. He didn't know how she could tolerate that smell all the time, that lingering reminder that what existed here could kill you, had killed others already. As if reading his mind, Rhodie looped an arm through his. He gave her a tight smile.

Besides the unpleasant smell, he sensed the magic here, like a pulse, powering not just the lights and the heat, but the heart monitors, the X-ray and dialysis machines . . . Even inside the Veil, non-tech magic existed as a healing remedy. Rhodie considered herself too much of a scientist to stoop to such "mumbo jumbo," as she called it. But now, with his friend lying before him, tubes sticking out of his chest, an oxygen mask over his face, his body too still, Parker understood the appeal for the first time. At least if he tried a traditional magical remedy, he'd feel like he was doing all he could, like he was doing *something*.

Everyone stood at his arrival, and he motioned them to sit back down. Simonson and Saint came over for firm handshakes, the most they could do in public, though he'd honestly have preferred a hug. Nothing too touchy-feely, mind you, just a strong one-armed embrace with a back slap at the end. *Is that weird?* he wondered.

Rhodie's colleague, Dr. Pasqual, was waiting for him. The three men gathered around, arms crossed, to listen.

"We're glad you're here, Your Majesty. There's a lot to be thankful for," she said, her light accent easy to understand, her tone even and comforting. "The bolt collapsed his right lung but missed the heart entirely, and that's going to help him a lot going forward. It did nick his superior vena cava, the vein that carries deoxygenated blood into the heart. He also has two broken ribs, likely from how he hit the ground." She turned to his two friends. "You did great with the field triage. If you hadn't kept pressure on his wound, we might be having a very different conversation. We were able to repair the vein, but he lost a lot of blood. If either of you would be willing to donate, it would certainly speed his recovery."

"I will," Parker said, regaining her attention, and her eyebrows lifted in surprise. "This isn't just any soldier, Doctor; Lieutenant James and I have been friends for many years. I'm also a universal donor."

She nodded, and he thought she looked impressed. "We'll arrange for a private room for your use while you donate, Your Majesty. Thank you."

He looked around for Rhodie, who was also a universal donor, and found her paging through Arron's chart, frowning. "Dr. Broward? Do you want to donate blood?"

His sister nodded distractedly, then turned to the nurse at her elbow, asking questions about the type of antibiotics they'd already administered and what percentage oxygen was flowing through the mask, her eyes rarely leaving Arron's sleeping face. *It's so weird to see him so stoic. We can hardly get him to keep a straight face long enough for his military ID photo.*

"How long does he have to stay here?" Parker heard how bad that sounded as soon as it was out of his mouth, and quickly tried to remedy his mistake. "We're extremely grateful for your help, but I'd like him somewhere more comfortable, closer to home, you understand."

Dr. Pasqual nodded. "We'll need to monitor him for another few days to make sure there's no complications from the surgery such as blood clots or the lung re-collapsing, but after that, he'll be free to do his rehab in Orangiers. That'll take six to eight weeks, depending on his diligence with his exercises."

"Oh, he'll do them diligently," said Saint darkly, and the doctor looked like she wanted to take a step back, but held her ground.

"Shouldn't he be awake?"

Dr. Pasqual pressed her clipboard against her chest. "It's a bit early for that. We'd expect him to wake up in the next two to four hours. He's been under heavy sedation for the pain. Trust me, the pain will wake him up soon."

Parker nodded, then turned away from the conversation, texting Abbie the salient information as promised, hoping the notification wouldn't wake her. He kept Rhodie in his peripheral vision, more out of curiosity than brotherly protection instincts.

Simonson stood at his elbow and cleared his throat. "His mum and sisters are coming down tomorrow."

"Good. Let's help them with the cost, quietly. I know it's expensive to fly."

"Right, sir." He looked wiped.

"Why don't you and Saint go to the house and get some rest? Rhodie and I can stay here with him."

Simonson looked at Rhodie, and she caught him staring and smiled. He looked away, embarrassed.

"Oh, come on. Still?"

He nodded. "She's a princess, sir."

"I'm a king."

"It's not the same." His voice had dropped to a mumble.

"It is to the women." Parker elbowed him, and Simonson grinned, still staring at the ground. Parker jerked his head at Saint, who came over.

"You can get the details on the house from Waldo. It should be more than large enough for all of us and his family, so don't let them get a hotel. Rhodie and I can share a room if needed."

"No need, sir," Saint muttered, grinning. "She surely doesn't want to hear your lovesick phone calls with your girl."

"Jealousy, thy name is Saint."

Simonson chimed in. "No, mate, it's more like, 'Abbie, darling, that's insane. You can't do that. No, you can't. No, you can't. Because I said so, and I'm a king. Yes, I am.'"

Parker chuckled harder. "That's much closer to reality."

"Things are good, though?"

He nodded, smiling. "Very good."

"What of these lawsuits, then?"

"We're fighting them. I expect they'll give up eventually."

"Can you marry before they're resolved?"

He shook his head. "But we're planning for Twelfth Month, end of the year."

Saint stepped closer. "And what of the death threats? Do we need to change our mission?" He stroked his light beard thoughtfully. "I've never been to Gardenia."

"No need. I've deployed two of my best security, and she has begrudgingly accepted them, as I knew she would. Hashtag—"

Saint groaned. "Don't say #kinging. It's ridiculous."

The young royal crossed his arms. "Abbie laughs."

"She won't once you're wed. Might as well quit now. My brother's girlfriend used to laugh at every dumb thing he said, and now she just tells him that she'll laugh when he remembers to rinse out the sink after he brushes his teeth. He's a bit of a slob, though."

"Get out of here, both of you. I bet Kurt doesn't have to put up with this ballast."

They gathered their packs, grinning, and Simonson muttered, "Kurt is a lonely jackass. You're lucky to have us."

"So you keep telling me. I'll have the gaming systems set up by the time you get back."

"King Edward? Your donation room is ready," Dr. Pasqual said.

He glanced at James, then said, "Waldo, you're with James. Dean, you're with Rhodie and me." He wasn't sure if she was actually going to leave Arron's side, but he heard her stilettos on the tile trailing him, however hesitantly, as he followed the nurse down the hall. Most rooms he peeked into had at least two patients, and he made a mental note to thank the hospital for giving Arron a private room, though he was sure it would be reflected in the bill. He knew many Attaamish citizens felt ashamed that they'd allowed Lincoln to wage his war on their soil; perhaps this was subtle compensation.

They settled into the donation chairs, Rhodie finally removing her coat.

"All right, love?"

"Yes," she said, still distracted. Her phone was in her hand.

"I know you're tech-noring me." She shot him an annoyed look and he smiled.

"Is that an Abbie-ism?"

He nodded, looking away as the nurse rolled up his sleeve. He wasn't afraid of needles, he just didn't like to watch them go in. He began to sweat and forced his arm muscles to relax.

"It's when people use technology to ignore people around them."

"Yes, I deduced that, actually . . ."

"How do you feel about the level of care he's being provided?"

She shifted in her seat as her own technician came over. "Please use a butterfly needle. I have small veins." The nurse appeared to Parker to be suppressing an eye roll, but she complied.

Parker chuckled. "Doctors make terrible patients."

Rhodie lifted her chin. "I just know my body better than most. It's not a sin."

"Still waiting on your answer."

She sighed. "He's being very well cared for."

The nurse was smirking, but stopped when Parker met her gaze.

"Why do you sound disappointed, Dr. Broward?" he said.

"I'm not disappointed." Her voice was steady, but her eyes betrayed her stress.

"Don't worry. You can still stay. I won't send you home."

Her shoulders dropped a little. "Thank you."

"How long have you been seeing each other?"

Her shoulders shot up again. "We're not *seeing each other*," she snapped.

"Why not?"

She stared at him. "You wouldn't disapprove?"

"Of course not. Why would I?"

"He's not *royal*."

"So? It's the year 517 A.B., and there's a dwindling number of royal partners available. I think you're capable of choosing your own life partner, within reason. Plus, you're after Andrew in the line of succession, and you could always refuse."

She stared at him again. The technician touched her arm and she jumped, glaring at her, then turned back to her brother.

"Well," she sniffed, "it's not like that. We're not . . . we're not together."

"I see," said Parker, even though he was fairly sure it was at least a little "like that." "Well, that's a shame. I think you'd be brilliant together. You could use someone to make you laugh."

The young king peered at the cookie tray, trying to find one with chocolate chips he could take without touching the others.

"Your Majesty, if I may, your security checked them, and they're all for you, so it's okay to touch them." He grinned greedily and the technician smiled. He'd skipped breakfast, so he and the lads could easily put all these away. He passed the tray to Rhodie but she waved it away. He'd forgotten. She never ate sweets.

"Finish up, I want to get back to Arron, and I can't go without you because I didn't bring my security." Rhodie was digging in her purse and came up with a peppermint.

Her technician frowned. "Dr. Broward, that's not enough sugar to compensate for—"

"I'll be fine. I take full responsibility for my blood sugar levels."

The technician shook her head a little, and Parker sighed. "Dr. Broward, please eat a cookie. It will make the staff happy."

Rhodie glared at him and silently selected the smallest cookie on the tray, holding her right hand under it as she ate to avoid getting crumbs on her outfit. "It's very inconvenient to be ruled by my second brother."

"I can just imagine," he drawled, and she laughed softly. *Better than being ruled by your first brother,* he thought, but he didn't dare say it. They never mentioned Lincoln anymore in the family; he might as well have been dead, killed by his own ambition. Parker knew his youngest brother missed Lincoln especially, but Simon's developmental delays made it tough for him to understand what had transpired to send him away. A shudder went through Parker as he imagined whom Rhodie would've been married off to—not to mention the twins and Forsythia—under Lincoln's rule in order to benefit the kingdom.

Rhodie stood and walked to the door. "All right, let's go."

"So impatient." He stood and turned to the technicians. "Thank you both for the good work you do; you have done us an important service today, and we are most grateful." Both ladies blushed and curtsied.

He and Rhodie exited and had started down the hall when Parker noticed his sister watching him out of the corner of her eye.

"Is Abbie charmed by you, Second Brother?"

Unable to stop himself, Parker snorted, and Rhodie smiled.

"I guess I have my answer." She was quiet, realization blossoming on her face. "You like that she's not charmed by you?"

"More accurately, I like that she's not intimidated by me. She makes me work for it."

She kept a straight face. "'It' being . . ."

He scowled. "Her affection."

Her face broke into a teasing grin. "Yes, of course, her affection, her *affection*."

"We haven't married yet. How could it be anything else?"

"Well, it could be—"

"Not for me."

Her gaze shifted down the hall. "Good for you."

CHAPTER ELEVEN

THE ROYALS ARRIVED back at Arron's room and made themselves as comfortable as they could in the hospital's thinly padded chairs, Rhodie sitting by Arron's head, Parker across the room with his feet up on the end of the bed, computer on his lap. He had some work to do . . . okay, a lot of work to do. Mostly, he was rescheduling and reordering things he was supposed to do this week, putting off everything he could, arranging video conferencing for the most important tasks. He politely pretended not to notice Rhodie brushing Arron's red hair off his forehead and holding his hand, staring at his sleeping face. He'd been working for the better part of two hours when he noticed some movement across the room.

His friend was blinking, looking around. He pulled off the oxygen mask.

"Edward? What are you doing here?"

Parker turned to his guard. "Dean, please let them know he's awake." Then he set aside his computer and crossed to the head of the bed. "You're in the military hospital in Briggin. You were shot. I came to see how you were doing. Rhodie, too."

At her name, Arron looked around, clearly startled to see her holding his hand. He held her gaze, then a slow smile spread across his face. "What a nice surprise."

Rhodie seemed flustered—a state Parker had never once observed her in—and she dropped his hand, fussing over him. "Are you in pain? How much on a scale of one to ten?"

"When I woke . . . a nine. Then I saw your face . . ." He chased her gaze without moving too much. ". . . and that number dropped significantly."

She scowled. "You're not funny."

"Not trying to be, love." He coughed, and Parker could see the agony on his face.

Rhodie grabbed an extra pillow and put it on his chest. "Hug the pillow when you cough, it'll help. Edward, don't touch him."

He held up his hands, confused. "I wasn't going to."

"Yes, *Edward*, don't touch me. I'm fragile."

He wanted to laugh, but the stern look Rhodie was dishing out sobered him.

"Oh Woz, I've broken my funny bone. I can't be funny. I've no reason to live." He turned to Rhodie. "Just pull the plug, love."

Her anger bled into her voice. "Which one? Your thoracostomy tube? Your IV? Your oxygen? You've had a serious medical event, Lieutenant . . ."

"Your choice, flower. Just make it quick. Be merciful."

Rhodie sniffed, and Parker knew she was fighting feelings. "You're impossible." A covey of doctors and nurses flew into the room, and Rhodie was relegated to the back of the crowd. Though they were too polite to say so, Edward sensed he was in the way and moved aside for temperature taking, blood pressure monitoring, and head-to-toe "how are you feeling?" questions by the medical staff. When they were sat-

isfied that he was making the necessary progress, they disappeared as quickly as they'd come, leaving the two friends
alone.

"Where's my princess?" Arron asked, trying to lift his
head, and Parker crossed to crank his bed so he could sit up
more.

"She must be just outside; she's using my security." He
lifted an eyebrow. "And she's hardly *your* princess."

"Who told you that?"

"She did, if you'd believe."

"She would. She invented playing hard to get, you know.
Just because I'm trapped in this ruddy bed with more tubes
than the Barrowdon underground, she thinks she can just
walk out whenever she likes. As if I'll just lie here until she
comes back."

"James, she can't hear you, just relax, all right?" Where
had she gone, anyway? Edward peered toward the door to
see if he could spot her through the window.

"Edward."

Surprised by the use of his first name, he turned toward
James and found his friend's face strained.

"I need meds. Stronger stuff, yeah?"

Parker nodded. "I'll speak to Dr. Pasqual."

"You know horse tablets?"

The king nodded, one eyebrow raised.

"Yeah, forget those. Go for elephant tablets."

Parker chuckled and nodded. "She's right, you are impossible."

"Don't tell her, okay? About the meds."

"She has access to your chart. She's going to know. Nothing I can do about it."

He tensed visibly, and the heart monitor's tempo increased. "Where's Saint and Simonson?"

"I sent them off to rest. They hadn't left your side since it happened. They'll be back in a few hours."

"But they're not . . ."

"No, they're fine. Everything's fine, everyone's fine. Lie down and relax."

"But my princess . . ." He seemed a bit loopy; Parker was pretty sure the pain meds the staff had administered were starting to kick in.

"Your princess will be back in due time, I'm sure."

"I'm going to hold you to that, sir. Don't let her go running back to Orangiers to her responsibilities. That's just the sort of sneaky trick she'd try."

AS IT TURNED OUT, THE hospital staff would not let Edward set up their video game system in Arron's room, citing the potential for noise to disturb other patients, so they were forced to entertain him in less advanced ways. Parker doubted that their card game was really any quieter than their video games would've been, but at least there weren't any weaponry noises; the other patients might not be keen to listen to that in a military hospital. His pile of tongue depressors that Dr. Pasqual had offered as chips for their poker game was dwindling, but he still had an ace up his sleeve. Not literally, of course; he'd never actually cheat. But orchestrating their distraction . . .

"Dr. Broward? Sure we can't deal you in?"

The other men raised an eyebrow at him, seeing through his attempt to fluster them, but Rhodie just shook her head, eyes trained on her laptop screen.

"I don't think you could keep up, anyway. Your feeble female brain isn't suited to the sophisticated strategy of card playing."

"Nice try, Second Brother."

"Leave my princess alone," James said. "She's working hard over there, saving the world. What are you curing now, love? Cancer? Measles? Acne?"

"Measles is cured already, and acne hardly seems worth my time."

"What then?"

"Alzheimer's. Specifically, examining how it's impacted by blood sugar, and its strong correlation with trisomy 21."

"My princess is so brilliant." He grinned at her, but she didn't look up. "Additionally, I can say whatever I want, because I'm in hospital. I'd no idea injury gave me license to be a twit. I'd have shot myself years ago if I'd known."

"Are you sure you didn't?" Edward asked coolly.

"It's to you, James," Saint muttered.

"What's to me?"

Simonson snorted. "He's so busy flirting he's forgotten the game."

"I'm losing anyway." James replaced two cards.

"Edward far worse." Saint grinned.

"I'm just lulling you into a false sense of security before I make my comeback."

The others chuckled, and Arron's face contorted at the pain of laughing, but he recovered quickly. "Well, I can't lie around all day, so what shall we do this weekend? Rock climbing? Skydiving? Spelunking?" More chuckling.

At this, Rhodie raised her head, her walnut skin reflecting the blue glow of the laptop. Only James and Parker could see her tortured expression, the tears threatening to fall. She quickly set the laptop aside and darted for the door.

"Rhodie?" At Edward's voice, her royal training compelled her to stop. "Where are you going?" She didn't turn around. Edward glanced at James, and there was a new kind of pain on his face, his eyes trained on her back.

"Deal me out," Parker said under his breath. "Let's take a walk . . ." He grabbed their coats from the chair by the door and touched her elbow to lead her into the hall.

"What's going on with you?" he said once they were out of earshot of the others.

"Not here." Her lip was trembling.

"Where, then?"

"Outside." Though she was supposed to trail a step behind, he offered her his arm so she could lead the way inconspicuously. Rhodie wound them through the catacombs of hallways, Dean a few paces back. They stepped out into the warm summer afternoon rain, and the city smells of horses and wet wood washed over him. She was marching now, practically dragging him along despite her stilettos.

"Rhodie," he complained, "I'm getting wet." She strode into an alley behind the hospital that had an overhang coming off the building. Dean handed him an umbrella—apparently courtesy of the hospital—and he gladly accepted it.

"All right. We're alone now. What's going on?" he asked, lifting his voice over the pelting of the rain.

"This is your fault. You should never have sent him after Lincoln. He wasn't properly prepared, he wasn't . . ." She heaved a sob, and he moved toward her, but she stepped away, her hands up. "Don't. I just want . . . I just need a moment." She paced under the overhang; it seemed like she was talking more to herself than to him. "He shouldn't be joking at a time like this! There was a real chance he'd never do any of that again, never skydive, never even walk again, let alone live to be an old man! And the mere thought of that breaks my . . ." Her voice trailed off.

"He doesn't mean anything by it, love. That's just who he is. Life's a joke to James."

She was folded over, hands on her knees, trying to slow her breathing. "Well, it means something to the rest of us. He could at least have the decency to be sorry for putting us through this."

"Sorry? Why? It's not his fault he got shot. And frankly, it's not my fault, either. I sent the best man for the job. I make no apology for that. If there's anyone to blame here, it's Lincoln."

"Well, I can't shout at Lincoln, can I? So perhaps you'll indulge me if I shout at you instead." She rolled up slowly and dabbed at her eyes with a handkerchief she'd apparently had in a pocket.

"I've never seen you so emotional."

She stiffened. "I apologize for my outburst. I'll hold it together; I hope you weren't embarrassed in front of the others."

"That's not what I meant, Rhodie. I just meant it's unusual for you. You're allowed to have feelings, especially about people who are important to you. I just didn't realize Arron was important to you . . ."

She stared at him. "Neither did I," she said softly.

"Would you accept a brotherly embrace?"

She squared her shoulders, waved him away. "Unnecessary. Don't worry about me."

"Oh, I don't worry about you. Mum's got that covered." He thought she might chuckle, but she didn't. "Do you want to go back up?"

"No, I think I'll go on to the house, rest a bit, eat something. Get some work done. Hard to focus with you four chattering like gibbons."

"Fair enough. Who would you like to escort you?"

"Waldo's fine. My security is supposed to be coming in this afternoon; I wasn't sure if I was going to stay."

"James asked me not to let you sneak home to your responsibilities."

She smiled. "I've no doubt he did. Will you bring me down my computer? And my purse?"

"Certainly." Parker texted Waldo to come down, and he and Dean went up to gather her things.

"My princess is leaving?" James asked.

Parker nodded. "She's tired, she's going to head to the house."

"We left her the nicest bedroom," Saint said, not looking up from his cards. "Top of the stairs on the right."

"What am I, fish guts?"

"Sorry, sir. To quote the damaged one, she makes us weak. Security wanted you elsewhere regardless." Simonson glanced at James, who didn't laugh. He stared at his cards.

Saint nudged James. "Your turn, mate."

"What?"

"Your turn."

"Oh, right. Sir?" Parker turned in the doorway, and James was still fixated on his cards. "Would you thank her for coming? And tell her I'm sorry?"

"Sorry for what?"

"For making her want to leave," he said, laying down his cards.

"Certainly," said Parker. He was beginning to feel like a carrier pigeon and hoped these two would figure out how to talk to each other sooner rather than later.

CHAPTER TWELVE

118 days to the wedding

EDWARD ARRIVED BACK home to Bluffton Castle the following Sunday night. Arron's rehab and transportation were arranged. The hospital room was just too congested once Arron's mother and sisters arrived, and he wanted them to have some private time with him. Truth be told, he was missing his own family . . . He hadn't had dinner with them in weeks, and they'd all agreed to remedy the situation that night, school night bedtimes be damned.

The family dining room at Bluffton was his favorite room in the castle, though he expected that would change once Abbie shared his bedroom. The long oak table was old, scratched, and lacked the mirror shine of the formal dining room table. They never used china in this room, just the hand-painted hummingbird pottery dishes his parents had bought on their honeymoon in the Trellan Archipelago. Despite his recent demotion, Ignatius still sat at the head of the table here; Parker was just the Second Son, and even that made the space feel more comfortable. Everyone stood up when he and Rhodie came in and put their phones in the basket on the center of the table, then both went around the table, greeting each family member.

He put a hand on his youngest sister's shoulder. "Forsythia. Painted any new pictures lately, love?"

"No." She pouted. "Teacher's had lessons for me every day." That was the pain of being twelve and royal; he knew his parents were trying to nail down Thia's marriage contract to a prince in the Forgelands, of all places, and as such, her dress and deportment lessons had been kicked up a notch.

"I'll speak to him." He winked at her, and she grinned.

He made a show of bouncing his gaze back and forth between the twins, who were giving him identical Cheshire grins. They were different enough in personality that he didn't usually have trouble telling them apart, but when they weren't speaking, it was tougher. "Hello . . . Ginger." He was quickly forgotten.

Dahlia stuck her hand out to her sister. "Five quid, please."

Ginger slapped her palm against it. "I don't have it with me. How does he always know?"

"Never bet against a brother—that's my motto."

"And hello, Dahlia, thank you for the vote of confidence."

He ruffled both their heads and was rewarded with unison squeals of displeasure. Parker continued around the table.

"Andrew." The young man grunted and offered his hand, but Parker used it to pull him forward into a tight yet brief embrace.

"Hello, Simon."

"Eddie!" Only Simon could get away with calling a king "Eddie," but the eight-year-old pulled it off with panache.

He threw his arms open and hugged Parker ardently before he could get his arms out, and then prolonged the experience, rocking them side to side. All Parker could do was laugh, and those close enough to notice laughed, too. Simon's open affection was a steady source of joy. The boy broke the hug and looked up at Parker, about to ask the question he asked every time Parker came back from a trip, the question Parker always dreaded.

"Where's my other brother?"

Parker forced half a smile. "Still away, mate. He'll be away for a long time, remember?"

"You say that all the time!"

Parker pulled a new keychain out of his pocket, his traditional gift, and Simon grabbed it.

"It's a ship!"

"I thought you'd like that." His mother had suggested bringing a gift to distract from questions about Lincoln's absence, and it had been an effective strategy.

Lily cleared her throat. "Say 'thank you,' Simon."

"Thank you, Simon," he said, absentmindedly turning the tiny ship over in his hand, examining it carefully from all angles.

"Hello, Mum." Parker kissed her cheek.

"Hello, son. How is the James family holding up?"

He squeezed her hand. "Well enough. Arron should be released in a few days, but I paid up the rental house for two weeks, so they can stay as long as they like. They're relieved, but shaken by what could have been. They're still processing it all, I think."

Lily took his face in her hands, examining him from both sides. "And you? How are you holding up?"

"Well enough, too." He smiled, used to her scrutiny. She let her hands drop and gave him a sad look.

"I'm so sorry your bride couldn't come this weekend as planned. I'm sure you could use her comfort now. Such a sweet girl..."

I don't think she met the right princess, but I'm glad she thinks so. She'll be disabused of the notion soon enough.

"Well, between the eight of you, I have an adequate substitute."

She glowed at him. In his family, "adequate" was higher praise than it sounded to most.

"Oh, darling—I keep forgetting. Abbie sent me with an envelope for you. She didn't elaborate, but she said you'd know what it was."

Parker closed his eyes, shaking his head. *That's low, Abs, involving innocent family members in our feud.* "You can donate that to your trisomy 21 foundation, Mum. Please be sure to send her a thank-you note." *Round three to her...*

He moved on to his last stop, his father. Ignatius gave him a warm smile and a warmer embrace. *No one hugs like my dad.* "Bear hug" didn't begin to describe it; "cobra hug" came closer, being crushed with style when you least expected it.

"Dad."

"Son." They sat down, signaling the start of the meal, and everyone began to dig in.

"So Abbie was supposed to come this weekend...," his father began.

"Yes. We postponed to next week since I was gone due to Arron's situation."

Parker glanced around. Rhodie was notably quiet; she had been since they'd left Briggin. Everyone else seemed to be ignoring him, engaged in side conversations about how many vegetables were required to get a lemon square for dessert and arguing over what Ginger's nail polish was called.

"We should strategize your military response. Later." Ignatius, too, seemed to be checking to make sure their conversation was private.

"No need. I'm bringing Saint and Simonson home."

His dad gave him the scrutinizing stare he knew all too well. "Why?"

"Because it's not worth the cost. He's retreated. I'm just going to let him be."

Ignatius lowered his voice. "You can still send out a contingent. Just don't send your best friends this time." The comment stung.

"They were the best men for the job."

Parker saw the disagreement written on his father's face. "Why do you think so?"

"Because I can trust them; they're loyal. If I sent a Black Feather unit, I was concerned that they . . ."

Ignatius swallowed his bite. "You were afraid they'd kill him."

Parker nodded curtly. "And respectfully, I don't want to discuss it. I'm not a pushover; there's just no reason for it. I've had enough of pointless killing."

"No Black Feather will disobey you, son. He'd rather die than disappoint you."

"No, Dad, he'd rather die than disappoint *you*. Their track record with me is untested. At this point, I don't even know for certain who's on Lincoln's side and who's on mine. He wouldn't persist unless he thought he had some popular support."

Ignatius rubbed at his full beard. "I still think they're an important resource you're not using for a faulty reason. If you don't try the Black Feathers, you'll never find out—"

"No work talk at the table." Lily's voice floated over the top of the conversation; she was giving Ignatius a censorious look, and he smiled at her, going back to his food. You could put whoever you wanted at the head of the table, but his mum often had the last word.

Ever the peacemaker, Ignatius changed the subject to appease her. "I didn't know Abbie was meeting you in Imahara. Business or pleasure?"

"A bit of both," Parker said. "After our time in the Unveiled, she's very interested in social justice issues. I'm hoping to put her in contact with some foundations for future involvement and advocacy. And then she'll stay the weekend."

"At a hotel?"

"No, at my rental. There's ample space, and the security situation is better. Rolls, please." Parker took the basket from his mother, who passed them over Simon's head.

His father chuckled, low and knowing. "Oh, you made sure of that, did you?"

"Meaning what, exactly?"

"You have a talent for keeping your bride close by, now that you've got her back . . ."

"I would remind you that she's still living across the continent, and I don't think you'd do any differently with Mum."

"Fair enough. Do you have things planned for the weekend?"

Parker shook his head. "We're both pretty exhausted most of the time."

"Well, running around can be helpful in keeping you both distracted . . . Too much sitting around can lead to . . ." Ignatius paused cutting his chicken as he leaned forward. "I know your contract's signed. Just remember, 'good as married' isn't good enough for certain activities."

Parker wanted to glare at him, but didn't dare. He sipped his wine to cover his annoyance.

"Give me a little credit; we're both adults."

"That's what I'm afraid of, son. I remember those days . . ."

"You needn't worry or fear. It will all be entirely proper."

"Very well. By the way, Mum really enjoyed getting to know Abbie better in Gardenia."

"Good. She said the same. Well, reversed, of course, but you know . . ."

"Yes."

"Eddie"—Simon was tugging his sleeve—"you're on my team."

"Oh?" Parker looked down at his youngest brother. "What are we playing, pray tell?"

Simon threw out his arms to punctuate his words. "Hearts!"

"I don't excel at games of deception, but I admire your enthusiasm. I'm in." Parker wiped his mouth and pushed back from the table to stand up, but Simon plopped himself on his lap.

"Oof," Parker winced. "You're getting a bit big for this, Si."

"You're weak."

He knew he shouldn't argue with him, but little brothers sometimes needed to be taken down a notch. "I'll have you know that I'm in peak physical condition."

Simon shook his head. "You're weak. I'm little. I'm not too heavy."

"Fine. We'll settle this right now," Parker said, slapping the table. "Arm wrestling, let's go." This captured the amused attention of the rest of the table, even Rhodie.

"Five quid on Parker," both twins said simultaneously, and their mother gave them a sobering look.

He turned Simon and showed him how to plant his elbow on the table.

"You can't use your other hand, just this one," he explained, ignoring his mother's anxious face over his brother's shoulder. "Are you ready?"

"I. Am. Ready," Simon answered, serious.

"One-two-three, go!" Parker flexed his abs so the vein on his forehead would stand out, like he was trying as hard as he could. Simon's grip was surprisingly strong, but he didn't have the leverage to push Parker over. Parker resisted just enough to keep it an even match for a few moments, then he let Simon win.

The elated surprise on his brother's face was totally worth it. "I won! I beat Eddie!"

Their father held up a hand for a high five, and then Simon needed one from everyone, lapping the table to collect them, and Parker's abs hurt from how hard he was laughing. *Abbie would love this.* The thought surprised him—not that he was thinking about her, missing her, but that he assumed she wanted family time like this. *Does she like kids? I know we've talked about having them, but it was a bit of a foregone conclusion, given our royal status . . .* He made a mental note to ask her when his reflection was interrupted.

"How is you versus Simon a fair fight?" Andrew complained.

Parker sat forward to see Andrew better. "Perhaps you're right." He paused. "Perhaps you and I should go." *Even better; this brother needs it more anyway.* Forsythia looked nervous, as she often did when the siblings wrestled and roughhoused, and he touched her shoulder reassuringly as he came around to Andrew's side as the rest of the family chattered about this new development.

Parker dropped his voice so only his brother could hear. "If you think you're getting the Simon treatment . . ."

"Not necessary. I'll beat you fair and square." Andrew's jaw was set, and Parker grinned.

"One-two-three—" Andrew started early, but Parker recovered quickly. He slammed Andrew's hand onto the oak so fast, his brother's mouth dropped open. Andrew pulled his hand back, shaking it out.

"That stings!"

"One hundred push-ups, every morning."

Andrew's mouth pulled to the side. "I only do fifty," he muttered.

"Yes, that's why you *lost*," Parker chuckled. "Let me know when you want a rematch."

"All right, son."

Parker thought he was being chastised until he turned to look at his father, only to find his arm set, ready to be his next opponent.

"You're not getting the Simon treatment, either, old man."

Ignatius chuckled. "Sure you don't need it yourself?"

"Peak physical condition."

"So I heard. Hard to resist quelling an ego like that."

"You're a leftie; you okay with my right?"

"Just fine, son. Enough talk."

Parker put an open hand to his chest, offended. "You believe me to be stalling?"

"You're definitely stalling," his mother offered from down the table. "Show him, Ig."

"Yeah, show him, Dad!" Forsythia called, and Parker glared at her playfully.

"Don't forget who's approving your marriage contract in a few months, Thia." He sat down and took his father's hand, as the twins quietly worked out a new bet. "On three?"

"I'm old and feeble; you'd better count it out," Ignatius said with a straight face.

"Fine. One-two-three, go." Parker's shoulder was already burning by the time he got to "go." *Come on, Broward, you're better than this.* Both of their arms were shaking; his dad was definitely trying his hardest. *Should I let him win, so he can save face in front of the kids?* He caught his dad's eye and noticed the tiny smirk on his face, even under his thick gray beard. *That's it.* Parker gave a final push and won, and Ignatius laughed as the room exploded into congratulations for Parker.

"Oh," Lily sighed, rising. "My poor husband. Bested by his offspring."

"Yes, my pride is gravely wounded," Ignatius quipped over the chattering kids and the money being exchanged that Ginger did have on her after all. "I'll need a lot of consoling later."

Lily smiled, leaning down to kiss his lips. "I think I can manage that."

"Gross," Andrew said, and Parker snickered. *I hope Abbie still wants me after thirty years together . . .* It was hard not to think about their legal problems when he thought about their future together. Everything was at risk. They'd know more once she had her first court date, but that was still a few weeks away. *But I'm going to see her in a few days. Just a few more days.* After what happened to Arron, he wasn't sure which he needed more: to hold her, or to be held by her. Thankfully, he could do both at the same time.

CHAPTER THIRTEEN

116 days to the wedding

ABBIE HAD FORGOTTEN: traveling with security was nice. People treated her differently. It was tough not to let it go to her head. Since her appearance at the ball had been publicized anyway, she'd decided to travel under her real name. The special treatment started on the blimp.

"Ms. Porchenzii, you and your security have been upgraded to first class."

"Oh." She gave the flight attendant a gracious smile. "Thank you."

"Absolutely, ma'am, and anything you need, please don't hesitate to ask your valet, Drake." Drake, as it turned out, was the tall, blond young man who'd been assigned to take care of them on the three-hour ride.

"He's certainly fit," Georgie muttered. Tezza nodded slowly, and her eyes said it all. Abbie snickered. First class also meant a table and a complimentary meal. The food was only slightly better quality than in coach. Still, free food was free food, and they got silverware and plates instead of cardboard and wood. She wished she didn't have to be so picky.

"Are you going to finish that?" Georgie asked quietly. Abbie liked how familiar Georgie felt she could be with her. It made the whole security experience more comfortable, more like traveling with friends than trained assassins. She assumed both women could kill someone without detection if they wanted to.

"No, I can't eat the rest. Please help yourself."

Tezza passed her plate across as well before Georgie could ask. Tezza's healthy physique made sense: she ate almost nothing. But Abbie had no idea how Georgie stayed so impossibly thin, given that she often ate her own dinner, plus Abbie's leftovers, and now Tezza's as well.

"Dessert, ma'am?" Drake asked.

"I'd better not. Thank you, though." Georgie looked disappointed. Abbie wanted to save her off-plan eating for the ball; she tended to eat when nervous. *And I am nervous. There's a good chance I'll see some of my old classmates. Considering I'm the prep school dropout and runaway princess who's marrying a king, there might be resentment.* Parker had told her that Crescena was expected, and her brother would also be there.

She pulled out a book and tried to read for work, but couldn't focus. She wrote her brother another email instead, letting him know she'd be at the ball in case he still disliked surprises. She'd heard nothing from Kurt since she left Brevspor after her father's funeral. She needed someone to walk her down the aisle, and he was pretty much the only person available. It wouldn't hurt his political stature, either; emphasizing close ties to Orangiers despite her non-reign would work to his benefit. Abbie had expected a terse "no" when she asked . . . but silence was something else. He was probably still angry that she'd recommended he be named prince regent until a female heir could be produced by him or named from another line. It was better than seeing him rejected outright, tossed on his backside from their childhood home. She'd done him a favor. But clearly, he didn't see it that way.

If he didn't answer her, she'd have to go and see him eventually, maybe on her way back from Orangiers in a few weeks. He needed to get engaged ASAP if he had any hope of holding on to political power, preferably someone from a royal line. Eighteen was young to start trying to attract a wife, but he could be charming when he wanted to be. He could pull it off, if he got started now. She should ask around tonight, see who was available and interested.

There was a carriage waiting for them when they exited the airport after breezing through the diplomats' line, even though she'd resisted it. *Yes, some serious perks I'd forgotten about.* Parker promised he'd have appropriate dresses for all of them, so she'd packed light. It was nice to get away from her normal life; she couldn't afford to travel when she got vacation time. And at least they'd be in a house, not those guest houses and "hotels" they'd stayed at in the Unveiled. The experience had been hard to shake; why were things so different there? Was it just money? If they veiled it, surely that wouldn't fix the racism, the ignorance? Was it really any better inside the Veil, or had she just never noticed? Parker had relayed to her an interesting conversation he'd had with Pap, where he compared people to a tapestry . . . But what was holding it all together? If you tried to pull out a few of the loose threads—violence against women, poor medical care, child slavery, illiteracy—would the whole thing unravel? Maybe she should write to him . . .

The carriage turned up a steep hill, and the women braced themselves against the sides. Georgie was close to Abbie's age, but Tezza was older, probably nearly thirty. Yet something resonated between them, something hard to define. Outwardly, they had very little in common, except perhaps being more severe than necessary. Yet there was a dark grief in Tezza, some unspoken tragedy. Abbie could feel it. She knew she shouldn't push her to talk about it, but she was curious.

The driveway flattened out, and Abbie could see Parker waiting out front for her, grinning. *I should play it cool,* she thought. *You know, saunter up to the front door, classy, collected like his mom and sister.* That's what she was thinking as she climbed over Tezza and threw open the carriage door before it was even stopped, leaping over the carriage stairs to land on the cobblestones. Hair flying out behind her, Abbie felt her excitement build as she took the natural stone steps two at a time and launched herself into his arms, expecting a warm tangle of lips, tongues and teeth; the peck on the forehead and stiff-armed squeeze she received was more disappointing than an oatmeal cookie when one is expecting triple-chocolate layer cake. An oatmeal cookie *with raisins.* She blinked at him.

"What the Jersey was that?"

"So impatient," he muttered, still grinning. "Come inside."

Georgie approached him and stopped at a respectful distance. "Apologies, Your Majesty; Macias and I will need to check the premises before Ms. Porchenzii can enter."

"It's been checked, Addington. My security have gone through it thoroughly."

Georgie pursed her lips, and Abbie could see she was holding back objections.

She stepped away from Parker to see him better. "So, she should just take their word for it? Let her do her job. You can wait a few minutes."

He lifted his gaze from her face to Georgie. "Apologies; go ahead and do your checks. I'd expect no less from my own security. Dean, would you please show them around?"

The large man nodded, and Georgie followed him inside. Abbie stepped out of the sun, remembering herself, suddenly self-conscious about Parker's lack of response to her arrival. She felt like an obstacle and moved to step out of the way of staffers unloading the carriage.

"Abs," he softly called her attention back to him. His eyes were impossibly warm, like sinking into a hot spring. "I'm very happy to see you, I am. But out here, in front of other people, when I'm technically still working, I can't properly show you . . ."

"No, I know, I just . . . forgot. Sorry." She twisted her rings and avoided his searching look. She really wanted to ask him about Arron, but decided to wait for a bit more privacy.

"How was your trip?"

"Fine."

"Are you hungry? I could poke around the kitchen on your behalf . . ."

"No, thanks."

"Will you take a turn around the grounds with me?" She smirked at his reference to his seven-year-old self's ridiculous question.

"No, thank you. I'm just going to sit here and wait."

Parker made a guttural noise, and she turned to find him glaring at her.

She pointed at his slightly disgruntled face. "Your royal facade is slipping, hon. And don't be ticked with *me*, they're not *my* stupid touching rules. If you don't like them, change them."

"So if you can't be kissed, there's no other use for your lips? You can't chat to me while we stand here waiting?"

"I'll need my energy tonight. Travel tends to wear me out."

"No, you're just irritated about my job. As usual."

"Parker, I'm just tired, okay?"

He turned and stalked inside, and Abbie felt a pang of guilt. She rose to follow him, but Tezza stopped her at the door, arms crossed.

"Almost done, ma'am."

Abbie heard him say something to the staff waiting for him in the foyer and watched him take the wide staircase up to the second level. She brushed the hair out of her face, stepped back. "How long does it take to look into the bathtubs? Seriously, T. Just let me in."

"Patience."

"I *hate* being patient." To her surprise, Tezza smiled, shaking her head. "Are you laughing at me?"

"No," she said, still shaking her head, still smiling. "When I was engaged, I didn't want to wait for anything, either. I was sick to death of waiting."

"Yes, exactly. Finally, someone gets it. Wait, when were you engaged?" Abbie didn't think about the question before she asked it, and Tezza flinched as Georgie came loping back into the foyer.

"All clear, ma'am."

Abbie charged up the stairs, and Tezza calmly followed her. *I'll probe that mystery later. Talk about bad timing.*

"We're getting in the carriage in forty-five minutes!" Georgie called after them.

That is not long enough to yell at Parker, take a shower, and get dressed up to the nines. Well, I guess I'll be fashionably late. There was only one problem: she had no idea which room was his—or hers, for that matter. She knocked on the first door, and Ms. Scrope answered, who was delighted to see her. She pointed her down the hall to her room. Abbie didn't want to ask where Parker's room was, lest she seem whorish. Then she spotted Dean and Waldo outside a door at the very end of the hall, right across from hers. *That's dangerous*, she thought, *but at least there's two people who might stop us if either of us tried to cross the hallway in the night. Then again, they might just open the doors for us . . .*

"Ma'am?" Tezza asked, and Abbie nodded, waving her off. She disappeared into her adjoining room. Abbie had forgotten that she was usually just getting up at this time of day; she only had a few hours to sleep before her shift started.

Abbie knocked on Parker's door. No answer. She turned to Waldo. "He's in there, right?"

Waldo nodded hesitantly.

"Parker, open the door. I need to talk to you." Silence. Letting her temper get the better of her, she pounded on Parker's door with her fist. A moment later, the door handle clicked, and the door swung open slowly.

CHAPTER FOURTEEN

PARKER STOOD IN THE doorway to his bedroom with his phone to his ear, wearing most of a tuxedo. Abbie turned bright red, embarrassed by her own rashness. He waved her into the room and shut the door behind her.

"Yes, Mr. Ambassador, I can understand that, but I'm sure she meant no disrespect." He listened to the caller as he tried to put on his cummerbund without dropping anything. Abbie came over and tied it in the back for him.

"Sir, I will speak to her about it, but I can assure you, this is a simple misunderstanding. I'm not willing to discuss reassignment until we can sit everyone down together and discuss it." He turned around to face her and tucked a stray curl behind her ear. All the yelling she'd been prepared to do faded away under that tender gesture; that was all she'd wanted earlier.

She mouthed, "I'm sorry," and he nodded, stroking her cheek with his thumb.

"No, sir, I'm afraid I cannot promise that. However, I would be willing to send a mediator—"

Abbie checked her phone. Time was ticking away, and she did need to get ready. Abbie pressed her lips to the cheek that was away from the phone and moved toward the door, but he caught her by the wrist.

"Sir, I will send a mediator next week. Currently, I'm running late to an engagement for the human rights summit tonight, and I need to see to one more thing before I leave, so I'm afraid we'll have to postpone the rest of this conversation to a later time." Parker was staring at her lips, currently curled into a coy smile, and she was pretty sure she was the "one more thing."

"Very good, Mr. Ambassador. Yes, you have a pleasant evening, too."

He set down his phone on the desk and sat on the edge of it as he pulled her between his knees, smirking.

"A bit anxious to see me, darling? I thought there was an ogre out there."

"You know what they say about a woman scorned."

"I hardly scorned you."

"Well, it felt that way a little, since I couldn't follow you."

"Did it? I'm sorry. I don't think either of us were communicating well."

"I'm sorry if I was cold. I was just embarrassed. I wasn't trying to punish you."

"Okay. I wasn't trying to snub you, Abs."

She put her hands on his arms and rubbed lightly. "How are you doing with everything that happened last week?"

He shrugged. "Arron's okay. I will be, too. Scared me, though."

"Of course it did. How could it not?" Truth be told, it had scared her, too. She knew what it was like to lose people you loved in the blink of an eye. Strange how something that happened eight years ago could still rip you wide open like a sword, how even a "healed" wound never really was. Losing her sisters in that fire was still fresh, four times over.

"Rhodie took it quite hard as well."

Abbie's hands stilled as she considered this. From what Parker had told her, James flirted with lots of women; he loved getting a laugh. Hopefully Rhodie didn't think it was more than that.

"Really? How would you even know? She's so polished I can see my own reflection."

Parker laughed, then stopped suddenly, like he felt guilty about it. "No, Abs, really. She was crying."

"Super Princess was crying?"

"I know, it shocked me as well."

"Did you comfort her, at least? How do you comfort someone so proper?"

"I offered her a hug, but she refused. She's never been physically affectionate, unlike someone else I know." He was leaning toward her, but she caught sight of the clock over his shoulder and sighed.

"I really have to go get ready if we're going to be on time. I'm sorry." She started for the door, but Parker pulled her back against him.

"Where do you think you're going?" He brushed her hair away from the back of her neck and trailed kisses down it, then back up under her ear.

"I told you, I'm going to get dressed." Her breathing was becoming tough to keep even . . . and he smiled like he heard it.

"Maybe I can help . . ."

"Not yet, you can't. Let go of mmm . . ." The last word caught in her throat as his tongue flicked her earlobe; she felt her skin flush. He had one arm wrapped around her middle, and she put her hand over his, but didn't push him away.

"What was that, darling?" He barely paused his kiss for-ay. "I didn't quite hear you . . . let go of what?"

"I blame you," she whispered.

He chuckled low. "What for?"

"Everything." She reached back with her other hand to run her fingers over his short hair.

He squeezed her tighter, then sighed and buried his face in her hair. "I release you to go take your clothes off."

"But not to put them on again?"

"I'll think on it."

"How will I know what you decide?"

"Obviously, I'll have to text you."

She laughed and wriggled out of his grip, blowing him a kiss on the way to the door. Her head was buzzing with happy feelings . . . until she opened the door to her own room.

"Where the Jersey have you been?" Georgie demanded. "Never mind. Go pick a dress and I'll start the shower." When Abbie hesitated, the blonde shook her head, then began pushing Abbie toward the en suite bathroom. "Never mind, too slow, I'll pick for you."

"No strapless. My girls need support," Abbie yelled as the bathroom door closed.

"Clothes off!"

Abbie took the world's fastest shower, and the moment she shut off the water, the bathroom door flew open, and Georgie paired each of her commands with a clap of her hands.

"Get out! Get dry! Let's go!"

"Georgie, relax!"

"Look, lady, I've never been to a ball before, and you are not going to ruin a moment of this for me."

"For you? I thought this was *my* night . . ."

"Yeah, you got that wrong, sister."

Abbie's skin was still damp when she pulled the dress over her head. She had no chance to see how it looked full-length on her before Georgie sat her down at the vanity and began to dry her hair. In line with her request, her security had picked a royal-blue dress with a strap—one, anyway. The gown fell across her right shoulder; it was made of gathered chiffon and had appliquéd white flowers with pearl centers at the top that twisted down into more flowers, swirling around her waist. At the bottom, the color faded to a lighter blue. She looked in the full-length mirror approvingly. Ms. Scrope had styled her hair off to her left side in a ponytail holding a mess of tight curls, and she'd brought pearl earrings. "I gotta get going, it's already ten after, and I don't know how far the venue is."

She was most of the way down the hall when she heard Ms. Scrope clear her throat behind her and Abbie turned. She held out a pair of nude pumps, and Abbie grabbed them, trying to put them on as she started down the stairs.

"Slow down, Abs; you don't need any broken bones." Parker caught her by the elbow, stabilizing her descent.

Woz, he could make anything look good. It's like he's not even trying. "You look very handsome."

"And you look lovely, as always."

Abbie leaned into his arm and whispered, "Make sure you tell Georgie she looks lovely, too. She's been looking forward to this apparently."

"Yes, I heard quite a bit of shouting after you left . . ."

"It was intense. Next time I'll just make up with you in the carriage."

"But then your pretty makeup would get smeared . . ."

Abbie grinned. "Worth it."

AS IT HAPPENED, THE venue was not far, and they were still mostly on time. She saw several women she'd been friends with in secondary school, and they seemed surprised and pleased to see her, from what she could tell. With this crowd, you had to be careful; it might be an act. But Abbie felt it was genuine, and when Parker asked her if he could go speak to a foundation chair he'd been trying to connect with, she waved him off gladly.

Cherry Reynolds squeezed her hand, peering after him. "Abelia, I can't believe how handsome Edward's become! He was such a nerd before . . ."

"Oh," Abbie said, munching a carrot stick. "He's still a nerd, he just has cooler glasses now." The women giggled.

"Are you getting involved with foundation work?"

She nodded slowly. "I'm thinking about it. I was very moved by my experience in the Unveiled. Things are very different there."

"It's so sad, the way people out there live. But even though they have nothing, they're just the happiest people," Marigold Chester put in. "I did a trip to the Forgelands, and it changed my life."

Abbie worked to keep her face straight. "That's not quite what I meant; I saw lots of people who didn't have nothing.

People would offer us a place to stay or food, even not knowing who we were. They were very generous."

"And simple!" Marigold put in. "We taught them to sew handbags from coffee sacks."

"Who's going to buy those?" She hoped the question didn't sound rude.

"There's a charity that sells them in Gardenia. It's a wonderful thing."

"Hmm. Well, that's interesting." Abbie meant Marigold's perspective, not the charity's work, but didn't say so. She looked over Cherry's shoulder and saw Edward standing alone with his hands in his pockets, watching her, and her pulse quickened. "Excuse me, ladies—wonderful to catch up with you . . ."

"Enjoy your time with your man!" Cherry called, and Abbie smiled over her shoulder.

CHAPTER FIFTEEN

"DID YOU MEAN TO GIVE me a 'come hither' stare?"

He grinned. "I was just enjoying watching you. I didn't know it would summon you, but I'm not sorry it did." He held out a white-gloved hand. "Would you like to waltz with me?"

"Are you any good?"

"I excel at many things, dancing among them."

Abbie rolled her eyes, but she set down her plate on the nearest table and brushed any lingering food particles off her hands, lest she dirty his tuxedo. "I think you just wanted a way to touch me in public."

"If you're waiting for me to deny that accusation . . ." He led her toward the center of the room. ". . . you'll be waiting a long while."

Oof, it's been a long time since I've done this. Yet as Abbie placed her right hand in Parker's lifted left, she was surprised how good it felt to be in his arms, however removed the rest of their bodies were. Abbie smiled as she remembered her lessons from Mrs. Andel, the famous Trellan dancer who'd married a member of Brevsporan aristocracy. *Let your hand perch upon his shoulder like a baby bird . . .* He put the right amount of pressure on her upper back and held his arm out stiffly, gently supporting her hand, and she stepped backwards following him into a basic box step.

"Well, that answers that question."

"What question?" Abbie asked.

Keep your gaze over your partner's shoulder, children, well to the left; romantic as the dance is, if you try to look at your partner, you'll drift right and get all tangled up. There had been rampant snorts and giggles at that.

"The question of whether you know how to follow," he said, and she could hear the teasing in his voice.

"That all depends on who's leading."

Keep your hips up, Abelia. She'd had no desire to touch her hip to Norman Barkus, who smelled like sweat and potato chips and kept pushing on her hands instead of indicating turns with his lower body like he was supposed to. But Parker's hip seemed glued to hers, and she could sense him turning before she knew what was happening.

"*I'm* leading."

"I sensed that." She tried to hide a smile. "You're good at it."

"I should be. I've had ample practice."

With whom? Her mind demanded to know. *Whose hips have you been touching? Those are my hips.* She did not ask, but she was glad she didn't have to make eye contact with him, lest he see her question there.

"My first sister loves to dance but often lacks what she considers to be a suitable partner. I have accompanied her and her book club friends on numerous occasions. Or I did, before I became intolerably busy."

Her jealousy subsided with this new information and she felt a little foolish.

"You should still go. All work and no play makes Parker a grumpy Gus."

"All work and no Abbie, you mean."

"Aww." Now she really had to keep her focus over his shoulder; the last thing she wanted was to step on his toes and cause a scene. *Stand up tall, keep your back a bit arched.* That's when she noticed. "Parker?"

"Hmm?"

"People are staring at us."

"We make a handsome couple. I can hardly blame them." He took her into a running spin turn, and she couldn't stay focused on their observers if she wanted to stay with him. And she did want to stay with him, and not just because people were watching her . . . She squeezed his hand, and he returned the gesture. A few moments later, the song ended, and she tried to look subtle as she led him away from the dance floor toward the art gallery wing of the venue. The lights were mostly off in the quiet space. It was almost time for her to go home; Edward was obligated to stay for another few hours.

"No collywobbles tonight?" he asked as they took in the oil paintings.

She pursed her lips. "Don't invent words."

"I'm not." He turned. "Addington, what's a collywobble?"

Abbie turned suddenly. She hadn't noticed Georgie lurking there in the dark.

"When your nerves are in your belly, churning it up. Why? Does Abelia have collywobbles again?"

That rankled, but she knew it wasn't Georgie's intention. "No, all my wobbles are in my ankles due to these ridiculous shoes, thank you very much."

"It doesn't show," Parker said.

Abbie let the words tumble out without thinking. "I know it does. Don't lie to me."

Much like he had on the dance floor, he used his hips to smoothly turn and back her up against the white wall between a landscape and a portrait of a child on a rocking horse. He cradled her face in both hands and waited to speak until she looked him in the eye.

"I do not lie to you. Ever."

His sudden intensity flustered her. She pushed back her shoulders and opened her mouth to rebuke him, but he shifted his thumbs over her lips.

"And someday, my darling bride, I hope you'll find it unnecessary to lie to me. You'll finally know deep down that all your secrets are safe with me. Someday, you'll trust me all the time like you did during that waltz. It was a thing of beauty."

"Parker," she breathed, shocked that he felt that way, tears stinging her eyes. "I don't lie to you that much." She brought her hands up to his wrists. "I do trust you, hon. I trust you."

"No, you don't. You get a wild notion and then you try to hide whatever foolish thing you've done. You lie to protect yourself. You think you're sparing my feelings, keeping me from worry, trying to handle it all yourself. You needn't do that. I wish you wouldn't."

Abbie wanted to pull him closer, to reassure him of her love and devotion. She also wanted to get away, out from under his ardent gaze and frank insights into the workings of her mind; she felt laid bare. Glancing around, she started to pull him toward her, then stopped.

"Can I kiss you?"

He rewarded her restraint with his ten-thousand-watt smile. "Best not to, for the moment . . ."

"I'm going to need a code word, then."

He lifted one eyebrow, still leaning dangerously close to her. "Code word?"

She nodded. "A secret word between us that means I wish I was kissing you, something innocuous others won't pick up on."

"Hmm. I'll think on it."

She sighed. "Couldn't you have been a shoe salesman?"

He laughed, his head falling back. "That wouldn't help; you'd have just been engaged to some other prince, then." Her mind was drawn back to her discussion with her father just before he died . . . *Lincoln. It would've been Lincoln. Woz, I'm so lucky.* Her face fell, and he saw it.

"What's wrong?"

"Nothing." She smiled and gently pushed him away, back toward the party. Abbie saw the president of Anti-CYST, the Anti-Child and Youth Slavery Trust, standing near the front of the room, and she was moving to intercept her when Parker leaned close to her ear.

"Strawberries."

"Huh?"

"That should be our code word. Strawberries."

She held out a hand to seal the deal, and he shook it.

AFTER AN ENGROSSING conversation with the Anti-CYST president, Jenise Brandon, they set up a time to meet when she returned to Gardenia to see how she might be helpful to them. Parker escorted her and Georgie to the carriage, squeezing her hand as he helped her in, promising to be home as soon as he could. Georgie waited to be unprofessional until the door slammed.

"Oh Woz, what a night! I met the king and queen of Op'Ho'Lonia, Princess Heather, and more royals than I can count." She pulled out her phone and showed Abbie the photos she'd taken surreptitiously.

"Don't do that next time. You don't want to get into trouble. Royals are touchy."

"I won't," she said. A black-and-white photo caught Abbie's eye over her shoulder.

"Wait, who's that?"

Georgie stiffened and stammered, "I-I'm sorry, ma'am."

"We're back to ma'am now? I swear, Addington, I cannot keep up with you. Hand over the phone."

Georgie did so, blushing. The photo was of Abbie with Parker in the art gallery. Georgie had caught them engrossed in their conversation about trust, and since the party was behind them, it blew out the background so they were no more than silhouettes in profile. Abbie could see the powerful longing in both of their postures, the tender way he was touching her face, pressing his body against hers; the way she clung to his wrists, tipping her head back to look into his eyes.

"I know I shouldn't have invaded your privacy, but you just looked so perfect together . . ."

Abbie touched the screen and sent the photo to herself, then deleted it from Georgie's phone.

"I'm sorry, ma'am. I shouldn't have. I got caught up in the moment. I apologize."

Abbie squeezed her arm. "You're forgiven. You have a gift for photography. You captured a very precious moment between us, and I'm glad."

ABBIE WAS BACK AT THE house in her pajamas with her feet up, reading, by ten. She intended to wait on the couch downstairs until Parker came home, so they could finish their conversation about trust . . . but she woke to him gently shaking her shoulder.

"What time is it?" she asked, rubbing her eyes.

"Late. You should be in bed. Come on; I can't carry you."

"Why would you carry me?" She yawned. "I'm not a child."

"I thought women liked that."

"Only in novels, hon. Lots of fantasy between those pages . . ."

He chuckled and offered her a hand up. She took it and stood up, wobbly. "Just a minute," she said. "I'll be right back." Abbie walked quickly toward the oversized kitchen, hoping he wouldn't follow. He didn't. She checked the stove: it was off, and she hurried back to where he was waiting, ignoring the question on his face.

Fingers intertwined, Abbie and Parker stumbled upstairs to the end of the hall, ignoring Tezza and Parker's night guards, who trailed after them. Not ready to say good night yet, Abbie pulled him into her room. "I need to show you something real quick. Just for a minute . . ." She pushed the door most of the way closed, but didn't latch it. He knew what she wanted, of course, and his gaze heated. He backed her into the wall, just as he had a few hours before, but this time, Abbie grabbed his shirt and pulled him into a scorching kiss that had them both gasping for breath.

"I've been wanting to do that all day," she whispered.

"Me too."

She pulled him in again, clasping her hands behind his neck to avoid inadvertently straying to areas that might be too incendiary. It seemed like they were already running pretty hot; their light, happy noises had deepened into quiet groans and gasps. Abbie wanted to lie down, and she backed Parker up until his legs hit the edge of her bed. She pushed him, and he sat down hard on the mattress, stunned. Before she could blink, he'd stood back up.

"Not a good idea," he murmured, pulling her close to him again.

"I love you, Parker. I trust you. The door's still open."

He grunted like she'd gut-punched him.

"Just for a minute . . . I just want to be close to you."

"Don't, Abs."

She kissed him again, caressing his tongue with hers. "Don't what?"

"Don't say those sweet words." He kissed her back with as much heat as she'd ever felt from him. "Don't tempt me. You don't know how badly I want to do that with you." He pulled back with a tortured sigh, shifting his kisses to her neck to whisper in her ear. "But when I cross that line, when I get into your bed, I want it all. And we've got to wait for that."

But for how long, Parker? This isn't getting resolved; we're going nowhere. I can't hang out in limbo like this, living with this tension, this ache to be with you . . . this fear.

Abbie huffed and voiced the part she could safely say aloud. "I'm tired of waiting."

He dropped his voice. "I promise to make it worth your while."

She shivered, and he felt it.

"Oh, you're not making this easy."

"Do I ever?"

He chuckled at that. "No, never." The joke broke the tension a little, and he gently set her away from him by her hips. Abbie scowled at him, and he laughed again. "I promise, darling; you'll get everything you want, as soon as your name's on that marriage certificate." He kissed her forehead. "Sweet dreams, Abs."

"You too."

"Oh, don't worry," he said, looking her up and down once more from the doorway, "I'm fairly certain mine will be delightful."

CHAPTER SIXTEEN

115 days to the wedding

AS USUAL, PARKER ROSE at 5:00. He opened his laptop and sat at the desk, glasses off, answering emails until the sun started to come up. He had dreamt about Abbie . . . and as such, he considered taking a cold shower before he spent all morning with her. But he might as well save it until after his workout. Maybe he wouldn't need it by then.

He paused in the hallway. Abbie's door was open a crack; Tezza was nowhere to be seen. He went on immediate alert. He turned sharply to Dean and Waldo for an explanation, but they both shrugged, apparently anticipating what he wanted to know. Quietly, Parker pushed Abbie's door open and stepped hesitantly into the room. His fiancée was sprawled in bed, sound asleep, a bare leg out of the sheets, one pillow against her chest and one under her tousled head. Soon it would be his chest she'd be using instead of a pillow; he expected it would make his 5 a.m. wake-up all the more painful, leaving her. He sighed, but his breath arrested as a large curved blade met his throat.

"Tezza?" he said softly, raising his hands as a show of compliance. She came around to see his face and dropped the weapon to her side. She gestured toward the hallway. They exited quietly and shut the door; Abbie didn't stir.

138

"I'm sorry, I didn't see you around. I just wanted to make sure she was all right."

The dark-haired woman crossed her arms. "Some people want to be seen," she replied, gesturing with her chin to the two large men outside his door. "Some don't. But I assure you, sir, I know how to do my job. If I do it differently, that's on purpose."

"I apologize. I shouldn't have doubted you."

"No apology needed. Just a reminder in case you cross the hallway in the dark . . . and you don't see me around." She lifted an eyebrow, and he grinned.

"Would you like to come running with me?"

"No, thank you, sir. I can't exercise right before bed. Also, I'd hate to stick anyone else with her in the morning. She's a bear."

"I can't disagree, I'm afraid." He continued down the stairs and out the front door, trailed by the other two men. Parker knew it made them nervous when he wanted to run in unknown territories, but he couldn't help it. He hated exercise, but he detested indoor exercise. He ran outside even in the rain at home; it was rarely so inclement that he had to use a treadmill.

The steep terrain around the house would be an interesting challenge. He reminded himself of that three miles in, when his lungs and thighs were on fire. He continued to set a brisk pace, determined to be back and showered by the time she woke up. *Abbie's here. I don't want to waste any time on work today that could be spent together; I've done nothing but work all week.* But despite pushing himself (and his out-of-breath security), he was only on pushups when she wandered out the back door, still in her modest pajamas, feet bare, robe open, her hair a cloud of untamed curls around her, coffee in hand. Abbie curled herself into a bamboo lounge chair, watching him.

"Good morning," he panted, holding himself in a plank to see her better.

"Mmm. It is now."

He laughed and dropped to one knee, pausing to catch his breath. "I've had an audience for all sorts of things before, but never a workout."

She took a sip of coffee. "You're doing just fine. Continue."

"Yes, ma'am." He finished the last fifteen push-ups and wiped the sweat off his brow with the bottom edge of his white cotton shirt. Abbie's eyes flared with interest as he flashed his abs. Winking at her, he took his shirt off and watched her melt into a puddle of lust. *Woz, I love this woman.* He lay in the cool grass to start his crunches, but he kept his eyes on her.

"Will you join me tomorrow morning?"

This earned him a low chuckle. "I'd be out before the first mile."

"When do I get to ogle you, then?"

She reddened, stammering, "I-I'm not ogling."

"Oh, darling; you're definitely ogling. Just admit it." *Woz, she even lies to herself.*

She glared at him good-naturedly over her mug. "Fine. Maybe I'm ogling. It's hard to do from a distance."

"I could send you pictures . . ." She reddened again, and he laughed. "Not dirty pictures, Abs. Just the regular kind. You know, selfies. And you still didn't answer my question."

"About when you get to ogle me?" She stretched thoughtfully. "I don't really *do* anything ogle-worthy, hon. I read. I cook. I clean."

"I think the carriage needs a wash. Did you bring a swimsuit?"

She snorted and her hand flew to her nose to keep coffee from shooting out. He grinned and picked up speed with his crunches, showing off. He had assumed the conversation was over when she suddenly said, "I guess I sometimes do yoga."

His crunches slowed to a stop. The mental image of Abbie with her backside in the air, wearing skin-tight clothing, ought not to be brought to mind when his heart was already pounding. He flopped back on the grass, his chest heaving. *This engagement is going to be the death of me. That will be an unfortunate epitaph: Here lies King Edward, slain by lust for his fiancée, who sometimes did yoga.* Parker took off his glasses and covered his eyes, trying to get the image out of his head before the rest of his body caught on.

"Oh no, I've killed you. Do you need mouth-to-mouth?" She grinned as she walked down the steps and stopped next to his prone body.

"That's the last thing I need right now."

"You're all talk, Broward. That's what I just learned." She offered him a hand up, and he accepted it.

"I do love looking at you, you know," he said, heading back into the house.

"I know." She followed him up the stairs, and an awkward silence took hold of the conversation.

"Do you want to know my favorite part?"

"No."

Is she blushing? he thought.

Pivoting to her room, she noticed Georgie standing there and her blush intensified. "I'll let you get your shower now."

He grabbed her by the elbow before she could escape, pulled her into his room, shutting the door. *No, this isn't the ideal place for this conversation, but she'll have to get used to the constant security presence eventually.*

"Why don't you want to hear about my favorite part?" She didn't meet his gaze, and he stepped into her personal space, letting his hands rest on her shoulders. "You're spectacular, you know."

"Don't comment on my body," she whisper-yelled.

"Why?" He felt his comments were innocent enough.

"Why? Wha—why? What do you mean, why?"

"Just what I said. Did I stutter?"

"Don't be flippant," she said. "I don't comment on your body, I just want the same courtesy."

"Darling, you just spent fifteen minutes drooling over me outside. Granted, there was no verbal commentary, but based on your expression, I'm fairly sure your internal narrative would have been damning evidence . . ."

She stuck a finger in his face to reprimand him, but he grabbed it and held on when she tried to pull away. "I mean it, Parker: don't comment on my body."

"That's going to be tough when I'm making love to you," he said, bringing her arm up to kiss the inside of her wrist. "I can hear it now . . . 'Oh, Abbie, I love your beautiful, perky . . . thoughts. I can't wait to kiss your sweet, soft . . . personality.'"

Clearly flustered, she pulled her arm away from him and pressed her other hand over his mouth. "Stop talking like that."

She's upset, but her pupils are dilated. That's interesting. She can't decide if she likes dirty talk or not . . . It was difficult not to show his amusement. He gently tugged her hand away. "No one can hear me but you . . ."

"Yes! And at this stage in our relationship, I do not want to hear what you plan to say when you . . . when we . . ."

"Yes?" he asked, grinning. *Is she going to say it? Please say it.*

"You know what I'm saying."

"Sorry, I'm not sure to what you're referring. When we . . . play table tennis? Go sailing? Avoid nightstallions? What?" He didn't know why he was goading her, except that it felt imperative. She should start getting more comfortable with physical closeness; saying the word *sex* felt like step one.

"Knock it off, Your Majesty, or I'll knock it off for you."

He stepped closer to her ear to whisper. "You're too shy to even say the word? Why?"

Her face flushed, and he couldn't tell if it was out of anger or embarrassment. She whispered back fiercely, "I am *not* shy!"

Anger. "Then say it," he whispered. "Say it, just for me."

"Why? What does it prove?"

Don't laugh at her. Don't laugh.

He chuckled. "Abs, you're a scientist!"

"So?"

"So you should have an appreciation for how we're made, our basic urges."

"I do. I just don't talk about it."

He laughed harder. "I can't believe you right now. You're so forthright normally. How did you not die of embarrassment when your mum had the talk with you?"

"She never did."

He felt an unexpected rush of anger. "What?"

"My mother never talked to me about . . . that. Nor my father." Parker already hated her mom, but now he thought Faith must have hated him, too. *Jersey, couldn't she at least have wanted her daughter to have a happy marriage?*

"Who, then?"

"My sisters. Friends in boarding school. Both sets shared some very inaccurate information . . ."

"I can imagine."

"And then later, anatomy and physiology class in college, as well as library books. Oh, and Patty and Lauren have both been fonts of information, whether I wanted it or not."

"Wow." This prompted a whole new set of worries. Was she not as interested in him as she seemed to be? How could he begin to broach the subject? He wasn't putting this off another moment. "Sit down."

She drew away to see his face better. "Why?"

"Just sit. Let's talk about this." He drew her toward the desk chair and gently pulled her down to sit on his lap with her legs together. He put his arms around her and squeezed.

"I'm sorry."

She was whispering again. "What are you sorry for?"

"For teasing you. I wasn't trying to embarrass you."

She shrugged, looking away. He'd hurt her. *Damn.*

"I'd like to go on record about a few things, and then I'll leave it alone. Is that all right?"

She nodded.

"One: I adore your body. I think it's perfect the way it is. But if you don't want me to comment on it, I won't."

"Thank you," she whispered.

"Don't take that to mean I'm not *thinking* about your body, however . . . especially at night." He cleared his throat meaningfully and she smiled warmly. "Two: Just like many other areas of marriage, I'm told communication is key when it comes to sex. I want to talk with you about your expectations before we have sex . . . and I want to tell you mine. I'll try to be more understanding now that I know that sex is a difficult subject for you . . . but you've got to meet me partway. Talk to me, Abs. I don't want you to feel uncomfortable, but new things are often uncomfortable at first. Practice makes perfect . . . a proverb a good Brevsporan like yourself should be familiar with." He repeated the word intentionally, trying to build up her tolerance to it.

She blew out a deep breath she'd been holding. "You're right, communication is important, and I will try to talk more openly about . . . sex." She still whispered the word, but she said it.

Parker grinned, triumphant. "There, was that so hard?"

"Yes!" She covered her crimson face with both hands.

"You're extremely adorable, you know that?" His legs were starting to fall asleep, and he planted a quick kiss to her neck to signal that the conversation was over. Her next words were so quiet, he almost missed them.

"What kind of expectations?"

"Pardon?" He turned her words over in his head, confused, and his heart went double time as he realized she was trying to talk about sex. *Forget my legs; I'll cut them off before I end the conversation here.* "Did I pique your curiosity, darling?"

She nodded, her hands falling away from her face. She didn't meet his gaze, but she leaned into him more fully.

"Well, let's start with an easy one: I expect that you'll be honest with me about what feels good and what doesn't. I can't read your mind, and I never want to hurt you or, worse, bore you—"

"Do you own handcuffs?"

Parker was stunned. He stared at her profile for a moment before he burst out laughing, burying his face in Abbie's neck, his face hot. "No, I don't. Do you?"

"No. I don't."

"Would you like me to procure some?"

"No, thank you," she whispered, grinning, and he laughed again.

"You are certainly full of surprises, Abs . . ." He drew her closer for a deep kiss, still laughing. "Well, I guess now I know one of your expectations and you know one of mine . . . Maybe we'll share another one tomorrow?"

She nodded, then glanced at the clock. "I need to go get ready now."

"Me too."

She got up and left without saying goodbye, and Parker got the impression that she might have reached her emotional limit. Hopefully she'd be able to recharge a little before the breakfast.

CHAPTER SEVENTEEN

THEY ENDED UP RUSHING, but they arrived in time to hear the keynote speaker, a former child prostitute who was now a lawyer in Imahara, fighting to free others who had been enslaved. Abbie seemed transfixed; she was taking notes. Parker noticed that she often did that if something was important to her; she didn't trust her memory to be sharp later. *Maybe I should slip a note into her phone that says "Find a better apartment" or "Stop trying to repay Parker for a debt you don't have" and see what happens.*

"Would you like to meet her? I can arrange it for you, if you'd like," Parker asked as the applause died.

Abbie was still typing. "No, I'll get her contact information from Jenise if I need it."

"Who's Jenise?"

"The president of Anti-CYST, Jenise Brandon. I told you, I talked to her last night. We're meeting up when she comes to Gardenia in a few weeks."

"Oh, right."

"Good morning, King Edward." Parker turned to see Crescena standing behind him, smiling.

"There you are!" He stood up and gave his old friend a long embrace. "Where have you been hiding? I sought you last night, but didn't find you, obviously."

"Yes, my apologies. My obligations at home delayed my arrival. Good morning, Abelia."

"Good morning, Your Highness."

Parker glanced at Abbie; he couldn't read her expression, but it wasn't a happy one.

"Please, call me Crescena."

I wish they could be friends . . . Maybe I can put them on the path.

"Will you join us?" he asked, and Abbie's mouth opened and closed silently.

"Certainly, thank you." She turned to Abbie. "What a pleasant surprise to see you, Abelia. I do not believe we have met in person yet. It is overdue."

Abbie nodded slowly. "No, we haven't met yet. I met your dad, though."

Parker gave her a hard look. *Stop it,* he said with his eyes. *Be nice.* She must have sensed it, because she seemed to be purposely avoiding his gaze.

Crescena smiled graciously. "Yes, Edward said the Silicon King is well. I cannot say that I have heard much from him as of late, but perhaps that is for the best."

"Blair's a different person than he was when you knew him."

"Abbie." It came out harsher than Parker meant it to.

"No, friend, it is all right. I do not mind." She turned to Abbie more fully. "I am sure that is true, and I am different, too. I have had some unique life experiences because of him. His absence has shaped me just as his presence would have."

"What kind of experiences?"

"Forgive me, Abelia, but we do not know each other well enough for me to disclose such details. Perhaps someday we will. After all, Edward and I have been friends since childhood, and our families are so close. It would be good to be friendly with you as well."

Parker figured Abbie would hear this as a threat, though he didn't think Crescena meant it that way. *This situation could escalate quickly . . .*

"Sure. Let me know next time you're in Gardenia. I'll take you to lunch."

Have your food tasters check that meal thoroughly, Cress . .
.

"Oh." Crescena tucked her hair behind her ear. "I would enjoy that very much, thank you. I will certainly accept your kind invitation in the near future." She turned to Parker. "May I please speak with you privately for a moment? I promise I will not leave your bride without a breakfast companion for long."

"Certainly," he said before he caught Abbie's stony expression. He hesitated. It was too late to take it back now . . . "I'll be right back, Abs." She was pushing her eggs around her plate. "Abs?"

"Yeah, I heard you. Enjoy your little . . . *chat.*" She had all the sincerity of a beauty pageant runner-up congratulating the winner. Parker offered Crescena his arm, and he led her toward a small conference room that had been used for the panel discussions the day before, their security trailing. He'd barely latched the door when he noticed silent tears on her cheeks.

"What's this?"

She was wringing her hands in almost comical way. "Oh, Edward; I am in trouble. I need your help."

"Of course, anything. Tell me what's going on, first of all." He led her over to a chair and she offered no resistance. He meant it. They'd been friends their whole lives; he would help her any way he could, if only to try to make up for Blair's abandonment.

"Someone is giving me his attention, and I do not think I can refuse him." The fear in her eyes was obvious, and it concerned him deeply.

"He wishes to marry you?"

She nodded. "My mother, she does not know what to do. She knows that our nation needs the economic benefits of a royal marriage as soon as possible, and he has much to offer."

"Who is it?"

"He wishes his offer to remain a secret until it is final. If I must go through with it, I do not wish to face his wrath later."

Wrath? Even a political marriage should be civil. This smelled like several wicked men he could think of . . .

"Well, it's difficult to help with such meager details."

She looked down at her hands. "Yes, I . . . I am sorry. I should not have involved you. Please forgive me."

"No, no, you can come to me. You can always come to me." He crossed his arms. "What can I do? Tell me."

"Could you help me arrange another marriage quickly? Perhaps if I am unavailable, his attentions will shift to someone else."

Is this why she'd been dropping hints that she was interested when Abbie seemed like she wasn't going to fulfill our contract? That would explain a lot. He hadn't thought she was attracted to him, and he certainly didn't see her that way.

"Well, I will certainly reach out to some eligible parties . . ."

"Thank you, Edward. You are my savior again. I do not know how to thank you."

"Oh, I don't know that I'd go quite that far . . . Let's see if I can get any results first. No promises, but I will make a diligent effort."

"That is all I can ask for."

He hated to see her like a beggar, trying to escape a forced marriage with someone who frightened her. *She deserves better than this. Jacking Blair.*

She rose from the chair, wiping her eyes with the back of her hand. "I will let you return to Abelia. I am sure she is not anxious to make small talk with strangers when she could be with you."

She moved past him toward the door, but he put a hand on her shoulder.

"I'm sorry for what Abelia said. Truly, I am."

Crescena shook her head a little. "She wants me to know you belong to her. I would do the same in her position. Please do not berate her."

Parker put on an expression of mock outrage. "How often have I berated anyone?"

"Well, I do not know for certain, but you and Abelia have always been like flint and steel."

"I assume I'm the steel in this scenario; that sounds more manly."

"I could not say," she replied with faux sincerity. "All I know is that the sparks seem to fly."

He opened the door for her, and they said goodbye with a friendly kiss on both cheeks. Parker walked quickly back to his table, only to find Abbie gone. *Fish guts. Did she leave?* He felt a sharp desire to speak with her, and there would definitely be some berating, but he also wanted to unpack what he'd just learned with her. Looking around, he found her auburn head nodding in the crowd, talking to the Brevsporan ambassador to Imahara, Mr. Van Hecke.

"So you see," the man was saying, "we're concerned. We respect your needs, your private life, but if there is anything you can do . . ." His mouth snapped shut as he noticed Parker approaching, and the king put a protective hand on Abbie's lower back.

"There you are, darling. Ready to go?"

"So ready." She turned back to the ambassador. "I will see what I can find out, Mr. Ambassador."

"Thank you, Your Highness. Your kindness to the land of your birth does not go unnoticed."

Parker led her toward the front doors. "What was that all about?"

"Guess who was supposed to show up to this?"

"Kurt."

"Bingo. They have no idea why he flaked. He's making them look bad. They want my help to figure out what's going on."

"I see. And will you help them?"

She shrugged. "I've had no luck getting a hold of him lately myself since I left Kohlstadt. I don't know why they think he would respond to me." She stopped in the shade to wait for the carriage to come around. "How was your talk with *Crescena*?"

"You don't have to say her name like that."

"Like what?"

"Like it's a virulent strain of a sexually transmitted disease."

Abbie snickered. "But that's just what she sounds like. Can't you just hear it? 'Oh man, that chick I picked up last weekend gave me crescenas all over my—"

Seeing the Trellan ambassador to Imahara exiting the building in his peripheral vision, Parker cleared his throat to indicate that they had an audience. Abbie fell silent, but her eyes were still twinkling, even as he gave her a hard look. Their carriage arrived, and he opened the door for her, glad to be taking this conversation into relative privacy. There would only be three other people within hearing distance . . . three people who had signed nondisclosure agreements.

"Speaking of saying things you shouldn't . . . let's discuss how you spoke to Crescena."

She lifted her chin. "You *ditched* me. We're supposed to be spending this weekend together."

Parker rolled his eyes, even though he knew his parents would've cringed to see it. "Abs, you started in on her the minute she sat down."

"And *why* did you invite her to sit down? My weekend. My time."

He took off his glasses and massaged his temples. "Abs, she's one of my very oldest friends. I know you don't want to hear it, but she is special to me. You cannot treat her like that."

She held up her hands. "Fine. I'm . . . sorry."

He put his glasses back on and looked around the heavily brocaded carriage, as if searching for the right words. "You've built her up to be this villain in your mind, and you could not be more wrong. She is one of the most sensitive, bright, sweet people I've ever known. She's not tough like you, darling. Her father's departure during her childhood is a wound that still hasn't healed. Your attacks will be deeply felt."

"I said I'm sorry!"

"Actually sorry this time?" he asked.

"Yes. I shouldn't have brought up Blair. That was wrong . . ."

"I feel like there's a 'but' coming."

"But she deserves it for throwing herself at you."

"For your information, she's in a very difficult spot. She's uncontracted . . ." Parker ignored Abbie's snickering this time, guessing that it harkened back to STD jokes again. "And she needs to marry quickly. Someone is giving her unwanted attention. Someone who frightens her."

"Who?"

"She wouldn't say."

"Interesting. I wonder . . ."

He leaned forward. "I'm listening . . ."

"Well, two things. First of all, Kurt needs a bride."

"No. No way. Sorry, but they'd be like oil and water."

"With enough surfactant, you can make that work. Maybe they would, too. Need is a powerful motivator. They don't have to love each other."

"Not happening. What's the second thing?"

"You're not going to like it, hon." She sighed. "When I negotiated the withdrawal of the mercenaries with the Warlord-in-Chief of Gratha . . ."

"You're referring to the unfortunate incident when he scarred you and humiliated you while I wasn't there to pound him into next week?"

She crossed her arms. "Who's telling this story?"

"You are. You're simply telling it incorrectly."

She sighed again. "When I met with him, he mentioned that he was looking for a bride."

Parker felt a wave of nausea rise in his throat that had nothing to do with the bumpy carriage ride. The very idea of someone like him having unfettered access to someone like shy, sweet Crescena was . . . unthinkable.

"You're right. I don't like it."

CHAPTER EIGHTEEN

114 days to the wedding

"BUT IF YOU LOOK AT the economic factors, there's no way the Forgelands could have kept the Trellan faction happy long-term," Parker said. Tall bamboo trees grew thickly on both sides of the path they were hiking on, providing heavy shade, and birdsong echoed.

Abbie shook her head. "Forget economic factors. That's nothing. They broke away from the motherland because they were underrepresented in the government. They treated anyone east of the mountains as irrelevant." It was Sunday morning, and the pair was hiking through an Imaharan state park that Parker had discreetly arranged to be closed to all other traffic. Abbie loved it; leave it to him to arrange the perfect date.

Parker rolled his eyes at her as he adjusted the heavy backpack he was carrying. "Yes, and why were they unhappy about their representation? Because government resources were being directed heavily toward the western half of the country. It all goes back to money."

"No, it doesn't. There were cultural and social divides between the two halves going back generations. The indigenous people groups never got along, and that tension only increased once the settlers came in. I can carry the backpack for a while."

"Where is this drivel coming from, Frank Tacker? No, I'm good."

Abbie lifted her chin. "I think Tacker has a unique perspective on Forgelander history."

"Oh, come on. Abs, the guy still argues for reconciliation to exclusion of all other solutions, after 150 years. He's living in the past."

"There are worse insults for a historian."

He reached out and took her hand without asking as they walked along the level path, and she smiled inwardly at the familiarity of the gesture.

"I would pick you a flower, but I was told in no uncertain terms that I would be fined if I did, diplomatic immunity or no."

Abbie chuckled. "I didn't know Imaharans were so uptight about the environment. That's false anemone. Isn't it pretty?"

"It is pretty. It looks like a miniature lotus flower."

"Yeah, it does. But lotus is always aquatic. Ironically, it's also called a water lily, when in reality, lilies are from an entirely different order. Lotus flowers aren't even monocots! Isn't that hilarious?"

Parker nodded slowly, but his eyes had glazed over.

"Uh-oh. I over-nerded on you." Abbie pointed at some bellflowers. "Look, pretty."

"Oh good, we're back to a conversation I can participate in." He pointed at another purplish flower. "What's that one?"

"Fawn lily, I think. This one is a true lily, though it's more closely related to tulips." She stooped to look closer and felt Parker's blatant stare on her backside. "Yes, fawn lily; we have a slightly different variety in Gardenia. It's redder."

"Nice."

Abbie straightened and leaned into Parker, staring deep into his eyes. "My backside or my knowledge of flora?"

He grinned. "Both."

She whacked him lightly. "Have you no shame?"

He shrugged. "As you said, it's hard to ogle from a distance. I've got to seize the opportunity when it presents itself . . . Are you thirsty?" He let one strap of the backpack fall from his shoulder and twisted to get some water. But his eyebrows came together, and she knew his hand must have fallen on the envelope.

Rats. I knew I should've put it in his suitcase, not his backpack.

He affected a calm expression as he pulled it from the bag, but she knew he was unhappy. "Care to explain this?"

"I think it's self-explanatory."

Holding her gaze, he threw it over his shoulder, then zipped up the backpack and re-shouldered it.

"Hey," she reprimanded. "Don't do that." Abbie snatched the envelope up off the ground and dusted it off before stuffing it in her back pocket. She expected to find his eyes on her backside again, but he stared down the path, clearly distracted, and she followed his gaze. She didn't see anything except Waldo, keeping a respectful distance.

"What are you looking at?"

Parker didn't hear her. Abbie snapped her fingers.

"Hey, where'd you go?"

"Sorry, I was just . . . sorry. My brain took off." He started them walking again, his gaze bouncing between her face and the path ahead.

What in the world? What was that all about?

They walked along in silence. Abbie's mind was trying to formulate more questions to draw out what had just happened, but she didn't know how to be more direct than "where'd you go?" and that clearly hadn't worked. She watched a little stream that rolled along with them, sweeping leaves over slippery rocks and over orange fish, congregating in a large natural pool. They stood there, watching the fish. The silence was deafening; she couldn't take it anymore. Abbie took a breath to speak, but he beat her to it.

"Sorry about earlier, I just . . . I wanted to ask you something, but I didn't have the right words."

"Sounds serious."

"Just a little bit." He licked his lips. "Do you like kids?"

"What do you mean? Like, all kids?"

"Yes. Are you a kid person?"

Now she was the one staring off into space. "Sort of. It depends on the kid. I like well-behaved kids. I don't do well with hellions, and I'm not great with infants, mostly from lack of experience. Sometimes I watch Jenny; she's Ward and Patty's daughter."

"Your friends from under the bridge? When you first got to Gardenia?"

She nodded. "But Jenny's a really good kid. Lots of energy, but she likes me and we go to Dempsey Park. She hates being inside. I think they're still trying to get her used to the idea of living in a house. They started by sending her to my house, but it's not working." She looked up at him. "What about you?"

"I love kids. Especially my siblings."

"Yes, Rutha had mentioned you all were very close."

He nodded, playing with her engagement ring; he'd offered to get her a nicer one, but she was quite partial to the one he'd brought to her in Imahara the first time.

"We are. And I think it's partly due to Simon."

"Your youngest brother?"

He nodded. "He's got trisomy 21. It's been a challenge, but we've all pulled together to help, to support Mum and Dad. He had some heart issues, had to have surgery as a baby." Edward would never forget sitting with his family in the hospital, waiting those three long hours during the operation to fix the small hole in Simon's heart. It hadn't been easy to endure at age fourteen; he couldn't imagine how his parents must've felt. Though Simon was only five months old, the whole family had already been so enamored with him.

"Oh man. I knew he was disabled, but I didn't know it was that bad . . ."

Parker scowled. "He's not *disabled*. He's sharp as a tack. He notices things I've missed constantly."

"Sorry, I just meant he's . . . delayed. Special needs." Parker still looked ruffled, and she laid a hand on his chest. "I wasn't trying to offend. Really. Tell me more about Simon."

"I just hate that word, *disabled*. It gives you no useful information about *Simon* whatsoever. Even when I tell you he has trisomy 21, it doesn't really tell you what he can do and what he can't. How are his needs *special*? He's eight years old.

He needs his family, food, shelter, education . . . Don't we all need those things? Why do we settle for pat labels?"

Abbie shrugged one shoulder. "It's easier. People don't want to take the time to get to know him."

His face was showing all his vulnerability. "Will you?"

She kissed him. "Of course I will. He's your family, he's important to me. They all are."

"You know," he said, musing, "there's a good possibility we'll have twins." He tugged her forward down the path again.

"Oh Woz, you're right. We've got them on both sides. I hadn't thought about that." She groaned. "I'm going to be as big as a house. We'll have to build a new castle to hold my girth." She glared at Parker, who was gazing at her contentedly, his previous unreadable mood now gone. "I really think you're getting the better end of the deal with this whole procreation thing."

"Can't argue with that."

"Why'd you ask if I'm a kid person?"

He shrugged. "I guess I didn't want to assume you wanted them, just because we're royal. I realized I'd never asked you." He glanced at her, and she smiled at him encouragingly. "My mum was a different kind of queen as we got older. Rutha raised us until Simon, when she wanted to be more hands-on. But even before that, she spent significant time with us. I guess I'm hoping you'll be a mum like that . . ."

"And less like mine?"

His nostrils flared. "I didn't mean it like that."

She squeezed his hand. "I know, it's okay. I don't want to be like her. Though in some ways, I get it. I mean, queening is a full-time job, and so is parenting. Something's gotta give."

"I suppose so." He looked like he was holding back a smile, and he glanced over his shoulder at their security, before his voice dropped to a register harder to overhear. "So I shared an *expectation* with you . . ."

"That's not exactly about . . . sex."

"It's about kids. I think it counts." He squeezed her hand. "But you don't have to."

"No, it's okay," she said, mentally fidgeting with the words she wanted to say, trying to arrange them. "I guess mine is more about kids, too." *How can I explain this?* She felt the long-forgotten tremble that accompanied truth-telling for her. Lies were so much more comfortable. "I want a small family. I know both of our family traditions dictate that we have as many kids as we can, but I don't think I can handle that, health-wise or personally. I just don't have the energy. I think it's wiser if we limit ourselves to two or three kids."

Parker said nothing, staring down the path, but his pace quickened.

"Did you hear me?"

"Yes, I . . . I heard you."

See, this is why I hate telling the truth. Now I feel like a terrible person, and he's clamming up and our day is ruined . . .

"And?"

"And . . . I'm thinking." He noticed her troubled expression and stopped. "You can't get upset just because I'm thinking. I'm allowed to think about what you say."

"I'm not upset," Abbie spluttered. "I just don't see what there is to think about. You either agree or you don't agree. I've never known you to lack opinions about anything."

He crossed his arms. "My opinions are formed by scrutinizing all the facets of an issue, giving it due consideration. No, I don't lack for opinions, but I don't come to them lightly, either."

"I'm not suggesting you should! But you must have given it some thought before this moment."

"Yes, of course I have. But I'm not ready to give a pronouncement yet, unlike you, who never met a snap decision you didn't like."

She stabbed a finger into his chest. "Not even forty-eight hours ago, you asked me to trust you, tell you the truth, but you can't handle it. You're getting all bent out of shape."

His eyes flashed. "Me, bent out of shape? Ha! You're demanding I give my approval for a huge life decision without giving me even five minutes to think about it. For your information, I was trying to think of a way to talk about this without starting a damn argument!"

"Don't you jacking curse at me, Edward! I did what you asked me to do, okay? I told you the truth. And look where it got us."

Feeling antsy, Abbie turned and strode down the path as quickly as she could without running. He caught up to her easily, coming into stride with her. If she could've hiked with her arms crossed over her chest in perturbation, she would have. Ten minutes later, their accelerated pace had her perspiring, and she swiped a bead of sweat away before it could sting her eyes.

"Are you crying?"

She didn't bother looking at him. "No!"

"Because I hate it when you cry."

"Well, I'll inform my emotions of your preference, but alas, you don't reign over them." She felt his finger brush her shoulder, and she jerked away. "Don't, Parker."

"You had a bee on you! Am I supposed to let it sting you just because we're having our first big fight?"

"Of course not!"

"Then stop yelling at me!"

"I'm not yelling at you!"

"Yes, you are!"

Abbie's brain caught up to his words, and she shouted, "Are we having our first big fight?"

"Looks that way," he yelled back.

"Well . . . I . . . ," she stammered, "I don't know how to feel about that!"

"I don't either!" Parker slowed to a stop and put his hands on his narrow hips, and she slowed with him. "I don't like fighting with you."

"I don't like fighting with you, either."

They stared at each other, then the corner of Parker's mouth lifted ever so slightly.

"What's so funny?"

"I don't know. We're being dumb, both of us."

She crossed her arms. "*I'm* not being dumb!"

"Okay, okay, fine." He edged toward her, his smile growing. "You didn't storm back to the carriage. I feel like that's progress."

"Yeah, maybe." Abbie looked down and dug in the dirt with the toe of her boot.

"You know, what happens next sets a precedent for the next fifty to seventy years."

"You mean, what we decide about how many kids?"

"No, but we'll discuss that again later. I meant how we decide to make up."

Abbie glanced up briefly and noticed his hands stuffed deep into his pockets. *I bet he wants to touch me, but he doesn't want his head bitten off. He's no dummy.* "Well, I'll give you an hour to think about it and you let me know what you think."

Parker was the one looking at his boots now. *Okay, maybe I am being dumb. That was a dumb thing to say. Why am I dragging him?*

"Sorry," she mumbled. "I shouldn't have—"

"Actually," he said, "I can tell you right now."

She looked up, wary.

"I think we should hug it out." He held his arms out, straight-faced.

She chuckled. "I don't think so."

"I do," he said, stepping closer, and Abbie back away down the path out of his reach. His eyes flashed, and she knew his pursuit was imminent. *He never could resist the chase...*

"Stay away from me," she said, shaking her head. Her grin gave away her lack of actual resentment. "I'm warning you."

"You know, kings are terrible at taking orders," Parker said, returning the grin. He dropped his arms suddenly and broke into a run. Laughing, Abbie turned and took off down the path, not daring to look back lest she lose ground. He didn't catch up as quickly as she'd feared he would, but when he did, he slammed into her like a linebacker, almost knocking them both to the ground. He regained his balance just in time, his arms wrapped firmly around her, pressing her side into the front of his chest.

"You almost knocked me over, you loon!"

"And you loved it. Don't deny it."

"Whatever. You're very sweaty."

"So are you. It's disgusting, really." He buried his face in her neck, inhaling deeply, and Abbie cracked up.

"Why are you *smelling* me?"

"Pheromones. Can't help it. You should've run faster, darling, we're done for now. It's biology."

"It is not," she laughed. "There's no evidence that humans emit pheromones."

He lifted his head. "Really?"

She nodded. "Really. Sorry."

"That's disappointing. I'd really like to be able to blame my behavior on something other than myself."

"Wouldn't we all," she sighed, pivoting in his arms to face him, then she kissed him. She intended a peck, a simple conciliatory gesture, but he wasn't wrong on one count: being surrounded in a cloud of Parker's scent was slightly intoxicating in a completely illogical way. His arms were still tight around her, and she made the mistake of looking into his eyes. *Lord, this guy has no poker face. Forget his sleeve; he's got his heart in his eyes, everything he's feeling.*

So when he drifted closer, she didn't notice until his lips touched hers again, a teasing brush, a long, lingering draw against hers. The blood rushed to her head so fast her scalp tingled, and she deepened the kisses, reveling in the scent of lilies, the sound of running water, and the feeling of being in love.

CHAPTER NINETEEN

109 days to the wedding

EDWARD KNOCKED ON HIS friend's apartment door. A full minute passed.

"James?" He knocked again. "Open up, it's me."

"Coming," James called. "Keep your silk shirt on." The door opened.

"I'll have you know this shirt isn't silk. It's cotton."

"Slumming it for your visit to my place? Smart." Arron's place wasn't even close to slumming; the man liked nice things. The trust he'd been left by his anonymous father meant that he didn't lack for much. In stark contrast to Abbie's place, Arron's was light and open, with a view of Grammarless Park. Still, in contrast to his place, yes, this was slumming. Pretty much everything was.

"I'm here to do your exercises with you."

James scowled. "But I don't have a leotard in your size."

"Not those exercises, mate." Edward chuckled. "Your physical therapy."

"What happened to Saint?"

"Called away."

"Just as well. He always seems like he wants to murder me by the time we're done. I'd hate to have to haunt that prickly bastard for all eternity."

"He prickles because he cares," Edward returned.

He didn't mention what a mess sturdy, stable Saint had been just after James was shot. "I don't know what the Jersey happened," he'd kept saying, his voice hollow. *That was a phone call I'm not likely to forget anytime soon.*

"And until you agree to a nurse, you're getting the Saint treatment. Now, how do we begin?"

James shuffled back to the leather couch where, based on the number of dirty dishes and food wrappers adjacent, he'd been spending a significant amount of time.

"Surely you have better things to do than watch me breathe deeply."

"Better things? No. Other things, certainly. But more important? No." Parker whipped out his phone. "I'm setting my timer. Get going."

Muttering under his breath, James scooted himself to the edge of the couch to sit up straight. In order to exercise his lungs, he had to practice deep breathing...without talking. Torture for someone like James, who lived to entertain. "Tell me about Imahara," he said, quirking an eyebrow at his friend suggestively. He breathed in deeply through his nose, then let it out slow through his mouth, like he was blowing out a candle, impeding his part in any potential discussion.

"Funny you should mention, there was some heavy breathing there, too . . ."

James laughed, sending himself into a coughing fit. "It's okay," he rasped as Edward looked on, concerned. "It's good to cough, it keeps my lungs clear." He gave him the hand signal for "Keep going" as he started over.

Edward sat down on the fashionably distressed coffee table across from his friend. "It was great. It was . . . a tiny taste of what it's going to be like to be together all the time. Minus the sex, of course."

James waggled his head in understanding.

"But we had some really good talks. Not too much arguing . . . though we didn't really resolve the worst argument. It's hard to leave things just hanging in the air like that . . . but she's not ready to talk about it again. I called her on her lying, and I made her cry."

His friend's eyebrows bounced in surprise as he pulled in another deep breath.

"I know. She's so tough, I didn't think it would bother her that much. And if it did, I thought she'd yell, not cry. I hate it so much when women cry. So much."

James nodded vehemently, holding his arms out even with his chest to indicate a large amount.

"I know, you're the same." He was thinking back to Rhodie at the hospital.

"What base?" James wheezed at the end of his exhale.

Edward grinned. "I'm not telling you that."

James held up his pointer finger in a "one," and Edward held up his middle finger in response.

"She did attempt to snog me in her bed at one point." Edward chuckled as Arron's body language went nuts, all to indicate "AND?" "And I refused her. She's so naive, James. She just has no idea about anything. She wants me, I know she does, but she doesn't realize what kind of exquisite torture it would be for me touch her in her bed. Oh—I finally got her to say the word 'sex.' That was an achievement."

James turned his exhale into a low whistle, and Parker laughed.

"But it was good. We waltzed; she actually followed my lead. We hiked; it was nice to do something besides sitting around inside. We talked. We made out. She insulted Crescena, that was nice."

James smiled and gave two thumbs-up.

"Not you, too."

James pantomimed "You see picture?" quirking his finger like a camera trigger in front of his face.

"What picture?"

He pulled out his phone and opened a celebrity news app. Someone had taken a picture of him and Crescena giving their goodbye kiss, chaste though it was, outside the conference room, paired with the headline "King Edward indulging in Descareti dalliance?"

"Woz-condemn-it," Edward seethed. "There were no journalists there—who sent this to them?"

James shrugged, clearly apologetic.

"Never mind. It doesn't matter," he said, trying to convince himself. "Abbie won't care. I just hope it doesn't give the litigants hope that their lawsuits are succeeding." Edward paused. "You're not interested in marrying Crescena, are you?"

James sneered at him, waving his arms in front of him.

"No," Edward chuckled, "she's not quite your type, is she? You'd be queen's consort, though. That's something."

His friend waggled his hand to say "Sort of."

"Speaking of your type, has Rhodie been by to check on you?"

James shook his head, but he pantomimed texting with his phone.

"Texting? That's good. She's been busy. I'll try to bring her next time I come." He paused, considering his next statement. "I don't want to raise your hopes, either, but I actually think she might be warming to you . . ." He watched his friend's response closely. James laughed, coughing again, and Edward could see it hurt this time, but he didn't lose his smile. "Can I get you anything? Water? A pillow for your fragile chest?"

He shook his head, but his eyes twinkled.

"You know, she's going on an expedition in a few months to Trella. Should be easy duty for whoever guards her. You interested?"

James nodded slowly, grinning.

"You'd have to behave yourself."

James gave him a "Who, me?" innocent expression, his hand to his chest.

"Yeah, yeah. Save it. You'd also have to be back to perfect health, which means you have to do your PT every day, not just when one of us shows up to make you do it."

James touched his thumb to his pointer finger, making the sign for "Okay."

"Arron, this might be the finest conversation we've ever had."

James didn't need his pointer finger or his thumb for the next thing he said.

CHAPTER TWENTY

100 days to the wedding

ABBIE ARRIVED IN ORANGIERS just before dinner-time Friday night, and he'd been giving her long looks all evening. Distracted when people asked him questions. Their legs were pressed together, his fingers circling her knee. She returned the favor by sliding her foot against his under the table. Any time they lost contact for a passed basket of rolls or bowl of salad, they found each other again quickly. Abbie had forgotten how much fun it could be to eat with children, especially children whom you didn't have to bathe and wrestle into bed afterward. She was fairly sure Parker had wrestling of a different sort in mind, and she enjoyed raising an eyebrow at him when the others were distracted. After dessert, she excused herself to go to the restroom and found him waiting for her in the hallway when she was done.

"Sadly, the party began to break up when you left, as parties are often prone to do."

"Ha ha."

"Did you want a tour?"

Was that code for "Do you want to see my room?" It sure feels like it. And she sure did.

She reached for his hand, and he led her down the hall.

"That's the game room." He didn't stop to open the door. "That's the nursery." He pointed to the left. "That's the dormer, and that's a guest room." He pointed to the right. "That's the movie theatre."

"Ooh, really?" Teasing, she tried to slow his steps, hanging back to peek into the red-carpeted room. "I love home theatres. We didn't have one in Kohlstadt." Parker continued to pull her down the hall without acknowledging her comment. She was laughing harder and harder the farther on he charged, and it only seemed to spur him on. He only slowed down when he had to drop her hand to open the ornate double doors in front of him.

"And this is your future home, the residence."

Despite the opulent front doors, inside it was fairly simply appointed. Oh, the artwork on the walls was priceless, and there were a few antique pieces, but most of the furniture was angular, modern. It was painted in blues and grays, offset by the large white sectional, and the effect was oceanic. *That sectional will be the first thing to go when we have kids, though . . . if we have kids,* Abbie thought. She heard the doors click quietly shut behind her and felt Parker at her back, his hands on her hips, guiding her forward, shifting her hair over her shoulder to kiss her neck.

"Do you like it?"

She pivoted to see him, but he buried his face in her neck as if he didn't want to see her reaction.

"Of course I do. It suits you perfectly."

"And you? Will it suit you?"

"I'm sure it will."

"We're into double digits, you know. Less than one hundred days . . ."

"Mmm."

"My office is that way. Our bedroom is the other way," he said between long, lingering kisses.

Abbie laughed. "Are we still adhering to the tour ruse? I thought maybe we could drop that, now that it's just the two of us . . ."

He didn't seem to be listening to her. His hands were roaming up and down her sides, restless. He'd directed them to the couch, not bothering to turn on more lights, and to her surprise, he pulled her down onto his lap. His intensity was intoxicating; whatever percentage of his brain was currently in use, it was 100 percent focused on getting her as close as possible. She felt rational thought melting away like an ice cube in boiling water. She unbuttoned her cardigan, revealing her tank top underneath, and his hands immediately went to her arms to push the sweater off them. He seemed to need as much contact with her skin as possible, and she felt her eyebrows go up as he pulled off his T-shirt. Abbie shifted to put one knee on either side of his lap, grinning at him. But Parker wasn't smiling; this was no lazy Sunday make-out session like they'd had at her apartment. His frantic kisses were drifting lower on her chest. Abbie suddenly realized they were on a runaway train, barreling toward part of the track that hadn't been built yet, the line with a comically large red-and-white "Do Not Enter" sign. *Brakes*, she thought, so mindless that even her thoughts were somehow breathless. *We need brakes.*

"Parker . . . ," she said on a gasp. It only served to encourage him, and he groaned in response. Abbie forced her breathing to slow so that she didn't sound like she was having so much fun. "Parker, honey, slow down." She put her hands over his and tried to press them in place, but he shook her off, reaching under for the lower edge of her shirt. "Edward." Her voice was firm, and she pushed his hands away. He grabbed her backside to pull her flush against him, and that's when she slapped him; the sharp sound reverberated through the quiet room.

Immediately, she covered her mouth with her hands. Tears sprang to her eyes at the shock and hurt on his face. He shook his head like waking up from a dream, and he reached for her, but she pushed off his bare chest and quickly stood up, backing away.

"Abs . . ."

"Eddie!" Both their heads snapped toward the door where Simon stood in the now-open doorway, his arms lifted in triumph. "I won spoons!" Parker stared at him, chest still heaving, his mind apparently beyond words.

"Simon, that's fantastic!" Abbie gushed, picking up her sweater and pulling it on quickly. "Well done, you! Let's plan another game for tomorrow and we'll see if you can defend your title."

"My title is Simon Daniel William Ford Foster Broward, Fourth Son."

"Yes, I know that's your royal title," she said, genuinely amused, ushering him toward the door. "I meant your new title, Spoons Champion of Bluffton Castle."

"Oh! Why are you in the dark?" She was met at the door by Lily, who looked relieved and apologetic at the same time.

"Deepest apologies, Abelia, he said he was going to the toilet . . . Come on, love. Remember how we said we were going to give Edward and his bride some alone time?" Lily grimaced at Abbie as she led an oblivious Simon away from the residence and mouthed "Sorry" again. Abbie waved her off, silently conveying that apologies were unnecessary, and quietly shut the door, locking it this time. Parker's elbows were on his knees, his head in his hands.

"Are you sure you want to be in close quarters with me?" He didn't lift his head.

Abbie crossed to the couch and sat next to him. "I like to live dangerously." He flinched at her hand on his shoulder, and she drew back. "I'm sorry if I hurt you."

He let out a pained laugh. "Do *not* apologize. If you hadn't, I don't know if . . . I am so sorry, I did not intend to—"

"I know you didn't. It's not only your fault; I encouraged it. I'm sorry I didn't speak up sooner, but I kind of like being adored." Her attempt to make him laugh fell flat again. She decided to try sincerity instead. "Frankly, it just caught me off guard because it felt pretty backwards. I'm usually the pusher, the rule-bender. You're Mr. By-the-Book. And that felt more like setting the book on fire."

"And dancing by its light." He finally lifted his head, but didn't look at her. Abbie reached down and handed him his shirt, and he put it on.

"It's not like this is unexpected, though. It'd be weird if we didn't feel a strong attraction to each other. You're supposed to want me. I'm supposed to want you. "

He stood up suddenly, pacing to the window. "Yes, but I'm not supposed to take without asking, disregarding my promises. I'd be furious if you came on to me like that." He paused and his voice became firmer. "I am furious. I'm furious with myself; I broke your trust. How can you not be furious with me?"

"Because I took off my sweater. Because I straddled your lap, for Woz's sake. I returned every one of those kisses until I realized things were getting out of control. I should've realized you were too on edge. I saw the hot looks you were giving me at dinner."

"Was I? Woz, I didn't even notice."

Abbie cleared her throat. "I'm assuming you don't think we should've . . ."

"What, given in? Absolutely not. No certificate, no sex."

Good. Rational Parker is back. "Well, then it appears we need a plan. Because I don't think we want to depend so heavily on my self-control in the future. That's not my strong suit, and I know where our bedroom is now, thanks to your extremely cursory tour."

He chuckled softly, and Abbie felt her shoulders drop. *Finally.* He moved toward her, his arms crossed over his chest, but stopped a foot away.

"Are you okay?" His face was so full of concern, remorse. It was painful to see.

She nodded.

"I didn't hurt you?"

She shook her head. "It was delightful until you stopped listening to me. Then it was a little scary, only because I knew how much you'd regret it if we . . ."

"I should've stopped right then, Abbie. I am so sorry."

She stood up. "Should we rejoin the others? I hear there's a game of spoons happening . . ."

He pinched the bridge of his nose. "Can you imagine if Simon had come in a few moments earlier? I'd have never heard the end of it. My father would've killed me."

"To be fair, he didn't knock . . ."

Parker's hand dropped. "You go ahead; I need a few minutes yet to recover. I'll be out soon."

She grinned at him. "Maybe take a shower . . ."

"I'm not sure what that would—" She shot him a meaningful look. "Ah, a *cold* shower. That does seem an appropriate punishment."

She headed for the door, stopping to lean in for a short kiss . . . and stumbled when he stepped back.

"Maybe in a few minutes," he muttered, arms crossed again, looking at the hardwood floors. "Sorry."

Abbie swallowed her disappointment and nodded, closing the door quietly behind her. Dean and Waldo were just outside the doors now.

"Where the Jersey were you a few minutes ago?"

They shrugged, and Dean offered, "You seemed like you wanted to be alone."

"Yeah," she muttered under her breath, "but that doesn't mean we should be."

CHAPTER TWENTY-ONE

99 days to the wedding

THE NEXT DAY, PARKER kept her running: up for an early breakfast with his grandmother, then cake tasting, then on to pick out chairs and tables for the reception. They met with her lawyers and did some preliminary paperwork, despite it being a Saturday. He convinced Rhodie to take Abbie out to a lupus-approved lunch spot, and she hung out with the twins the rest of the afternoon, indulging their magazine "Is he into you?" quizzes and viral videos. The two of them made an appearance at a late-summer concert in Chapel Park with a picnic dinner, much to the delight of most of the audience. She was happy to just say good night and stumble down the hall by the time they got back to the castle.

But not the day after. He tried to overbook them: he made her go to the gym with him at six, breakfast with the family at seven thirty, shopping at nine, premarital counseling at ten thirty, lunch at noon. He had some work to do in the afternoon, so Abbie took a nap. Then he took her sailing the rest of the afternoon, getting back in time for a quick shower and dinner with the family, then games afterward . . . but he could feel things winding down, and it was too early. It was time to make a quick getaway. They hadn't yet had dessert when he sauntered over and kissed the top of her head.

"I'm off to bed, darling. See you in the morning."

His mother looked mildly perplexed, but said nothing. His father smiled knowingly.

"Off to bed? It's eight thirty!" Abbie protested.

He gave her a glance that said "Drop it" and strode out of the room and down the hall, feeling seven sets of eyes on his back. He hadn't even reached the game room when his phone plinked.

Abbie: Don't avoid me. I haven't been properly kissed in days.

It was the nap, he thought. I should never have let her nap. Annoyed, he leaned against the wall and typed back.

Parker: How can you say I'm avoiding you? We've spent most of the day together. I'm tired. We've got tomorrow together as well.

Abbie: You're punishing yourself for the other night. But you're punishing me, too. That's unfair.

Parker: I won't put you in a compromising situation again.

Abbie: So you'll hold me at arm's length instead? Smart. That'll fix things.

Parker: Hush, woman.

Abbie: I hope you dream that I'm massaging your shoulders, trailing light kisses down your neck . . . my reckless red hair tickling your chest . . .

Parker: Stop it. Kings don't sext. It's not proper.

Abbie: Now I'm blowing in your ear, nibbling your ear lobe, pressing my generous chest against your back . . .

Parker: I'm turning off my mobile.

Abbie: Good, maybe you'll actually sleep.

Parker: Bully.

Abbie: When you avoid me? Yes, I will bully you. With my love.

Parker: You're nonsensical at this hour.

Abbie: Again, it's only 8:30.

He sighed. She wasn't wrong; this wasn't solving the problem, ultimately, and as usual, she'd seen through him. Maybe they did just need a plan, some ground rules for being alone. He went back to the dining room.

"Please excuse the interruption. May I borrow Abbie?"

Simon shook his head, throwing an arm around her neck, nearly pulling her out of her seat. "No. She is on *my* team. You left. Go away." Parker grinned at the sight of his youngest brother getting chummy with his future wife.

"Someone's become quite enamored with your bride." Lily smiled.

"And here I thought I was hiding it so well," Ignatius deadpanned, and they all laughed except Simon, who nevertheless looked around, smiling.

Abbie turned to the boy, her face serious, pressing their foreheads together. "Well, hearts buddy, will we be done soon so I can talk to your silly brother, who can't decide if he's coming or going?"

Simon held up his fingers. "Two more rounds."

She turned back and smiled at Parker. "We'll be done in a few minutes; where shall I meet you?"

"Your sitting room?" She nodded and he turned to leave.

"Wait up." Parker turned to see Andrew waiting in the doorway, and he grinned and jerked his head down the hallway. His brother caught up quickly; his legs seemed longer every day, and his head was above Parker's shoulder now. "I want to talk to you."

"Of course. What's on your mind?"

"Lincoln."

Parker's easy stride faltered, and he turned to look at his brother. "What about Lincoln?"

"They won't tell me anything, especially when the girls and Simon are around. But you know. You know what will happen when they catch up with him. I can handle it." Andrew's voice cracked, and he rolled his eyes, as if frustrated that his body wasn't on board with his brain's agenda. Parker knew that feeling well.

"There are soldiers out looking for him. If they find him, their orders are to bring him back alive."

Andrew nodded, serious, copying Parker's wide stance. "And then?"

"And then he'll be tried in court, and if convicted, he faces life in prison."

Andrew lowered his voice, glancing over his shoulder. "Not . . . not death?"

"No, I won't ask for that. I'll ask for life in prison. You'd be able to visit him."

Andrew sniffed, and Parker knew he was trying not to show his relief. "Why would I want to see him? He's garbage. He's ballast. Fish guts."

Parker hid his surprise at Andrew's harsh language, nodding slowly. "Well, you may not always feel that way. He's still your oldest brother."

"Is he still aiming for you? For us?"

Parker shook his head. "That's rather tough to determine. My expectation is that he'll continue to gather allies, perhaps to try again. But we're ready for him. We won't let him win." He pulled the young man in for a strong hug, clapping him on the back as he released him. "You can ask me anything, all right? Man to man."

Andrew nodded, then gestured over his shoulder. "They dealt me out, but there's still pie." He patted his belly, then disappeared back into the dining room. His mother had privately asked him to encourage Andrew to eat. Parker had discounted her concerns at first, but during their hug, he'd noticed how thin the boy was. He wondered if Andrew was grieving more than he let on; perhaps he should see a counselor. He'd speak to his mother later.

Parker: On second thought, meet me in the game room. It's less intimate.

Abbie: I'm rolling my eyes at you.

Parker: There's an emoji for that.

Abbie: Honey, there's emojis for lots of things . . . but you said kings are too proper for that.

By the time she got there, Parker had rearranged the room to put a couch in front of the old chalkboard and dug around until he found some chalk. The game room had been the tutoring room, long ago. He had all the lights on, and she squinted as she walked in from the dark hallway.

"Hey." He met her at the door and shut it behind her. "Did Team Simon take the hearts title, too?"

"As a matter of fact, we did. I see you had a change of heart about hitting the hay."

"I did." He guided her over to the deep leather couch, and she sat down. "I realized you were right."

"I hear that more often than you'd think."

"From kings?"

She grinned, but said nothing. He stationed himself in front of her like a professor, and he hoped the posture would draw out the beta side of her for once. He tossed the chalk to himself while he talked, nervous.

"I've been reflecting on the incident the other night." To his mild surprise, she appeared to be listening quietly. "Having you in my space, which I think of as our space, provoked some powerful emotions. This us, away from everyone staring and whispering and judging, this us is so different. We have so little that's ours; we're public property. But pulling you into my arms behind closed doors, no security just outside, no nosy neighbors . . . I felt like I could breathe. I finally felt as close to you physically as I do emotionally. Having you all to myself went to my head. I apologize again." He took a deep breath and looked into her eyes. "Any questions so far?" She raised her hand and he narrowed his gaze, then called on her.

"Will you be grading on a curve?"

"For you? Definitely. Please come to my office after class . . ." He shook his head. "See, I could never make that joke except in privacy."

She grinned, then dropped her gaze to her hands. "Thank you for sharing that with me." She fidgeted with her engagement ring. "I know what you mean about feeling watched. I feel that, too."

He nodded. "Normal couples, having too much closeness, could take a stroll through the public park or down to the coffee shop. That's not a luxury we have. So the question then is how we're going be close without being . . .

"Too close."

He nodded. "So. Suggestions for a set of guidelines?"

"No straddling each other's laps."

Parker winced at her frankness. This was so improper. It grated on all his royal training, not to mention his cultural propensity for implying uncomfortable facts rather than stating them outright, which seemed to be Abbie's propensity, always.

Her eyes turned hard. "You said suggestions!"

He put his hands up in surrender. "Yes, I did. I'm sorry. I'm . . . writing it."

Parker wrote it on the chalkboard in script, which made it look even dirtier. *Maybe I should print it.*

"Keep hands on top of clothing," she dictated.

"Good. What else?"

She cocked her head. "I want to hear one of yours."

Parker rubbed the back of his neck, avoiding her gaze. "I don't know . . ."

Abbie crossed her arms over her middle. "So let me get this straight: you can kiss me breathless, caress me under my top, and grab my backside with mind-blowing confidence, but you can't sit here and have a frank discussion with me about what intimacy should look like going forward in our engagement?"

He nodded vigorously, and she gave him a low chuckle.

"Well, forget it, Your Highness. I'm not doing your dirty work. We're a team. We can't be on the same page unless I know how you feel about things, too."

Parker's shoulders slumped and he slowly walked to the chalkboard. He paused, then began to write, stepping away so she could read it. She squinted to read his writing from a distance. "Does that say 'No snogging while intoxicated'?"

He grinned and Abbie fell over laughing, then he laughed, too.

AN HOUR LATER, HAVING finished their list and taken a picture before erasing it lest the siblings find it, Parker walked Abbie back to her room. He gave her a good night kiss he was fairly sure would give her sweet dreams, waiting to leave until he heard the lock click. Back in the residence, he toed off his shoes, leaving them in the living room; they'd be back in his closet by the time he woke up in the morning, thanks to the housekeepers. He unbuttoned his dress shirt, removing it, and stripped off his gray pants, stepping out of them and leaving them outside his room. There was an envelope on his perfectly made bed, the only bit of housework he ever did himself. His grin widened. *When did she slip in here?*

He pulled the chain on the lamp on his nightstand and felt the blood drain from his face. That wasn't her handwriting. He tore the envelope open.

I will rip her from your arms like you ripped my kingdom from mine.

Parker ran. Deep down, he knew she was probably okay; he'd just seen her a few moments ago. But the only word his mind could form was "no," over and over, over and over.

CHAPTER TWENTY-TWO

DESPITE HIS BARE FEET and being in his boxers, Parker blasted out of the residence and sprinted down the hall at a dead run that left Dean and Waldo scrambling to catch up.

"Abbie!" He bellowed as he beat on her door. "Abbie, open up! Open the door!" He looked around frantically. "He's here," he told his security as they ran to him. "Lincoln's here."

"Step aside, sir." Waldo unlocked the door and threw it open. She was standing next to the four-poster bed, a quilt wrapped around her, blushing to high heaven.

"Parker, what the Jersey?"

He pulled her into the hallway despite her vigorous protests.

"Search her room, then we'll go about searching the rest of it. Wake everybody up. If Lincoln is here, I want him found now."

The young king held his fiancée to his chest, and she stopped struggling when she heard Lincoln's name. He felt a shudder go through her, and he rubbed her back. "Just a minute, darling, and I'll get you some clothes. I'm sorry about this. Just hang on a moment."

"This is definitely breaking the new rules," she said quietly, nestling against his neck with a shaky sigh. Glancing down, he saw that she wore a bra but no shirt. She must have pulled the quilt off the bed to cover herself when she heard them coming in. He let himself look one more time, then forced his eyes away. *I'm still chivalrous. I'm not staring.*

"Did you see anything unusual in your room?"

She nodded. "There was an envelope . . . a big one."

"Did you touch it?"

Even in the darkened hallway, he could see her blush increase again. "Not yet. I thought it was from you, I-I-I was going to read it in bed . . ." She looked up earnestly. "Don't judge me."

"I had the same thought, I just got there first."

Dean stood at attention in front of Parker. "The room is clear. The rest of the family is awake. You'll all be evacuated to Hearth House for the night."

"Harbor House is closer," Parker pointed out.

"Yes, sir, but it's still undergoing renovations."

"Oh, that's right. Well, Hearth House it is, then."

"Is that really necessary?" Abbie asked.

"That's SOP, ma'am. You're all to come with us. There could be explosive devices, booby traps, chemical weapons, magical enchantments, anything. We'll need to sweep the castle thoroughly before you can return. Grab the essentials and let's go."

Abbie charged back into her room, her blush still high, and Parker fought the urge to follow her. He pointed at Dean.

"As soon as she's got a shirt on, she doesn't leave your sight."

"Yes, sir."

"And find out what's in her envelope. Waldo, let's find me some trousers."

Parker hurried to get dressed. *I have to get Abbie out of here, somewhere safe.* Even a few minutes ago, he would've said there was no place safer than Bluffton Castle. He tried to focus on packing: there would be clothes already at Hearth House; he grabbed his laptop, his phone, and his toothbrush, and hustled back down the hall to see how she was coming.

She was just pulling out an empty suitcase, and he grunted.

"Too slow, Abs. I'll help." He started dumping the contents of her dresser drawers into the suitcase.

"Hey!"

"You've got five minutes, and then we're leaving. Essentials only." He turned to Dean. "Get Macias back on duty."

"She went to Op'Ho'Lonia, sir. Couldn't get here until tomorrow afternoon at the earliest."

He swore. "Addington, then."

"Yes, sir."

"Okay," he said, turning back to Abbie. "Let's go."

"That was *not* five minutes!"

"Nevertheless." He pulled on her elbow, and she wrenched it away.

"Parker, I cannot leave without my passport. I had it in the drawer beside the bed, and now I can't find it. I will not travel in a foreign country without it."

Grumbling, he dropped to his hands and knees, looking under the bed. "It's not down here. Did you check your backpack?"

"Yes. Twice. And the bathroom drawers." She was rummaging through the outer pockets of her suitcase, when her head suddenly lifted. "You don't think he . . ."

"What? You think he took it? It's possible."

"Why would he do that?" she whispered, wide-eyed.

Parker rubbed his temple. "Because if you can't leave Orangiers . . ."

"He knows right where I'll be." She shuddered, and he gave her shoulders a tight squeeze.

"I'll get you home somehow. But we can't remain here any longer. I'll send people to find it in the morning, I promise." She hesitated, and he ignored the surge of panic that she was going to demand to stay, gentling his voice instead. "Please, Abs. We have to go." *Don't make me carry you out of here over my shoulder.*

She nodded, and he zipped up her suitcase and dragged it into the hallway as the rest of the family emerged from the extended family wing. Under other circumstances, he would've felt amused by the sight of his mother and sisters in their pajamas, putting on raincoats and high heels, their locks still carefully wrapped in silk scarves. His father carried a sleeping Simon.

He reached for Abbie's hand and didn't let go until they were in the armored carriage, settling in for the two-hour trip. Without a word, Abbie lifted his arm and settled it around her shoulders, pressing her cheek to his chest. She was asleep before Bluffton was out of sight. When he finally dropped off, his fingers were still raking through her auburn waves, his lips still pressed to the top of her head.

Georgie was waiting out front of the two-story stone mansion when they arrived.

"She got here quickly," Parker muttered, and Dean nodded.

"Her folks live just up the road in Cobbleford." He opened the carriage door, and she stepped forward to help them down.

"Good evening, Your Majesty. I've cleared the building; there are no pre-existing traps or curses that I could detect. I've placed enchantment enhancers around the perimeter, but I need help setting them. Where's Macias?"

"Op'Ho'Lonia. I think Roman has some non-tech magic skills. I'll have someone locate him for you. Help me get Abbie inside first, will you? She sleeps like the dead." He'd been rubbing her arm for some time now, but she showed no sign of stirring.

"Hang on, I've got this." Georgie slapped her leg. "Oh no, someone's dumping used motor oil into that bubbling mountain stream!"

Abbie's head jerked up, and she looked around, tense. "Don't let him," she muttered, as Georgie pulled her forward by both hands down the narrow steps.

"No, we won't let him. Oh good, he's stopped. Let's go inside and go to bed."

"Where am I?"

"Hearth House."

"Oh, right." Despite being under Georgie's arm, she stopped. Pivoting, she held out a hand to Parker, and his heart flipped. He was next to her in three long strides, tucking her against his side, leading them into the stone house.

"I want her in Lincoln's room, not a guest room."

"Yes, sir." Yawning staff members yielded to them as they took the stairs to the upper level, some still in slippers and pajamas, their arms full of clean linens and extra pillows. He opened the door to find the bed already made, so he left the light off. She sat on the edge of the bed, looking dazed, and he couldn't help but grin.

"Now, darling," he said, kneeling to remove her shoes, "we've got to stop meeting like this in the dead of night." Her forehead furrowed, as if she was trying very hard to understand his joke but couldn't quite get there. "You're lucky I'm not a man to take advantage." Parker pulled her to feet in order to draw back the covers, but before he had the chance, Abbie nuzzled his neck and sighed deeply.

"Don't be scared," she whispered, smoothing her hands up and down his back.

Parker froze. *Is she even awake? Does she know what she's saying?*

"He can't get us here, Parker. I'm okay, we're okay."

He felt like she'd tenderly punched right into his chest and squeezed his heart. Tears? He wasn't supposed to be shedding tears; that was for later, when he was in the shower, when the sound of running water could cover all evidence of his unwanted feelings. He was supposed to be soothing her, protecting her, assuaging her fears . . . but for once, it felt nice to have someone do it for him instead. He wiped the tears away with the heel of his hand even as he shifted closer to her.

"I know," she said softly, pressing his head to her shoulder. "We're safe here. Just breathe." She rubbed his back in

big, soft circles, and he found himself drawing her even closer, reaching around to hook his hands over her shoulders,
shaking as he let her shoulder muffle his quiet tears.

"I thought he'd hurt you. I thought you were gone."

"I know, hon."

"Even those scant seconds until I got to your door . . ."

"They were too long, I know."

"I will not let him hurt you, Abs. I won't." He drew back
to look into her eyes, convey the sincerity of his promise.

"I never doubted it."

"Thank you." His heart was on fire. *She hasn't even kissed
me.* This kind of desire felt different: he wanted to give more
than he wanted to take, wanted to try to offer her even a frac-
tion of the comfort she'd given him, then fall asleep holding
her. She must have seen the thought on his face, because her
hands slid to his shoulders, and she gave him a tender shove
toward the door, her eyes shy.

"Good night, hon."

He swallowed hard, swiping at his eyes once more for
good measure, then moved toward the open door. "Good
night, pleasant dreams."

The whirlwind of activity was slowing . . . The younger
kids were all tucked in, their doors shut, and his parents were
climbing the stairs. They each gave him a tight hug before
they disappeared into the master suite; it should've been his
by right, but it was the only room in this wing with a queen-
size bed. He'd rather be next door to Abbie, anyway. Not that
it was close enough. Not by a long shot. Purposely avoiding the gaze of the two rows of guards, he went into his
room. He pulled the quilt and a pillow off the twin bed and

dragged it out into the dimly lit hallway. *If I can't fall asleep holding her, this is the next best thing.* Edward lay down on the hardwood floor in front of his fiancée's door, punched the pillow until it was comfortable enough, and fell asleep.

CHAPTER TWENTY-THREE

97 days to the wedding

ABBIE WOKE TO WHAT sounded like crying. She sat up, listening. *Is it a cat? Maybe a goat? No, someone is definitely crying.* Figuring she could always hit the bathroom on her way back if she was wrong, she put on a bra, slipped out of bed and opened her door.

"Look out!" Startled by the whisper-yelled warning, Abbie stumbled, and a female hand caught her just before she tripped over Parker.

"What is he doing here?" Abbie whispered, exasperated.

Georgie shrugged. "He's been here all night."

Well, one problem at a time, thought Abbie. "Who's crying?"

Georgie pointed down the hall, on the boys' side. When Abbie entered the dark room, Simon was sitting up in bed in pajamas with goldfish on them, rocking forward and back.

"Hey, buddy . . . what's wrong?" *Should I rub his back? Try to get him back to sleep?* Based on the warming gray out the window, she estimated it was almost dawn.

"Where am I?"

"You're at Hearth House . . . We got to take a little vacation, isn't that fun?" She sat down on the edge of his bed.

"Where's Mum?"

"Oh, she's sleeping. Just down the hall, right across from my room."

He scowled. "That's Lincoln's room."

She smiled. "That's true. But I'm borrowing it while he's away, just until your brother and I get married."

He was still snuffling, but he wiped his snotty nose on his pajama sleeve as he considered this.

"Your own room."

Abbie blinked. "What?"

"You can have your own room. Don't share with him. Our house is *big*." He threw his arms out to demonstrate.

"Um . . ." Since she certainly didn't want to try to guess what he already knew about sex and marriage, she defaulted to her usual tactic with children. "Would you like pancakes?" Simon's eyes lit up, and Abbie chuckled. "Okay, but you'll have to help me because I don't know where anything is. And you'll have to be quiet as we tiptoe past Edward, who is foolishly sleeping in the hall."

"Eddie is a goose. Like me."

"You said it, brother."

This seemed to satisfy him, and he grabbed her hand as they silently walked down the hall, trailed by a tired Georgie. Abbie felt her stomach tighten as Simon led her toward the kitchen . . . Her presence here was unexpected. They probably wouldn't have the food she needed. *Oh well, I can still make pancakes for them. Surely they have eggs.* Abbie had a love/hate relationship with eggs. They were cheap, nutritious, and easy to cook, and after eating them every morning for years, she could barely stand to look at them.

She squeezed Simon's hand. "Is there anything you can't eat?"

He stared up at her, his expression serious. "Vegetables."

She stifled a laugh. "Any ones in particular, or just . . ."

"All of them. All vegetables, I can't eat."

Abbie schooled her expression to match his. "I see. That's so sad. I love vegetables."

He considered this for a moment. "Because you're white."

Don't laugh, don't laugh. "That's got nothing to do with it, bud." She tied her long hair back and washed her hands in the sink as she looked around. Unlike the sleek, stainless-steel kitchens at Bluffton, this kitchen was homey. It still had professional touches, like double ovens, an eight-burner range and two fridges, but it also had homemade jams and jars of tomato sauce lining the shelves with handwritten labels and floral calico lids that matched the cafe curtains. *First things first . . .* She started the kettle for coffee, winner of Most Essential Beverage twenty-one years running, and also for tea, the runner-up.

Abbie pulled out a batter bowl, then found flour, baking powder, salt, and sugar as Simon noisily dragged a stool over to the counter. She pulled up a recipe on her phone, then measured the flour, and Simon plopped it into the bowl so that a poof of white powder rose into the air around them. They both giggled. Abbie went to the fridge, realizing she'd never checked for milk or eggs. A fresh pitcher of buttermilk was waiting for her, as well as a basket of speckled eggs in various shades of brown and white. How was it even possible? They'd arrived in the dead of night with only two hours' warning. Was it . . . magic? Like, actual magic? If so, she wouldn't mind having one of these fridges. She carried the ingredients back to the counter.

"I don't do eggs," he announced, sounding every bit a member of the royal family.

Abbie raised an eyebrow. "Oh?"

"They're messy. I don't like it."

Abbie put her hands on her hips. It was a little thing, really, making pancakes, but she didn't want to see him grow up spoiled. She could tell Lily babied him a little too much; he was perfectly capable of cracking eggs.

"Mr. Simon, if you want to help, you can't cop out of the parts you don't care for. Commit to the project."

"What?"

She paused. "Let me say it another way: don't give up. Find a way. Finish what you start?" Simon pouted, but nodded slowly. They compromised by breaking them together, her hands over his, into a measuring cup with a handle and letting him pour them into the batter bowl.

"You do have a way of bringing the Broward men to task, don't you?"

Abbie turned to see Ignatius leaning against the doorframe, arms crossed over his chest, a warm expression on his face. *Is that a compliment?* Before she could answer, the kettle shouted that it was done and she hurried to turn off the heat before it woke the whole house.

"We're making pancakes, Pop," Simon said, stirring the batter frantically.

"I see that, son. Good work; I wasn't looking forward to more of Mum's poached eggs."

"Leave some lumps, Mr. Simon. It's better that way," Abbie said, putting a staying hand over his, as she glanced at Parker's dad. "Can I get you anything? Coffee? Tea?"

Ignatius grinned. "When did you start working here?"

Abbie blushed. "Just trying to make myself useful." *It's my fault we're here, after all . . .* This probably wasn't how Parker's whole family had planned to spend the day. She turned her attention to lighting the burner under the cast-iron frying pan so he wouldn't see the guilt on her face. She put the bacon in cold and stood back for a moment to think.

"Abbie?"

"Yes, Simon?"

"I'm sorry I took your book."

"My book?" She had no idea what he was talking about.

"It had your picture in it. I wanted your picture after you leave."

My passport. "This book, was it small and blue?" He nodded. "Well, that clears up one mystery . . . Thank you for being honest about it."

"But don't think this means there won't be a discussion later with your mother present, Simon," Ignatius rumbled. Simon didn't seem too concerned.

"Abbie, why was my second brother in the hallway?"

She poured the hot water into the percolator, stalling. Ignatius crossed to the cupboard and pulled out a mug and tapped some loose tea from a tin labeled "Lemon Lover" into a metal tea ball. She glanced at him somewhat desperately for help, but he just focused on his task, muttering, "He didn't ask me. He asked you."

Sighing, Abbie crossed back to Simon's side. "Well, I think he just wanted to make sure I was okay in the night."

"Why?"

"Because he worries too much, bud."

"About what?"

"Who knows?" she lied. She couldn't help it. She didn't want to be the one to put ideas in his head about what a terrible person his beloved brother Lincoln was. Abbie felt Parker at her back, wrapping his arms around her.

"No one has ever given me more reason to worry than Abbie, Si." He gave her temple a brief kiss, and she fought a blush when she noticed Ignatius grinning down into his mug, stirring his steeping tea.

It makes no sense, really, she thought to herself. *I want his display of affection in public, where it's not allowed, but not in front of his family, where it's perfectly allowed.* Abbie turned to face Parker and smiled at him. He looked a little better than last night . . . still pretty exhausted, though. Maybe she could get him to rest a little more today.

"Good morning."

"Good morning. Thank you for not tripping over me this morning."

"You're welcome, but it's Georgie's fault, she pointed you out when I went to check on Simon."

At the sound of his name, Simon jumped down from the stool and held up his chosen spatula like a sword. "Stay out, brother."

"Simon," his father warned. "Be polite."

Parker lifted an eyebrow at Simon over her shoulder, rubbing Abbie's back slowly with both hands. "Why should I, squirt?"

"Because when you're here, she only talks to *you*."

Parker and Ignatius both burst out laughing and Abbie's face flamed. It was a fair assessment. *I should probably work on that* . . .

"Si, you expressed that very well; I'm impressed. I've got some work to attend to anyway, so I will heed your wishes this time . . ."

"We'll call you when it's ready," Abbie said, kissing his cheek.

"I'm using your office, Dad," Parker called over his shoulder as he left.

"So just because you're king now, you think you own the place?"

Down the hall, Parker laughed, "I do own it, old man!" and it made Abbie relax a little. She hadn't meant to make him cry last night, and she wondered if he felt embarrassed about it now, in the light of day. At least they'd been alone. She certainly respected him no less for it. Abbie removed the bacon from the pan and poured some of the drippings into the batter.

"Abelia, are you trying to give me a heart attack?"

She grinned at Ignatius. "Don't believe the hype; animal fats are good for you." Together, she and Simon scooped batter into the hot pan and watched the bubbles form.

"Three's not enough," he complained.

"You just start with three, then you do three more, and so on and so forth . . ."

Simon leaned over the pan, sniffing. "I smell it with my nostrils."

"Well, technically," Abbie said, "you smell it with your brain."

He stared at the pan as she flipped them over. "I eat them with my brain, too?"

Abbie thought for a moment. "No, you taste them with your brain, but you eat them with your mouth." She took them out of the pan. "Speaking of which . . ." Abbie trolled the shelves of preserves until she found applesauce. "I don't know if you've ever tried it, but pancakes with applesauce is my favorite way to eat them. Are you up to try something new?"

"No. I want maple syrup."

She looked to Ignatius, who shrugged. "If Lily objects, I'll take the blame. He doesn't have to focus on any lessons today, lots of room and time to run off that sugar." He turned to his son. "How about a little applesauce on the side as a compromise?"

Simon nodded and jumped down, eager to claim the freshly made pancakes for himself. Abbie looked on in wonder as the child inhaled his food. She grabbed a piece of bacon for herself, afraid it would all be gone before she got the chance.

When he looked up, he simply said, "More?"

Ignatius chuckled, shaking his head. "Go play. Don't wake Mum or the others." He jumped down and wandered off and Ignatius put his plate in the sink. "I'm not being cruel; he has a lower metabolism than some, and Lily's particular about his diet."

"Should I not have . . . ?"

Ignatius paused mid-sip and shook his head, his gray dreads following the movement. "No, no, he can have pancakes, that's fine. Good to have something special on a special day."

Checking over her shoulder that they were alone, Abbie moved toward the eggs to cook her own breakfast. "I'm sorry, by the way."

"Why, have you burnt my breakfast? You're fired."

She chuckled lightly, breaking an egg into another pan, moving to flip the current set of pancakes. "No, your breakfast is safe. I'm sorry we had to leave Bluffton."

He waved away her concern. "That's not remotely your fault."

"I know . . ."

"Do you?" He watched her with interest, and her shoulders slumped.

"No, not really." She glanced toward the open door again. "Tell me about him."

Lincoln's father needed no clarification regarding to whom she was referring. "He was always a game-player. Loved chess, loved World Domination or Peril—did you ever play that game?"

She sipped her black coffee, lacking coconut milk. "Often."

"He's still playing games, he's just doing it with my kingdom now." He stroked his beard. "He doesn't know how to lose. He'd try to press you into check with just a bishop and a rook, never concede. Get him down to a pawn, and he tries to get it across the board to exchange it for a queen."

"So if he doesn't know how to lose, how does this end?"

He put down his tea and crossed his arms. "If I knew that, it'd be over."

"Who is he close to?"

Ignatius flattened his mouth into a line. "Few. He was one of those who passed between groups without ever really becoming part of them. But he was close to one of his college professors, Dr. Langham; he taught literature, I think. And his roommate, Charles Groves. Princess Heather, his contract fiancée; they chatted a lot. Exchanged letters, of course."

"Have you reached out to any of them?"

He shook his head, staring out the window, and Abbie knew she was pushing the limits of his comfort zone. She was about to change the subject when he spoke again.

"Lincoln always dominated Edward as a child. He didn't always mean to; their personalities are just very different. Lincoln's decisive, outspoken with his opinions. He took a lot of things for granted, made a lot of assumptions. When they didn't turn out to be reality, he took it badly."

Abbie blamed what she said next on the lack of caffeine in her system. "I'm sorry about what he did, what he tried to do."

Ignatius held her gaze, his face somber. "So am I." He looked down into his mug. "But thanks to Edward, he was unsuccessful."

She leaned forward. "How did he walk into your study with a knife unnoticed?"

"He'd hidden it there, in the room. He pulled it out of a book safe."

"Hmm." She tried to imagine the scene, how shocked Ignatius must have felt, how indignant. How scared.

"Why all the questions about Lincoln?"

She shrugged. "I like solving problems. I'm good at it. He's a problem for my husband."

"Husband?" he asked, his voice quiet.

"Well, future husband," she said as she flipped more pancakes and stacked them neatly. "If we can ever get this legal mess worked out."

"Perhaps that's what we should be discussing."

"I think we need a mediator . . . That's what my lawyer in Gardenia suggested. Can you think of any candidates?"

"No, but it's an interesting idea. I'll give it some thought."

"Thank you; I appreciate it." Abbie felt her heart tugging at her to be less formal with Ignatius, but it was hard to let go of the image and embrace the man. *I'm glad I knew Parker as a skinny, long-legged nerd before he was a handsome ruler. That's who he still is, deep down.*

CHAPTER TWENTY-FOUR

ABBIE SETTLED INTO a rhythm, pouring pancakes, frying bacon, flipping pancakes, boiling water for more tea. And it felt like home, felt like her space more than any other place with the Browards had, because she knew exactly what to do here. She wanted to hold on to the feeling so badly, she waved away the kitchen staff when they hurried into the house at 7 a.m., red-faced and apologizing. When everyone was up, she went to the office to get Parker. The door was cracked open, and she raised her hand to knock.

"No, there's no way we can wait that long. Abelia needs to get back to work as soon as possible. Press them for a temporary passport for her; she's royalty, surely they can do better than that." He paused, listening. "Good, I want an update in three hours. What was in the envelope that was left on her bed? Were his prints on it?"

She heard him sigh deeply and his glasses clattered onto the desk as he whipped them off. "They were *inside* her apartment?"

Abbie's hand covered her mouth in surprise. She didn't want to hear any more. She pushed open the door silently and waited for him to notice her. "It's ready," she whispered, and he nodded. Abbie closed the door quietly behind her and wandered back to the safety of the kitchen . . . wondering if it really was safe, after all. Maybe she could lean on Georgie for the rest of the report later. She didn't want to stress Parker out any more.

When he finally appeared at the breakfast table, he was quiet. When his siblings tried to engage him, they were met with grunts and nods and too-small smiles. When he pushed away his unfinished meal, Abbie caught his eye.

"Want to go for a walk?"

He cocked an eyebrow. "In your pajamas?"

She rolled her eyes. "I will dress first if you insist, but you're stifling my natural vacation state." By the time she got back to the foyer, he was waiting—with Simon. *Well, I was hoping for a private walk, but it looks like that's not happening . . . oh well.* His face conveyed regret, but she smiled at them both.

"Has Simon offered to chaperone our walk?"

"He has indeed; in fact, he's gone one step further and suggested that we go fishing." The boy's face was silently pleading with her. She checked her cell phone.

"Well, it's a bit late in the day, but maybe the fish would like a midmorning snack."

Lily poked her head out of the kitchen. "It's up to you, Abbie. If you wanted a moment alone with Edward, I'm sure Simon would understand . . ."

"No, I would *not*. I want to go, too."

The queen's stern look sobered him, and Abbie wondered if she would teach her how to do that; she seemed to have a veritable treasure chest of "looks" that subdued her offspring.

"Simon's welcome to come with us. Be glad to have him." Before anyone could respond, he ran off to the shed to grab poles.

"Would you be willing to help me dig worms?" Parker asked.

Abbie nodded. "Do you have a compost pile?"

"I've no idea."

She cleared her throat dramatically. "My first act as un-queen . . ."

"Woz preserve us."

"Hush. As I was saying, my first act as un-queen will be to mandate compost piles at all my residences."

"I think you mean *our* residences, and aren't they quite smelly?"

She shook her head. "Not if they're done correctly. And they're a good source of wormage."

"I defer to my resident doyenne on such matters."

"I'm not a resident yet, but I appreciate that. Also, I asked your dad to think about who might be impartial enough to mediate our legal disputes."

"Whom did he suggest?"

"No one sprung to mind."

"The problem is that most countries sided with one brother or the other in the . . ." The word *war* died on his lips as Simon came bounding back into the foyer.

"Why are you standing here? Let's go!"

"Okay, sorry, squirt . . . It's Abbie's fault."

"My fault? Excuse you, Your Majesty . . ." She shoved him good-naturedly and he grinned.

"You started the conversation. Also, I don't want to be on Simon's bad side. That's never worked out well for me."

"Go get the shovel, Mr. Self-Preservation." Abbie went to the kitchen and poked around until she found an empty mason jar. She found the guys outside, tackle box and net at their feet. Parker took the jar and handed her the shovel.

"Oh, I see now," she laughed. "So when you asked if I'd help you, you were asking if I'd do it for you . . ."

"As I said, I defer to my resident outdoors doyenne. Your dad always handled the procurement of bait."

"We're hardly procuring them; more like ripping them from their warm, cozy compost bed in order to send them to their watery deaths." She found ten good night crawlers near the bottom of the pile, and they were off.

They trailed behind Simon, who led the way down a narrow dirt path along the edge of the lake. Tall cedars shaded the path, bumpy from gnarled roots popping up through the packed earth. Parker took her hand to help her over a fallen log, and then didn't let go. She squeezed his hand, and he rubbed his thumb against hers.

Simon was carrying all three poles, and they kept slipping down and catching on the ground.

"Need some help, squirt?"

"No." He scowled. "I got it."

The couple exchanged a look, then Parker shrugged. Abbie cleared her throat.

"Edward, weren't you just saying you were hoping to carry the green fishing pole?"

He cleared his throat. "Yes, I was, as a matter of fact. Simon, may I carry the green one? I really want it."

"Well . . ." The boy hesitated, and Abbie found it wholly adorable to see the Broward pride taking root in someone so young.

"It would really help him out. Edward, that is. You know how he falls down a lot? This will help him. He can use it like a walking stick."

"Okay." He handed it over. Edward's reply was flat.

"Thank you, Simon . . . for helping me out."

"You're welcome. You do fall down a lot."

The point he'd been leading them to was lovely at this time of day, Abbie thought. A light mist rested on the surface of the water, and she could see that it dropped off deeper on one side. There were no boats out, just the occasional ripple from a fish jumping. Even the mosquitoes weren't that bad. Parker rigged the poles while she chatted with Simon.

"What do you like about fishing, Simon?"

"I like rainbow trout."

"Not lake bass? Perch?"

"No, rainbow trout. Cooked with butter."

"Ah, I see, so it's about your stomach, not the thrill of conquest. You're a connoisseur, not a sportsman."

"What's that?"

Parker passed him a pole. "It's a compliment, Si. It means you know what's good when it comes to food."

The boy whipped it over his shoulder. Abbie didn't move fast enough and took the tip of the pole in the shoulder.

"Easy, mate. Watch where you're swinging that thing, we don't want to hook Abbie."

"No. She's not a keeper."

Her mouth dropped open, and both Browards laughed. "I am totally a keeper, thank you very much. And to think I made you pancakes . . ." She shook her head, but Simon showed no remorse. "Fine. Just wait until I put you both to shame with my mad fish-catching skills."

She moved down the point closer to where the shelf dropped off underwater, then cast and landed her bobber just on the far edge of it. As she thought, it didn't take long before the fish were interested. At the first nibble, she held her breath, waiting for another, bigger bite. Two, three more nibbles . . . Did she leave too much bait hanging out? Then it came: the chomp she was waiting for, and she flicked her wrist to set the hook.

"Already?" Parker asked as she began to reel in. She nodded, smiling smugly. He came over to help her net it and held it up for Simon to see.

When she reeled in her third one, Simon decided there was something better about her spot, and he came over to sit next to her. She helped him perfect his cast to hit the spot he wanted, giving Parker a chance to finally get his own line in the water. *We do make a good team. I wish there was more I could do to help with this Lincoln situation . . . Maybe there is.* She was in such deep thought about it, she didn't hear Parker's question.

"Sorry, what?"

"Simon's stepped in the lake and doesn't care for soggy shoes, so he's ready to go back to the house. Are you coming?"

She nodded, untying the stringer from the fallen log she'd employed to keep her catch from floating away. Five wasn't bad for this time of day. Maybe they could save them until tomorrow and catch enough for everyone . . . Then again, maybe it didn't matter. They trudged back, lugging all the equipment between the two of them as Simon went ahead.

"He's our passport thief, by the way."

"Oh really?" Parker sighed. "That's a relief, actually. Confessed, did he?"

Abbie nodded. "Which is good, because I'd never have guessed to ask him." Simon ran down the path ahead of them.

"I wish I had his energy," Parker muttered as the house came into view, and Abbie nodded. She needed a nap.

"Is there a hammock here?"

"Several, I think."

"I think I might crash for a while."

He kissed her temple. "I approve the idea, but not the location. Please sleep inside."

"Didn't you hear Georgie? She enchanted the whole property . . ."

"I did hear her. And yet, if you insist on being unconscious, I would prefer you do so inside stone walls that have stood for more than five hundred years. Indulge me."

She tried to keep her tone kind. "Do you promise not to sit in front of my door? Because I won't be able to sleep if you do."

His shoulders tensed, but he nodded. "You look dead on your feet. I've got this stuff, you go." She didn't need to be told twice.

"Just what every woman wants to hear . . . You're lucky you never had to woo a woman."

"Darling, I've been wooing you for fourteen years . . . with no plans to stop now."

She just smiled and shook her head. Abbie dropped off her catch in the kitchen, then went straight upstairs toward the siren song of her temporary bed. The covers went over her head to block out the midday sun . . . but it wasn't enough. It was too warm to be under the quilt, but without it, she couldn't relax. Fatigue wasn't sufficient . . . She wasn't sleepy, just tired. Still, she knew she'd be dead later if she didn't try.

Her eyes wandered around the room . . . Lincoln's room. He was still a puzzle. She'd never spent much time with him as a child; her memories were vague. Everyone seemed content to tell her generalities, but something must have set him off, triggered him. Someone professional had obviously decorated the room; even this far inland, it was still all sailboats and seashells. A stuffed seal sat on the bookshelf next to a generic collection of children's classics . . . but next to those, the titles were more intriguing. Poetry? *Glass Birds in Rusty Cages: A New Collection* by Thusnelda Greene. *My Love on the Darkest Night* by Thusnelda Greene. *Peering Between the Alders*, more Thusnelda Greene. Interesting. Abbie sat up, crossing the room to the bookshelf. *Section Hiking the Mapphorn Range.* She wasn't familiar with that one, but it didn't sound like anywhere around here. *The Fear, the Fury* by Luca Thias; that one was a novel. *He's from Kiriien, isn't he?* Abbie grabbed her phone and started taking pictures of the titles she wasn't familiar with. Maybe it would lead nowhere . . . but it didn't hurt to dig around a little.

She chose the book with the most worn spine, the most dog-eared pages, *Linen and Sage.*

LINEN AND SAGE

> Days I should have been in school
> Booking and writing and arithmaticing
> Instead I sat upon a wooden stool
> Fuzzy-headed, sick as anything
> In my mother's kitchen, warm and light,
> Reading to her as she baked our bread
> Chopped onions and carrots into bright
> Round circles, pausing the story I read
> To say "no mushrooms," she'd smile.
> Smile as if to say, "Do you know who bore you?
> Do you think me a stranger after all this while?"
> And when my soup was done, a sure cure for the flu,
> She'd leave me to read for—a day? For an age?
> Kept warm by the scent of linen and sage.

THE POEM MADE ABBIE cringe a little. Stories about warm mothers were hard to swallow; they read like fiction in her mind. Then again, Lily was an obvious counterexample. She fell asleep thinking about motherhood and being sick and what could have been.

She didn't get to spend much time with Parker that day. He spent most of it working in his dad's office, conference-calling into the different meetings he'd been scheduled to attend in person. Abbie spent the afternoon trying to cheer up Rhodie, who was grumpy about having to get other people to check on her experiments and take down the data to her satisfaction. It turned out that the gardens still had some ripe blueberries, so Abbie made a cobbler, which was a big hit after dinner. She was staring into the fire, contemplating going to bed when Parker strolled in.

"Hey."

"Hey."

He closed the doors to the library behind him, and she sat up.

"You're supposed to leave the door cracked open, remember?"

He tapped his temple. "That's right. Thank you for reminding me." He unlatched the door and pushed it open a little. Coming over to the sofa, he sat down on the floor between her feet. "Can I have one of your patented 'put you to sleep' shoulder rubs?"

She smiled. "Only if you promise to sleep in a bed tonight."

"Very well. I'll get the village priest up here for a quickie wedding if you insist, then you can share my bed."

She dragged her knuckles just inside his shoulder blades, and he groaned.

"Just to sleep?"

"I haven't the energy for more. Look at me, I can barely even banter with you. My mind is fried." He took off his glasses and put them on the oak end table next to her.

She squeezed him with her knees, still rubbing the knot she'd found. "You should go to bed."

"I will in a minute. I just wanted to be sure you were okay."

"Me?"

He nodded, waiting.

Why wouldn't I be okay? "Yes, I'm fine."

"You had a good afternoon with the others?"

"Yes, I beat Rhodie at rummy several times. That was fun."

"You're not freaked out about Lincoln's notes?"

She shrugged, moving her hands to his stiff neck. "A little bit." She thought for a moment, trying to figure out what she wanted to ask. "Do they know how he got onto the property?"

Parker sighed. "As far as we can tell, Lincoln himself hadn't been there. Dean thinks he used a transportation spell to put the notes there. Either that, or he had an accomplice."

"Someone inside the castle?"

He nodded. "But he doesn't think it's likely." He groaned again as she worked the muscles at the base of his skull. "That's heaven, by the way."

"Good." She pushed her hair over her right shoulder, then leaned over and kissed his neck. Then she kissed it again, and again, enjoying the way the firelight danced over his skin.

"Correction: *this* is heaven." Abbie chuckled and wrapped her arms around his chest for a tight embrace before she went upstairs so that he would, too. He did sleep in a bed; she knew because she tucked him in, just like he'd done for her the night before. She agreed to leave their connecting door open if he promised to stay in his room unless he had a very good reason not to. He was so exhausted, she doubted his eyes would open again before sunrise.

"Is wanting to snog you a 'very good reason'?" he asked, half-asleep.

"Nope," she said, affecting the sternest tone she could muster.

"Damn."

WEDNESDAY AFTER LUNCH, they got the all-clear to go back to Bluffton. The rest of the day was a whirlwind of packing, carriage travel, reclaiming her passport from Simon's toy box, more packing the things she'd left at Bluffton, goodbyes at the airfield, and finally, collapsing back into her own bed in Gardenia after one o'clock in the morning. As she drifted off, she realized she'd never asked Georgie about the pictures of her apartment that security had found in her room at Bluffton, and her dreams were understandably disturbing with that thought in her mind.

CHAPTER TWENTY-FIVE

94 days to the wedding

ABBIE WENT TO WORK on Thursday, but it was a grave error. She should've seen the warning signs; the fatigue, the excess hair in the shower drain, the rash. Her lupus was flaring so badly by lunchtime, she went home early and fell into bed, ignoring Georgie's concerned glances and mouth pinched shut with unasked questions. She got a nasty email from Hall about her "unpredictable schedule causing significant disruption."

It's not like I asked to be trapped in Orangiers. It's not like I wanted to be sick. Let him come and see if he doesn't believe me. She was still annoyed about it when Parker called around five.

"How was work today?"

He doesn't need to know. It will only worry him or make him feel guilty for last weekend's stressors affecting this week's work.

"Fine," she said, wary. Georgie wouldn't meet her gaze.

"Anything interesting happen?"

"Not really." Warning bells were going off in her head. *Something in his tone . . .*

"Not surprising, I guess . . ." He paused. "Since you came home early."

"When did you become such a drama king?"

"I'm not joking, Abs. Do not lie to me about this."

"What's the point in telling you the truth?" she snapped. "You've got your spies in place. You don't need my honesty." Her energy immediately waned, sapped by the strong emotion.

He kept his voice low. "Do not make this about me. You have manipulated the situation to conceal your illness in some twisted protection scheme. I'm asking you nicely: please do not do that. Not when you're really sick, Abs. I need to know."

"Why? What can you do about it?" she asked, her voice flat.

He huffed. "Nothing."

"Then how is you knowing better than you not knowing?"

"Because I care what happens to you, damn it. I care what's happening in you. I care whether you go to work, whether you enjoyed your dinner, whether your body is rebelling against you. I care about the details. I'm supposed to be the one who gets the details. Especially when you're far away. Just give me this."

"It doesn't matter."

"We've been over this countless times. You've exhausted my forbearance in this regard."

She rolled her eyes. "Here come the ten-dollar words..."

"Fine, I'll speak plainly: How sick are you? Do you need a hospital?"

"Parker, I don't have the energy to be interrogated right now."

"Have you called Dr. Honaker?"

"Leave it alone, I said."

"Why haven't you called? She said she wanted to know if you flared on this new med—"

Abbie hung up. She didn't intend to answer when he called back, but she knew he'd just keep calling, or worse, involve her security. His face popped onto the screen again, and she swiped to answer, but kept the camera off.

"Did you just hang up on me?" Outrage laced every word, then silence.

She said nothing, her head pounding as she lay back down.

"Abbie, answer me!"

"I told you to leave it. I don't owe you answers, Parker." She felt like she was dying inside, physically. Why shouldn't she feel dead emotionally, too? Her heart didn't even ache. It had simply shut down.

"I can't believe you're acting like this. I can't believe . . . No, you know what? This is so unbelievably predictable, Abbie; the minute I try to exercise any authority in your life, you push me away. Tune me out. Tell me to shove off. Treat me with that self-righteous disdain, like I could never understand."

"You could never understand!" she shot back. Even though it was a gut response, it took everything she had. She'd have to sleep after this, if she could get comfortable enough.

"You never give me the chance!" he shouted.

She rubbed her head, trying to engage it in the fight she didn't want be having. *When did he get so pushy? He knows how I am. He knows what I am.*

"Forget this," he said. "I'm not coming out tomorrow. We just saw each other, and I'm way behind. I'm not going to waste seventy-two hours traveling, arguing, and watching you sleep. I sincerely hope you feel better soon."

Shock and fatigue relieved her brain of the burden of forming a response. She held the phone away so he wouldn't hear her breathing quicken. He scoffed, then hung up. She waited to cry until she was in the shower so Tezza wouldn't hear.

ABBIE HEARD THE FRONT door open early the next morning. *Georgie's back,* she thought as she turned over. She'd say hi later. She was hungry but too tired and stiff to get out of bed. Her bedroom door opened softly without a knock first, and she lifted her head, confused.

Parker.

He came. Abbie let her head fall back to the pillow as she fought tears.

He said nothing, but he toed off his shoes, took off his tie, removed his coat and tossed them onto the futon. Then without a word, he climbed into her bed.

"The rules . . ."

"The rules don't apply in this situation." He brought his body against hers, spooning her, bringing their hands together to intertwine their fingers. "Nothing's going to happen. You have my word." They lay quietly together. He sighed a heavy sigh.

"Why are you here?" she whispered, not trusting her voice to remain unwobbled by emotion. "You said . . . you said you weren't coming."

"I did, I did say that. Apparently, I get cruel when I'm afraid."

She twisted in his arms so she could see his face. "You were afraid?"

He nodded, burying his face in her hair and inhaling deeply. She turned back so he wouldn't have to hide.

"Why were you scared?"

"Because you wouldn't tell me how bad it was. My imagination got the best of me."

His thumb was stroking the back of her hand absentmindedly, innocently. *It feels good to be held, even when everything hurts. I'm so tired; he's so warm and cozy . . .*

"Are you going to be mad if I fall asleep?"

"No, darling." He kissed her shoulder and brought his hand to rest on her hip. "Are you in pain?"

"Yes. I took medication, but it's not helping."

He paused, and she could tell he had something to say.

"Out with it, Broward." She felt him smile against her shoulder.

"Dr. Honaker said I could give you gentle massage if your muscles and joints were bothering you."

"That's right, she did." *I forgot about that . . . He has a good memory when it suits him. Just not when it comes to his belongings.*

"If I promise to keep it very chaste, very appropriate, will you let me try? Let me help you?"

Abbie pulled her lips to the side. It sounded nice, but she didn't want to get his hopes up. *Then again, what do I have to lose?*

"Okay." Her voice came out small, and she cleared her throat. "But the second it starts to go the other way, I'm shutting it down."

He sat up and slid off the end of the bed. "Be right back."

"Where are you going?"

He threw a thumb toward the living room. "I brought lavender oil."

She sat up. "You did?"

He grinned. "Yes, I came prepared. I also purchased several assorted gluten-free muffins from that bakery you like. Would you like one now?"

"Sure." She watched him go and decided maybe she'd been wrong to shut him out . . . and that if she hadn't already decided to marry him, this might've turned things in his favor. Baked goods, lavender, a massage, and that face? *Happy sigh.*

He came back with the bakery box and she picked a chocolate one, despite the early hour. He raised an eyebrow at her, made a show of checking his watch to see what time it was, and she gave him a shy smile.

"Hey, if I'm going to get rubbed down by a handsome man, I might as well elevate the experience with chocolate." He chuckled as he took off his dress shirt, leaving him in his white T-shirt. She swallowed hard. "Leave the door wide open."

"Miss Porchenzii." He shook his head, feigning shock. "What do you think is going to happen here? I promised a chaste, appropriate massage, and that's exactly what I'm going to deliver. I just don't want to get oil on my nice shirt. Lavender," he said as he knelt in the middle of the bed, his knees almost touching her backside, gently lifting her left ankle to rest on his shoulder, "is supposed to have anti-inflammatory properties, which is why I chose it." He began working her calf with his thumbs in even strokes. "Personally, I find the scent a bit intense, but it does remind me of our time in the Unveiled at Molly's, and that was a happy time."

She found another shy smile. "You can try to distract me all you want, I still know your hands are on my leg."

He gave her a knowing smile. "I know physical intimacy is sometimes—"

She wrinkled her nose. "This isn't *intimacy*."

"It isn't? Who else would you let do this?"

"No one."

"Well, by definition, anything you draw a boundary around creates a potential for intimacy, don't you think?"

She shifted to lie flat on her back. "But even when I drew a boundary around my whole life, I still had friendships."

"But you created exceptions for them. Lauren knew where you'd come from, knew about your illness. You allowed her to know the truth. That creates intimacy."

She watched his face. He was clearly concentrating on his massage technique, even as he talked about other things. His eyebrows pulled together, his gaze was far off. She found his commitment to his work adorable.

"But back to my previous point: intimacy, proximity, whatever you want to call it—I know it sometimes makes you uncomfortable."

She nodded. "Sometimes. But it's not like we're alone. Georgie is in the next room."

"And Waldo and Dean."

"Oh, right. I forgot about them."

"It's a regular party out there." He smirked as his thumbs inadvertently brushed behind her knee.

Abbie tensed. "Unh—don't," she choked out. *Holy Jersey, who knew THAT was there? I don't think he did it on purpose, but HOLY JERSEY, YES, PLEASE, WITH WHIPPED CREAM AND A CHERRY.*

His hands paused, but he looked genuinely confused. "Don't what?"

"Behind my knee, don't . . . don't touch behind my knee." Abbie's cheeks flamed.

"Oh?" He was fighting a smile. "My apologies . . ." He did not look sorry in the slightest. Parker dutifully shifted his hands above her knee. "This may be an appropriate massage, but if you think I'm not noting that for future interactions, you're mad."

"Parker," she warned, her face still hot.

He gave a low chuckle. "I can't wait to put that look on your face again . . ."

"Stop," she whispered. "They'll hear you."

"Only because you made me leave the door open. That's your doing, not mine."

"So I'm just supposed to let them think I'm the kind of woman who lets handsome men come into my bedroom with massage oils and baked goods and close the door? I don't think so." He hit a sore spot too hard, and she winced.

"Sorry, love." He reduced the pressure, and she relaxed again. "Does it feel good, though?"

"Yes," she admitted begrudgingly.

"This is where you thank me."

She bit the inside of her cheek to hide a smile. "Thank you for suggesting it. You're better than I would've thought."

"So, correct me if I'm wrong—there *was* something I could do to help . . ."

"Don't gloat." She finished her muffin and stretched. "That lavender is putting me to sleep."

"I forgot to mention, that's the other thing it does. I know you don't sleep well when you're flaring."

"That's true," she murmured, snuggling deeper into the pillow. "I wish you could do my hips," she said, then tensed when she realized how it sounded out loud.

"Relax, Abs. I know what you meant."

"I am relaxed."

"Liar," he cooed.

Abbie glared at him, and he switched legs, pausing to get more oil.

"For future reference, Georgie is a licensed massage therapist."

"What?" Abbie's head snapped up. "Why isn't she the one in here, then?"

"Because you're my fiancée, and I would never pass up the opportunity to touch you." He winked. "This isn't precisely what I have in mind when I dream of being between your legs, but I'll be damned if I let Georgie do it. It's the flip side of love, the unglamorous part."

"You're such a philosopher today."

He looked into her eyes. "Have I mentioned that I love you?"

"No, you haven't."

"I do love you. And based on the tears in your eyes when I walked in the door, I'd say you love me, too, even when I say idiotic things."

She closed her eyes and turned into her pillow again. "You should give up kinging for detective work."

"Can't you just see me with a pipe and a deerstalker hat? A regular Gerald Botham."

She giggled. "I can, actually. Who's that?"

"Gerald Botham? Oh, he's a famous detective in Orangiersian literature. A classic. You've never read any?"

"I guess not."

"I'll bring you some next time."

"Maybe you could read it to me . . ."

His hands paused, and she opened one eye to peek at him. The massage resumed.

"We could do that long-distance, too. Do you miss my voice?" he asked, lowering it suggestively.

She nodded, not looking at him. *Maybe this is intimate . . .* His hands, his closeness, were breaching her emotional perimeter, each of his musings an arrow in the chest of her inner sentinels, and it made her bold to ask the question she'd been guarding in the keep all these months.

"Parker?"

"Abs."

"What if we can't get married?"

He went to the door, closed it, then crossed the room to kneel near her head. She rolled onto her side to see him face-to-face.

"I am going to marry you. No one and nothing on earth can stop me."

"That's not true," she said, letting her tears fall. *Great, now the moat is leaking, too.* "They are stopping us. They're not going away, they're not giving up."

"Let them. I'll outwait them all."

"We don't have time for that, if we want kids. My clock's ticking, hon."

"We're only twenty-two. Your fertility won't begin to decline until what, thirty?"

"Maybe for a healthy woman. Not for a sick woman. Dr. Honaker says we should start trying now, as soon as possible—months ago, ideally."

He frowned. "I didn't realize you'd spoken to her about it."

Abbie nodded. "She recommended a perinatologist to me, but I haven't called him yet. There didn't seem to be a point until we actually . . ." She sighed. "What if this legal trouble is still going when Twelfth Month arrives? What if we can't come to some kind of agreement with them? What if this stalemate stretches into—"

He put a finger to her lips. "I'll make you a deal. If it's not resolved within a year, we'll . . ." He looked down. "I'll abdicate."

"No." Her voice was firm. "You're a good ruler. That's not an option. I'm not letting you do that for me. I'm not doing that to Andrew."

"What, then? Marry in secret?"

"It would kill you to live a lie like that. I know you. You'd hate it. I want our marriage to be a source of joy, not misery, especially for you." She chuckled wryly. "Plus, the cat would be out of the bag if I did become pregnant."

"What's the solution, then?"

"That's what I'm asking you. I don't know. Maybe we should just . . . before any more damage is done, before any more time passes, we should just go our separate—"

"Don't you dare finish that thought, Abs." His hand came to the side of her face and he kissed her fiercely, possessively. "You're mine. I'm yours. The rest is just paperwork. I am never going to let you go. I didn't cross the Unveiled and fight a war to lose you over some ridiculous legal squabble. I stand by my original statement: I am going to marry you, and I have the contract to prove it." He paused. "Although, sneaking around to have secret married sex doesn't sound so bad."

She smacked him on the shoulder, and he grinned, undeterred.

"There's a few forgotten ancestral properties where I could hide you away, have you all to myself . . ." He ran a hand from her side to her hip. "And the nearby villagers will gossip about who I've got up there, crying out in pleasure late into the night . . . multiple times."

She rolled her eyes, then decided to play along. "And visit me how often? Once or twice a month? That doesn't sound satisfying."

He gestured between the two of them. "And this is?"

She groaned. "How did you turn a serious conversation about how we can't get married into an argument about your dirty fantasy?"

He put his hands on his hips, glaring at her with mock resentment. "What's dirty about the logistics of making love to my secret wife?"

There was a knock at the door, and Abbie quickly wiped her tears.

"Enter," Parker called. Georgie poked her head in the door.

"Sorry," she muttered, "they need the toilet."

"Then why aren't they the ones asking?" asked Abbie.

"Because they don't want to see something they won't be able to unsee." She looked at Parker. "They revere him more than I do, apparently."

Abbie laughed, propping herself up on an elbow. "That's fine, they can come through."

Parker stood up. "We'll continue this conversation another time," he said, putting on his king voice, as though they'd been discussing something important. He winked at her when no one was looking as Waldo quickly passed through her bedroom to the bathroom.

Abbie sat up and grabbed his hand. "Where are you going?"

"Nowhere." She didn't let go of his hand, gave him her best beseeching look, and he laughed. "Seriously, nowhere. You can let go."

"You can't declare your love and then disappear."

"I'm not going to!" he exclaimed, his eyes shining. "I'm just getting a chair to sit on." Waldo came back through with neither eye contact nor comment.

"What's wrong with the futon you foisted on me?"

"It's too far away."

She swung her legs over the side of the bed and got to her feet gingerly, slowly, to keep her head from spinning. He offered his arm, which she accepted. Her eyes met Dean's as she limped over to the couch, and she saw a fleeting glance of pity. She grunted, her anger stirred. She resented her need, her pain, and she resented him for seeing her in the middle of both.

"Just ignore him," Parker murmured in her ear. "They don't know better. They don't know what a badass you are. I've seen you deny nightstallions their prey. I've seen you cross mountains. I'll set him straight later."

"Don't bother. That's just how the world sees me."

"Don't let them. That's not who you are."

"It is in part." She sat on the couch, pulled her knees to her chest, rested her head on his shoulder, and closed her eyes. She felt dizzy. She felt tired. She felt tired of being tired. She had dishes to do, laundry, work reading. She'd already chewed out Tezza for cleaning her bathroom when she was asleep. T's only response was a glare and a nod of respect.

"I've been thinking," she said.

"Uh-oh. More thinking?"

"Just listen for a minute. Do you remember what you said when you first came here, and I wanted you to step out so I could clean up the mess?"

"There was no mess."

"That issue aside, do you remember your words?"

Parker shook his head slowly.

"You said you wouldn't fight me because you didn't have to." Abbie stared out her bedroom door. "We've been going about this all wrong."

"How so?"

Her voice was low. "We've been chasing him. We've been chasing Lincoln, letting him stay one step ahead, when we should be setting a trap and letting him walk into it." She ticked off on her fingers. "He's got the ego to think he won't get caught; he thinks he has an advantageous knowledge of the castle, your home. He may have someone on the inside. But he's just reckless enough to risk a confrontation if it meant seeing the look on your face when you think I'm gone."

"If you're proposing that I use you as bait, you can just stop right there."

"But if we pick the forest, and the snare, and the cover, why does it matter what we bait it with?" She threaded their fingers together. "That is our house, Parker, that he drove us out of," she said with a fierceness she hadn't used in a while. It took extra effort to muster it during a flare. "That is our kingdom, our home. But let's fight our way: let's lay a trap so perfect he'll never see it coming until it's snapped." She looked away, even as she squeezed his hand. "I ran away from the fight in my own house, and I lost out on so much. I'm done letting you and your family suffer." She leaned away to see him better. "But it's ultimately not my fight. I leave the choice with you."

Parker was quiet for a long time, and she let him think. Then he slid off the couch, kneeling, to face her. He leaned forward until their foreheads touched, a whisper away from a kiss. "I can't lose you, Abbie. The thought alone crushes me." He paused, swallowing hard. "So this would have to be the most foolproof plan in the history of foolproof plans."

"It would be, hon. I promise. I promise, it would be." She brought her hand to his unshaven cheek and gave him a deep kiss. "We can do this. Trust me."

"Did you have something in mind?"

She nodded. "I do, actually. In Brevspor, when a woman asks a man to marry her, there's a big engagement party . . . and traditionally, that party is a masquerade." She looked in his eyes, trying to convey her sincerity. "It might be the perfect thing to entice him."

He sighed. "I'll think on it. No emails, no phone calls about this, all right?"

"Okay." Her need for sleep was dizzying, disorienting.

He stood up. "Stay." Parker walked out of the bedroom, but came back with a glass of water and his e-reader. He gave her the water. "Drink." He watched her empty the glass with concern on his face, then took the glass back. He pulled a pillow off her bed and sat back down next to her on the futon, putting the pillow on his lap. "Lie down."

"So bossy," she yawned as she complied, without the energy for wit. To her mild surprise, he laced the fingers of his left hand with hers, rested them on her hip, and began to read aloud . . .

"'*The Crankshaft Affair*, Chapter 1. My work as Gerald Botham's assistant nearly came to an end before it truly began. On my fifth day of work, he had sent me a telegram, asking me to meet him at the St. Damien's Hospital in Badger's Square. I waited outside an unreasonable amount of time, more than two hours, before he appeared. Though it was his coin that employed my time and talent, I resented him for wasting it . . .'"

"Damn straight," Abbie muttered. She didn't get to hear who'd been murdered before she fell asleep.

CHAPTER TWENTY-SIX

87 days to the wedding

ABBIE WALKED INTO THE orphanage late on a Thursday afternoon, her palms sweating. She didn't know what she'd expected, but it wasn't this. Twelve metal cribs lined the walls of a big, open room, each with one baby, sometimes two. Most were awake, but only one was crying. A pasty white baby stared up at her. Abbie made a motor noise with her lips, but his only response was wider eyes. She popped her lips softly like a bubble popping . . . nothing. This had always gotten big laughs with Ward and Patty's daughter, Jenny. This baby just stared.

"Do you want to hold him?" The nanny who'd let them in was hovering at her elbow. "Most of the visitors like that. You can take a picture with him, if you want."

"No, no," Abbie said quickly, "that's okay." She wasn't all that comfortable with babies anyway, but she definitely wasn't comfortable holding these babies. Her shields were up; she would be seduced by no motherless, adorable bundles. She would care from a safe distance. All that shattered when Theresas and Fadline saw her across the room and ran to her. Their hugs almost knocked her over, and she felt a surge of joy she hadn't expected as they beamed at her. They hadn't been told about her true identity, but they knew she'd called the authorities to investigate their situation. They didn't seem to notice Georgie, who was having a conversation with a little girl who was looking at the pages of a tattered book.

"How are you, girls?" She leaned back to see them better. They were both still quite thin, but their clothes fit better. The bruises were fading on the outside, but she knew that may not represent the inside. Those kind of wounds didn't respond as well to the balm of time.

"Good," they chorused.

"What did you bring us?" Fadline asked, grabbing her hand, and Abbie laughed in surprise.

"Nothing, sorry. I didn't know I was supposed to."

"Most visitors do," Theresas said, lowering her voice to a conspiratorial whisper. "But give it straight to us, not Miss Glynn. It all disappears when the gifts go to her."

"I see." She didn't like the sound of that. Suddenly, she wanted to get them away from here, just for a little while, to hear more.

A slim, middle-aged blonde lady emerged from an office, smoothing her suit skirt set.

"You must be Miss Anderson." She smiled, holding out her hand, and Abbie shook it firmly. Probably too firmly. "My, that's quite the grip you have."

Yeah, I'm sending a message, lady. Do not mess with my girls. Abbie knew they weren't hers; it wasn't as if she wanted to adopt them. She looked around at the other kids, most of whom were much younger. *Is anyone going to want to adopt them?* The girls hadn't been sure how old they were, exactly

. . . Authorities had estimated Theresas at ten and Fadline at eight.

"Yes, I'm Abbie. I was part of the mission to remove the girls from their former living situation, so I thought I'd come by to visit."

"Oh, how nice. If you'd let me know you were coming sooner, we could have arranged for the kids to sing to you."

Abbie cringed inwardly. "Oh no, that's not necessary, but I appreciate the . . . gesture."

"Oh, they love it, they love welcoming visitors to our home. We're just one big family here."

"Oh. Perhaps I misunderstood the situation here. You're not adopting them out?"

The lady's face twitched, and Abbie smiled inwardly. *Subtlety never was my strong suit.*

"Well, yes, of course, we are finding them forever families . . ."

"Then you'll forgive me for saying so, but this isn't a family. It's a nice place, but I had a family once, and they never tried to give me away." *Though they probably wished they could on more than one occasion . . .*

Miss Glynn's eyes narrowed for a moment before she reclaimed her compassionate, collected demeanor. "It breaks our hearts to say goodbye to our kids. We love them like our own; that's all I meant. But we know that our loss is their gain, so we do what's right by them. We can't wait to find the right placement for Fadline and Theresas. Isn't that right, girls?"

"Yes, Miss Glynn," they chorused.

Abbie tried to keep her demeanor casual. "Would it be all right if I took the girls to lunch in town? We'd only be gone a few hours."

"I'm afraid not. My government license doesn't allow me to let them off campus with people who aren't blood relatives."

Surprise withheld Abbie's voice for a moment. "Why would children in an orphanage have blood relatives who aren't caring for them?"

Miss Glynn shook her head, her expression somber. "Their families just don't have the resources to feed another mouth. They know the children are better off here, and we are happy to help."

Abbie looked from Fadline to Theresas, who were still grinning up at her, oblivious to the strained tone of the conversation. "Well," she said to the girls, "give me the ten-cent tour." She was dragged from room to room, their hands never leaving hers. Abbie noted the bright murals of fruit trees with nursery rhymes inscribed below in Common Tongue, which most of the kids probably didn't speak. She noted the lack of books and toys compared to the number of children present.

How desperate would I have to be to leave my own child here with strangers?

Where do the kids who don't get adopted go?

Do the kids go to school? Is it a good school? What about the ones who are behind? Surely Fadline and Theresas aren't proficient enough to be in the right grade, though they can both read . . .

She read to them. Other kids came over, curious, wanting her attention as well. She made a mental note to bring art supplies next time; both girls showed an interest in art, creativity. When their lunch was served, sandwiches and fruit, they gobbled it all down. The nannies were politely deferential with Abbie, but none of the children seemed to have any warm feelings toward them. They spent a fair amount of time on their phones . . . but so did normal parents. She'd been reading about abuse in orphanages, and it was a little hard to imagine it existing here, in such a bright, sunny place . . . but that didn't mean it wasn't present. She knew that some of it stemmed from the caretakers' jealousy that the children they looked after had things theirs didn't, anger that they had to work and spend their day caring for other people's kids while their own lacked basic necessities.

What a mess. When she and Georgie walked out a few hours later, she had more questions than she'd had before they arrived. They drove back in the dark for their red-eye flight to Orangiers . . . It was finally time to face their opposition in court. As she was boarding, she got a text from Parker.

Parker: Safe flight, darling. See you soon.

Parker: Forgot to mention—Dad found a mediator. Hoping to get her approved at tomorrow's hearing. Lawyers are working on it now.

She'd wanted suggestions, not for them to charge ahead without her. It was such a pain to be apart.

Abbie: Okay, thanks. Who is it?

Parker: Queen Annette Richard from across the Sparkling Sea. Lethos. Can't remember all her names . . .

Parker: It took some convincing, but she's agreed.

Annette, Annette . . . it rang a bell. Maybe she'd had a treaty with her mother at some point? Oh, wait . . .

Abbie: Wait, Annette Friedrich?

Parker: Yes, well, she married, so it's Richard now.

Abbie: Not the Annette who was my mother's nemesis in college?

Parker: They were acquainted, I believe.

Abbie: WHY WOULD HE ASK HER?

Parker: Refrain from yelling, please. She disdains all parties involved and is therefore impartial.

Abbie: This sounds like a bad idea.

There was a long pause, and she used it to find her seat and stow her carry-on.

Parker: Got a better one? Hmm?

Abbie: No . . .

Parker: Then this is it, toots.

Abbie: . . . toots?

Abbie: What?

Parker: What? What what?

Abbie: You sound weird.

Parker: Rubbish. I'm a proper king who says proper things, sexypants.

Parker: Now send me that bathing suit selfie you promised me earlier.

Perplexed, Abbie dialed Parker.

"Good evening, fair princess! Is your day going well or falling ill?"

She grinned. "James. I should've known."

"Whatever do you mean? Can't imagine."

This guy. As nervous and screwed up as she felt inside, she suspected James would always be able to make her laugh.

"Arron, does Edward know you have his phone?"

"Of course not. What do you take him for, woman? Oh, oh, here it comes . . . Goodbye, princess, pray for me." There was a scuffle, and Abbie chuckled.

"Abs?"

"Oh, much better. James is a poor substitute for you, by the way. Don't let him attend parliament sessions in your stead."

Parker laughed. "Sorry, darling, I went to the toilet for two seconds, and James managed to make a nuisance of himself. A NUISANCE," he yelled, holding the phone away from his mouth, "WHO IS SUPPOSED TO BE DOING HIS PHYSICAL THERAPY. SILENTLY."

"Yeah, I didn't think you'd call me 'toots.'"

"What? Toots? Oh, for the Woznick's sake . . ."

"Do you still want that picture?"

"What picture?" She heard him scrolling back through the texts. "JAMES!"

"It was for you, Edward, it was for *you!* I was doing you a favor! Ouch, hey!"

"Run, James!" Abbie laughed and hung up.

CHAPTER TWENTY-SEVEN

83 days to the wedding

"SO?" LAUREN PROMPTED before she'd even sat down at the wrought-iron outdoor table. "How did it go?"

"Fine." Abbie put away her phone; the device was becoming a constant in her life, much to her chagrin. "It was very brief, actually. I said nothing, my legal team got our mediator approved, and we worked out our next date to meet."

"That's great!" Lauren gushed. "How soon?"

"I'll meet with them to set the conditions of our mediation next month."

"When's the actual mediation, though?"

Abbie let the air in her lungs out slowly. "Not until Eleventh Month. Her schedule was pretty packed."

"Are you guys going to push back the wedding?"

"I don't see how we can . . . Everything's booked, invitations are going out any day now to a bazillion people I don't know since I have no friends . . ."

"Hey!"

Abbie grinned at her. "Fine, few friends. Speaking of which, are you bringing Shane? I'm trying to get a head count for my people."

"Yes." Her tone was terse.

"What's your deal with this guy? It's like you like him but you hate that you like him."

Lauren paused. "That's an excellent way of putting it."

"What's wrong with him?"

Lauren sighed and leaned back from the table as the waitress put down the sandwich Abbie had ordered for her. A glare from Lauren made her shrug.

"You always get the same thing, why wouldn't I order for you?" Abbie swallowed a bite of her salad. "I repeat: what's wrong with him?"

"He's just not . . . cool."

Abbie blinked. "Like, he's not charismatic?"

"Yeah. And that sounds really lame when I say it out loud. He's a perfectly nice guy, and he likes me, and I like him . . . but he's just not the kind of guy I pictured myself with." She leaned forward like she was telling a secret. "If I leave him alone at a party, he just stands there and drinks."

Abbie chuckled. "What do you want him to do, juggle?"

Lauren threw her hands up. "I just want him to mingle! I want him to be social!" She picked up her sandwich, then stopped halfway to her mouth. "It's like he only wants to talk to me. I think he only goes because I'm there, even though we basically live together."

"It sounds like you're in love with an introvert, hon." Abbie smiled. "As a fellow introvert, I think that's nice."

"I'm in love with an introvert," Lauren said, as if it were a foreign language she was trying to translate for herself. "I'm in love . . . with an introvert."

"How did you meet again?"

"My mom set us up at a dinner party. He's a nurse in her clinic. I make twice as much as he does, which he doesn't resent one iota." She shook her head. "I'm in love with an introvert who's secure enough in his masculinity to do a job normally relegated to women."

"Is he a sensitive guy?"

Lauren wrinkled her nose. "Not really. Like, he's not real emotional or a crier, thank Woz, but he's a good listener. The other day, I was telling him about my client who's divorcing her—"

"GET DOWN!"

Georgie tackled Abbie to the sidewalk just before the crossbow bolt sliced above them where her chest had been a moment ago. Before she had time to think, Georgie was hauling her up off the ground, pushing her toward the building, shielding her with her own body, muttering enchantments under her breath that caused the air around them to thicken, congeal. Abbie felt encased in a bubble of gel; her own movements were slower, the sounds of people around them screaming became muted, like they were all underwater. She couldn't run, could barely move, pressed against the building by Georgie's spell. Her security stepped away momentarily to retrieve Lauren and shove her into the bubble with Abbie. Several others who attempted to approach them were rebuffed by the spell, and Abbie watched, fascinated, as they bounced off the air around her. She'd never experienced anything like it.

"Are you okay?" Lauren asked, her voice shaking. "Oh, Abbie, you're bleeding."

With effort, Abbie touched her forehead; she must've knocked against the corner of the table as they went down. Still, it was far better than the alternative.

"I'm okay, I'm okay." She made her voice soothing and turned Lauren toward her more fully, looking her up and down. "Are you okay?"

Lauren nodded. "It came from that building across the street. A couple of floors up."

"How did they know where we'd be?"

"Do you think they hacked your email? Or your phone?"

Abbie shook her head. "We didn't say a location, I don't think. They must have been following me, learning my routines." That was far more terrifying to her, that someone had been following her whom she hadn't noticed, whom none of them had noticed.

A large armored carriage came to an abrupt halt in front of the deli, and Abbie felt herself drawn toward it as Georgie moved her enchanted shield forward. Lauren was swept along, too, and a moment later, they were inside the carriage. Georgie dropped her shield and her hands went to her charge's head immediately.

"How did your injury happen? Was it the bolt?" She didn't wait for Abbie to answer before she looked down, lowered her voice, murmured more enchantments, and Abbie felt the surge of magic around her like a cloud. Her wound suddenly felt as if she had frostbite.

Abbie whimpered, and Georgie's eyes met hers. Something swirled just beneath the surface of her gaze, and Abbie was suddenly in what felt like a memory: her mother was holding her, stroking her hair, rocking, singing.

"Don't!" Abbie cried out, trembling. "Don't—don't show me that. Please . . ." Abbie felt the static as Georgie shifted focus for a moment, and the "memory" disappeared. Another image appeared in its place: she stood on the banks of a roaring river, mountains rising up on the other side, the deep woods below her engulfed in mist; a crow flew over, cawing. Abbie felt her body relax at that, and her eyes fluttered closed.

"Stay awake," Georgie ordered. "I'm checking that the cursed bolt didn't affect you; I'm almost done." The magic itself seemed to shake her awake with invisible hands. Abbie opened her eyes and Georgie dropped her hands to her shoulders. "The arrow didn't touch you, did it?"

Abbie shook her head, unable to speak.

"You hit your head on the table?"

Abbie nodded.

"Your mother never held you like that, did she?"

Abbie shook her head, her lower lip trembling, her wound still throbbing.

"I'm sorry, Abbie; I didn't know. It won't happen again." The "memory" was already fading, nearly out of reach, and she felt only relief. She looked out the window; they were leaving the city, heading north. "Where are we going? I have to get back to work . . ."

"Sorry, ma'am, not today. You'll spend tonight at a safe house. We'll call your work and give them a plausible explanation for your unavailability." She turned to Lauren. "Ms.

Drake, we can arrange transportation for you wherever you'd like to go, once Ms. Porchenzii is safe."

"No, no, I'll stay with her." Lauren grabbed Abbie's hand and squeezed.

"Parker . . ."

"He'll be notified of the incident soon. You'll be able to speak to him on a secure line when we arrive at the safe house."

Abbie nodded and kept staring out the window. "Georgie?"

"Ma'am?"

"Thank you."

"PARKER, CALM DOWN. I'm fine, really." She was sitting on the porch of the log cabin, curled up on the swing. Ten other people, eight of whom were security personnel, were hanging around nearby, both inside and outside; she had no illusions that this was a private conversation. It was warm, but they'd insisted on wrapping her in a blanket, and the heaviness around her shoulders felt better than she'd expected it to. She wondered obliquely if Georgie had done something to it magic-wise to make it more comforting.

"I will destroy them. I will track them down and obliterate them. I will mutilate their bodies so badly, their own mothers won't know them."

"Parker . . ."

"And if this is my wicked brother's doing, Woz help him when I get my hands on him. Family or no family, I will end him."

"Parker . . ."

"He'll be begging for death by the time I'm done with him."

"Deep breaths, hon."

"Why can't I see you? Turn on the video."

She shifted the phone to her other ear. "I'm too tired for that . . ." she lied. If he saw the purpling bump the size of a goose egg on her forehead, he'd freak out even more, and he was just now starting to calm down.

"It's not a request," he snapped. "Turn it on." She sighed and complied. When he spotted her injury, he released a string of curses she didn't know he was capable of. *Probably learned it in the military . . . probably from Saint. He seems like the type.*

"I'm coming out there."

"No," she said gently. "No, you're not. There's no reason for that. Georgie did her job, and I'm fine."

"What's that lump on your head, then? That's not fine! That is NOT fine, Abbie!"

"It's better than a cursed bolt in my chest. That was the alternative." This was not the right thing to say, and she realized it when the look in his eyes went murderous again.

"I'm sorry, but I'm disregarding your opinion in this instance; I'm coming out there. Then I can at least hold you."

"I don't need holding. I have ice packs and ibuprofen and Dr. Drake. I'm okay. Really."

"Look, I know you're a badass, but in this case, it's *me* who needs to hold *you*. I almost lost you today."

"Nope." She shook her head slowly to minimize the ache. "We were nowhere close to losing. It's a bump on the head. Plus, Georgie has the most amazing non-tech magic skills I've ever seen." She stopped herself from telling him how deeply the implanted memory had upset her; this wasn't the time for him to be doubting Georgie's abilities.

"Good, that's why I hired her. Don't leave the safe house. I'll be there by dawn."

"I've decided something."

He paused. "Am I going to like this?"

"I'm not sure." She sighed. "I'm moving to Brevspor."

His face fell. His voice was quiet. "Not here, with me?"

"No. I considered that, but I think it will aggravate our opponents, like I'm moving in already, like we're disregarding their concerns and legal action. I think it would be better if I moved back to Kohlstadt, to the state castle." She paused. He set his phone on the table, propped up, and he weaved his fingers together, resting his forehead on his joined hands, almost like he was praying. He was so still, she thought the video was frozen. "Parker?"

"I'm here," he said without lifting his head.

She paused again, but he said nothing. "Are you thinking?"

"Yes. I'm thinking."

"Okay." She was learning this about him, that he needed a caesura now and then . . . that it was better not to count the beats of silence, but rather let him resume the music of the conversation when he wanted to. She waited, watching him.

Parker looked up, his face still partially obscured. "Would you take Addington and Macias?"

"Yes, of course."

"You'd be a lot closer. And the state castle would be secure."

"Yes, that was my thinking, too. You'd be able to stay with me when you visit."

She waited again, trying not to let her face show her anxiety. *I want him to approve. I've made the decision, but if he fights me on it . . . I can't take it. No more fighting. No more arguments. Why does distance bring out the worst in us?*

"Have you spoken to your brother?"

"Not yet. I wanted to speak to you first."

"Thank you," he said quietly. He sounded sad. She didn't want to make him sad.

Abbie swallowed. "Since I never formally renounced my title, I have a legal right to live there. And even if he's unhappy about it, it's a big enough place that I'm confident we can successfully avoid each other."

"Okay."

"Okay, you approve?"

"Yes. I approve, with a few conditions."

"Why do I feel an argument coming on?"

"You'll need money if you quit your job. I'd like to issue you a stipend."

"That's not necessary. The Brevsporan government has been badgering me to come on in an advisory capacity until Kurt turns twenty-one. They think I'm playing hardball, so they've now offered twice what my current job pays, and they said I can set my own hours."

"Does that interest you?"

"Not particularly, but I don't see that I have much choice. And maybe it would help me mend my relationship with Kurt. He's all I have left."

"Except me."

"Yes, of course, except you," Abbie amended hastily, trying to see if she'd hurt his feelings. "But isn't this what you wanted? Me living somewhere safer?"

"I thought so. It turns out I really wanted you to live here, with me . . ." He sighed. "But your plan is more sensible."

"And I will live there with you, in eighty-three days."

"Too many."

"I know," she said.

"You're very stubborn, you know that?"

"I do, as a matter of fact. I've always thought it one of my best qualities."

She watched his smile grow. "Well, one of your qualities, anyway . . ."

They said good night, her promising to keep him informed as her plans developed, him promising to get some rest tonight and not just pace and fume. The next call was tougher. Kurt didn't answer; no surprise there. So she called Mrs. Braun.

"Abelia?" The reserved woman's voice held a hint of astonishment.

She smiled. "Yes, Mrs. Braun, it's me."

"To what do I owe the pleasure?"

"I'm coming home."

"Wonderful. We'll prepare the queen's suite, and—"

"Mrs. Braun?"

"Yes?"

"There's been an incident here. It's not safe for me anymore. So until Edward and I can marry, I'll be living at the state castle."

When she finally spoke, her voice was guarded. "I see. Tell me, have you spoken to Kurt recently?"

"No, I haven't been able to get ahold of him since I left."

"I see."

"Why do you ask?" Abbie's voice was sharper than she meant it to be.

"You'll see when you arrive. When shall we expect you?"

"In a few days. As soon as I can get packed and moved." Her phone plunked with a text message.

"Wonderful. We await you with great anticipation."

"Thank you, Mrs. Braun. See you soon."

Abbie hung up and checked the text.

Parker: I'm sending a naval transport for you and your things.

Abbie: Are you sleep-texting? Because you're supposed to be asleep.

Parker: I don't want you flying right now. Please don't fight me on this.

Abbie: I'm not fighting. That's fine.

Parker: They'll be there on Wednesday afternoon.

Abbie: Okay . . . now GOOD NIGHT.

Parker: Good night, darling. I love you.

Abbie: I love you, too.

GEORGIE CAME AND SAT next to her on the swing, rocking it gently. "Are you okay?"

Abbie nodded slowly, not sure how to voice what she was feeling.

"I'm sorry again for the projection . . . The magic knew your mother was important to you, and it misinterpreted what I was asking for."

"I didn't know you could enter my mind like that . . ." She swallowed hard. "Have you done that before?" *And would you tell me if you had?*

Georgie shook her head vehemently. "No, never. I promise. And I wasn't actually there . . . In my bond with the magic, I've developed what's known as a secondary bond on your behalf. It's basically like talking about you to a friend who hasn't met you yet, so that when you meet, you feel like old friends. So the magic allowed us, as friends, to share a calming vision while I scanned your body for corruption."

"Corruption? What does . . . what does corrupt magic even feel like?"

"Like a rabid dog's bite. It feels . . . sick. Manipulated, controlled in an unhealthy way." She shuddered a little. "And I won't even tell you what has to happen to get it off you."

Abbie squeezed her hand. "Thank you again. And thanks for getting to Lauren, too."

"Was he upset about the head injury? Please tell him I'm so sorry . . ." Her voice was thick with stress and regret, but it trailed off under Abbie's scornful glare.

"You saved my life, George. I think he can begrudge you a head bump." Abbie gave her a one-armed hug, then wandered back into the house, still yawning, dead on her feet.

She went into the kitchen and checked the stove . . . *Parker isn't here. Why did my feet bring me here? Oh, because Lauren and Melinda are here.* She sighed, rubbed her tired eyes. Whenever there was someone she loved in the house, she had to check. If she didn't check, she just lay there, staring at the ceiling, no matter how exhausted she was.

What the Jersey is going on in Brevspor?

CHAPTER TWENTY-EIGHT

81 days to the wedding

DEAN HADN'T BEEN WRONG: it didn't take long to pack her things. In the better part of a day, she had everything boxed up, given away, or sold. Lauren took her plants, promising to have Shane water them, and Davis wanted the guitar she'd never learned to play. Most of the furniture went to Ward, Patty, and Jenny; their apartment was finally starting to take shape, feeling less like squatting and more like stability. They'd been so good to her when they lived under the Sixth Street Bridge together . . . No gift would ever feel like too much.

It's good, she thought, staring out her window, wiping tears. *My treasures are going to treasured friends. Nothing's going to waste. I'm just getting on with my life.* But it was hard not to look around and see memories . . . The first piece of artwork she'd bought herself. The free bed frame she'd repainted in the middle of winter with all the windows open so she wouldn't pass out from the fumes. The bedsheet curtains. The place on the rug where she spilled red wine one night when Lauren was over, and the hours they spent trying to get it out again. Outside, the train went by, but there was no lamp to rattle.

Getting to go back somewhere is a luxury, she decided. Life was cruelly progressive in that way. She would come back to Gardenia to visit, assuredly . . . but Lauren might have a new guy by then. Jenny would grow. Old buildings would get knocked down, condos would go up. Home was fragile, fragile. This nebulous mix of people and place that makes your shoulders relax, the familiar feeling that draws your feet to the coffee table. She'd never come back here, to this room, when it meant as much to her as it did right now. She wiped tears again and lifted her chin. *I'll be fine at the state castle, and then I'll be fine at Bluffton. I'll be fine . . . but I won't be here.*

They went down to meet the ship in the bay, and she put on her seasickness bracelets even before she boarded. A broad-chested white man was waiting for her at the top of the gangplank.

"I'm Lieutenant Saint. Nice to finally meet you, ma'am." The appraising look he gave her made the hairs on the back of her neck stand up. He kept his fawn-colored hair a medium length, and he'd gone to the trouble to style it with gel, in an attractive wave curling away from his face. Somehow, with only a firm handshake and eye contact, he silently communicated that he had her number, knew her secrets, and wasn't afraid to use them. She felt a pang of fear at what Parker might've told him, then regarded the notion as nonsense. *It was nonsense, right? . . . Right?*

"Sorry you got stuck escorting me around the edge of the continent."

"It's nothing to concern yourself with, Highness."

"You can call me Abbie," she said, as he took her backpack from her.

"Yes, ma'am." If he realized his incongruity, it didn't register on his face. He led her forward across the deck, past the communications center to her cabin. They'd put her in one of the junior officer's staterooms between the troops' and the officers' floors, which meant she had plenty of privacy. And if she was throwing up all night, there was no one to keep awake with her retching.

"Did he tell you I get seasick?"

"We have a medical officer on board. We're running some training exercises, so we have a full contingent of support staff."

"Thank you," she murmured. It was hard not to find the special treatment embarrassing. Saint noticed Georgie and Tezza for the first time.

"You'll be berthed down the hall. Follow me."

"You go," Georgie said to Tezza, who nodded and took her bag. "Get some sleep."

From the doorway, Saint turned back to her. "I'm your liaison. Whatever you need, you ask me. Understood?"

She wanted to throw him a salute, but decided to wait until she knew him better. "In that case, would it possible to get a few more supplies before we ship out? I'd like to do something for the crew, but I want to make sure we have the necessary provisions. I don't want to put a strain on limited resources."

"It's your sail, ma'am. We'll leave whenever you're ready. I'll have the supply sergeant come speak with you as soon as possible." He paused. "But you have to tell Edward that you caused the delay. He's very anxious to see you."

She smiled. "Of course, Lieutenant. How do I find you if you're not around?"

"You can have me paged in the communications office."

"I know where it is," offered Georgie. "I have a schematic of the ship."

"Can I wander around?"

"Yes. You can go topside. Just don't go into the machine rooms. And take your security."

"Of course."

"Good," he grunted as he left.

After confirming with the supply sergeant that they had what she needed, Abbie got to work. She only had three days . . . Her time with the Browards at Hearth House had taught her that she was most comfortable in the kitchen, so that's where she planned to be. Abbie grief-baked her way across the southern edge of the continent. There were few things she couldn't make. The chocolate chip cookies and the Brevsporan apple crumble pie were both a big hit, but she wanted to see if they had any requests for their final night . . . The lemon meringue certainly stretched the limits of her ability, but it came out pretty good. It took her most of the day when the regular kitchen staff wasn't in the kitchen to bake for that many men. She and her security happened to be the only women on board, but everyone was perfectly polite to them, as far as she knew . . . In fact, they seemed anxious—no, *eager*—that Georgie especially feel welcome on board. Tezza remained bored by everyone as usual.

"What do you do for fun?" Abbie asked between puking sessions the second night, lying in bed, miserable.

"Shoot things."

Abbie crinkled her nose. "You're in the right profession."

"Yes, I am."

"Don't you knit or bake or anything?"

T just stared at her. Abbie rallied her courage, made bold by the darkness and her burning desire to be nosy. Tezza was a vault when she didn't want to talk. Abbie made the mistake of trying to badger information out of her once and promptly found herself on the ground with her hands behind her back. How she'd managed to throw her to the floor without leaving a single mark was still beyond Abbie's comprehension. But she knew Tezza felt sorry for her when she was sick . . . and she didn't mind using it to her advantage.

"In Imahara, we had that talk about patience, and you mentioned that you were once engaged."

"Yes." Her voice was light.

"So . . ."

The meagre light coming under the door was just enough to let Abbie see Tezza's grin.

"My husband's name is Rocco Macias. We were married about ten years ago."

"But you don't wear a ring."

"Right."

"But you still have his name."

"Right."

Abbie huffed impatiently. "Come on, T. Are you going to make me play twenty questions? Can't you just spit it out? What happened?"

She shrugged. "I don't like sad stories." Then, after a few moments of silence, Tezza said softly, "I'll tell you, but I don't want meddling. No favors."

Abbie sat up, trying not to look too eager for a sad story. "You have my word."

"I know what that's worth . . ."

"Hush. I mean, go on."

"Rocco is in the Op'Ho'Lonian special forces. He went missing some time ago."

Abbie wilted. She'd imagined her divorced, but she should've known the pain went deeper than that.

"I'm sorry."

T shrugged.

"How long is 'some time ago'?"

"Two years on the seventh."

"That's a long time."

"Yes."

"Where was he when he went missing?"

"Beyond the Sparkling Sea. They wouldn't be more specific than that."

"Did you love him?" It was a stupid question to ask, Abbie knew; if Tezza hadn't, perhaps she'd be embarrassed now, and if she had, it would just make it all more painful.

"Oh yes," Tezza said, smiling, but her voice caught on the last three words. "Since we're still married, I still do."

HER REUNION WITH PARKER was regrettably brief; he had budget meetings to get back to, but she got a long kiss when no one was looking while they moved her things to his private train car to take her to Brevspor. After the extended journey she'd already had, another four hours on the train seemed interminable; she was ready to get to Brevspor and get settled. *A hundred men may make an encampment, but it takes a woman to make a home.* She'd made a home before. She could do it again. And she had good people around her . . . Warner had retired when her father passed away, but Mrs. Braun had proved herself useful during her absence. The rest of the staff was pretty good, too. She'd talk to them about her needs, be up-front. This wasn't like before. It would be better this time.

She thought that all the way up to the front door of the state castle. There stood Mrs. Braun, grim-faced. That was just her way, Abbie knew; she didn't expect sunshine and roses.

"Hello, Mrs. Braun."

"Hello, Abelia."

"Where's Kurt? Out of town?"

She shook her head slowly. "He is here."

"Okay, so why isn't he *here* here to welcome me?"

Mrs. Braun shook her head again, sadly this time. "I am sorry. We tried."

"What does that mean, 'we tried'?"

The woman straightened her slumped shoulders. "I will take you to him."

"All right." She followed her up the stairs. "Is he still mad at me?"

"Yes. As always, he is angry . . . but since your father died . . ."

She put a hand on her arm. "What's going on, Mrs. Braun?"

"It will be easier to show you."

She followed the matron deeper into the state castle, a little shiver working up her spine. It was so quiet. The Browards' castle was alive with servants, family, friends. This place felt dead and buried. Mrs. Braun paused at the door to Kurt's quarters.

"Just . . ." She sighed. "We tried, Abelia. I promise we did." Then she opened the doors.

Abbie gasped. There were books everywhere, stacked as high as her shoulder. He must have hauled half the royal library into the hallway. There was a path over the blue carpet that wound between the stacks. No one would have been able to clean in here; no way could they get the cart through, not to mention a vacuum.

"Hello?" She called as she carefully worked her way down the hall. She cautiously poked her head into his study and found him bent over a book at his desk, taking notes. "Kurt?"

He didn't look up.

"Kurt?" He wasn't wearing headphones . . . *Can he not hear me? He should be able to hear me. What the . . .*

Sliding between more books on the floor—there were fewer, in here—she scooched her way toward the desk and put a hand on his shoulder.

"I TOLD YOU NOT TO—" He turned toward her angrily. "You."

"Kurt." He seemed completely livid with her, and all she'd done was come into his study and touch his shoulder. "I'm back."

"Right," he snarled. Abbie felt her chest constrict.

He shoved back from the desk, pacing over to a bookshelf before pulling three more books off. He carried them over to the door without looking at them and added them to an existing stack before returning to his desk.

"What's with the books?" she asked, switching back to Common Tongue.

"They keep out the worst ones."

"The worst ones . . . what? The worst *what*? Servants?"

He scowled at her for a long moment. "What are you doing here?"

"I'm moving back in."

"Like Jersey you are. This is *my* house."

She crossed her arms. "It's mine, too, by ancestral right. More mine than yours, actually, as sole remaining female heir. Perhaps I should kick *you* out?"

"You wouldn't dare," he sneered.

Being with Parker has corrupted me, she thought.

"You're right, I wouldn't. But I could. So be nice to me. And for Woz's sake, let the staff clean your quarters. It smells like a bachelor pad in here." She turned to leave. "Oh, and one more thing. Your government is unhappy with your lack of involvement and your unresponsiveness to their concerns. They've hired me to supplement your deficits while I'm living here."

"Oh, JERSEY NO. You stay out of my government, Abelia, or I'll—"

"Oh, you'll do nothing, little brother," she said in Brevsporan again, "except cooperate."

Abbie edged back through the crowded hallway to where Mrs. Braun was waiting, hands clasped, her knuckles white.

"How long has he been like this?"

"Since you left. He just . . . fell apart."

"Why didn't somebody call me?"

Mrs. Braun shook her head, her lips pursed and white. "He forbade us."

Abbie let out a deep sigh, then clapped her hands. "Okay, first things first. Get some men in here to make the hallway more passable. Don't remove all the books, just enough to get by more easily. It's a fire hazard as it is." She sighed. "I'm going to take a shower and go to bed."

"We've prepared a meal for you . . . just as you told us last time you were here."

"Okay, a quick dinner." She paused. "Does he come out to eat?"

Mrs. Braun shook her head sadly.

"You just take him a tray or what?"

"We presume he comes to the kitchens at night when everyone's asleep. We leave a plate in the refrigerator."

Abbie nodded slowly. "I see. Okay. Thank you, Mrs. Braun." She pulled out her phone as she walked away; she'd missed Parker's text.

Parker: You get in okay?

Abbie: Yes, thanks. Still in your meetings?

Parker: Yes. Snore.

Abbie: LOL. I miss you.

Parker: Talk to Kurt?

Abbie: Yes. It was . . . confusing.

Parker: How so?

Abbie: All I did was talk to him, and he was livid with me.

Parker: Strange.

Parker: Perhaps more investigation is warranted . . . just be polite.

Abbie: I'm always polite.

Parker: LOL.

Abbie: Go back to your meeting and mind your own business.

Parker: I love you, too.

CHAPTER TWENTY-NINE

76 days to the wedding

"THIS IS THE LIST?"

"This is the list, yes. Of course, you can feel free to make additional suggestions . . ."

"Certainly." It was her first meeting with Kurt's cabinet as his "appointed personal advisor." His popularity, at an all-time low before her arrival, had since risen since word had gotten around that she was back, even temporarily. It made no sense, really. What made them think that she was fit to rule, beyond the circumstances of her birth?

"I'd like to read through it thoroughly tonight, but give me the highlights."

"Of course, Your Highness. We—"

"Sorry to interrupt. I prefer to be called Ms. Porchenzii or Abelia."

Rudolpha Van Liesing shifted uncomfortably, a light sheen showing on her forehead. "Of course, A—Ms. Porchenzii." She cleared her throat. "We'd like to see him attending more cabinet meetings and conferences. He does send long letters outlining policy he'd like to see enacted, but we'd like more face-to-face time. We're also concerned about his lack of connection with other heads of state. He hasn't attended any of the conferences or summits that we've managed to get invites to. People are starting to talk, calling him the Hermit Prince."

"Well, I'm sure if I threaten to go in his place, he'll shape up. He's not anxious to have me involved."

"The way of a fool is right in his own eyes . . ." Mrs. Van Liesing quoted, and they all nodded.

"What's he doing well?" Abbie asked.

There was a long silence, and several cabinet members reached for their water glasses.

"He speaks often of equality for the sexes," Mrs. Lange offered. "I don't know that it's very popular rhetoric, but he is passionate about it."

"And his policies on development are very positive. He's not afraid to say no to corporations who would change the landscape of our cities if history is at stake. It's a surprisingly mature stance for a male so young."

"Good," she murmured, still looking at the paperwork they'd given her. "I can work with that. What's this about an upcoming marriage?"

"Oh, yes." Mrs. Van Liesing beamed. "He's had a marriage offer from a prominent Brevsporan family. The Fuchs' eldest daughter, Klara."

Um, what? "Klara, my second cousin?"

"That's right." Abbie thought back. *Klara, who pinched me black and blue during the opera so I wouldn't tell on her? Klara, who read my diary and snickered about it with her sisters? Klara, who called me Scabby until my sisters died, when she acted like we'd always been best friends?* She leaned back, arms crossed over her chest. "Traditionally, a female family member should vet his bride. Why wasn't I consulted?"

No one answered.

"Is this decided already?"

"No, Ms. Porchenzii. But we anticipate that he will accept her offer. She would be a strong political queen. And her family has been very supportive of Kurt."

"His Highness."

"Pardon?"

Abbie leaned forward. "He's my brother. I call him Kurt. He's your leader. You call him His Highness." Meeting their blank stares, Abbie just shook her head. *We're as backwards as the patriarchies. They can't even respect him in private.* "What does His Highness think of the match with Klara?"

"He'll accept it."

"That's not what I asked, Matron. I'm sure he would accept it . . . It seems you have left him little choice in the matter. Has he voiced an opinion on it?"

Mrs. Van Liesing's mouth pulled into a tight line before she answered. "We haven't been able to get an answer from him. Perhaps he would share such thoughts with a close relative like you." There was an edge to the woman's voice, a challenge, and Abbie smiled.

"I'll see what I can do." Abbie stood, and the other women scrambled to follow her lead. "Thank you for your time. I'll make an appointment with your secretaries to meet again next week." She walked out before anyone could ask any more questions, taking the paperwork with her. She stalked straight to Kurt's study; the hallway hadn't been cleared . . . or if it had, he'd reconstructed his fortress of reference material. He was asleep on the antique yellow-and-green love seat, one arm cast over his face to block out the light of midmorning.

"Wake up, jackass."

"Wha . . . You."

"Yes, me. Why didn't you tell me about Klara?"

"Klara?" He sat up, rubbing his face.

"Yes," she said, grasping her fragile patience as though holding a slippery fish. "Klara, our awful cousin who'd like you to sire her heirs and rule your queendom."

"Oh, that."

Abbie laughed. "Is that all you have to say about it?"

He scowled. "I thought they'd forget about it if I just didn't answer them."

"Priests and women never forget," Abbie quoted. "You can't just ignore your way out of your problems."

He glared at her. "Better to run from them, I suppose?"

She sat down on the love seat, and he moved his legs to avoid being squished. "Stop deflecting, Kurt. Do you want Klara or not?"

"Does it matter?"

"It matters to me." She wanted to reach out and touch him; he looked so guarded.

"I can't marry," he said quietly, staring at her hands in her lap.

"Why not?"

"I have . . . problems." He met her gaze for the first time, then stared at the bookshelf behind her. "Personal problems."

"Don't we all?"

"Not like this," he said, shaking his head.

Was it a guy thing? Was there something wrong with his . . . plumbing? Was he sick?

"Would you rather talk to Edward about it? He'll be here two weeks from now."

His face brightened to cautious optimism. "Edward?"

"I'm sure he'd be happy to talk with you. He's a very good listener."

He smiled, and Abbie remembered how young he was. "You'd know; you talk too much."

"Probably," she acknowledged, smiling back. "He knows the kind of pressures you're under, Kurt. Talk to him. Maybe he can help you get some perspective."

He nodded slowly. "I'll think about it." He picked up a book, but didn't open it. "What did they say about me?"

"Who?"

"The vipers you met with this morning."

She ignored the slight. "They said they liked your development policies."

He snorted. "Of course they do. They hate change of any kind, and I've preserved their precious queendom just as it is."

"I won't let them marry you off if it's not what you want, Kurt. Okay? I'll protect you. I'll find you someone else. You can trust me."

"Like I trusted you to advocate for a kingdom instead of a stewardship at my hearing?"

She pressed her lips into a white line. "You know what? I deserve that. I'm sorry. I should've done what you asked me to do."

He gaped at her, letting the book fall to his lap.

"What?"

"You've never apologized to me before. Ever."

Abbie stood up. "Then I'm sorry for that, too," she said, then turned to leave.

"Wait!" he called. She paused in the doorway. "What time is dinner on Saturday?"

CHAPTER THIRTY

67 days to the wedding

THINGS BEING WHAT THEY were at the state castle—i.e., majorly messed up—Abbie decided that her wedding dress date with Lily and the sisters would be better done at a hotel. The last thing she needed was Kurt cursing at her proper future in-laws. Georgie was chatty on the way, and she thought she might be trying to distract her. Last time, when they'd picked colors, had gone fine, she told herself. *Today, too, will be fine. It will be fine.*

It was not fine.

From the moment the double doors opened, Abbie felt anxiety dragging her away from calm like an undertow, sucking at her ankles. She struggled to stay on her feet emotionally. The room was full of white dresses—there must have been upwards of three hundred. The Broward women had turned the suite into their own personal bridal boutique, complete with four full-length mirrors surrounding a circular stage. This was not what she'd been expecting; yes, they'd asked for her measurements, but she had no idea . . .

Someone thrust a champagne flute with orange juice into her hand, and Abbie stared at it. How was she going to try on all these dresses when she was sweating like she'd just run a marathon? Georgie touched her elbow.

"Ma'am? Are you all right?"

Pushing off her stupor, she nodded unevenly. "Of course, yes. I'm . . . I'm fine."

Thirty fashionably dressed men and women were milling around, yet somehow, Lily noticed her.

"She's here," she announced calmly, and the noise level rose considerably. The girls swarmed her for a hug, and everyone was hovering near, the crowd of bodies moving her toward the center. Many wanted to express their congratulations on her upcoming marriage or condolences for her father's passing. *This is too much. I can't . . . I can't stay here.*

"Go use the restroom, Abelia, because after that, you're ours for the next few hours!" Lily's aide Bernice joked, and everyone laughed. Abbie bolted so hard for the bathroom, she stepped on strangers' toes, and Georgie had a hard time keeping up through the group. Once the door was shut, she sat on the closed toilet lid, her hands shaking as she called Parker.

"Hello, beauti—"

"Can't do this, Parker. I can't do this. Too many of them, it's too much . . ."

"Okay, slow down. You're trying on dresses?"

"I haven't even gotten to the jacking dresses yet! Oh Woz, my chest hurts. I can't—I can't breathe . . ."

"All right, hold on, darling. I'm texting Rhodie. She'll be discreet. Just hang on."

Her shaking hands couldn't hold on to the phone anymore, and it clattered to the tile. She could still hear his voice on the phone, and she tried to switch to speakerphone. *Why is it so hot in here?* She would've killed for a fan right about then. Her stomach was twisting uncomfortably. She slid off the toilet to kneel on the cool floor and finally got her fingertip on the speakerphone button.

"Are you still on the line, Abs?"

"Yes," she gasped, raising her arms over her head to breathe better. "I'm here."

"Rhodie's on her way, okay? Is the door locked?"

"I don't know. Don't hang up."

"Don't be absurd!"

She gasped a laugh at his tender disdain. There was a soft knock, and Rhodie opened the door.

"Abelia? Are you—oh, no, you're not all right. Let's get you up. Ms. Addington, a little assistance, please." She and Georgie lifted Abbie by her arms back onto the toilet, the only place to sit, and Rhodie gently pressed Abbie's head between her own knees.

"Are you having trouble breathing?"

She nodded.

"And your chest hurts?"

She nodded.

"Is it a stabbing pain or a squeezing pain?"

"Stabbing...," she gasped out.

"Do you have a heart condition?"

She shook her head.

"You feel warm. I'm going to check your pulse, if that's all right..."

Abbie chuckled, because only a Broward would ask for permission before touching you during a medical emergency. Rhodie and Parker were so alike.

"Okay, Abelia, based on your accelerated heart rate and other symptoms, I believe you're having a panic attack. Have you had one before?"

She shook her head. *Is this a joke? I don't crumple. I don't fold. And I sure as Jersey don't panic.*

"I'd like you to focus on long breaths out, as long as you can, okay? So breathe in for two and out for five. In for two, out for one, two, three, four, five . . . Good," she murmured, rubbing her back, "just like that. Keep it going, please. Edward, can you hear me?"

"Yes, I can."

"I think she's doing okay now, but you were right to alert me." Rhodie turned her attention back to Abbie. "You've been under a bit of stress lately, mmm? The passing of your father, separated from your fiancé, death threats and lawsuits, new security, an assassination attempt, moving unexpectedly, planning a wedding, and of course, your chronic illness on top of all that . . . it's a lot to deal with."

Abbie sat up slowly and stared at Rhodie. Her vision was spotty, and her head felt too light; she felt it might float away if it somehow came untethered from her body. She wanted to stand, but she wasn't sure her legs would hold her. Every ounce of energy felt siphoned out of her.

"Parker, I thought you said she was a medical doctor."

Rhodie blinked, and Parker snickered.

"I know, darling, but I wouldn't deceive you; she only *sounds* like a shrink. Older sisters can be insightful sometimes, independent of their degrees." The casual observer might have interpreted Rhodie's quiet amusement as the onset of a cold or an otherwise itchy nose, nothing more than bouncing shoulders and a few dignified sniffs.

"I'm so embarrassed," Abbie whispered, pressing her palms into her eyes, her breath coming back.

Rhodie waved her concern away. "Whatever for? We all overextend ourselves at times. You were overtaxed and your body told you so, in no uncertain terms. Evolutionarily, you should thank it."

Abbie stared down at her hands and muttered, "Thank you, body," and Rhodie laughed audibly this time. Her laugh was so typically princessy, Abbie was jealous; it was soft, lilting, musical all at once. It put her throaty chuckles to shame.

The princess put a hand on Abbie's wrist. "Would you like a cup of tea?"

"Orangiersians think tea fixes everything," Parker said through the phone. "We're very predictable that way."

Abbie blinked hard and sighed. "I would, actually. Do you have Duke of Darlington?"

"Is the ocean a mile deep?" Rhodie must have seen Abbie's confusion. "Apologies for the turn of phrase. Yes, of course we do. The king's preferred blend is always available. And actually, the Orangiersian Ocean is closer to five miles deep in the Crow's Nest Trench, so I can't fathom how that expression got started."

Parker sighed. "Fathom, Rhodie? Really? Puns at a time like this?"

She grinned, glancing slyly at Abbie. "Laughter is the best medicine, especially when you're chronically stressed. Just medicating my patient."

Parker cleared his throat. "Abs, I think you should call Lauren or Patty. They should be there with you next time. And Rhodie, we need to speak to Mum about curtailing the circus."

"I believe I can accomplish that . . ."

Abbie held up her hand. "No, I can talk to her. It's my problem. I'll handle it." *I want Rhodie's respect, not her pity, and this whole situation has taken me a step backwards.*

"Abs, could you please take me off speakerphone?"

She picked up the phone off the floor and put it to her ear as the others politely wandered out of the room.

"Okay. It's just me."

"I'm worried about you; this is so unlike you. Are you certain you're all right? What can I do for you right now?"

"Well, I could use a hug and a nap, but I don't think either of those things is going to happen."

He sighed. "I hate this. I abhor it. I despise, detest, and loathe it."

"Me too, hon." She turned toward the door. It was strangely quiet out there. "I should go talk to your mom."

"What will you say?"

"Something near the truth; that I'm not feeling well. And try to gently remind her that I left a royal life for a reason and can't take high levels of stress."

"Promise me you'll rest this afternoon."

"Yes, I will."

"Oh, that was too easy. Now I'm truly concerned."

Abbie chuckled. "I love you, too. Bye, hon."

Abelia walked back out to the living space and found it nearly abandoned. Lily was sitting on the couch, and she patted the spot next to her. A steaming cup of tea was waiting for her as well. Abbie sat down hesitantly.

"Your Majesty, I'm sorry I ran off. I'm not feeling well this morning . . ." She trailed off under Lily's hard look. *Uh-oh. She's got her truth stare out. Maybe it's a mom stare and my mom just didn't have one.*

"You don't have to pander to me, dear."

"Did Rhodie . . . ?"

"She didn't have to say a word." Lily shook her head. "I saw your panicked look as you exited and I sent them off for a while so we could chat. Have some tea."

Abbie obeyed, lifting the teacup painted with violets to her lips and blowing.

"It appears that in my zeal to help, I've overstepped. Is that so?"

Abbie's wince wasn't just because the tea was too hot.

"I see. Well, I don't excel at frank conversations, but if you'd like to suggest some changes to my method, I would certainly be open to that."

"This is hard for me." Abbie swallowed. "I don't know why. Normally, I have no problem expressing my opinion, but you're Parker's mom, and with how I abandoned him, I guess I don't know if you . . ." *Nope, not ready to go there just yet.* She hurried on. "I just want this wedding to honor his cultural traditions, too, and mine are all different, and I feel like I have no clue what I'm doing because Brevsporan women never plan their own weddings, and I just wish my mom and dad . . ."

There it was. The truth she'd been trying to drown in bravado. Being with Parker's mom made her miss her own parents, even though they were nothing alike. They would've both delighted in seeing her married. Letting her mother's critical voice go had done strange things to her; lately it had been easier to remember the good times they'd had . . . watching her reserved, proper mother curse when her marshmallow caught fire while camping; racing each other on horseback in the Thundercreek Highlands; playing ongoing games of World Domination or Peril, Christmas mornings in her parents' suite.

Lily put a gentle hand on her arm. "I can't imagine how you must miss them. And while I have no intention to replace them, I do hope we can be close. I'm so pleased that you're Edward's bride; I've never seen him so smitten as he is with you. And more than that, you have a strong friendship on which to build your love, just as Ignatius and I do. Many royal marriages are no more than political alliances, as you know. I wanted more for my children," she said, moving to push Abbie's hair behind her shoulder. "When you went missing, we feared the worst. Woz knows how many nights I fell asleep praying you were all right. Having you back is better than we could've hoped for." She straightened her posture even more and leveled her gaze on her face again. "But we want to keep you this time. So you'll have to instruct us on your needs. I'd hate to spend my golden years in the stockade for upsetting Edward."

Abbie grinned at her gentle teasing, but wiped away a tear as well. "Thank you, Lily. From the bottom of my heart. That means a lot to me." She laughed softly. "And if it helps, I suggested we elope as a joke, and he quite seriously informed me that he couldn't, because you'd never speak to him again."

Lily laughed almost silently, just like Rhodie had a few minutes before, her shoulders shaking. "I'm glad he understands what's at stake."

"Where are the girls? Where's Rhodie?"

"They're in the bedrooms."

She nodded. "When are all the designers coming back?"

"Would you like them to come back?"

Abbie shrugged. "Maybe one or two of them? Or the wedding coordinator?"

She put a hand on her arm again. "Let me explain what we did here, and then you can decide how you'd like to proceed today. We wanted to expose you to a variety of styles and fashions, so we had some noted designers come up with ten dresses each. The dresses are organized by designer, so if you look through them and decide you like one set in particular, perhaps we could invite that designer up. Keep in mind, too, that a dress often looks different on the hanger than it does when you're wearing it, and of course, everything would be tailored to fit you precisely."

Abbie nodded. "And I'd like the girls and Rhodie to help me look through them, too, if they don't mind. I don't always know what looks good on me . . ."

"No one does, darling. You think I picked this out? No." She turned and nodded to Bernice, who was standing nearby.

Abbie stood up and wandered over to the closest rack . . . Many of the gowns were very couture, outlandish designs that relied heavily on things like feathers and boning to create unusual silhouettes. They had slits and holes in what she considered to be very unflattering places. She was much more traditional than that. The twins came cautiously out of the bedroom, and she felt a wave of guilt rising up. Abbie smiled as warmly as she could and gestured to them.

"Come help me look, girls. You've both got an eye for this."

They perked up at this. Though they were identical twins, they couldn't have been more different: Dahlia's choices reminded Abbie of cake frosting: fluffy, soft, layered. Ginger, on the other hand, went minimal, clean lines and slick, shiny fabrics. Abbie tried on several dresses for both of them, but she didn't care for any of them. Lily and Rhodie were good at pointing out the aspects of each dress that were working for her . . . She favored bateau, illusion, and irony of ironies, Queen Anne necklines. She looked best in A-line and trumpet silhouettes. She didn't want a long train; she was clumsy enough as it was. While she was distracted, the wedding coordinator wandered back in and quietly came to her elbow, noting what interested her. They invited three designers back into the suite, and they asked her questions until Lily noticed the fatigue in her face.

"All right, everyone, I think that's enough for today. You've got your assignments: bring us back some A-line beauties for Edward's bride."

"And bring some with sleeves next time," Abbie added. "It's a winter wedding, after all."

They chuckled and scribbled.

"I would invite you to stay with us for lunch, but I think you've had enough excitement for one day. But we'll see you the weekend after next, correct?"

"Yes, that's right. I'm looking forward to it. And thank you, Your Majesty, for putting this together; it really was very helpful, even if I didn't find a dress today."

"My understanding is that several attempts are usually required," Rhodie put in, and sipped her tea.

Abbie nodded. "That makes sense. With your permission, Lily," she said, still stumbling over her first name, "I'd like to invite two of my friends to join us next time."

"Oh, I'd be delighted."

"Well, perhaps hold off on that delight until you meet them. Until just recently, one of them lived under the Sixth Street Bridge, and the other one is a lawyer."

"Any friends of yours are welcome here. Please invite them, and we'll make a party of it." Lily noticed her guarded expression and quickly amended. "A quiet, intimate party."

Abbie smiled. "That sounds nice."

CHAPTER THIRTY-ONE

60 days to the wedding

ABBIE: You awake?

    Parker: Yes. . .

    Abbie: I miss you.

    Parker: I miss you, too. Why are you awake?

    Abbie: Because I miss you.

    Parker: That's rather flattering.

    Abbie: I don't even care anymore.

    Parker: You're no longer worried about inflating my ego?

    Abbie: No, I just miss you.

    Abbie: I need you.

    Parker: I need you, too, darling.

    Parker: BTW, that would be a good thing to say if you wanted to have sex.

    Parker: I hope/expect that you'll start things sometimes, too . . . It would get tedious to be the only one who initiates.

    Abbie: 1. Good slang texting (BTW).

    Abbie: 2. That's not exactly how I meant it, but good to know.

    Abbie: 3. Thank you for sharing that expectation . . . It might be awkward at first, but I think I can do that.

    Parker: It might be easier than you think . . .

Parker: Let's practice.

Abbie: What, now?

Parker: Why not? Nothing's going to happen, we're four hours apart.

Abbie: I thought kings didn't sext?

Parker: Leave the eggplant emojis out of it and I'll be fine.

Abbie: If you say so. . . ::ahem::

Abbie: That's a nice shirt, but you know what would look better on you?

Parker: What?

Abbie: Me.

Parker: LOL.

Abbie: It's handy that I have my library card . . .

Abbie: Because I'm totally checking you out.

Parker: Eh.

Abbie: My doctor says I'm low on Vitamin U, can you help me out?

Parker: Where are you getting this nonsense?

Abbie: The internet, duh.

Parker: But there's no sentiment in it.

Abbie: I didn't think men needed to be wooed. You guys always seem so . . . ready.

Parker: I object to that. I'm not always ready.

Parker: Sometimes I'm asleep.

Abbie: LOL

Abbie: I guess I could always just take your pants off. That should send a clear message.

Parker: It would be hard to miss your intentions, yes.

Parker: Let's just hope we're alone. The rest of my family might not appreciate the gesture.

Abbie: Sorry, hon. I kind of suck at words.

Parker: I liked the speech you gave at the press conference when we announced our engagement.

Abbie: It wasn't bad, was it?

Parker: Not at all.

Abbie: You can't tell, but I'm yawning.

Parker: That's because it's after midnight. I thought you passed out at 9.

Abbie: Not when I'm lying in bed thinking about my hot fiancé . . .

Abbie: Imagining he's here with me, so I can gaze into his amazing, expressive eyes . . .

Abbie: touch his face . . .

Abbie: taste his lips . . .

Abbie: feel his warmth under the sheets . . .

Parker: Okay, that's enough practice, you've got it, good night.

Abbie: Sweet dreams. ;)

Parker: Sadist.

PARKER ARRIVED TWO days later for their weekend together in Brevspor. It was the first time he'd been back since her father's funeral, and it was hard not to see it all in a new light. He'd spent a lot of time here, getting to know her parents, her father mostly. Tradition dictated that they meet regularly, and he'd made time for it as an obligation at first, but then found he really enjoyed Paul. Kurt began tagging along more after he graduated high school. They went fishing, ate, hiked in the mountains around Kohlstadt. Paul was an active guy before his cancer. It'd killed Parker to watch him fade away.

But today, he wasn't thinking about Paul. After their hot texting exchange, he was more than ready to see his fiancée. Weekends just weren't coming fast enough. It was only six more weeks until their wedding . . . if things went well with their mediator, that is.

Abbie was sitting on the front steps waiting for him, and she descended slowly as his carriage pulled up.

"Hi." He'd been greeted more enthusiastically by the guards at the front gate.

"Hi, beautiful. Everything okay?"

"Yeah." Since no one else was paying attention, he leaned toward her for a chaste hello kiss, but she turned and went back up the stairs. *Oh. Well, then. Am I expected to guess what she's upset about? Great. Four hours of train travel, now this.* He followed her up the stairs.

"Are you ready to go for a hike?"

"No."

"What, then? A movie?"

She sighed. "We'd have to watch it in my father's study. It's the only room with a screen besides Kurt's quarters. Which is a waste, because he never stops reading long enough to use it."

"As ranking royal, have you thought about commandeering it? He might not even notice."

She huffed. "And reinforce every negative stereotype about how overbearing women can be? I don't think so."

Parker said nothing. When he couldn't say anything right, it seemed the thing to do. He'd just follow her around for a while. He stuffed his disappointment down deeper. He followed her into her quarters and sat down on the futon he'd bought for her. Why she'd brought it from Gardenia, he wasn't entirely certain; she didn't need it here. It didn't fit with the decor at all, which was all rather spartan. Was she being sentimental?

"May I inquire why you brought this?"

She shrugged and flopped down on her bed, facedown. "There was room."

"By that measure, you could've brought all your furniture."

Abbie grunted.

What's her deal? And why can't she just be honest about it?

"Well, it's a quality piece of merchandise, I made certain of that. It should last for many years. And they have a generous 'restuffing' policy, should the interior batting prove insufficient over time."

She lifted her head to look at him as she rolled her eyes. "It has nothing to do with quality," she snapped. "It's a piece of you. I just wanted a piece of you here with me."

Interesting. Perhaps she's more romantic at heart than I imagined . . . even if she's expressing it poorly.

"Well, I'm glad."

Abbie snorted, then let her head drop again. *Lord, she hasn't been this grouchy since last month, the last time she had her . . .* Parker subtly looked at his watch to check the date and quickly did the math in his head. *Ah. That explains it. Perhaps I didn't do anything wrong, except be a man.* He recalibrated himself to tread lightly around her . . . This time of the month seemed to be full of landmines. And since he was indeed a man, his mind skipped again to calculate the next few occurrences in order to record them, the last one falling . . . over their honeymoon. His heart fell. Surely not. As much as he loved her, he had little desire to be trapped with her grumpy self on an island, finally alone, unable to consummate their marriage. Yes, there were other things to do, but . . . but . . . his insides were whimpering. He had to say something.

"Say," he started, "is there any chance it's your . . ." She glared at him, daring him to continue. "Time of the month?" Her face reddened, but before she could start yelling, he rushed on, "And I only ask because it seems like it might put a cramp in the festivities during Twelfth Month, pun intended."

"You like to live dangerously, Broward?"

He grinned. "I suppose I do."

"It shouldn't be an issue. My cycles are short. I usually only go twenty-three days between."

He did the math again. She was right, it wouldn't intersect with their honeymoon. *Whew.*

He paused. "Is there anything I can do to ease your suffering?" She wrinkled her nose at him, and he chuckled. "I'll take that as a no. When's this dinner I'm having with Kurt?"

"Tomorrow night."

"Are you nervous about it?" She shrugged, but he couldn't see her face. "Come on, don't just lie there. Tell me about your day."

She rolled over and sat up. "You want to hear about my day? Fine. My guts hurt, and the acetaminophen I took isn't doing anything for it." She took a deep breath. "My brother yelled at me for touching his books when I tried to talk to him earlier about the budget clarifications that the committee wanted back three weeks ago. I'm dropping everything, I found a hole in my favorite sweater this morning. Everything in my closet is either too big or too small, and I have no appropriate work clothes because my last job required a uniform."

"Well, that last one's easily solved. Let's go shopping."

She sighed. "I love you, but you're an idiot." He suppressed the desire to tell her not to be abusive.

"But you just said . . ."

"Hon, I'm totally bloated and exhausted. I don't want to go out."

"Come on, it'll be fun. I never get to dress you up."

She lifted one eyebrow. "What do you even know about women's clothing?"

"Plenty. I've got four sisters who talk too much." He reached for her hand and pulled her to her feet, circling her, looking her up and down. Abbie's hands were fidgeting at her sides under his assessing gaze, and he smirked. *Get used to it, woman. I'm going to be spending a lot of time looking at you very soon.* "I bet you look great in a flouncy skirt and an off-the-shoulder sweater, cashmere. Or we could go more traditional and put you in a pencil skirt and an oxford blouse . . . but that wouldn't be as comfortable." He was more talking to himself now, but he kept going. "Ooh! Or we could get you a tunic and leggings. I bet your legs look fantastic in leggings and ballet flats, and they'd be cozier in the winter. Did you know they make fleece-lined leggings? They do. I'm almost jealous of your legs." She was watching him with a look of bemusement. Without a word, she walked over to her desk, grabbed her purse and tilted her head toward the door.

He must've done something right, because she held his hand in the carriage. He had security call ahead, and by the time they got to the mall, the stores they were interested in had been checked out. Since it was the weekend, there were more people than usual, but it wasn't crowded. *Thank you, internet shopping.* The first place was kind of a bust; mostly petites or "women's" sizes, which he quickly learned wasn't Abbie's size at all.

"I'm a size twelve, thank you very much," she'd fumed when he'd offered her a striped knit dress that looked quite comfortable. "That's way too big." Lesson learned, he always pulled sizes that looked smaller than hers after that. The second place seemed more like her style: bohemian, loose, natural fabrics . . . but maybe not quite right if she wanted to be taken seriously at work. The third place was a jackpot: he loaded her up with silky skirts, pants, and blouses with lace at the edges and sent her off to the dressing rooms. Prepared to kill time, he sat on the couch with a dozing middle-aged man who'd clearly been dragged along on the shopping expedition. Giving the guy a nod, he pulled out his phone to work for a few minutes while he was waiting, just to check in . . . and when he looked up, twenty minutes had gone by.

"Abs, are you ever coming out?"

He heard her grumbling from the stalls, and the other guy looked up. "You're not . . . You're not King Edward, are you?"

"Yes, I am." He smiled. "And you are?"

"Luke Gregoff . . ." He dropped his voice, so as not to be overheard. "And I'd like to apologize in advance for my wife's response when she sees you, if she ever comes out of the dressing room."

"Yeah, what do they do in there? What takes so long?"

"No idea. No clue. But my wife's never going to let me leave once she finds out Princess Abelia shops here."

"Princess Abelia *doesn't* shop here, because it's all polyester and rayon." Abbie had come out while he wasn't paying attention, looking peeved . . . and fabulous. Parker was momentarily speechless. The pinstriped gray dress pants made her legs look a mile long, and the violet lace cap-sleeve wrap top showed just a little of her cleavage.

She crossed her arms and went on. "Do you know how bad polyester is for the environment? Spoiler alert: it's terrible."

"You're kind of ruining this for me," he murmured as he stared at her, and he heard Luke chuckle.

She blinked for a moment, then gave him an embarrassed smile as her cheeks glowed. "You like it?"

"I love it. And you may not be able to keep the same standards here as you had in Gardenia, love." He could see her stewing about that, considering her options. "But just think, other women may share your concerns. You and Kurt could work on that, make Brevspor come into the modern age of clothing production."

"But what kind of example am I setting if I just cave and wear it anyway?"

The waiting man's wife stepped out of the dressing stall and stopped. "Your Highness?"

"Yes?" Abbie said, distracted, as she tried to see herself better in the full-length mirror.

The woman gave her husband a wide-eyed look, which only intensified when she noticed Parker sitting beside him.

"Your Majesty . . ."

"Yes." Parker smiled. "I've just had a nice chat with your husband. You're a lucky woman."

She emitted a garbled sound that might have been agreement, then quickly left the dressing room area, still clinging to a large armful of clothing. Luke raised an eyebrow at him, as if to say, "See?" then hurried to follow her.

"Hang on," Abbie said, "I think there were a few that were tencel . . . Let me go see, I'll be right back." She paused. "Are you okay just waiting here?"

"Of course."

She smiled and bit her lip a little; that tiny sign of attraction that drove him crazy.

"What?"

"You just look so cute, sitting there, chatting it up with the other husband . . ."

"Cute?" Kittens were cute. Babies were cute. *I'm not cute.* His face must have telegraphed his thoughts, because she full-on grinned at him.

"I'm sorry, I thought cute was a compliment. You're a stud. You're a stallion."

"That's better." His response sent her chuckling back into her stall, and she shut the door. He'd just opened an email from his father when her shrill voice came over the top of the door.

"How is this $100? It's a *shirt*, for crying out loud . . ."

"Don't worry about it, I'm paying anyway."

"No, you're not," she sang back.

He silently signaled to one of the roaming saleswomen, slipping his credit card into her hand with instructions not to let Abelia pay for a single damn thing. *New job or no, I'm taking care of her. Whether she wants me to or not.*

She glared at him when they went to check out, but her anger was quickly spent. She'd bought enough clothes to get her through an average work week; he'd even found her a blue cocktail dress for their joint bridal shower which she'd seemed to love.

"Would you like to talk through the guest list for the masquerade now, without prying eyes or ears?" he asked as they climbed back into the carriage.

"Sure," she said.

He pulled out his phone. "I've got king and queen of Op'Ho'Lonia, the Forgelands, New Pyet, Lethos, Trella . . . no Gratha for obvious reasons, though he'll probably crash and be pissed like he usually does. I didn't think we'd invite Blair, either, since the Descareti will be there."

"No Kiriien?"

He pulled his lips to one side. "It's a bit awkward because of Heather."

She blinked. "Lincoln's fiancée Heather?"

"Yes."

He ignored Dean's irritated gaze. His lead security still wasn't sold on Abbie's plan to lure Lincoln to them, but then again, he wasn't integral to the plan, so it didn't really matter. Still, Parker didn't like to go against his wishes . . . They had trust; Dean was almost a friend. He didn't want to break that.

"Oh my Woz." Her tone was hushed. "I just figured it out." She held out a hand. "Give me your phone."

"Why?"

"I need to see the letter that was on your bed."

"I have it," Dean offered, scrolling to the right photo and passing it across the carriage.

She shook her head, letting her hand fall to her lap. "How could we have been so stupid? It was right in front of us!" She showed Parker the screen. "There's no signature on this note. Is this Lincoln's handwriting?"

Parker furrowed his brow. He hadn't looked at it that closely before; panic had overtaken him at the message, leaving the handwriting unexamined. "No, come to think of it. So whose is it?"

"Who else stood to inherit your kingdom?" she asked.

"Heather."

She nodded, pointing at the phone for emphasis. "Heather. She's part of this, far more than we realized." Abbie pulled out her phone and scrolled until she found the picture she was looking for. "These books were at Hearth House."

He took the phone and peered at it. "Poetry anthologies? I've never known Lincoln to read poetry. He was more of a sports guy, honestly."

"Exactly. What if they're hers?"

"How would they have gotten to Hearth House?"

She raised an eyebrow. "How indeed. Didn't she go to college near there?"

He nodded. "In northern Brevspor, just across the border. Guttencrat, I think."

"So," she said, "is it possible they met at Hearth House to . . ."

"To what?"

"I'm not going to say it, Parker."

"What—you think they were going there to have *sex*? How do you get from random poetry books to *sex*? Couldn't they just be meeting to hang out? Why does your mind jump immediately to—"

"Stop saying that word," she hissed, glancing at his security, who appeared to be trying valiantly to keep a straight face. "The spines were worn. The pages were dog-eared. And if you'd read the contents of said books, you'd know why." She passed him her phone and pointed to another picture. She'd taken a picture of one of the poems on a marked page.

FIREFLY

> Like a summer night,
> My lover is sense and heat
> A storm of lingering touch
> Like falling rain, his kisses come
> Fat, wet drops fall on my skin
> And my restraint won't be called back
> It drifts away like a firefly

When I open the jar.

PARKER FELT HIS FACE heating as he read the poem. Abbie was watching him with her eyebrows raised.

"I do see your meaning about the contents, but how do you know it's from her?"

She shook her head. "I don't know for sure, but the poet is Kiriien, just like Heather. Thusnelda Greene is famous there. I'd never heard of her; have you?"

"No," he said, "but honestly, I don't go in much for poetry."

"Someone in Lincoln's life does. He *hid* those books up there. Why weren't they at Bluffton?"

He stared at the photo again. "I can't answer that."

"Unless he's leading a much more alternative lifestyle than we've been led to believe, his only other friends were guys. It's got to be Heather. She wrote this note; she's the only person that makes sense. Think about it: How would you feel if you thought you were going to be queen, only to find out you're ending up with nothing but a marriage contract to an exile?"

"I'd be pissed," said Dean. His thoughtful, determined gaze toward Abbie made Parker think his head of security was coming around to Abbie's scheme . . .

"Exactly. You'd be pissed. You'd want it back. And if you're the man in love with her, you'd do almost anything to get it for her. And that kind of desperation is exactly what we're counting on."

Dean's eyes came to Parker's. "I'm in."

CHAPTER THIRTY-TWO

57 days to the wedding

FIFTEEN MINUTES INTO dinner Saturday night, Kurt still hadn't shown. Abbie's huffy annoyance was grating on his own nerves, so Parker wiped his mouth with his napkin, patted her hand, and went to Kurt's study to fetch him. He edged between the stacks of books, stopping to look at the titles... They didn't seem to be related. Most were historical.

"Kurt, mate, you in there?" he called genially. Something crashed in the study, and Kurt's face appeared in the doorway, his smile brilliant. When he wasn't sulking or complaining, he was a handsome young man; Parker saw a lot of Faith in him, more so than Paul. Faith's beauty had been downright intimidating, even before he was old enough to feel any kind of attraction toward women. Abbie's beauty, though still captivating, was more subtle; she didn't feel the need to wield it as a weapon as Faith had.

"You're here. Is it Saturday already?"

"Don't you have a secretary to remind you of engagements?"

Kurt waved away the question. "I fired him. Couldn't stand him just sitting around, staring. Come in, come in. Did you eat?"

"Well, we were in the process of . . . Abbie thought you were planning to join us."

"Yes, of course. Why didn't anyone call me? I was just absorbed in this book . . ." His voice trailed off to a mumble Parker couldn't understand. Parker started back toward the hallway, but he could see that Kurt was struggling to leave.

"Abbie won't mind waiting a bit for us," Parker said, but Kurt snorted. "Well"—Parker grinned—"perhaps she will mind, but she can't have her way *all* the time . . .Woz knows I bend to her will often enough. Let's talk in here, just as mates. Tell me what's on your mind."

Kurt sat behind his desk, and Parker took a place in the chair across from him. It was slightly odd to be on this side of the balance of power, and he nudged the distracting thought away. He could hear Kurt's knee bouncing under the desk.

"Abs said you can't marry. Is that right?"

Kurt nodded, avoiding eye contact.

"And why's that, mate?"

"No one's going to understand. I just . . . it's impossible. That's all. It's impossible."

"Impossible because . . . ," Parker prompted, folding his hands across his flat belly, leaning back. "You don't like girls?"

Kurt gave him a lascivious grin, and Parker mirrored it.

"All right, you like girls. Impossible because you fear commitment?"

Kurt shook his head.

"Impossible because you hate Klara?"

Kurt picked up a book and hugged it to his chest like a child might do with a teddy bear. "It's got nothing to do with

Klara, though I do hate her. She treated Abelia like trash as a girl. Check that: she treated all of the younger heirs like dirt, including me."

"So, marriage is impossible because . . . Are you injured, mate? Some kind of accident?"

Kurt laughed without humor. "If only. That'd be a lot easier to explain." Parker could see his throat bob as he struggled to swallow. "I hear voices."

Parker froze. "What?"

"I hear voices in my head. Mostly when no one's around."

His fingers itched to text Abbie, to send out an SOS, but he forced himself to stay calm.

"That's not good, mate." *I have never felt more out of my depth than I do right now.*

Kurt laughed again, wiping a tear with the heel of his hand. "I know, Edward. Trust me, I know."

"What do they say, these . . . voices?"

Kurt shrugged. "Some are okay; they speculate. They ask questions. Sometimes they even encourage me . . . But some of them"—he glanced toward the doorway, as if he were afraid who would appear in it—"some are cruel."

Parker wanted to scoop Abbie up, put her on the train and take her back to Bluffton tonight. Away from here, away from Kurt. But this wasn't just a disturbed roommate of hers; this was her *brother*. That didn't keep his protection instincts from kicking in full force, but it tempered them a little. Kurt obviously needed help. What if this were Andrew sitting there, tears on his face, bearing his secret, the secret that could end his career if his opponents knew?

"Thank you, Kurt. Thank you for telling me that." He leaned forward. "I realize this is a delicate situation for you, but we're friends—we're almost brothers. I'm not going to tell anyone without your permission, all right? We'll keep this between us for now, but mate, we've got to get you some help eventually."

Kurt nodded, still wiping tears away. "Okay." That one word was so tortured; it was just one word, but there was suffering and relief both in it. *Had Paul known about this?* His mentor certainly would've gotten his son the help he needed; Parker couldn't believe that he would've let Kurt spiral like this.

"Can I tell Abelia what we spoke about?"

Kurt met his gaze. Conflict lay just below the surface.

"The worst voice . . . ," Kurt choked out, "it sounds just like her. I don't know why," he sobbed. "I'm sorry. I'm so sorry."

Parker was out of his seat before Kurt stopped talking, coming around the desk. He knelt in front of him, one hand on Kurt's shoulder. "We're going to get you some help, brother. I promise. She'll understand; it's not your fault. You tell us what we need to do, and we'll do it."

"Okay." He nodded, gave a shaky sigh, still trying to wipe away all the tears. "Okay."

"You're right about one thing, though, mate . . ."

"What's that?"

"You can't marry until we can work on this . . . You'll scare the shit out of her."

Kurt laughed, and this time, it wasn't all pain.

A FEW MINUTES LATER, Parker sat back down at the dinner table.

"Well? Is he coming or what?"

"No. Not coming." He shoved a dinner roll, now cold, into his mouth.

She clanged her fork down onto her plate. "Of course not. Why do I even bother?" She crossed her arms. "Did you talk to him, though? You were gone basically forever."

"Now you know how I felt outside the dressing rooms yesterday," he said, smiling, then sobered. "Yes, I spoke to him."

"And?"

"And he's right; he can't marry. Not right now, anyway."

"Is it Klara, does he not like her? What about someone else?"

Parker shook his head slowly, spearing a forkful of salad. "It's not just Klara."

"Why then?"

"Why?" Parker echoed, trying to figure out how to get her to back off without actually telling her anything, as he'd promised Kurt. Her cold gaze told him that her patience was expiring.

"I can't tell you that, yet. But I can tell you that his problems are real and valid." He chewed and swallowed a bite of food. "And he and I are going to work on it. We may have to bring you into it eventually. In the meantime," he said, taking a sip of wine that turned into a huge gulp, "I suggest that you email him if you need something."

"He's that angry with me?"

Seeing the tears in her eyes, he reached for her hand and squeezed it. "Actually," he started gently, "it's not 100 percent about you in this case, love. It'll be okay, darling. Just give him time."

CHAPTER THIRTY-THREE

52 days to the wedding

ABBIE SPENT THE REST of the week giving Kurt space, as Parker had suggested. When she did see him in person, he regarded her warily, but with less vitriol. When she emailed him, he wrote back; Parker had set up his phone to receive emails so he didn't have to sit in front of a computer. Abbie was still working at 8:23 at night, trying to finish reading some committee notes that they wanted Kurt's feedback on. Her phone plinked.

Unknown contact: Good evening, Abelia, this is Rhodie.

Unknown contact: I wanted to extend you an invitation to my book club next week; you'd have to come out a bit earlier, as it's on Thursday night.

Unknown contact: I hope you'll be able to join us.

Abbie called Parker.

"Hello?" From the sound of it, he, too, was still working.

"She invited me to book club, what do I say?"

"Hello, beautiful," he chuckled.

"No time for chitchat, man—*what do I say?*"

"Who invited you to book club?"

"Super Princess."

"Oh, how lovely."

"You didn't put her up to it?"

"Not me. Perhaps Mum did. Do you want to go?"

"I don't know. I think so. I want her to respect me. It feels significant that she's asking."

"Then say yes." Parker yawned.

"But what if she's just trying to be nice?"

"Then you'll be trying to be nice, too, plus you may make some new friends in Orangiers."

"Oh, you're no help."

Parker chuckled again. "So sorry, darling. I do try."

"It's not your fault."

"That's generous of you."

She paused. "I'm going to go."

"Good."

PARKER OFFERED TO DROP her off, but Abbie preferred to go alone. She wanted a few minutes to do her presocialization routine: *You can do this. You're reasonably likeable. They're probably not judging you too hard. Your hair isn't that big. You'll be fine.* She drummed her fingers on her knees in the carriage. Maybe her psych-up speech needed work; it was realistic, but not all that encouraging. She felt itchy—not physically, just emotionally. These were Rhodie's friends. They were used to the princess thing. But they were used to Rhodie's version of it, not hers. *So perfect, so controlled . . .*

She knocked on apartment 401, Tezza in tow. *Wait,* she thought, *shouldn't Rhodie's security be out here?* The door swung open, and a smiling redhead in a tight-fitting purple top greeted her.

"Abelia, right?"

At least she didn't call me Your Highness.

"Yes. Carla, right?"

"Carlie. Yeah, come on in, Rhodie should be here anytime now . . . She's usually late."

No wingman? No buffer? Abbie could feel the sweat already gathering on her back. The host handed her a glass of red wine, and Abbie said nothing to stop her. *I'll just hold it. I won't drink it. No one has to know.*

"So Abbie, you're in waste management, is that right?"

She nodded, grasping for something more interesting to talk about than the job she'd just quit. "I just started consulting for my brother a month ago . . . not on waste management—though given the state of his quarters, he could use some advice."

Carlie laughed, and without thinking about it, Abbie took a sip of her wine. It was good. *So good.* Everyone else was drinking . . . Surely she could have just one glass. She didn't want to be different right now, couldn't lay it all out for them, all her issues, the moment they met.

There was red-haired Carlie, the bookkeeper at the geology firm. *The redhead keeps the rock people out of the red. I can remember that.* Black-haired Bridgette, who used to be a nurse but stayed home with her kids now (a boy and a girl, five and two), married to Carter, a doctor; they'd met at work. *Bridgette checked the blood pressure before the big doc bought the big rock, now she bounces babies.* Mariona from Op'Ho'Lonia was single; also dark-haired, but hers was curly. She'd been in medical school with Rhodie but dropped out to be an artist; she was still waiting for her big break, but working at her parents' furniture store was cool, too . . . Abbie couldn't think of a mnemonic for her. Such an eclectic group of women, and yet they all seemed to get along so well.

Abbie had made it to about half of the participants to learn their names, family status, and professions when Rhodie finally arrived. The mood in the room shifted, as if they'd all been subconsciously waiting for her, and the women moved toward the seating. Touching her elbow,

Rhodie whispered, "Pardon my intrusion, but should you be drinking that?" Abbie paled when she realized her glass had been emptied and refilled twice over. She hurried into the kitchen to put the glass far away from her, even knowing that it was likely too late to prevent a reaction with her medication.

They were funny; she hadn't laughed so hard in weeks. She especially liked Bridgette, who seemed to have a forthright way about her that Abbie appreciated.

"We're gonna want details when you get back from your honeymoon, love," she said with a wink. "We've been dancing with Edward long enough to know . . ."

"Stop right there," Rhodie said, holding up a prim hand. "I've no desire to hear any of this. That's my little brother, and I lent him to you with the promise that you would not objectify him."

"Oh, *we're* not objectifying him." Mari giggled. "We want *Abbie* to objectify him, then tell us all about it!" Rhodie rolled her eyes, and the room filled with laughter. Abbie just shook her head.

"An un-queen never kisses and tells, ladies. I must maintain royal discretion . . ." Then she stage-whispered, "At least until Rhodie goes to Trella!" More fits of giggles, and she saw even Tezza was smirking.

"Enough tangents, back to the book," Rhodie announced over the chatter, and they dutifully quieted. The meeting broke up around nine and Abbie was in bed by ten.

SINCE ABBIE WAS VOMITING again when Parker knocked on her bedroom door at ten thirty the next morning, she decided not to answer. It would be awkward, she decided, to explain her current state. It was a bad reaction to mixing alcohol with her methotrexate, not a hangover, but it was still going to cast a pall on her day. He was bound to be . . . displeased. A knock sounded on the bathroom door this time.

"Abs? You okay?"

"No." *Damn it, couldn't he give me another ten minutes to get cleaned up before he finds out the truth?*

"What's wrong?" He tried the door, but she'd wisely locked it. He had a bad habit of entering without asking . . . She assumed it was a lifetime of royal privilege, but maybe he was just presumptuous. She did not think that marriage would encourage him in the right direction, either. "Open the door."

"You're not going to watch me throw up, Parker. That's weird."

"Fine, open the door, and I promise to stare at the ceiling if you start to vomit. I'm not great with bodily fluids anyway. Have I mentioned that you're changing all diapers, forever?"

She groaned, her stomach lurching again. "Don't make me laugh, please."

"What's going on, Abs?" She didn't say anything, tried to get to her feet, but her legs weren't cooperating. "I'm not going to leave, so if you're planning to wait me out . . ."

"You're awfully pushy sometimes, you know that?"

"I give as good as I get, woman. Now *open the door*."

Abbie crawled across the tile and unlocked the door, then sat back as he blasted into the room, concern knitting his brows.

"Are you sick?"

"Not exactly, no."

He crossed his arms, his skepticism plain on his face.

She shook her head. "But I did drink."

He stiffened. "You're not supposed to drink."

"I know. I did anyway."

"Why?" His question was laced with such scorn that it lit her anger like a rocket engine.

"Because I was uncomfortable and everyone else was doing it, okay? Because Rhodie was late and I was alone in a room full of women I didn't know and I wanted to feel like I belonged there. That's why!"

"But you know better!"

"Of course I jacking know better! But knowing doesn't have anything to do with how it feels to be excluded, even inadvertently. Knowing is in my head, and it just didn't translate."

"Don't make excuses. You have to take better care of yourself."

Abbie's eyebrows bounced so high, she was surprised they stayed on her face. "Excuse you?"

"I said—"

"Yes, I heard what you said. And it was *the wrong thing to say*, you idiot." She pointed at the door. "Now get out of my bathroom. I need to throw up again."

"I have absolutely no sympathy for you," he said as he stormed out.

Despite her roiling stomach, she moved to the doorway to yell after him. "Yes, Your Majesty, that's patently obvi—" Whoops. Well, she almost made it to the toilet.

ABBIE WAS STILL FUMING over his words as she went to see what lunch was available; despite her nausea, her stomach was painfully empty. *You know better? Of course I know better. I know it twenty-four seven, and it gets old. I do nothing but take good care of myself, almost all the time. But I screwed up, and I don't need my nose rubbed in it like a puppy being potty-trained. If I wasn't trying to establish detente with his sister, I never would've been in that position! I've taken care of myself just fine on my own for years now. I don't need his guilt trips and badgering . . .* And speaking of guilt, her own was now piping up, reminding her that he wasn't entirely wrong, even if he was being a jerk about it, that she didn't need to call him names . . .

She pulled out her phone.

Abbie: I'm sorry I called you an idiot.

No response. She tucked her phone into her back pocket as she sat down to lunch, but the conversation and his lack of response stayed at the front of her brain. A sandwich definitely held no appeal, so she spooned herself some melon, trying not to think about their shape . . . *Chunks* was a very unwelcome word in her brain right now. Almond milk tasted weird in her mouth, and she set it aside, opting for water. Maybe some applesauce would taste good . . .

She pulled out her phone again. Still no answer.

Abbie: Did you get my message?

The three dots appeared immediately.

Parker: Yes.

Abbie frowned.

Abbie: And?

Parker: And I don't like being insulted.

This is ridiculous, she thought. *We just need to talk this out, face-to-face.*

Abbie: Where are you?

Parker: Went for a run.

Abbie: I'll come meet you.

Parker: No.

No? Um. What? It wasn't that they didn't disagree or argue opposing viewpoints . . . but this was different. He never turned down a bid for attention, time together. Until that moment, she'd mostly felt annoyed at him for being too sensitive . . . but now, real panic started to set in. *Since when does he not want to see me? That's . . . new.*

Abbie: Get back here. We need to talk about this.

No response. Her anger roared back to life, a booster rocket to ease her transition back into the argument.

Abbie: Are you seriously ignoring me right now?

No response.

Abbie: Last chance before I do something drastic.

Parker: I don't like being threatened, either.

Abbie: Have it your way.

Rage made her efficient. Abbie had her things packed and back on the train in under twenty minutes. By the time Parker got back to the castle, she hoped she'd be halfway back to Kohlstadt.

CHAPTER THIRTY-FOUR

44 days to the wedding

ABBIE HAD TEXTED MRS. Braun that she'd be back early, figuring she would fill Kurt in if it suited her. He probably wouldn't care either way. She was answering emails on the train, trying not to think about what she'd just done, when her phone plinked.

Parker: I'm back. Where are you?

She read it on the lock screen, then turned off her phone, so it wouldn't mark his messages as read. *You want to ignore me? Fine. Two can play at that game.* But another voice, a more sensible one than the enraged one she was currently listening to, muttered that this tactic wasn't going to work after Twelfth Month. That she should start adapting now . . . if only she knew how. She had no model for this. Her father had always done what her mother said, publicly anyway, not only because she was his queen, but because that's how they worked. She knew he'd manipulated things in the background, but he never openly defied her. No one had . . . until Abbie ran away. Now she was stuck trying to rule her relationships in the same way . . . *If he loved me, he'd obey me.* The sensible voice chimed in again at that . . . *If? You know he loves you. That's why he wants to see you healthy, not lying on the bathroom floor ghostly pale with the contents of your stomach in the toilet . . . or near it, anyway. Don't be a fool.*

It was too late for that, though. She'd taken off, probably the worst thing she could've done. She'd made him look foolish: he'd have to ask his staff if they knew where she was, feel the sting of embarrassment when they informed him of her departure. His family knew she was supposed to stay all weekend; they'd ask why she left, and knowing him, he'd tell them the truth. Abbie swore softly under her breath, and Georgie looked over.

"Everything okay?"

"No." Abbie massaged her temples. "I screwed up. Twice. Three times, actually . . . Woz, it's been a great weekend, huh?"

"Want to talk about it?"

"You're my employee."

Georgie said nothing but looked away. Tezza was fast asleep with her coat over her head a few seats over.

"Sorry, Georgie; I shouldn't have said that. Woz, what is wrong with me?" She shook her head, putting her hands back on the keyboard.

"Technically, I'm *his* employee, if that helps."

Abbie laughed softly. "I don't know if it helps. I'm so screwed up."

"Who isn't?" Georgie tossed back a handful of complimentary nuts. "It's okay. We all make mistakes. Just talk to him."

ABBIE, GEORGIE, AND a half-asleep Tezza trudged into the state castle in Kohlstadt. It was only a four-hour trip, but it was exhausting and dirty. She decided to go shower. Abbie went straight to her quarters and whipped her shirt off before her door had even shut all the way.

"Ahem."

Abbie screamed, covering her chest with her shirt. Parker stood in the corner of her bedroom, his skin blending perfectly into the dark. Georgie had the door open before she could blink, then upon seeing her boss, quietly excused herself.

"What the jack, Parker? You scared me half to death!"

"*I* scared *you* half to death?" He stalked toward her, and she backed up instinctively even before she could see the rage in his expression. "*I* scared *you?* Do you have any idea how terrifying it was to come back from my run and find you just . . . gone? Like you'd been snatched? Like Lincoln made good on his promise?"

Her lip trembled, and she bit it. *Oops. Yeah, that never occurred to me . . .*

"And then to have your phone not even receiving my messages when I was desperately trying to reach you, trying to make sure you were okay, even though I was still insanely livid with you?"

Her voice came out as a whisper. "I didn't think about it like that . . ."

"Yes, the first part of your sentence is correct: you didn't think. You just reacted, to the benefit of no one but yourself. We didn't figure out you'd left of your own volition until an underbutler heard the commotion and said he'd carried your bags out to the train!" His volume increased even more. "I had half the palace staff searching the grounds for you!"

Abbie's temper flared, and she wanted to put her hands on her hips, but still needed to cover her chest.

"I did warn you I would resort to drastic measures." He stared at her, slack-jawed, and she pressed on. "Why didn't you come back and talk to me?"

"Are you . . . are you actually trying to blame *me* for this?" he bellowed.

"You're at least partly to blame," she shouted back. "You can't pin it all on me, either." Her lip was trembling violently, and she felt the tears coming. *He's* yelling *at me. He's never yelled at me like this.* Not just tears, sobs. She choked the first one back, but there were more—a lot more. She needed to get rid of him. Now. She lifted her chin defiantly. "You should leave."

"No, that's your role, apparently."

Abbie flinched like she'd been slapped, and it helped her swallow the sobs down. He stepped closer to her, and she could smell the sweat still clinging to his running clothes. He hadn't even stopped to change.

"I told you in the Unveiled," he growled, "we're not going to succumb to dramatics, we're not going to act like loons. I meant it. You've got a problem with me, you stick around long enough to talk it out."

"Oh, because flying in a blimp to beat me here isn't dramatic? And I tried to talk it out, but you stonewalled me. You wouldn't listen, you wouldn't even see me. What would've been the point in staying?"

"I was coming to talk to you. I just wasn't ready. I needed to blow off some steam first! Woz, Abbie, I was only gone an hour and a half!"

"Well, it was too long. I tried to make things right and you didn't want to. You don't get to treat me like fertilizer then avoid the fallout. You've got a nasty habit of that lately."

He threw out his arms to both sides. "What the Jersey are you referring to?"

"I'm referring to you forcing me to take security. I'm talking about you pressuring me to move. I'm talking about you abandoning me at the diplomatic breakfast in Orangiers to talk to your 'friend.' I sat there squirming, awkwardly making conversation with Van Hecke while you gave her a very friendly goodbye, and then treated *me* like the villain. What about that?"

"What about it? There was absolutely nothing inappropriate about my interactions with her, and you know it."

"Do I? I didn't see you. I was busy getting roped into a job I hate. Because of you. And I'm living in Brevspor with my borderline-crazy brother because of you. And I have to do all of this stupid wedding shit because of you! So before you get in my face about my choices, maybe consider a few of your own for a moment." She stepped into his personal space and got into his face, wishing she were wearing heels so they were eye to eye. "This argument, this whole thing is on you."

The vitriol in his words hurt, but it was the coldness in his eyes that stung. "Perhaps I should spare you from interacting with me, since I seem to be the source of all your problems." He pushed past her bare shoulder and opened the door.

She could barely comprehend what was happening. "Where the Jersey do you think you're going?"

"Considering this has been one of the worst days of my life, I believe I'll go home." He was gone before Abbie realized she was standing alone, shirtless, in the dark.

THREE DAYS WENT BY. She felt the silence was going on too long, but she wasn't sure how to break it. On Tuesday, she finally had a valid reason to contact him. Abbie felt than an email might be better received than a text message. Secretly, she also believed that if he was busy and didn't write back right away, it wouldn't hurt her feelings so much. Self-preservation, it seemed, was not exclusive to the single life.

~~Parker,~~ *Edward,*

~~How are you?~~ Just wondering if you had a chance to look at those fabric samples for aisle runners. ~~I don't know if you cared about that.~~ The coordinator needs to get them ordered soon ~~assuming this is still happening.~~ Hope you're having a good week. ~~I miss you.~~ How did your meeting go with the Forgelands ambassador on Monday?

I am still planning to come next weekend to meet your friends. Please let me know if I should change my plans.

Love,

Abbie

Within the hour, she received his reply.

Abbie,

Choose whatever fabric you prefer. My week is going fine. I hope yours is too.

See you next weekend.

His Royal Highness Edward Kenneth Keith Francis Benson Broward

King of Orangiers

She looked around her quiet office at the antique desk lamp, her gleaming cherry desk, her neat stacks of paperwork. *What a very businesslike response.* He didn't even change his signature. That's what he gave everyone: polite distance. But it was never what he'd given her; he'd always given her more. She found herself pathetically searching celebrity news sites for indicators of how his week was actually going; not that they usually got things right. There was suddenly no one to say good morning to, no one to check in with at lunchtime, no flirty texts while she brushed her teeth for bed. For someone who was supposed to be the source of all her problems, her life felt painfully empty without him.

CHAPTER THIRTY-FIVE

35 days to the wedding

"HEY."

"Hello." They stood awkwardly together outside Bluffton as her things were removed from the train. Abbie twisted her rings, needing something to do with her hands. There had been no kiss in greeting, not even a peck for show.

"How are you?" she asked. He wouldn't give her his gaze.

"Fine, and you?"

"I've been better," she said. Based on the look on his face, her honesty surprised them both. Edward recovered quickly and started down the hall. She touched his elbow hesitantly. Slowly, he came to a stop and turned to face her, arms crossed.

"Look," she said quietly, "I'm not going to embarrass you. There's no reason for anyone to know that we're fighting. Let's just put on happy faces and get through this."

"Agreed. As far as they know, our situation is unchanged."

"I haven't told anyone, either," she said. His eyes met hers, and the mélange of emotions she saw there was almost dizzying. "But it isn't unchanged, is it?" she said softly.

His gaze hardened. "I'm not doing this with you now." He turned and strode down the hall. Abbie followed Parker into the game room, where two of his friends were already waiting.

"Lieutenant Saint you already know . . ."

"Good to see you again." She really was happy to see him, but her smile was forced and she knew it wasn't reaching her eyes. He gave her a friendly nod in return.

Edward gestured toward the other man. "And this is Simonson."

"Simonson." She got a handshake, but no eye contact. He kept his black hair shaved close to his head, and though he was black, his skin was much lighter than Parker's—redder, too. "Great to meet you, Sam." At the use of his first name, Abbie was rewarded with a fleeting glance in her direction and a tight-lipped smile as he looked away.

"Simonson's afraid of princesses, Abbie, don't take it personally," Saint said, grinning. He'd stopped calling her ma'am after he'd tasted her cookies on board the transport.

"I'm not afraid," Sam countered, "I just don't want to—"

"A. Look at them? B. Speak to them? C. Touch them? D. Acknowledge their presence, by accident or on purpose? The answer is E, all of the above." This came from James, who had strolled in while the others were being introduced. He stuck his hand out, and his V-neck T-shirt shifted so she could see some of the scars on his chest.

"I'm Arron. You may call me James, Lieutenant, or Arron. I also answer to Sex God."

Without batting an eye, Abbie volleyed back. "Sorry, I'm saving that nickname for someone else."

"Who, Edward? But he's a god as yet unworshipped, love, whereas I'm tried and true. I deserve it much more. But any god worth his salt appreciates loyalty, so may your devotion be rewarded." He crossed her like he was offering a benediction as he spoke, and despite everything, it made her giggle. "What are we playing?"

"If we bowl, everybody can play," Simonson offered.

"Oh," James cried, "I love how my avatar looks in his little shirt with all the flowers and the parrots!"

Saint and Parker protested, but Abbie interrupted.

"I can just watch, I don't mind."

Parker scowled and opened his mouth to speak, but he was too slow.

"Fair princess," James began, "art thy sensibilities too fragile, too feminine for all those pointy pins and large balls?"

"Look, I know you guys are usually blowing things up and storming castles when you play. You don't have to play kids' games for my benefit. I'm just here to hang out."

"Kids' games?" Saint asked, perplexed.

"You know, bowling, table tennis, Frisbee with the cute little dudes with no arms who bounce around."

All four men crossed their arms simultaneously, and it made Abbie want to step back.

"Don't blame her," Parker sighed. "It's my fault for not educating her."

Abbie crossed her own arms, feeling ganged up on. "What?"

"Those games are not just for kids."

"They're not?"

Simonson shook his head. "Not the way we play them."

"But Abbie can't drink, mates . . . ," Parker put in, and there was murmured sympathy. *I'd pay money to see them trying to play Frisbee drunk . . . They'd probably put a controller through the screen.*

"I'm not in the mood to murder anything," James said, "not with Sunshine here watching. We can't reveal Edward's true nature until they're wed. Let's race go-karts."

Saint grunted his approval. They stuck her in the middle of the long couch and put a controller in her hands.

"What does each button do?"

Parker sat down next to her, still keeping a careful distance. "It's better if you figure it out as we go. We'll do some practice runs."

"No, I like a plan of attack. I need to know how it all works first."

"But you'll remember it better if you learn it by touch. Don't worry about the letters. Your brain is pattern-seeking, you'll pick it up. Guys, back me up here."

Saint shook his head slowly. "Side against a woman, they never forget it."

Abbie lifted her hips and pulled out her phone out of her back pocket.

"What are you doing?" Parker asked.

"Looking up a schematic with directions."

"Oh no, you don't." He plucked the phone from her and tucked it under his leg.

"If you think," she said, diving for him, "that I'm afraid to go down there . . ."

"Stay away from his face," James said, cruising through the setup menu. "Our royalty have standards to maintain. We revere that face. Maim him elsewhere."

"Yes, but I need some of those other parts to maintain a dynasty . . . Woman, stop." He grabbed her wrists and held her away, and her traitorous heart started to beat faster, because he was touching her. A hundred years had passed since that happened.

"You also need a willing wife to create a dynasty, Your Majesty."

He shoved the controller back into her hands. "Pick an avatar."

She glared at him, but he leaned closer and pressed his forehead against hers.

"Trust me, Abs." *It's an act,* she told herself. *It's just an act.* The tenderness that should've made her feel warm and fuzzy just made her tense; she did not want to be kissed in front of "the guys," but she wanted him to stop withholding himself, too.

Growling, she turned back to the screen. She scrolled through the characters until she found one that suited her: a dragon.

"Wow," Simonson said. "I did not see that coming."

"She doesn't have to pick a princess, idiot," said Saint.

Abbie sniffed. "I'm going to torch my fiancé. Only virtually, of course."

"You sure about that?" Saint smirked.

She stared at the giant screen. "Mostly."

"Well, your passive-aggressive revenge will have to wait a bit," Parker said, "because I'm going to coach you through the first few rounds. Now, when the start whistle blows, you're going to move that little stick on the right forward." It was counting down from five on the screen, and she only had a moment to find the stick with her thumb before they were off. "You're the bottom right-hand square."

"I see it," she said. "Now what?"

"Now you want to pick up stuff to chuck at the other players."

"How do I do that?"

"Run over those little exclamation point boxes." Parker put his arm behind her on the back of the couch, and she jumped when his fingers traced her upper arm lightly.

"That's distracting, hon." *But he's touching me. I should've let him.*

"Sorry." He moved his fingers, but left his arm where it was.

"I'm distracted, and he's not even touching me," quipped James.

"Okay, I picked up some kind of bomb thing. How do I chuck it at James?"

"Oy! Why me? Simonson's in the lead!"

"Well," said Parker, "first, you'll have to catch up to someone. You're last."

"Damn it. You said this was practice!"

"It is practice. Good news, though; they're about to lap you, and then you'll be able to lob stuff at them as they go by."

"Doesn't that mean they could also lob stuff at *me*?" she asked.

"Yes, but we won't," said Saint. "It's not worth it."

"Ouch."

"Economics, love," James said. "When you're a threat, we'll bomb the Jersey out of you, promise."

"Also, Edward said he'd demote us if we weren't nice to you," Simonson added.

"Did you? That's sweet, babe." Her heart swelled with hope.

"Hashtag—"

"Don't say it," all three of his friends yelled, and Abbie laughed, running her go-kart off the road.

"Oh no! I crashed . . ."

"It's all right, the mechanic will pick you up in a minute."

"But now I'm even farther behind . . . I need more practice." She paused, thinking, then took a chance. "Will you get me one of these?"

His voice betrayed his surprise. "A gaming system?"

"Yeah, then we can play when you come. And maybe I can coerce Kurt into playing with me if he ever shifts out of jackass mode." *Yes, I want to play with you, Parker. We're still friends, we'll figure this out. Don't give up on me, on us,* she silently begged him.

"Yeah, sure, makes sense."

His friends fell quiet for a few minutes, each man attempting to destroy his friends, leaving Abbie untouched as she navigated the curves of the track, Parker quietly offering more tips as she mastered each new skill. She finally got a shot off on James and he cursed.

"I was about to win!"

"Bam! Who's the sex god now, sucker?" Abbie crowed.

"Broward?" Saint muttered.

"Yo."

"She's cool."

"I know."

"Hashtag un-queening," Abbie muttered, and during the ensuing hysterics, she finally pulled into the lead.

"ABBIE. ABBIE, WAKE up." She stretched, arching her back.

"What time is it?"

Game night was breaking up; bottles and plates were being gathered up and disposed of by everyone except Parker, who knelt next to her. Based on the screen, they'd switched to some kind of fantasy role-playing game after she fell asleep.

"Around midnight."

"You guys are nuts." She tried to stand up, but her body wasn't quite ready, and she wobbled before Parker caught her elbow. His knuckles grazed her breast, but she was pretty sure it was an accident and decided not to draw attention to it. Then again, his eyes were wandering up and down her body. She gave him a soft look, and he turned away. He wasn't drunk, but he wasn't sober, either. Perhaps she could capitalize on his state of mind, but first, she had to get rid of the audience.

"Good night, guys. Really nice to meet you all."

"And lovely to meet you, Abelia, lovely Abelia, bride of Edward, Abelia, ruiner of go-kart wins, beautiful princess with a mouth like a sailor," James said, his words slightly slurred. He stumbled toward her, arms out, but Saint caught him by the back of his shirt.

"Look out, Highness, he's handsy when he's drunk."

"Found that out the hard way, did you?" she replied, yawning.

Saint grinned wickedly. "I didn't kiss him back, Highness, honest." He pulled a protesting James toward the hallway.

"You'll get him home?" Parker asked, and Saint nodded once.

"Where's Simonson?"

"Probably still cleaning."

"A man after my own heart," Abbie said.

"Samuel!" James bellowed, and the others shushed him. "Samuel, the wagon's leaving. Come, Francis, let's away."

Saint smacked James upside the head. "Don't call me that."

"But it's your given name. Your name from birth. Your mum gave you that name, Francis."

"DON'T CALL ME THAT."

Sam appeared a moment later, and Abbie could hardly hear him over James continuing to argue the point with Saint.

"Sorry, there were just a few more . . ." His mouth snapped shut upon seeing Tezza standing there. Even in her mid-sleep haze, Abbie registered a strange look on his face. He caught up with the group wandering toward the exit, and she looked up to find Sam at her elbow.

"Who's that?"

"Who?"

He gestured behind them with his thumb.

"That's my night security, Tezza Macias."

He glanced over his shoulder. "She doesn't look like security."

"Don't let the breasts fool you. Do you want an introduction? She's not a princess, you should be able to talk to *her*."

Sam elbowed her ribs gently, and Abbie grinned.

"You're gonna get demoted for sure," she teased. "Parker, Sam's bothering me."

"Is he? Oh, how sad. Nobody bothers my girl; back to private for you." His voice didn't quite carry the teasing; there was too much melancholy in it, and she hoped his friends didn't hear it.

Keeping up the show, Abbie rolled her eyes. "Your 'girl'? Really?"

"Yes. Shall I prove it?" Before she could respond, Parker turned, slipped his hand behind her neck and kissed her. He was warm and tasted like hops. His mouth was insistent, hungry, still angry. It would've embarrassed her if she wasn't so desperate for his affection; she leaned into him as hard as she could and wrapped both arms around him. Since they were missing the subtext, James broke into loud whoops and applause and Saint shook his head, grinning.

Startled by Arron's outburst, Parker broke the kiss, and Abbie could see the misery on his face. She opened her mouth to let it all spill out: the "I love yous" she'd kept for him, the "I miss yous," the "I'm sorrys" she knew were necessary. But he glared at her sternly, a silent warning not to air their dirty laundry here, and let his hand fall away.

"Good night, darling. Sleep well." He stalked after his friends to see them out, and Abbie turned toward her room, swiping at her hot tears, not caring who saw. She glanced over her shoulder. He didn't look back.

CHAPTER THIRTY-SIX

31 days to the wedding

"OKAY. IT'S GO TIME. This is it. We're locking this down today. Get your head in the game, because this is the fourth quarter, and our team needs a win."

Abbie angled her head away from her best friend's verbal assault, which was difficult given her grip on her shoulders. "I know you're just being weird, but this is kind of working for me."

"Of course it is. Now get out there, slugger." Lauren slapped her backside and pushed her through the double doors where the dress designers, Queen Lily, Rhodie, Dahlia, Ginger, and Forsythia were waiting for her.

"Don't mix metaphors," Abbie muttered as she pasted on a smile. She was still nervous as Jersey, but at least she had Lauren and Patty this time; they'd both flown out for the weekend, at Parker's expense, of course. She was pretty sure they were going to have to tranquilize Patty to get her back on the blimp, but they'd cross that bridge when they came to it. Today, Lauren was right: she needed to get her head in the game. The wedding dress game. Abbie looked around for Patty, and finding her hanging back, she doubled back to drag her into the room. The girl who'd grown up under the

Sixth Street Bridge was never going to be comfortable sitting next to royalty.

"They're just people, Pattycakes. And they have good food."

"Fancy people. And don't call me that." She pulled out her phone. "Just gonna call and check on Jenny real quick."

"Nope. Put that away. Ward's got her. She's totally fine."

Patty pivoted and crossed her arms. "Gave her pickles and vanilla yogurt for lunch while I was at work last week."

"Admittedly, that is an odd choice," Abbie said, steering her friend to the pale-pink loveseat with Lauren. "But in his defense, it did have vegetables in it."

Based on a cursory look through the racks earlier, she had it down to five. Maybe six. Okay, seven, but only because it had a very unusual material. Everyone had met last night over cocktails, and this had proven to be a good idea. They were already chatting away and mostly ignoring her as she pulled the first dress she wanted and went to change.

The Browards all oohed when she came out in the high-neck gown. It was white, of course, with a sweetheart neck-line for the satin part, with a lace overlay that covered her chest and arms. Even Abbie, who knew less than nothing about lace, could tell that it was very good quality and repre-sented a lot of man hours. The sash around the middle pulled her belly in nicely, not that she needed as much help there anymore, and she liked the covered buttons that went down the front to her middle.

"Well?"

Lauren was smiling, nodding . . . but she could tell there was hesitation.

This business with Parker had her emotions on high, and her patience was gone. Abbie held out her hands to her sides. "Just say it, Laur . . ."

Lauren opened her mouth, but then her gaze drifted over to the queen and her daughters, and it suddenly snapped shut again.

"I'll say it," Patty said. "Nice dress and all, but I wore my favorite hoodie when we tied the knot. Because it felt right, felt like me. This doesn't feel like you. "

Abbie pivoted to see herself in the mirrors, and she knew Patty was right.

"I like it because it covers my chest, in case I have a flare . . ."

"That makes sense," Lauren put in quickly, "but it just doesn't seem like your usual style."

Abbie lifted the skirts carefully as she descended the dais to try another one. "Well, by that measure, none of them are going to seem like my usual style, because my usual style is cotton and relaxed fit."

The second one was a satin dress (in white) with a high bateau neckline and no embellishments to speak of. The cut was flattering, but even as she put it on, she knew what they were going to say.

"It just doesn't seem very . . . ," Lily started.

"Interesting," Ginger finished. "I like things simple, but this is too simple." The others nodded, and she trudged back to the dressing room.

They rejected the silk strapless ball gown with the hand-beaded belt, and the mermaid cut that she couldn't walk in, and the low-cut tulle nightmare that she'd only thrown out there to see what Lauren would say. "Va-va-voom," she'd quipped. "You're gonna break him if you show up in that. A man has his limits."

Abbie was still thinking about her comment when she went back to the dressing room. *This should be about him, about us. It has to say so much more than it should: it has to proclaim my love out loud.* She still had two left, but neither of them seemed right. A quiet knock startled her.

"Yes?"

No one answered, and she cracked the door open. A satin hanger appeared as Forsythia slipped another dress in.

"Try this one," she whispered. "I just want to see."

Abbie grinned at her through the cracked door. "Of course, sweetheart."

She slipped the dress on. Even without the back buttons done up properly, she knew. She stared. *This is the one.* How had she missed it? She never would've tried it, even though it met all her criteria. *I guess Lily was right; no one should dress themselves.*

Since she'd been gone a while, the conversation was flowing like the mimosas; that is, freely. Patty was showing Dahlia pictures of Jenny. Ginger was arguing with Rhodie about their bridesmaids' dresses. Lily was nodding along to something her aide Bernice was saying. But all of this stopped when Abbie stepped onto the dais. Lily's hand went to her lips.

"Oh, Abbie . . . ," Lauren said, her voice catching.

"Damn," Patty breathed.

"Yeah," Lauren said. "I mean, that's just . . . it's . . . wow."

Abbie chuckled. "If it's rendering you speechless, loud-mouth, it must be good." She turned to the Browards. "Ladies? Thoughts?"

Lily and Rhodie just nodded ardently; Abbie wondered if they didn't trust their voices to come out normally. Dahlia and Ginger, on the other hand, had no lack of gushing and praise for the garment as Thia sat quietly by, beaming at her. The queen dabbed her eyes with a handkerchief.

"Okay," Abbie said, cutting them off. "This is it, then." She turned, unable to stop looking at herself. The ladies broke into applause, and Abbie sighed a happy sigh as she retrieved her phone from Lauren.

Abbie: Found a dress. No drama. Only a few tears, none mine.

Parker: Good.

Abbie: You're going to love it.

And hopefully, it'll remind you that you still love me, *too.*

"Get changed," Lauren muttered to her. "Patty and I are taking you out for a bachelorette party tonight, sans royals."

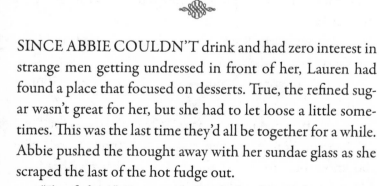

SINCE ABBIE COULDN'T drink and had zero interest in strange men getting undressed in front of her, Lauren had found a place that focused on desserts. True, the refined sugar wasn't great for her, but she had to let loose a little sometimes. This was the last time they'd all be together for a while. Abbie pushed the thought away with her sundae glass as she scraped the last of the hot fudge out.

"I'm fading," Patty said. "Let's do the unpleasant part now." Tezza and Georgie were both there, too, because it happened to be right on the divide between their two shifts, and Georgie was always up for free food.

Abbie tensed. "What unpleasant part?"

Lauren folded her hands on the table. "What with you being a motherless orphan . . ."

"That's redundant."

". . . we felt we should take it upon ourselves to get you some basic necessities . . ."

"Don't say it."

". . . for your wedding night!" Lauren's eyebrows bounced up and down suggestively, and Abbie groaned.

"Laur, I don't want it. I'll be fine."

"Don't make me get rough with you," Patty growled. "The other two can help me. Look like they'd enjoy it, too. Wouldn't stand a chance."

Abbie crossed her arms and huffed a sigh. "Fine."

Grinning, Lauren handed her a large gift bag, and Abbie accepted it warily. She peered into the bag. *Nothing looks too freaky so far . . .* Her face flamed as she pawed through the personal lubricant, ibuprofen (how much was this going to hurt, anyway?), razors (she could take a hint) . . .

"No copy of the Kama Sutra?" Abbie quipped, and Lauren shook her head.

"That's for your first anniversary. You won't need it until then."

Abbie frowned into the bag. "What's the towel for?"

"So you don't ruin your sheets. You know, blood." She did know, but she hadn't thought quite that far ahead . . . Maybe she should be thankful that they had. *At least they care.*

"Cranberry juice?"

"It prevents UTIs," Tezza said, surprising everyone. "When you're doing it a lot, you're at greater risk."

"Does that work? I always wondered," Lauren said, and Abbie tuned them out as they launched into a discussion comparing the effectiveness of cranberry juice versus antibiotics. She'd heard enough. She set the bag aside, and despite her embarrassment, she squeezed Lauren's hand.

"Thank you."

"Ooh, don't thank us yet, you haven't seen the skanky lingerie we got you!"

Abbie paled, and the rest of them laughed as they reached for their bags.

CHAPTER THIRTY-SEVEN

23 days to the wedding

"CALLED TO ORDER," QUEEN Annette's guard called, and the room quieted. Parker sat next to Abbie, who sat next to her lawyer, Mr. Morton. They'd finally convinced her that Morton was the best man for the job, despite the fact that he was, well, a man. Across from them sat Dr. Everett Harding, a thin, balding white man with a pinched expression, and several representatives of different historical preservation societies and royal watch groups whose names he did not remember. He didn't need to. Dr. Harding was the one to worry about, their most vocal opponent by far, giving press conferences and writing op-eds for months now. And he'd been elected the leader of the class action their opponents had been forced to form. Queen Annette had insisted her time not be wasted.

Parker turned his attention to her. She was an imposing woman: black, smooth hair that had been carefully coiffed, long red fingernails, a curvy figure, ice-blue eyes. She reminded him of an older Snow White. *Not a strand of gray; she must dye it. Or maybe it's a wig? It looks real. I wonder how I could figure out if it's real without touching her.* Queen Annette was from Lethos, a small island nation beyond the Sparkling Sea. As a favor to his father, she'd agreed to come arbitrate, but he had no idea what his father had promised her in return. *And I don't want to know. We need this settled. Now. Yesterday, really.*

"Thank you all for attending this mediation session today. It's an honor to help your two groups come together to find peace in a matter that is clearly dearly important to both you and your nation. As an impartial mediator, I can assure you that I hold no stake in either side's claim. I am merely here to help you communicate your wishes and come to a binding agreement of your choosing. Do we all understand?"

The participants nodded, and Parker nodded along, too.

"Good." Aside from a small imperial guard, she had no aides or secretaries with her, and she pulled out a yellow legal pad and a pen. "Now, start with your names."

"Dr. Everett Harding, professor of royal history at the University of Orangiers at Pebblestone."

Pebblestone. A miniscule town on the northern border. And he's so self-important, emphasizing the word doctor *like that.* There were other people talking, but Edward ignored them, figuring he could always just call them Doctor or Professor if he needed to address them. Technically, he was only here to support Abbie . . . and to remind them who they were really dealing with.

Abbie nudged him, and he realized they'd already gone down the other side of the table and it was his turn to introduce himself.

"I'm Edward Kenneth Keith Francis Benson Broward, King of Orangiers. I'm here to support my fiancée. I'm not a litigant."

"Very well. And you, young lady?"

"I'm Abbie Porchenzii." Parker didn't have to look at her to know how nervous she was; he'd planned to have a talk with her that morning about remembering her anxiety breathing, holding her tongue, saying as little as possible, keeping a lid on her temper . . . but she'd skipped breakfast, and he didn't feel like he could knock on her door anymore. Her words were said coolly, but he felt her foot tapping under the table.

"I knew your mother in college," Queen Annette said casually. "She was quite the opponent in our debate classes."

"I don't doubt it, Your Majesty. She was a force to be reckoned with, may she rest in peace."

"Indeed. You hold no royal title?"

"No, I do. I'm technically a princess. I was heir to the throne of Brevspor until earlier this year, but I've formally renounced that right."

"I see."

Her lawyer introduced himself, and the rest of their legal team. His father was in the gallery, as well as his security and hers.

"All right, Mr. Morton, go ahead and give me a rough overview of the events that started this lawsuit, from your perspective. And I should add that these are closed proceedings, the transcripts will not be shared nor your statements recorded, in order to preserve royal privacy."

"Thank you, Your Majesty." Morton stood. "In Sixth Month, King Edward, then Prince Edward, made a statement to the press that he and Ms. Porchenzii would be marrying, according to the marriage contract they'd made at age twelve. However, for personal reasons, Ms. Porchenzii has declined the title and role of queen, but will still honor her commitment to marry His Majesty and bear his children, who would be titled prince or princess as appropriate. Unlike most contracts, which spell out the responsibilities of each party, Edward and Abelia's was kept intentionally vague so that they might each rule if needed, since she comes from a queendom. It was not a provision of the contract that she bear any royal title whatsoever, and she plans to exercise that right under the law. Thank you."

"Thank you, Barrister. Dr. Harding?"

"Yes, thank you, Your Majesty. As we all know, the intention of the contract draftees was not simply a bride, but a partner in government and a union between our nations. This arrangement accomplishes only one of those objectives. It is her duty and contractual obligation to fulfill the role of queen. There is no precedent for interpreting a contract this way, and it reflects poorly on our government, nation, and people to allow her to avoid responsibility this way. We simply ask that she fulfill the entirety of the commitment that she made or stand aside. Thank you."

"Stand aside?" Annette's gaze was cool, exacting. "You're asking her to break her engagement?"

"If she cannot fulfill the spirit of the contract, then yes, Your Majesty."

"I see." She turned to Abbie. "Is that your client's intention, Mr. Morton?"

"As she has publicly stated, Ms. Porchenzii will not break her engagement. She is entitled to marry His Majesty and will not break her promise to him, both as a matter of principle and a matter of the heart."

Well said, Morton. Edward wondered if she'd told him that before or after their big blow-up. He didn't dare look at her for fear of breaking their masks, showing emotion that would tip things against them, make them seem desperate and vulnerable. Morton had been clear that overt displays of emotion would likely be received as manipulation by the queen.

"We'd like to put forth the title 'royal concubine.'" Though Mr. Morton delivered the line with steady confidence, a baffled silence descended on the already-quiet room, and Parker bumped her leg with his under the table to say 'told you so.' She didn't respond. *But she certainly responded when I kissed her in the hallway after video games . . .*

"You . . . you can't be serious."

"My client is quite sincere in her offer. Concubinage exists due to 'the inability to marry due to multiple factors such as differences in social rank status, an existing marriage, religious or professional prohibitions, or a lack of recognition by appropriate authorities.' That seems to fit their situation quite well."

"That's completely tawdry," Dr. Harding said. "There's no implication of her royal birth, whether she wishes to embrace it or not. What about the contract?"

"The contract would be enforced at a later date, at their discretion. It gives no mandatory time frame to be enforced. It indicates only that negotiations for a wedding date would begin at age eighteen, and given that Abelia's cosigners are both deceased, I think you'll find there's no push from either side to set a date."

"Discretion is hardly the word," the professor sniffed.

"But there is nevertheless a royal association," Morton went on, "a formal relationship, and that's one factor you indicated in your official complaint: that their relationship was made unclear by her civilian status. In her country of origin, her father was known as 'concubine' before Her Majesty became pregnant with Ms. Porchenzii's oldest sister, at which point he was elevated to king and given an exclusive relationship with Her Majesty. Many royals of many nations are known to take concubines, and our law does not prohibit it."

"We have no issue with Brevsporan traditions nor the traditions of other nations, so long as they keep them to themselves."

"Can you clarify that statement?" Queen Annette asked, not looking up from her note taking.

The professor's face reddened. "That tradition is not *appropriate* here. It makes her little better than a common *mistress*. It does *not* befit her station or his. She makes a *mockery* of the whole . . ."

"I'm not trying to mock you . . . ," Abbie blurted out. "I just want my responsibilities to be clear. And 'queen' does not match what I can offer."

"Neither does 'concubine,'" Harding said, spitting the word. "You can offer more than that. In fact, you're contractually *obligated* for more than that."

"Not sure how you'd have *any idea* what I can offer . . . ," she shot back.

"Ms. Porchenzii, please let me represent you," Mr. Morton said softly, resting a hand on her arm.

"Well, at least we have an opening offer," said Queen Annette briskly. "Let's hear some precedent now." For the next two hours, both sides presented obscure cases that very loosely applied to their situation. None of it was very compelling in Edward's mind, and he let his thoughts wander back to their argument. She'd basically accused him of ruining her life, of being controlling and manipulative. The more he thought about it, he did have to admit that their engagement had made him more jealous, more controlling. He was used to getting his own way, but that was no excuse, of course. His parents had raised him better than that. He didn't want to let the imbalance of power come between them. And he certainly didn't want his own stubbornness ruining things. They weren't ruined yet, but the tension between them had gone on far too long, mildewing the relationship. There were a few things to wash out and get into the light before they could move on, and he had already waited too long, expecting her to come crawling back to him. He should've known that his Abbie had too much pride for that. As uncomfortable as it might be, the discussion was overdue.

He glanced over at her, and shock washed over him. Abbie was crying. Silent tears flowed down her cheeks, and instinctually, he shot Annette a panicked look. She seemed to understand, and she interrupted Dr. Harding when he took a breath.

"We haven't had a break yet. Let's take a thirty-minute recess," Annette announced. Everyone stood up when she did, but Abbie sat back down immediately. When Parker put a hand on her back, he could feel her trembling—with fear or frustration, he didn't know. She looked up at him, her face still a mask . . . except her eyes. Their blue depths communicated sorrow, pain. He hated that he'd put that look there.

"Come with me?"

She nodded, and he took her hand and led her out the doors, down the hall. There was a dingy courtyard behind the municipal building, if he remembered correctly; maybe they could get a little privacy there. Rounding the corner, his heart fell: there were two men and a woman already there, chatting, smoking. Determined, he went out the doors and stopped in front of them, waiting for them to realize who he was. All three jumped to their feet, stamping out their cigarettes.

"I apologize for the intrusion, but would you mind yielding this space to my fiancée and me? We'd so appreciate your understanding." They were gone before the smoke had drifted away, and he started to turn to Abbie.

"I want to say something," she said, her voice catching. Her arms were folded tight across her middle, and she shifted her weight restlessly back and forth. "I know this isn't the right time or place to talk about our argument, but I just need to clear the air, and it's gone on way too long, and I was giving you space because it seemed like that's what you wanted, but I really need to talk about this . . ."

He sat on the bench of the stone picnic table, letting his elbows rest on his knees. "I feel the same. Go ahead."

She let out an unsteady breath and swiped at her eyes. "Just a minute. I'm sorry, I'm just really on edge right now, and sitting in that horrible, stuffy room, thinking about what I would do if I lost you entirely just brought to the surface how I feel like I already . . ." The tears were coming faster than her shaking hands could wipe them away, and his heart cracked a little more. "I feel like I lost you, Parker. I lost the real you, and that's the last thing I wanted."

"Oh, Abs." He couldn't take any more. He reached out and pulled her onto his lap sideways, and she cried into his neck. Parker let her go, just holding her, waiting until it seemed like she'd settled down a little, then he shifted to pull a clean handkerchief out of his pocket. She lifted her head and gave him a thin smile.

"Is it clean?" He smiled back and gently wiped the tears from her face, careful not to poke her. She watched him, sniffling, her eyes still guarded.

"I'm sorry," she said, looking at her lap. "I'm sorry for what I said to you, especially about Crescena. I just get so jealous of people who get you when I don't, and I don't trust her. I felt out of control. As you know, that's not my best thing."

He grimaced. "I imagine that wasn't made better when I left abruptly." She shook her head, wiping her eyes again. He debated a moment before letting out the thought that had been rattling around in his head for weeks. "That's the chink in my armor, you walking out. Disappearing again." Abbie looked into his eyes, and he saw guilt this time. "Still tender, that."

"I'm sorry." She bit her lip. "I should've thought of that."

He rubbed her arm and gave her a squeeze. "Well, now you know. And I apologize as well. I shouldn't have punished you like that, shut you out. I wasn't terribly understanding when you made the mistake of drinking at book club, either; I'm sure it was extremely stressful for you. I didn't even appreciate the effort you made to get to know Rhodie better. Will you forgive me, darling?"

Abbie was fingering the white handkerchief, rubbing the satin-stitched monogram of his initials with her thumb, and she nodded. "I forgive you. And I get it right with my health 95 percent of the time, but I'm human. I'm going to make mistakes sometimes."

"I do know that," he said quietly. "But I thought if I was perhaps there to help you, to support you, encourage you—"

"You can't fix me, babe." She was staring into his eyes, her voice still husky. "I know it's painful to hear, but you can't fix me. Your love isn't going to make me healthy."

His stomach clenched. "I wish it could."

"So do I. Woz knows, if it could, yours would do the job better than anyone's."

"I only want you to be healthy because I love you, darling. Because I need you. These two weeks were hell without you. I hated it." He paused as his fingers traveled up and down her arm without him realizing it. "I also forgot how soft your skin is. Woz, I missed you."

"Do you want to kiss a hot mess? Because she wants to kiss you . . ."

He needed no other invitation. "You always look beautiful to me, Abs," he murmured as he leaned toward her in a slow, tender capture of her lips. His security would keep everyone out of the courtyard. It was less than he wanted, but it would tide him over for now. He'd make up for lost time tonight in the hedge maze of Bluffton's gardens where they'd have a bit more privacy . . .

"We'll be okay," he said, pulling away. "Whatever happens today, whatever happens next, we're in this together. All right?"

She nodded, smiling, wiping the tears that had resurfaced. He was confident that they were mostly happy tears this time.

Their thirty minutes was almost up, and Abbie hurried off to the bathroom to fix her makeup and grab a snack before they reconvened.

Annette met his gaze as they re-entered, and he nodded his thanks. She smiled. Their arbitrator was clearly a romantic. The queen called the meeting back to order, and Harding continued his droning for another hour before they broke for lunch. He massaged Abbie's shoulders, feeling them locked up tight with tension, and she dipped her head forward.

"Feel good?"

She nodded.

"Want anything?"

"A glass of wine the size of Pigeon Lake."

"Anything I can actually get for you?"

She shook her head, placing a freezing hand over his warm one. "Thanks, though."

He bent to whisper in her ear. "Almost done, Abs. You're keeping your temper marvelously." When he straightened, he noticed Queen Annette watching them, weighing their interactions. He hastily removed his hands from Abelia's shoulders, feeling self-conscious, and she smiled down at the papers in front of her.

"Don't stop on my account, young man. You may attend to your bride."

Well. Maybe Morton was right about emotion, but wrong about affection.

"All right, let's get everyone back at the table. Shut the doors, please." Her guard complied, and people shuffled back to their places. "I would just like to offer an observation before we continue. I don't think anyone here would be able to look at this young couple and come to the conclusion that they shouldn't marry. That's not what anyone wants. They've been more than patient through all this, and I want to commend them for their love and commitment to each other and their submission to the legal process. I'm sure this hasn't been easy on them."

The opposition began to shift in their chairs, reaching for their water glasses. Parker didn't mind their discomfort one bit.

"I'm sure you'd all like to see their curly-headed babies waving at you from that gold carriage." Chuckles rippled through the room, and Queen Annette leaned forward. "So with that in mind, let's get down to brass tacks. What's the lowest title you'll approve of?"

Harding looked at the others, confused.

"The lowest . . ."

"Title," she prompted. "What's the lowest title she can have that will satisfy you?"

Harding's eyes gleamed, as if he could taste victory.

"You've rejected 'royal concubine' out of hand. Would you accept baronetess?"

"Baronetess! Be reasonable. That's for uppity banker's wives, not the king's bride!"

"Dr. Harding, you will address me with respect. I am eminently reasonable, and you are effectively a guest at my table. Don't make me kick you to the curb."

"I apologize, Your Majesty."

Parker made a mental note to do something nice for his father in appreciation for his cajoling the queen into this role; he couldn't think of anyone else who could've done it better.

"What about baroness?" She was inching up by degrees, and he could tell she was testing their patience by the tap of Harding's fingers on the table.

"Certainly no lower than princess. She can't lose rank when she marries a regent. It sets a terrible precedent . . ."

Annette's face showed nothing. "Why?"

"Because His Majesty must not be seen as depreciating his bride. Her rank and status must not be diminished by the marriage, lest future generations look with disdain upon our unions."

Can this man hear himself? thought Parker. *What a pompous bag of hot . . .*

"I see. So your concern is that this sets a precedent for potential royals of Orangiers."

"Precisely."

"You don't want them thinking that there's flexibility in the role, that they can be seen as something more than a royal."

"Yes, precis—well, no, not quite. It's just that we have an image to maintain."

Queen Annette smiled. "Yes, I'm familiar with those kind of expectations."

"I'm sure you are, Your Majesty."

Queen Annette tapped her chin thoughtfully. "Short of queen, then, that leaves grand duchess, grand princess and archduchess."

Mr. Morton cleared his throat. "I'd like to confer with my client for a moment."

"Make it brief. I've got a ship to catch."

"Yes, Majesty." Mr. Morton turned and spoke to Abbie under his breath, and Parker couldn't hear what they said, but he could see Abbie twisting her rings, squeezing her fingers together, and she nodded.

"Grand duchess is our final offer," Mr. Morton said to the room. "She'll go no higher than that. Refuse, and they may be forced to revert to a concubine situation." Edward nudged her until she looked up, and he took her cold, cold hand in his. With his gaze, he tried to see if this was really okay with her, and she gave him a tiny smile.

While the opposition conferred, Edward cleared his throat to gain their attention. He didn't look away from Abbie, but put in quietly, "She'd still be called 'royal highness,' and she'll still be my wife. I don't think history will frown on us for that."

"I still don't understand why all this is necessary," Dr. Harding said, scowling, "but it will satisfy tradition. If she gains the higher rank of grand duchess, his status is preserved and afforded the dignity it merits. But she must be given a territory. An excellent territory."

"That's not a problem," Parker said, leaning forward. "As reparations for their part in the Brothers' War, the Trellans have offered three islands. She can be Grand Duchess of the Lesser Wandering Rooster Islands."

"Great," she muttered, "more sea travel."

"Maybe we'll fly," he whispered back.

"Very well," Dr. Harding said, nodding.

"Is everyone satisfied? I'm not coming back here, people. This is it," Queen Annette warned, looking around. Seeing heads nodding, handshakes happening, she sighed. "I trust you all can draw up the paperwork yourselves. Meeting adjourned."

Abbie stood up and stretched, grinning at him. "Well, Your Majesty," she teased, "you're really stuck with me now." A look of faux thoughtfulness crossed her face. "You know, our legal victory has left me quite famished, do you know if there's any strawber—"

He was on her before she knew he was coming, and he felt her tense under his hands for a moment before she relaxed into his arms and their kiss. "Parker," she whispered, glancing past him as he moved closer, "we're in public."

"I know. But we're talking again and you're not mad at me and we're getting married." He kissed her again and again. Someone next to him cleared his throat to get his attention and he wanted to tell them to buzz off, but he was lost, so lost in Abbie; his fingers meshed with her hair, squeezed her rounded hip. Her lips were like a drug, and his uniform suddenly felt stifling. She chuckled and pulled away, her fingers still on his gold buttons, her eyes twinkling, her cheeks flushed. *Happy. Look how happy she looks. That's the greatest feeling in the wo—*

The lurker cleared his throat again, and Parker turned to glare at them. It was his father.

"Just wanted to congratulate you on your victory, but I see you are already busy celebrating." Ignatius winked. "Grand Duchess, you're going to be a Broward. Don't know if that merits congratulations or not, but . . ." Abbie grinned as she hugged his father ardently, then returned to his side. "I regret to inform you both that Her Highness the queen is back at Bluffton, preparing some kind of large party tonight. I could not talk her out of it."

"No, absolutely not," Parker fumed. "I'm spending tonight with Abbie—*only* Abbie. She'll get enough of us with all the pre-wedding stuff, I'm not—" He glanced at Abbie. She wasn't angry. She was still glowing at him, tucked under his arm, her arms around his waist.

His father continued. "Mum's grieving, son. She's never lost a son to another woman before. Just let her have this. She's trying to show her approval, get some closure."

"How on earth is she losing me? We live in the same castle, for Woz's sake. And there's going to be a masquerade in two weeks!"

"But she won't have the same influence over you as she does now. Abbie will have that place as the most important woman in your life. It'll be different. Just go with it."

Parker hesitated. A party was the last thing in the universe he wanted right now, just behind having his armpit hairs plucked out one by one.

His father lowered his voice. "Please, son, from one man to another. She's going to make my life a living Jersey if I don't get you there. Please?"

"Don't grovel," Parker grumped. "We'll be there. For part of the time."

Ignatius grinned. "She did invite your cohorts as well. I'm sure that will be entertaining."

"Abs, you get to keep James away from the hard stuff."

"Challenge accepted." She patted his chest. "As long as you make sure Sam doesn't hide in the corner the whole time. He's cute as anything; he needs a girl."

"One wedding at a time, love."

CHAPTER THIRTY-EIGHT

9 days to the wedding

ABBIE SURVEYED HERSELF in the gilded bathroom mirror. Emerald earrings, emerald pendant sitting on her chest. Hair neatly curled on either side of the furry gray mask that covered the top half of her face—the wolf. The bride always played the wolf at the engagement masquerade; her groom could play a variety of different prey, depending on his personality. They'd settled on the elk for Parker; he was tall enough that he was easy to spot, even in a crowded room, but the added height of the antlers would make him impossible to miss.

"At least it's not as emasculating as the goat . . . ," he'd muttered.

She'd grinned at that. "The elk is the pinnacle of male personas in Brevsporan culture. It paints you as a prize, as a challenge I had to win."

"But I'm still prey. You're getting the fun role."

"Now you're getting Brevsporan culture."

"I'm starting to see Kurt's point about gender equality," he'd grouched, but he'd kissed her sweetly before he left. She stuck both hands into the deep pockets of the shimmering green ball gown they'd designed for her. She fingered the pen-like device Tezza and Georgie had designed, touched the button with her thumb, then moved it quickly away.

"Don't play with it," Tezza said from across the room. "It's not a toy."

"Don't take it personally," Georgie said in Abbie's hidden earpiece. "She's just nervous. She's worried about you. It's her way, Grand Duchess."

Abbie smiled, then sobered for show. "I'm sorry, Macias. I won't play with it."

She grunted.

"You're not dressed," Abbie commented, turning back to the mirror to apply a little more mascara. She was still wearing her typical uniform of skin-tight black clothing.

Tezza smiled. "No. But I'm ready," she answered.

Parker stuck his head into her bathroom. "It's time."

"Okay." Neither of them had any energy for flirting for once. She took his arm, and he escorted her out of her guest bedroom and into the hallway. Normally, the event would be held in Brevspor, in the home of the bride's family, but they'd gotten away with having it here, since Kurt had "asked the Browards to host." Lincoln was more likely to get overconfident on his home soil . . . she hoped.

"Are they here?" she asked softly.

"Not yet," he said.

"You remember the plan?"

"Yes."

They were at the door to the ballroom. Abbie paused, unsure what to do. Tradition dictated that she go in first, but decorum dictated that he go first. They stared at each other for a moment, then laughed.

"Please," Parker said with a smile, gesturing toward the door, "after you, mistress wolf."

"Why, thank you, my dear prey," she responded, gliding through the door, her ceremonial sword bouncing at her side. She couldn't use it, but she adored how it looked. Besides, the room was practically bursting with weaponry, most of it decorative. Those already in attendance stomped their feet on the floor to herald her arrival, and she nodded in acknowledgment as it rumbled beneath her feet. Parker's personal assistant, Ms. Scrope, who knew nothing about the event's true purpose, smiled as she handed her a glass of pomegranate juice.

"Good evening, Grand Duchess."

"Good evening, Ms. Scrope."

"The ballroom looks very dramatic; I love all the candles. And you look very . . . feral."

Abbie laughed. "Thanks. I love your lamb mask, you look delicious."

"Ooh, that makes me nervous," she tittered. "Why do all the drinks look like blood?"

"Scholars disagree. Some say it goes back to the roots of the tradition, the husband as prey to be pursued, and serving a blood-like drink was the bride's way of announcing her victory before it happened."

"Yikes," Scrope muttered.

Abbie laughed. "But others say that it's a symbol of the marriage's importance: that they will only be separated when someone's blood is spilled in death."

"Again, yikes. Can't you guys just wear rings?"

Abbie patted her arm in an attempt to be reassuring. "We could. This is more fun. And it strikes fear in the timid hearts of the citizens of neighboring countries such as yours."

Ignatius and Lily approached; they wore matching his and hers clownfish masks that went dramatically with his black tux and her orange ball gown, symbolizing their coastal location. Their dreads gave away their identities immediately. They were not in the dark regarding their Lincoln plot, but if they were nervous, they hid it better than Parker had.

"Congratulations on the very good turnout, mistress wolf. Only the delegation from Gardenia has not yet arrived."

Then Heather is here . . . good.

"That's great news. We'll start the game soon, then, once everyone's had a drink."

"Game?" Scrope asked, and Abbie nodded, trying to casually survey the room for Heather.

"I will answer questions about Edward. If I get the question right, he takes a step forward; if I'm wrong, he takes a step back, so I have to answer even more questions. The game ends when the wolf captures her prey and begins the dancing." *Only my prey is a predator in his own right, and he and I have something else in mind . . . This has to work. It has to.* In an effort not to think about it, Abbie excused herself and began to make the rounds, greeting kingly peacocks, princely fawns, parrot princesses and dukes dressed as doves. *Lots of birds this time.* By right, she was the only apex predator in the room . . . based on the mask, anyway. She could feel Heather avoiding her, circling away from her into the crowd as she got close.

"Do we know how Heather is dressed?" Abbie murmured into the drink.

"Affirmative. Howler monkey," Georgie answered. Abbie smirked, but quickly wiped it off her face as her brother approached.

"Ready?" he asked. Mindful of his fear of her voice, she simply nodded. Kurt, dressed as a cobra, stepped onto the dais. "Who hunts this night?" It was so surreal to hear those ancient words asked of her, after hearing them so many times as a child.

"I am the wolf, and I come seeking a mate."

"Whom do you hunt, mistress wolf?"

"I hunt the elk." Feet stomped against the floor again until Parker emerged from the crowd five feet from the dais. This part of it had to be real; they hadn't told Kurt what to ask. Abbie felt her stomach tighten. *I shouldn't be more nervous about this than the trap . . .*

"Then let the questioning begin . . ." Kurt paced the dais solemnly, and Abbie almost laughed.

I never knew he had such a theatrical flare . . . The crowd was eating it up, grinning, elbowing one another.

"Mistress wolf, is your prey a morning person or an evening person?"

Good, an easy one. "My elk is a morning person."

Parker stepped forward.

"Mistress wolf, would your elk rather talk or text?"

Abbie scowled. "Master cobra, that's hardly a traditional question . . ."

Kurt laughed. "Just answer, mistress wolf."

She thought for a moment. "Text."

Parker took a step backwards, and she cursed. The crowd rippled with a giggle.

"Mistress wolf, would your elk rather dress up or dress down?"

"Dress up."

Parker stepped forward, and Abbie gave a mental fist pump.

"Mistress wolf, which one of you first suggested marriage?"

"He did," she said immediately. "Under the orange trees at Bluffton after I won another footrace. We were eleven."

The crowd held their breath as Parker stared up at her, lifted his foot . . . and took a step forward. Though he was supposed to stay silent, she heard him mutter, "But it was I who won the footrace, as I recall . . ." The attendees nearest him chuckled.

"Mistress wolf, does your elk prefer the comforts of the indoors or the wilds of outdoors?"

"Outdoors, master cobra."

Parker took a step toward her. *At least his legs are long.*

"Mistress wolf, what is your prey's prize possession?"

"His sailboat."

Parker hesitated, and she cursed inwardly; he might've said his video game system instead, but the sailboat was a gift from his father and worth more financially . . .

Parker took a step, and the crowd gave them rumbling encouragement as he reached the foot of the dais. Only three steps to go. *We can do this.* From her raised vantage point, a black-haired head caught her eye near the south exit. *Lincoln.* Abbie subtly signaled with her eyes to Tezza, who moved off in that direction.

"Mistress wolf," Kurt continued, "what does your prey love most about you?"

She slid her eyes to Kurt. "Can you clarify the question?"

"Certainly; his favorite aspect of your relationship."

Abbie stared into Parker's eyes, trying to get some sort of hint . . . *What does he love about me, anyway?* "My elk loves what good friends we are." This earned her an "aww" from the crowd, something no Brevsporan group would have given them, as Parker ascended the first step.

"You're doing well, mistress wolf. Tell us, who won your last argument?"

She couldn't hide her annoyance. "What? Master cobra, really, this is ridiculous . . ."

Kurt shrugged and gestured helplessly toward the cards in his hand as the crowd snickered and quietly speculated.

She huffed. "Fine. My elk won the argument." *Please don't ask what it was about . . .*

Parker took a step forward, grinning, and Kurt had to wait for the crowd to quiet down again before he asked his final question. This was always the hardest one.

"Mistress wolf, will your prey ever leave you?"

She could've kissed Kurt; he'd lobbed her a softball question for the last one.

"No, master cobra, my elk is mine until death parts us."

Parker bounded up the last step and swept her into a romantic kiss as the crowd cheered their approval. Over the noise of the cheers, Abbie heard George whisper through her earpiece.

"Grand Duchess, Lincoln is here. Iguana mask."

Gotcha, you slippery bastard.

CHAPTER THIRTY-NINE

"IT'S TIME," ABBIE WHISPERED to Parker, who gave her a nod.

"Let the dance begin," Kurt announced as Abbie led Parker down the steps. They claimed the center of the ballroom, dancing together for a few minutes, Abbie trying to ignore all the stares and whispers. Then they each broke off to find new partners . . . She didn't know Parker had a dramatic streak, either, but he made a good show of looking around before he chose Crescena, resplendent in her snow-white dress, glowing against her dark skin, complete with a dove mask: the picture of innocence. A lamb would have been better, considering she was their sacrificial victim; she'd be held up to public scrutiny until her role in all this could be made known.

Abbie chose her brother, but made sure she was staring daggers at Parker and Crescena every chance she got, huffing her displeasure without lowering her voice. Two or three rounds later, when they finally got back together, the audience was treated to the blow-up everyone expected.

"Why her?"

"Why not her? What's wrong with a dance, Abelia?" In the strangest way, that soothed her heart, since he never called her Abelia in real life. The latest argument still felt fresh.

"You're mine now. I don't know why you even invited her."

"You can't own a person, Abelia! This isn't Brevspor. I am no subservient male, and you'll never rule over me the way you want to!"

In the midst of the murmurs and the whispered speculation, Abbie turned and ran out of the ballroom, straight for the library. She stood with her back to the door, waiting—no, willing—Lincoln or Heather to show up. They'd have no way of knowing of the hidden cameras that had been installed a few days ago when the library was "closed for cataloguing." They'd have no way of knowing about the magical containment units that sat humming just behind the books on the shelves, no way of knowing about the trigger to arm them that sat in her pocket. The minute she pressed that button, anyone's ability to do magic would be neutralized; they'd be trapped. But in order to implicate Heather, she had to be caught in the act. And if Abbie's gut was right, catching Lincoln was nothing if they didn't get Heather, too. She was the real threat. Her name might not have been on that note, but her signature cruelty was. *Show up. Here I am, alone. Here I am. Come and get me.*

Footsteps. Lincoln was halfway across the room when she turned. He paused, taking off his iguana mask. She hadn't seen him in thirteen years . . . She'd only been eight when he'd signed his contract with Heather. But he still had a magnetic charisma as he smiled at her, and she suppressed a shudder.

"Hello, Abelia."

"Hello, Lincoln. I'd say it's nice to see you, but you've made my life a living Jersey lately, so you'll forgive me if I skip that part."

He swallowed hard. "You were never supposed to get caught up in this. I'm sorry."

"Why did you send that note?" Abbie asked softly, putting just enough vibrato in her voice to make her sound weak, helpless.

His brow furrowed. "What note?"

Exactly. "The one where you said you'd rip me from Parker's arms as he'd ripped your kingdom from yours . . . the one you left on his bed in the dark of night."

"What?" He turned sharply to the empty doorway. "You *did* that? You terrorized them? You said no one else would get hurt."

Abbie gasped as Heather materialized out of nothing.

"Stand aside, *jaat*." Heather stepped into the library, closing and locking the door behind her. It was the same way Tezza had locked her apartment door that first night; only she could open it to let them out.

Lincoln backed toward Abbie, keeping her firmly behind him. "No."

"No?" Heather's voice had gone dangerously soft, and Abbie played with the trigger, trembling. "Is that a joke?"

Wait for the evidence. Let them keep talking.

"Did she just say *jaat*? That's the word for 'lover' in Kiri-ien," Georgie said in her ear.

Not "husband" . . . Maybe she's holding out on fulfilling the contract until she's queen.

"Yes, I said no!" Lincoln shouted. "This is my brother's *wife*, damn it. You saw them in that ballroom, the true affection between them. This is the love of his life!"

"She stands between me and what's mine."

Lincoln was gritting his teeth. "Don't do this, lotus. Please. I'll give you anything, anything else, but we can't kill my little brother's wife. I can't hurt my family again."

Heather's voice was eerily calm. "They stand between me and what's mine."

Lincoln's shoulders squared. "If you'd just been patient, it all would've been yours! Dad was going to step down, and I was first in the Woz-damn line. But you had to have it sooner! Look what you've done! You've destroyed my life—both our lives!"

"Hang on, Abbie, His Majesty is en route," Georgie said in her ear. "You're doing great."

"No, I didn't ruin our lives, *jaat*. This is their fault. Us against the world, remember? Once I dispose of her, he'll crumble like sand, and you can reclaim our kingdom." Heather raised her arm and a crossbow appeared in her hand, glowing green.

Lincoln sucked in a sharp breath, and even Abbie felt her chest constrict at the amount of magic circulating in the room. *Will our device stop a crossbow that's been enchanted? Wouldn't it still shoot me without magic? Am I about to die?*

"Now stand aside."

"I don't think so." Tezza appeared out of the shadows like a ghost, launching herself at the princess with a menace that surprised even Abbie. With a startled yell, Heather released the bolt, which sliced through the air toward Abbie. She dove behind Lincoln as a shield just before she heard him shout in surprise; it had caught him in the arm. In the darkened room, she could hear Heather wrestling with Tezza.

"Punch it! They're not going to take you; she's trying to escape!" Georgie yelled into her ear.

Abbie realized with cold fear that she'd been distracted by the tussle; the trigger had slipped from her hand deep into her pocket. She stood up and scrambled for the button, but Lincoln noticed. He turned and grabbed her by the wrist, wrenching the trigger out of her grasp. Abbie's thoughts seized up as the back of his hand met her face in a sickening slap and sent her flying onto her backside.

"I'm sorry," he said, holding his injured arm, moving toward Heather. "But I can't let you hurt her, either. You should've stayed out of it, Abelia. You have no idea—" His words were cut off as Heather swept the two of them away in a black cloud of smoke just as Parker and his Black Feathers burst through the library doors.

"Abbie?" She could hear the panic in his voice.

"I'm over here," Abbie called, struggling to get up, rubbing her sore hip where she'd hit a sharp table corner as she went down.

Parker ran to her. "Are you all right? What happened?" He helped her to her feet, his hands running over her body to check for damage.

"I'm fine," she said, ripping off her mask in frustration. "She's behind all of this. All of it. He only went along with her plan when I was out of the picture. I don't think it ever occurred to them that you'd find me hiding in Gardenia." She ran a hand over her face as Parker pulled her into his arms. "I'm sorry I didn't hit the trigger in time. He got it away from me."

"I don't care about that. I'd rather have you here and whole than whisked away in a cloud of smoke to Woz knows where with that psychopath."

Abbie sighed. "At least she won't be able to keep pulling strings from Kiriien anymore."

"Right. She'll be forced underground, where we can't keep an eye on her . . ."

Abbie sighed. "I'm sorry, hon. I screwed this all up."

He tipped her chin up to meet his eyes. "Mistress wolf, you were brilliant."

"So were you, my darling prey. Are you still mine forever after our ballroom spat?"

He gave her a tired smile. "Yours forever."

CHAPTER FORTY

3 days to the wedding

"AND THIS ONE'S FROM Edward's aunt Elaine . . ." Ms. Scrope was hovering at Abbie's elbow, and Parker resisted the urge to ask her to roost somewhere. But his bride didn't seem to mind his assistant's proximity as much as she minded the truly extravagant pile of gifts on the table next to them and the hundreds of eyes on them. Despite her objections, they were currently seated in the throne room, with each giver being called forth individually to witness the acceptance of their gift. He'd convinced her that it would save time on the day of the wedding to do it now . . . getting them to La Bonisla quicker. That was the thought he consoled himself with as he opened Aunt Elaine's gift.

"Oh, how lovely," he said with as much sincerity as he could muster, and the older woman beamed. The Duchess of Rockwell had commissioned a nice portrait of the two of them, which would have been fine, had it not been six feet tall.

"Where are we going to hang *that*?" Abbie whispered, trying not to giggle.

"I have no idea, love. Mum will figure out something."

"Okay, just . . . I don't want giant Parker staring at me while we have sex."

371

He couldn't help grinning. After all, she'd just said "sex" without hesitating or stuttering. His plan was totally working.

"All right, I won't inflict anything but regular old me upon you."

"Thank you." She turned to face his aunt and smiled. "Thank you so much, Duchess, it's an incredible likeness." Right now, of course, it wasn't; Parker glanced again at the fading purple bruise on Abbie's cheek, which she'd tried to cover with makeup. When he'd watched the video of Lincoln's assault, he'd had to excuse himself and go find a punching bag lest he destroy the office.

The duchess gave a deep curtsy and moved off to the side as the next person shuffled forward.

"The ambassador from Trella, Your Majesties," Ms. Scrope announced.

Arms shaking, a small brown-skinned woman wearing a tailored suit carried what looked like a medium-sized cage covered in a floral-print fabric. "Your Majesties, I have brought you a symbol of our beautiful islands, a portion of which you, Grand Duchess, now preside over as guardian and patron. We hope this conveys how humbled and honored the Trellan people are to enjoy the hospitality of your wedding celebration."

If I had my way, thought Parker, *you'd be enjoying the hospitality of my prisons for siding with my brother and detouring my fiancée through Gratha.* With a flourish, the ambassador pulled off the sheet to reveal a bright-green bird with a red underbelly and a yellow beak. It was so brightly colored that it was almost comical. *Maybe we could donate it to the Bar-*

rowdon Zoo . . . He glanced at Abbie, only to find mischief in her gaze.

"Don't even think about it, Abs," he muttered, even as he smiled warmly at the ambassador.

"Oh, I'm thinking about it."

"Don't. We're not keeping a parrot."

"It's a Trellan amazon, for one thing, and they're endangered. Also, it's an excellent speech imitator. I'm gonna teach it to say the dirtiest things . . ."

"This from the woman who doesn't like to say 'sex'?"

"Fine. I'll let James teach it."

"There's a truly horrifying notion." Between that thought and the smell, he was definitely donating that thing somewhere.

"I'll call him Skippy."

"That's—no, darling, I'm not joking," he said, working to keep his voice quiet enough to contain their conversation to the two of them. "We can't have a bird in our quarters."

"What's going on in our quarters, by the way?"

"Hmm?" Parker pretended not to know what she was talking about.

"I said, what's going on in our quarters? I haven't been in there in weeks, and I sense that you're being cagey."

Parker motioned the next gift giver forward, even as Abbie bent over to see the bird better as he was carried up the stairs to the dais. "Who's a good bird? Skippy's a good bird, aren't you? Say, 'Abbie's right. Abbie's right.'"

Parker funneled his sigh out his nose to hide his irritation. "We'll discuss this later."

Ms. Scrope cleared her throat. "The Honorable Judge Burnham, Your Majesties."

He let Abbie tear into it, hoping to distract her curiosity regarding their quarters. He had to talk to her about money—and soon—or she'd never be able to accept the wedding present he was planning.

"*A Concise History of Orangiersian Conflicts, Conquests, and Coups,*" she read the title aloud, then paused before going on. "The Complete Six-Volume Set."

"A first edition, Your Majesties, and signed by the author. I think knowing our history is very important, don't you? It should be quite instructive for you, Grand Duchess."

"Yes, knowing our history is vital," Parker said, schooling his mouth into a solemn line, forcing himself not to react to Abbie's "Oh Jersey, no" expression that only he could see. She recovered quickly.

"Thank you, Judge Burnham. This is very thoughtful of you, and I am anxious to learn more about my new home."

As he retreated, she leaned over to Parker. "First of all, I am not reading that tome. Second of all, are we almost done?"

"I don't think so." They were four hours in, but the line was still long, winding around the edge of the room. *Why did I drink so much water after my workout?* "I'm going to need a break soon."

"Me too."

He looked up to see his father and mother approaching together, arm in arm. He gestured to Ms. Scrope, who led the rest of the line away to a more comfortable waiting room, giving them some privacy with his parents.

"Before you get any more worn out and all the gifts begin to run together, Mum and I wanted to give ours . . ."

"But you guys are paying for the wedding!" Abbie protested, hesitantly accepting a flat velvet box. "You didn't have to . . ." Her voice trailed off feebly as she stared down at the tiara he'd picked out for her. Her eyes were shining with tears when she looked between the three of them, speechless. She picked up the delicate piece, her fingers brushing gently against the vibrant blue sapphires that adorned the top of each scalloped ring of diamonds.

"Thank you," Abbie whispered, the tears finally falling. Lily reached out to lay a steadying hand on her wrist.

"The sapphires were gifted to Parker's grandmother Rose when she married his grandfather Damien, and she later had them made into this tiara. We thought it would match your eyes and let you carry a bit of Brevspor into the wedding as well. Your 'something blue,' hmm?"

Abbie nodded, then turned to Parker. "This is really happening, isn't it?"

"And not a moment too soon," he said, opening his own gift. It was a watch and a key. Not just any watch; it was the watch he and Lincoln used to sneak into his parents' bedroom to play with when their tutors thought they were "working independently." The pocket watch his father and grandfather had carried for years.

"I should've given it to you at your coronation, but it slipped my mind. Apologies."

"No, no—it's great. Thanks, Dad. I . . ." He cleared his throat as emotion clogged it. "It's really great." He picked up the key. "What's this for?"

"You know when Mum and I used to disappear on the odd weekend, and we told you were going to Harbor House?"

Parker nodded slowly, cocking an eyebrow.

His dad grinned. "We lied." He tapped the key. "This is the key to the retreat cabin our kings have used for generations. I'll draw you a map, but you have to burn it once you know it by heart."

"A *secret* cabin?"

Ignatius nodded.

"How did I not know about this? I'm now questioning everything I know about my childhood."

Ignatius and Lily chuckled, giving each other a knowing look. His mom added, "We know royal life is full of pressures, and this has been a place for us to escape all that. And if you're trying to start a family . . . you may wish for some additional privacy."

If Abbie's face turned any redder, he was going to have to get her a glass of water. He chuckled as he rose to embrace them, and Abbie followed suit. "Thanks, Mum and Dad. Love you guys."

"We love you, too," his mother whispered, and he knew she was going to cry.

"Come now, it's all right, Mum. I'm not even moving out of the house, for Woz's sake."

"I know, I know," she said, pulling a handkerchief out of some hidden pocket in her dress, then waving him away as she dabbed her tears before they could smudge her makeup. "It's just going to be different."

Abbie took a step forward and put a tentative hand on Lily's elbow. "I promise to take very good care of him, Lily." His mom hugged her shoulders with one arm, and she sighed, smiling through her tears.

"That's my one consolation: at least he's marrying a good woman." Lily's chin trembled. "Someone who's perfect for him."

Oh boy, that's done it. Now they're both going to start in, and I'll never get to use the toilet. That'll be a nice headline: King Edward puts off toilet use, bladder explodes; wedding postponed. But to his astonishment, his mother pulled herself together and changed the subject entirely.

"Abbie, dear, did you see that someone's brought you a ton of compost?"

She gasped. "A ton as a euphemism for a lot, or . . . ?"

"The unit, I believe: knowing your background and interest in ecology, one of the villages up north got together and brought you a metric ton of compost. They thought it would please you."

She gasped again, then turned to him, beaming. "Did you hear that, hon? Finally, something useful!"

CHAPTER FORTY-ONE

2 days to the wedding

IT WAS SNOWING. ABBIE loved the snow, and after a long day of wedding preparation and forced socialization, she dragged Parker outside.

"Let's go for a walk," she said, pulling him toward the gardens.

"I love how the snow is suspended in your curls," he said, digging in his heels, catching her around the waist for a quick kiss. "I actually have something for you."

"You do?"

He nodded, leading her down the garden path toward the woods.

"Remember this place?" It was their treehouse, the one they'd begged Ignatius for so that they could watch for pirates.

"Of course." She grinned. "Why, you wanna make out in it?"

"No, that's where your surprise is. Climb on up."

"Really?" She looked up skeptically. "It looks a bit rotted."

"You sounded like me when you said that. How flattering."

378

She rolled her eyes as she ascended the ladder. "Up here?" Abbie peered into the treehouse. "Are you sure?"

"Yes, it's right there. You can't see it until you get inside. Climb all the way up."

Abbie hauled herself up into the wooden structure, wishing she had actually accomplished her last New Year's resolution of learning to do a pull-up. She moved toward a green canvas bag and peeked inside.

"A sleeping bag? Pillow, blanket, flashlight, bug spray—what's all this for?" Abbie heard a scraping sound behind her, and she pivoted just in time to see Dean and Waldo removing the ladder, setting it carefully to the side.

"What the actual—"

"This was the only way," he said, crossing his arms, "to discuss this without you striking me, storming off, or otherwise sabotaging the effort."

She crossed her arms. "Discuss what?"

"Your attempts to repay me for your college loans."

"You put that ladder back *right now*, Broward, or so help me—"

"The game was amusing for a while, but I'm over it now."

"When the Jersey did you even plan this? This is just childish. You're being so immature right now."

"I gladly admit that it's not ideal . . . but it's your immaturity that brought it to this point, not mine."

"I am not above shrieking."

"Go right ahead."

"Georgie!"

Her security wandered to the foot of the tree and looked up at her. "Honestly, Grand Duchess, you get yourself into some interesting situations." She turned to Parker. "Did she agree?"

"Not yet."

"Well, it's not dark yet . . ." Georgie smiled at her, then wandered back out of sight.

Abbie huffed. "Dean? Waldo? You guys there?"

"Yup!"

"Yo!"

"Aren't you going to help me down?"

"Nope."

"No."

Parker took off his glasses, cleaning the lenses on the edge of his cotton shirt. "As you can see, anyone you think might come to your rescue is on my side."

"I don't care if they're on your side; this is a private, personal matter. And *you're* supposed to be on my side."

"But you see, that's the point: I am on your side. It's not like you borrowed the money to buy a flat-screen TV or a fast car; it was entirely necessary and prudent. I respect your career. I admire how much work you've done to accomplish what you have. But if the people who were supposed to take care of you had done so, you wouldn't have needed to take out a loan in the first place. I was merely righting that wrong, and I do not understand for the life of me why you resent that so deeply."

Abbie scowled. "Because it was my responsibility, not yours! You didn't sign, you didn't make the commitment. I did!"

"You've been talking about getting your bachelor's; are you saying that if you went back to college today, you wouldn't let me pay for it?" Abbie stared down at him; she wasn't answering that. For a long moment, she considered jumping, but she was probably fifteen feet up, and she didn't really want to walk down the aisle on crutches if no one broke her fall. She paced inside the treehouse instead.

"I don't want charity."

"For the love of Woz, it's *not charity*!"

"Oh, I've earned it, then? By what, making out with you?"

"Not every good thing has to be earned. Some of the best things in life aren't. Sometimes, a man just wants to do something nice for the woman he loves, even though she's a stubborn mule who has too many hang-ups to appreciate it."

Hang-ups, hmm. Maybe if I hang off the edge and then drop . . . that would take a good six feet off it. Nine feet's not that far to go.

"Abs, are you listening to me?"

"No, I'm planning my escape."

He shook his head. "Well, best of luck to you. I'll be back to discuss this in the morning; you should have everything you need in the overnight bag. If you ask nicely, I'll bring you breakfast." Parker turned and started back toward the castle at a leisurely pace, his security in tow. "Though it won't be easy getting eggs up there . . . ," he said, mostly speaking to himself.

"Hey!"

Parker didn't stop. "Maybe if I hard-boil them first . . ."

"HEY! You cannot leave me up here all night. That's creepy as Jersey!"

He waved over his shoulder. "Sleep well, darling. Love you."

"Wait! Fine, just . . . I can't . . ."

Parker stopped and turned. "You can't what?"

"Fine, you're right, okay? You're right!" she shouted. "I'm too proud. I can't handle you paying for my problems, I can't stand the idea that you're bailing me out. I don't care if it doesn't make any sense. It pisses me off. I've tried to get over it and I can't."

He strolled back to the bottom of the tree, hands in his pockets. "Darling, I have to watch you suffer through a lot of things, things I couldn't hope to solve. That's what upsets me: watching you sick, watching you wrestle with your difficult family issues. It makes me feel so helpless, so angry. But this, this is the one thing I can fix. This is something I can help with . . . but you won't let me."

She absorbed this new information. "It still feels like charity."

"Was it charity when you made us all pancakes at Hearth House?"

"No," she grumped.

"Was it charity when we took Simon fishing?"

She shook her head, her aching shoulders finally falling away from her ears.

"Was it charity when you took a day off work to meet me in Imahara?"

"No," she muttered.

"No, of course it wasn't, because your generosity toward us isn't motivated by a patronizing pity or a detached altruism. If I allow you to repay me, that would be admitting that my gift was a power play, rather than an act of love. And I could never let you think that, not for a moment."

"So, what do you want from me?" Her voice was small, but she couldn't help it: his argument had humbled her.

"Give up this game. No more repayments. Do you agree?"

She gave a terse nod.

"Sorry, darling, but I'm going to need verbal confirmation . . ."

"Yes," she spat out.

"And," he said, pointing up at her, "if you go back to university, I'm paying for it."

"If it's not an issue yet, I don't see why we have to . . ." Her voice trailed off as she saw his look harden. "Fine. If I go, you can pay. But a longer conversation is needed about how finances are going to work . . . when I'm not fifteen feet in the air."

He nodded and signaled to his security. Dean and Waldo moved to put the ladder back up. Despite his sweet monologue, her pride was still wounded. *I am going to make him suffer for this indignity . . .*

"Any bedroom-type favors you want to lock in while I'm up here?" she snarked. "You've got me over a barrel. Might as well take advantage of it."

Parker's eyes flared at the metaphor. She'd been trying to embarrass him, and his arousal was annoying as Jersey. He held up a hand, and his two security agents paused with the ladder, trying hard to fight smiles.

"It's an expression, you pervert!" she fumed. "Stop picturing me like that!"

He stroked his chin. "Now that you mention it, there's one or two things I've been meaning to ask about . . ." She knew from his smirk that her face was as crimson as a pomegranate. "But I'm fairly sure I can convince you better face-to-face. I wouldn't want to be accused of unfair manipulation."

"I am officially mad at you, Edward."

"Uh-oh," Dean muttered as they replaced the ladder.

"She used your real name, sir," Waldo added. "You're in it now."

"That was anticipated. I have gluten-free, dairy-free, refined-sugar-free gingerbread cake waiting for her in the kitchens. I'll be back in her good graces in no time."

She'd complained a few weeks ago about the dearth of holiday treats for people on a restricted diet. *Apparently, he was listening, curse him.*

"That's what you think, buster. Now turn around."

He gave her an incredulous look.

She raised her voice. "If you think I'm letting you check out my backside as I come down the ladder, you're sadly mistaken. Your touching and leering privileges are revoked as of now."

"That's unfortunate," he said, turning away, his shoulders shaking.

"I hear you laughing!" she yelled as she descended the rungs.

"Yes, I'm laughing, Abs. I'm sorry."

"You're sorry you trapped me up a tree, or you're sorry you're laughing?"

"Does my answer determine my punishment?" He bracketed her against the ladder with his arms and legs the moment her feet touched the ground, technically not touching her at all. The way he said *punishment* made it a dirty word, and she resented her body's reaction to the innuendo and his proximity. *If only I wanted him a little less.*

"Back up," she growled, her anger becoming more difficult to maintain.

"Not even one little kiss after my declarations of love? I stayed up late working on that speech last night."

"Time wasted, I guess. Step off, kidnapper."

Parker chuckled and leaned forward. "I think it was more intervention than kidnapping..."

She turned her face away from his. "We'll let the prosecutor decide."

"Oh, yes," he laughed, gasping for air. "Silly me. Of course, we'll let him decide." His eyes were twinkling. "I don't really leer at you, do I?"

"Sometimes you do. It's obscene, really."

"Well, I apologize for offending your delicate sensibilities, darling." He leaned back and offered her his arm. Abbie ignored it and brushed by him back toward the castle. He caught up with her easily.

"You know, a touch ban probably makes sense leading up to the wedding anyway. Lots of pressures on us both, lots of other things to do . . ."

She tossed her hair. "Whatever helps you justify it."

"Your cake is in the kitchen when you want it."

"I don't need cake."

"Nobody *needs* cake. I just thought you might appreciate the gesture . . ."

"I've got a gesture for you, mister."

He tsked his tongue. "Now who's being obscene?"

She whirled on him, her fists clenched, fully prepared to punch his arm, but he advanced toward her, and she backed up to avoid his touch. *That touch will break my anger. I like the anger. I want the anger.* It was already cracking though . . . She could feel the foundations were trembling, or maybe it was her hands that were trembling. It was very hard to tell.

"I said don't touch me," she said, but there was no fight in it.

"I'm not touching you," he said, so low that only she could hear. "I'm not going to touch you unless you want me to." He reached up, and despite his words, she thought he was going to touch her cheek; instead, he lifted a tree branch she was about to back into, then let his hands rest on it. "I trust that you'll let me know when that is . . ."

She nodded unevenly, and he gave her a slow smile.

"I said no leering."

"I'm not leering," he murmured. "I'm just looking at my future wife with all the love in my heart, the fantastic woman I'm finally making officially mine in a few days. I can't look at you another way, Abs. I'm sorry if it's making you uncomfortable." Like a bubble popping, her anger was gone.

"Woz preserve me," Abbie muttered, borrowing his phrase as she stepped forward, catching his face in her hands. There was a vapor of anger left in her kiss, but he didn't seem to mind; he gave it right back to her, sweeping his warm tongue into her mouth demandingly, leaning into her . . .

but something was wrong. She broke the kiss and looked up. Parker was still hanging onto the tree branch, quite tightly if she was seeing correctly in the waning light of sunset.

She smirked. "Parker, would you like to touch me?"

"You said I couldn't."

"That doesn't answer my question," she said, running her hands lightly up and down his sides.

"You know I would..." He glared at her, but he held still as Abbie moved her hands to his chest, running her fingernails over his pecs through his shirt, then she felt him shudder.

"This is payback, isn't it?" he asked, his voice tight.

"A little bit, yeah." Smiling, she pressed soft kisses to his neck as she brought their chests together.

"Abs?"

"Yeah?" she said as she toyed with his earlobe, ran her finger over the line of hair near his belt buckle.

"Are you attempting regicide again?"

"Oh, is this hard for you, hon?" She chuckled.

"A little bit, yeah." He groaned as she sucked on his bottom lip. "Don't make me beg."

"You know, I'm starting to understand the attraction of the whole handcuff thing..."

His eyes went wide, and Abbie laughed even harder.

"All right, fine. Touch permissions restored." His hands, despite being sticky with sap, went right to her hips, drawing her forward, and he kissed her again.

"I do have one more thing for you . . . ," he said, taking her hand and leading them back to the castle.

"A real thing? Not like the counterfeit surprise I just got?"

"Yes," he laughed, "a real thing." If she hadn't known better, she thought he looked almost nervous. She peppered him with questions all the way to the doors of the residence, but he just grinned at her. He took both her hands, looking into her eyes in that deep, sincere way of his.

"I know I couldn't plan our wedding like a good Brevsporan groom, but I wanted to do something to welcome you home, to show that I do know you. That I see you. I apologize for the ruses that kept you out of our space, but I just wanted it to be a surprise . . ." He swallowed hard and opened the doors.

Abbie was speechless. He'd knocked out the wall to his study and opened up the space to connect it with the living area . . . and given her a kitchen. Not just a kitchen—the counters were a gorgeous white quartz, and the rest of the kitchen had a tastefully retro vibe, from the baby blue of the refrigerator to the deep sinks. The stools that stood under the island had a reclaimed industrial look and had been painted a lovely oceanic teal. A coffee maker in the same color sat on the counter beside a stand mixer, behind which was a backsplash of white subway tiles.

And more than the gift itself, she thought, *he kept working on this while we were fighting. He didn't trash the project. He believed in us.*

"I didn't get pots and pans, as I thought you might like to choose them yourself. But I knew coffee was essential . . ." He was lingering behind her. "This way, if we have friends over, you can bake. Or just putter around in the morning if you're feeling sick or lazy." He put his hands on her shoulders and turned her back toward him. "Would you please say something? I'm concerned you're having a stroke."

She didn't know how she would've taken it if he hadn't just trapped her in a treehouse to bare his soul. She wanted to tell him how much this meant to her, how deeply understood she felt. But all she could do was cry. He'd given her so much more than a kitchen; he'd given her a domain. Independence. Normality. He pushed the hair away from her face and kissed her forehead.

"Darling, I was expecting a big reaction, but I didn't mean to break you."

She laughed at that, grabbing him around the waist into a tight hug. "Thank you," she whispered. "Thank you, Parker."

CHAPTER FORTY-TWO

Abbie and Edward's wedding day . . . finally

WHEN ABBIE APPEARED at the end of the aisle on Kurt's arm, Parker did not register the deep-red anemones or smoky-blue hydrangeas of her bouquet, nor the sea grass Abbie had tucked in herself. He did not notice the artful way her stylist had woven her hair around her head like a crown, nestling his grandmother's tiara inside, leaving a few trailing curls. He did not feel the way his white dress uniform was cutting into his neck or making him sweat. He did not see his mother and siblings beaming at his bride, nor his father's discreet tears. He did not hear his groomsmen's approving grunts, nor the bridesmaids' awed whispers.

He saw Abbie, though. His best friend. The love of his life. The girl who'd challenged him to footraces and ice-cream-eating contests would continue to challenge him, he knew, in new and interesting ways. Her dress was the only wedding detail that he did manage to take note of, and only because it suited her so entirely: white dimensional lace covered her chest and defined the top of her breasts. It cascaded from her shoulders, winding around her arms like ivy growing over her curvy body. It was not fluffy or ostentatious; its smooth, clean lines reflected her typical no-nonsense style. She looked like a wood nymph who'd just stepped out of an enchanted forest; he was afraid she'd disappear if he blinked. Over the string quartet, he could hear the dress swishing softly as she walked, and he was so entranced James had to nudge him when it was time for him to bring her up the stairs. They had about ten seconds to talk before the ceremony continued.

"Hi," she whispered.

"Hi," he breathed, feeling the word wholly inadequate. "You look incredible, darling."

"You don't look bad yourself."

"Compared to you, I'm rubbish. You're doing okay with all this?"

She nodded. "I'm just keeping my eyes on the prize." She leaned a bit closer. "That's you, by the way." His heart glowed brighter than all the candles filling the sanctuary.

Before he could respond, the priest began, "Dearly beloved, we are gathered in the sight of the Almighty Woznick to witness the union of this man and this woman . . ." Fortunately, the wedding planner, having seen Abbie's anxiety during the dress debacle, had arranged them so that Abbie's back was to the congregation, her train flowing down the steps. Unfortunately, this meant that the only contact he could manage, apart from a sidelong glance, was holding her hand. It felt appropriately innocent; he stroked her thumb with his, and she squeezed his hand in response. His mind wandered during the priest's short message, interspersed with Brevsporan proverbs likening love to mighty waters, unquenchable, as strong as death. He certainly felt that.

"Do you, Edward, embrace Abelia as your lifelong ship-mate, in storms and still water, in high tides and low, whether cruising or capsized?"

"I do," he replied.

"And do you, Abelia, embrace Edward as your lifelong captain, in storms and still water, in high tides and low, whether cruising or capsized?"

She had objected at first to the word *captain*, as he'd ex-pected she would. It would reflect poorly on the regency, he'd argued, if they were both shipmates with no leader at the helm. He didn't want people calling him a puppet king. And besides, he'd reasoned privately, it was true: they were a team, but sometimes, someone had to step up and pilot the ship. He felt certain he'd never wonder what her opinion was on a matter before having to make a decision, anyway. When they ran into sandbars and reefs, they'd navigate it together, even if he was at the helm.

"I do," she said, giving his fingers another squeeze before she dropped them.

"The couple will now ceremonially join their houses by the combining of water. Edward has brought the waters of the Orangiersian Ocean, Abelia, the waters of Lake Rhohn-rett, near the state castle in Kohlstadt." The tradition in Orangiers was sand, but that was a flawed metaphor, she'd pointed out. If you had enough patience, you *could* separate the grains of sand based on their chemical composition. On his mother's advice, they'd settled on water instead. Abbie had been nervous about her hands trembling as they poured it into the tall, clear vase, but she didn't spill a drop. He winked at her to share his congratulations, then poured his own water as well.

"Who then can separate one drop of water from another? Let these two people's lives be so saturated, so indistinguishable, so wholly intermingled as the waters in this vase."

Yes, Edward thought, staring at her, *it does feel like that. I don't know where she ends and I begin.*

The priest turned to his best man. "Do you have the rings?"

James patted his pockets, his brows drawing together, and Parker felt fear grip his heart.

"Just kidding." James grinned, pulling them off his fingers, and light laughter rippled through the crowd.

"I should've let Saint do it," Parker muttered, drawing smirks from his groomsmen.

"I'd say I'll do it next time, but there better not be a next time," Saint said.

"There won't be," Parker said, taking both Abbie's hands as they turned to face each other. She caught the congregation in her peripheral vision and stiffened. "Abs," he said softly, "stay with me." She looked up at him, her blue eyes full of vulnerability, but her shoulders dropped. He glanced at the priest to wrap it up quickly before she lost her cool.

"By the power vested in me by . . . well, technically, by the groom . . . ," the priest deadpanned, and the crowd chuckled again, "I hereby pronounce you husband and wife." He paused, and Parker felt his muscles winding up more and more by the second. Abbie had told him several times that she wanted their "first" kiss to be chaste, small, tongueless. She was giving him a warning glare now, as if she somehow sensed what he planned to do. But he wasn't going to let a single person walk out of this church wondering if he really wanted this woman in his life, doubting whether it was love or a contract that had brought them together.

"You may kiss the bride."

Quick as lightning, Parker slid his hand to the back of Abbie's neck and slung his other arm around her waist, dipping her over backwards as he kissed her deeply. She gasped and clung to the front of his uniform, more for stability than anything, he'd wager. But having little choice, she warmed immediately to the kiss, even caressing his tongue with hers. The crowd exploded into applause, and after a long moment, he put her back on her feet. She looked a bit dazed, and he carefully righted the priceless tiara that was now tilted to one side. In retrospect, he was rather lucky it hadn't toppled right off her head.

"May I be the first to present to you," the priest boomed over the noise, "King Edward Kenneth Keith Francis Benson Broward and Grand Duchess Abelia Olivia Jayne Venenza Ribaldi Porchenzii Broward."

"You're crazy, husband," she said, shaking her head, smiling. "You'd better watch out when we cut the cake."

"You married me, wife. Perhaps you're the one who's mad."

"Perhaps you're right," she said, taking his arm as the recessional started, and they made their way out of the sanctuary, "but I'm stuck with you now, aren't I?"

"TO THE BRIDE AND GROOM!" James yelled.

"To the bride and groom!" The table echoed, and Abbie took another bite of yet another strawberry she'd dipped in the chocolate fountain, giggling. Parker rolled his eyes; his friends were already a bit tipsy, and it was only two in the afternoon. He'd limited himself to one glass of wine, wanting to be sharp for what came next. Abbie was saying her goodbyes, giving out lots of hugs, getting lots of handshakes. They'd done their obligations; this was just bonus interaction with the people they cared about. It was hard not to be antsy, but he made himself keep from pacing or shifting his weight.

"All right, I know you're ready to go." She grinned, and his friends started hooting and howling, even Simonson.

"Get it, king!" James hollered. "Yes! It is *time*!"

"Saint?" Parker said, and Saint whacked James on the back of the head.

"Ouch? What was that for?"

"The whole county can hear you, you idiot."

"Thank you," Parker said. "You were closer."

"Of course, mate. Whatever you need," Saint said, lifting his mostly empty beer in salute.

Out of the corner of his eye, he could see his family gathering, and he gently tugged Abbie over to them by the elbow.

"See you all in a few weeks," he said. "You can relish the quiet of Bluffton without all the wedding nonsense happening."

His father was closest, and he wrapped Parker in one of his signature cobra hugs. "Take it *slow*," he muttered, "and have fun." Parker grinned at him over his shoulder as he moved toward his mother, who was crying again.

"Mum. Honestly."

"I know, I know. I'm sorry, son."

"They're happy tears," Abbie said, shedding a few of her own, and Lily nodded in agreement. At least he could count on Rhodie for a levelheaded, unemotional goodbye.

"Goodbye, Edward," she said, sticking out a hand for him to shake. "It was a lovely wedding."

"Thank you, Rhodie." He pulled her a little closer, then lowered his voice. "You want a postcard?"

"Absolutely not."

"Fine." He grinned. "Oh, before I forget, I'm sending Lieutenant James with you to Trella."

Her grip on his hand tightened. "No, you're not."

"Yes, I am. And you're hurting me."

"No, you're not."

"Yes, I am. Bye, Rhodie." Ignoring her frustrated expression, he wrenched his hand out of her grasp and turned to the twins.

"Girls, thank you so much for all your help with the wedding. You were indispensable. Truly."

They both blossomed under his praise, and he kissed their foreheads.

"Andrew."

"Congrats, brother. And I'll be ready to arm wrestle again when you get back, so don't slack off on the beach."

"Very well, I'll make you an appointment, but I'm very busy and important," he said, slapping him on the back. His brother rolled his eyes. Parker knew the hardest goodbyes were yet to come.

"Bye, Si, bye, Thia. Be good for Mum, do all your studies."

They both hugged him around his middle, and he put a hand on each head, chuckling. One of them said something into his shirt.

"Pardon? Didn't catch that . . ."

"Don't go." Simon lifted his head, his eyes brimming with tears. A cold realization came over Parker, and he took the boy by the shoulders.

"Are you afraid I'm going to disappear like Lincoln?"

Simon nodded, sniffling.

"Not going to happen, squirt. I promise. I'm just taking Abbie for a little holiday, and I'll be right back. All right? I will come back. You can count on it. In fact," he said, pulling out his phone, "I'm putting a spoons tournament into my schedule right now." He typed nonsense into his calendar. "There. The night I get home, it's on. You'd better practice." Simon hugged him again and sighed, happy this time, and he gave the boy a tight squeeze.

Parker stood and turned to Abbie.

"Ready, darling?"

She nodded, but said nothing. He helped her into her wool pea coat and they made their exit, waving to the many attendees waiting to throw rose petals.

"We're married," she said, as they climbed into the carriage.

"Yes." He grinned. "Happy?"

She nodded. "Very. Did you like my dress?"

"I *loved* your dress. I wish you'd brought it with us so I can unbutton it slowly . . ."

She blushed as she kissed him, ostensibly to shut him up.

"You didn't wait for me to stop talking."

"Nope. When you get going on sex, that could take for-ever."

"Well, good news," he said, kissing her again slowly, "we've got forever."

EPILOGUE

ABBIE GAZED OUT THE window. Parker was holding her hand, fiddling with her ring. Their blimp slowly descended toward La Bonisla, the Browards' private island. The staff did not disembark, she noted, and Parker spoke to them briefly before grabbing their bags himself. He started up the beach to the house perched on stilts just above them; she followed. Abbie unpacked on autopilot, leaving his suitcase untouched.

When she exited the walk-in closet, he was leaning against the bedroom doorway.

"Why don't you take a nap?"

She rubbed her face. "Because we just got here."

"So? We've got two weeks. Just lie down for a few minutes, and then we can explore the island all you want. I'm going to go read my book on the porch, and I don't want to see your lovely face for at least half an hour."

Abbie threw him a salute. *I must be tired if I'm just blindly obeying orders,* she thought, kicking off her sandals. The air was warm and scented with flowers; she could hear the waves throwing themselves against the white sand. She heard Parker turn on an overhead fan and felt him kiss her forehead as she dropped off into a hard sleep.

When she woke up, the sun was low against the mountains and the cicadas were starting to sing. She wandered into the bathroom and splashed water on her face. Parker came in from the screened porch, which apparently had a connecting door with the bedroom; she didn't know he'd been that close.

"So." He tossed his e-reader onto the bed. "What do you want to do now?"

Abbie shifted her weight uncomfortably. *We're in a bedroom. Our bedroom.* "What do *you* want to do now?" she echoed, twisting her rings. She glanced at him and then away. The half smile he was giving her said it all.

"I don't think I'm in charge here, darling." He was treating her like a frightened animal, avoiding sudden movements, not getting too close, as if he sensed the wild fear she was trying to contain. She hadn't been half as freaked out before she listened to Lauren and Georgie; she blamed them entirely.

"May I make some suggestions?"

She shrugged one shoulder. "You may."

"Would you like to take a walk on the beach?" The setting sun drew her eyes to the windows, as light streamed through the palm trees at the top of the mountains behind the house, bathing the sand in golden light. It was enticing, but Abbie found herself shaking her head.

"Are you hungry? I'm certain there's tons of food in the fridge."

"No." Abbie's heart was racing, and when she brushed the hair away from her face, she felt how cold her hands were. It had been such a long day, even with a nap. But her guilt at pushing him away was unbearable. He'd waited so long for this, been so patient. It's not that she didn't want to; she just wasn't ready to do it right this second, in this state of mind, after this amazing, incredible, exhausting day. It was the same old problem she'd always had; she struggled with transitions, coming down off the stress. Somehow, she hadn't anticipated having the same problem in this arena.

"How about a bath? You must promise to stay awake this time, though." He winked at her, and she tried to smile at him but found herself wrapping her arms around her middle, shaking her head a bit.

Girls in the romance novels never have this problem. They'd already be up against the wall with their legs wrapped around his waist.

The young king moved slowly toward her until he held her in his arms. "Abbie." His voice was so gentle, it cracked her heart. "There's no rush, you know." He rubbed her back lightly. "If you don't want to be together tonight, it's okay. This is not a command performance. We'll still be married tomorrow, and the next day . . ."

"Let's play a game." She didn't know where the thought came from, but it did sound appealing: limited physical exertion, maybe lighten the mood a little, distract herself with some good old-fashioned competition.

"What kind of game?" he asked, leaning back to see her better.

Abbie looked out the window, racking her brain. World Domination or Peril was too long. Go Fish was too puerile for her wedding night. War was certainly out, given the recent situation with Lincoln.

"What about strip poker?" he asked.

Perfect. A short reprieve while staying on the right track. "Are you good at strip poker?"

"Terrible." He smiled. "And you?"

"I've never played."

"Five-card draw okay?"

"Wait a minute; you're wearing twice as many clothes as I am. Nice try, Broward. Don't think you can pull one over on me just because I just woke up." Abbie disappeared into the closet, quickly stripped off her dress, and put on her sleep shorts, a camisole, a t-shirt, a sweatshirt, socks, and just for good measure, a baseball hat. She still had her bra and underwear on; that made nine pieces. At best, he probably only had seven: boxers, pants, undershirt, shirt, belt, and socks.

By the time she came back, he'd found a deck of cards and dealt, and turned on some mellow music through the house's sound system. He was stretched out on the white bedspread, killing time on his phone. At the sight of her, he cracked up.

"I've got to have a photo of this."

"Don't you dare."

"Too late." He grinned at her. "Now I can show our kids the sexy getup you put on for me on our wedding night."

"Lauren did get me something . . . else." *Does he want that? Should I change?*

Parker read the question on her face and shook his head. He pointed to the bed emphatically. "Come play poker with me. I'm literally going to beat the pants off you."

"You wish. I'm already cheating."

"I'd like to be surprised by that . . . You've got eight pieces?"

She shook her head, grinning.

"Well, I've got seven, so even it up, woman."

Scowling with mock consternation, she protested as she pulled off the hat and sweatshirt. "Someone who wants to get laid should let the woman cheat, FYI."

"Hey, you're the one who unwisely admitted her advantage. You brought this on yourself. Now sit down already."

Abbie sat on the bed, legs crossed like a pretzel, and picked up her cards. She already had two pair, jacks and threes. Three cards were also spades . . . She decided to play it safe and just trade in the seven. Parker appeared to be concentrating very hard, muttering under his breath, and it made her smile. He took two and glanced up at her.

"Full house: kings over eights."

She'd drawn a nine. Dang. "Who gets to decide what I take off?"

He kept a straight face. "I do. It's a real rule—don't ask questions. I choose your shirt."

Abbie set aside her cards carefully without breaking eye contact with him. She grabbed the edges of her shirt and watched his pupils dilate. In one swift motion, she pulled off the T-shirt, revealing the camisole underneath. His face fell in obvious disappointment, and she laughed.

"And that's exactly what you deserve for lying about the rules," she said, grinning, as she leaned forward onto her elbows and kissed him softly. His eyes betrayed his delight, and he grinned back at her. She sighed. Normal feelings. Normal feelings were good. The fear was quickly receding.

Seven hands later, things were not looking good for her win; they'd determined after a lot of heated discussion and an internet search that each sock was its own piece (he'd tried to demand they remain as a unit), and she still had on her underwear, camisole, and bra. But this hand was tricky; if she lost, something essential was coming off. He was staring at her expectantly, propped up on one elbow, his sleeves rolled to his elbows. Abbie was trying not to be distracted by his handsomeness, and she was fairly sure he was trying not to be distracted by her mostly bare body. She pulled her lips to the side, thinking. King of clubs, queen of diamonds, jack of clubs, nine of clubs, two of hearts. If she gave up the two and the nine, she had a chance at a straight if she pulled an ace and a ten or a ten and another nine. Then again, if she gave up the queen and the two, she could get a flush if she drew clubs. She arched her back, stretching, and he let out a frustrated sigh.

"Abs . . ."

"I'm thinking!"

"And yet it's time to play." His simmering patience had progressed to boiling anticipation, and she raised an eyebrow as she passed him the two and the nine. He slapped two cards down in front of her onto the white bedspread, and she peeked at the corners and cursed inwardly. A five and a two. That gave her . . . high card king. Wait; he was scowling, too . . .

"High card queen."

Abbie grinned. "High card king."

He shook his head, throwing down his cards. "I almost had you!"

"You almost did . . . but not quite. I choose your pants." Despite the fact that he was still wearing two shirts, Parker rolled onto his back and lifted his hips, pulling off his pants, revealing not only his gray boxers, but evidence of the growing desire they contained. Abbie's mouth went dry. She stared, her mind going off in several pleasant, distracting directions. When it came back, he had already dealt the next hand, never taking his eyes off her face.

She glanced at him over her cards. His burning gaze was getting to her. Her mind wouldn't focus, so she passed him all five cards. He passed her five more, a slow, hungry smile spreading across his face. Without looking at the cards, Abbie stood up and took off her camisole, then announced, "I need a drink," and fled into the kitchen before she could see his reaction. She took down a glass and filled it with water, trying to slow her heart.

Wait. What am I doing? Why am I trying to settle down? She checked that the stove was off, then marched back into the bedroom. Parker hadn't moved, hadn't dealt another hand.

"Get up."

He got off the bed and unbuttoned his dress shirt as Abbie took hold of the loose edge of the bedspread and snapped it to scatter cards all over the room. She slid under the covers, and he followed from his side, his hand sliding to her neck, drawing her into a deep kiss.

"Hello, Mrs. Broward."

"Hi there. You almost had me."

"I almost did. And now I will, if you don't mind."

Abbie smiled. "I don't mind at all."

Liked it? Hated it? Leave a review!

WHETHER THE PLOT MOVED too fast or too slow,
    Leave a review and let us all know!
    Was Abbie obnoxious? Was Parker a bore?
    Leave a review now; it's hardly a chore!
    Goodreads[1] and Amazon[2], wherever you bought,
    Please take a minute and share what you thought.
    Glowing reviews keep my business afloat,
    And at parties, they give me a reason to gloat.
    Thanks in advance!

Coming Soon: The Almost-Widow

Wondering what the deal is with Tezza? Is Sam ever going to quit being a wallflower? Well, wonder no more...their story will be released in episodes to my newsletter subscribers starting in July 2019! This novella was so fun to write, and I know you're going to enjoy watching these two fall in love. Here's a little taste of their story...you can sign up for my newsletter on my website: www.fionawest.net[3]

---

1.   https://www.goodreads.com/book/show/45888712-the-un-queen

2.   https://www.amazon.com/review/create-review/ref=cm_cr_dp_d_wr_but_top/error?ie=UTF8&channel=glance-detail&asin=B07S3XM6R6

3. http://www.fionawest.net

Episode One
SAM

"SIT DOWN, LIEUTENANT."

Sam Simonson sat down across from his commanding officer. The office was drab but orderly, much like the man who owned it. Colonel Pope folded his hands on the desk.

"First of all, we want to express our appreciation for your actions in the Heartwood Forest incident in Op'Ho'Lonia. You men spent a lot of time and effort looking for that traitor, Prince Lincoln, only to be attacked. You and Lieutenant Saint saved Lieutenant James' life. You're being awarded the King's medal for valor."

"Thank you, sir." He knew this already; being friends with the king had its advantages. He'd been friends with Edward since officer's training school. Saint had been as well, James even longer.

"But since your unit is going back into the reserves rather than active duty, we wanted to see if you'd be interested in a special assignment."

Why am I being given a choice?

"What kind of assignment, sir?"

"The king has requested you for his personal security staff. It seems that now he's a married man, he's a little more particular about who's standing outside his residence at night. But he made it clear that you should feel free to accept another assignment if you prefer." Sam was surprised that Edward hadn't said anything; he usually gave him a heads up about such things. Neither of them liked being put on the spot for a decision.

"What would that entail?"

"It's five twelve-hour shifts, 1700 to 0500 normally. You'd travel with His Majesty when necessary, but mostly, it's standing outside the residence with the Grand Duchess's security, Tezza Macias."

He remembered Macias. She was hard to forget, dressed head to toe in black, long black ponytail high on her head, toned stature. She was Op'Ho'Lonian; the winter weather had taken a toll on her skin tone, but it was decidedly more olive than the average light-skinned Orangiersian. The Grand Duchess, Abbie, had only had one close call with her opponents, and that wasn't on Macias's watch.

"Any idea why he asked for me specifically?"

Colonel Pope went on, "I believe His Majesty is concerned about the Grand Duchess's privacy as well as her safety...he expressed to me that he'd sleep better knowing that there's someone highly dependable outside their quarters."

Sam nodded. He considered himself dependable as well, and he was flattered to know that Edward trust him to keep him and Abbie safe. If that's what Edward needed, he'd be there for him.

"I'll do it."

"I'd also like to encourage you again to apply for a promotion, Lieutenant. There's no reason why you couldn't have your own command, especially now that you've got a commendation on your chest. It's the perfect time to think about moving up into your next role. You're a greater asset than you give yourself credit for."

"I'll think about it, sir."

The colonel's lips pressed into a line. "That's what you said last time, Simonson, but your request never crossed my desk." He gave him a pointed look over his reading glasses, and Sam looked away. He knew the colonel meant well, but he didn't know what to say. That problem wasn't likely to go away when confronted with a coworker like Macias...he hoped she wasn't chatty.

The colonel sighed. "You start tomorrow night. Report at 1630 for orientation. Dismissed."

"Thank you, sir." He left quickly, though there was no reason to. He'd be up all night anyway, trying to get his body on the right schedule. Maybe he could get James to stay up with him; he was always up for late-night shenanigans.

TEZZA

Tezza Macias set her groceries down on the counter of her bungalow and sighed. She'd gotten used to shopping late at night; after working the security night shift for months, that didn't bother her. Nor was she afraid to be out by herself. But the quiet in her house...that was something that still got under her skin, even now.

Two years, 105 days. Out of habit, she touched her husband's framed picture on the mantle as she searched for the remote to turn on the TV for background noise. The picture of her soldier used to live in her bedroom, but she'd relocated it to the mantle when she'd moved to Orangiers seven months ago to take this special assignment. She didn't know why. Grief was strange in that way; it never explained itself.

Magic gathered and pooled around her bare feet in a way that few could feel. Sighing, she flicked her wrist to turn on the TV, and she felt the magic ripple with pleasure. All her usage lately had been purely utilitarian, like most people inside the Veil. It wasn't that she couldn't do more, but lately, the drive just wasn't there.

Where are you, Rocco? Two years, 105 days ago, he'd called her to say he loved her just before he went incognito into a hostile area as a spy. According to the Op'Ho'Lonian special forces, they lost contact with him soon after that. She dropped to the floor and did some bicycle crunches, pushups, stretched her back. It was more productive than crying again. She'd fill her small house with the sound of exercise and television; it was better than letting the silence oppress her again.

They were showing footage of her employer's wedding again; she was amazed at this country's capacity for celebrity gossip. Then again, being meteorologically dreary this time of year, people did need something to keep them going, she supposed. King Edward, age 22, had married his fiance Abelia Porchenzii of Brevspor; they had been childhood friends, entering into an arranged marriage after signing a binding contract a decade before. It was a good match in many ways; both were a bit nerdy, bookish, intellectual, prone to banter and matching wits. Yet in Tezza's opinion, two stronger personalities had rarely been in the same room together, let alone shared a marriage. Abbie was now grand duchess rather than queen, due in part to a chronic illness that plagued her. Tezza didn't talk about that; silence was a virtue for a reason.

She'd been hired for her magical abilities; abilities that were now deteriorating from lack of use. As a non-tech magic user, she'd cultivated a relationship with the magic here in order to be able to protect the grand duchess during their engagement. Not everyone could feel the magic, but it had always been second-nature to her. And here, inside the Veil, the magic had been tamed—groomed, if you will—to be more open to sharing itself. Most people took advantage of this by purchasing devices powered by magic: cell phones, fridges, stoves, you name it. Even apart from the technology it powered, magic still required patience and the right words, but compared to the Unveiled, controlling it here was a cake walk. Tezza's abilities had been challenged just a few days before their wedding...but she'd protected the grand duchess when it counted. She'd take that secret to her grave; the spotlight held no attraction for her. Invisibility suited her best.

SAM

JUST RELAX. IT'S A job. A job you know well. Edward asked you. Sam stuck out his hand to the woman standing outside the palace security office.

"Good evening. We're assigned together, I believe. Sam Simonson."

She gave him a firm, business-like handshake. "Tezza Macias. Nice to meet you."

"Same."

They stood in silence. His nervousness began to extricate itself from his chest.

"Ready to go up?"

"Yes."

They climbed the back staircase to the king's residence and got a status update from the previous guard: the royals were in for the night. The previous watch had no issues to speak of. They'd be relieved at 0500.

They took up posts on either side of the double doors. *Am I supposed to talk to her? I've never observed Dean and Waldo working. They probably talk.* He glanced over at the woman, but she didn't acknowledge him. *Good. That's fine, silence is good.*

At 2200, he heard a noise that sounded like breaking glass. He immediately got a text.

Bluffton Security Central Dispatch: Outside sentries reported a crash inside the residence. Maintain radio silence.

Simonson: Investigating now.

He showed the screen to Macias, then pocketed his phone as he began to open the door to the residence.

"I can go," she said, putting a staying hand on his arm. *That's uncomfortably familiar,* he thought. There was a scent clinging to her...a perfume or shampoo or something...*plumeria. Gag.* "I'm quieter," she asserted.

His eyes narrowed as he stared at the doors to the king's residence beyond her. "What makes you think that?"

"Watch." She started into the residence, and then she...faded. He didn't know how else to describe it. It was as if someone put a transparency filter on her. She turned to look at him, as if to say, "well?"

He nodded, then flicked his hand to say, "go for it." She disappeared around the corner, and a few minutes later she came back with a look on her face he couldn't interpret.

"Find anything?"

"It was nothing."

"It was nothing because you found nothing or because you know what the sound was?"

"The royals knocked over a lamp while having intercourse."

"Ah. I'll let him know." She didn't seem embarrassed by this in the least. In fact, though he struggled to read other people's nonverbals, if he had to guess, he'd say she was amused. He was also a little amused, but didn't let it show. *Professionalism and all that.* The night shift was bound to have more intimate moments between them. They were lucky Arron James wasn't in his place or he'd be telling everyone within a five-mile radius.

She resumed her previous stance as he texted Central Dispatch back, giving them the all clear. He also let them know that the royals were awake and would likely be making more noise shortly. But in the back of his mind, the questions wouldn't leave him alone. He turned back to her.

"Did you speak with them?"

"No."

"Then how do you know they broke a lamp?"

"I could hear them laughing about it through the bedroom door, making bets on which of us was going to draw the short straw."

Sam grinned at his shoes; he was glad to hear they were laughing. Before Abbie, Edward didn't laugh enough. "Who guessed correctly?"

"She did. He thought you'd be more protective, more likely to burst through the door."

"A fair assessment." He wasn't embarrassed either. His friends had given him a hard time often enough about his naivete that it was no surprise Edward thought so.

"Perhaps in part, but I'm very protective as well. She's a good person."

"They both are."

"Agreed."

They settled back into the silence, broken a few minutes later by two muffled wordless cries from the residence, first hers, then his. Since Macias didn't react and he received no more text messages, he decided to follow her lead on this one. They didn't speak again until 0500 when their shift was over.

"Headed home?" He didn't know why he asked her that. It was probably intrusive.

"No," she shook her head, "I'm meeting my sister."

"Oh. Well, enjoy your time with her."

"Thanks. See you tomorrow."

"Yeah."

Edward was exiting the residence just as he started to walk away. "Hey, fancy a run?"

Sam shrugged. "Why not?"

"That's the spirit."

"How are you so chipper so early in the morning?" Sam asked.

"I have an exceptional constitution, mate, for I am exceptional person."

Sam grinned. "Bollocks."

"Cuts me right to the heart, that does. How was your first night of work?"

"Fine."

Edward glanced at him. "Fine? Just...fine?"

Sam nodded.

"How's Macias to work with?"

"She seems very competent. Last night, I watched her fairly fade away when she went to check on...um." He realized what he was saying too late and felt his face heat. Though they were both black, Sam envied Edward's darker complexion. He was sure Edward could tell he was blushing, given that he was grinning from ear to ear.

"Drat it all, Abbie was right. Don't tell her, all right?"

"Why, what'd you wager?"

"If she was right about who checked, there's a new horror movie she's going to make me watch. What Lies Underfoot, or something. She says my jumping and cringing is the best part." He gave an exaggerated shudder and Sam smiled at his shoes.

"Just let me change and I'll meet you outside."

"Sounds good."

Though they didn't usually talk much on their runs, Edward's confusion over his new bride's quirks seemed to give him plenty to discuss.

"She can't retire without doing in the dishes. Even if she's exhausted, falling-down tired. She'll stand there and wash them all up. You'd never know she'd been raised royal."

"I find that very practical. The scent of dirty dishes alone can ruin my morning."

"You're a bit more sensitive than most in that, mate."

"True." That hadn't stopped his mother from expecting him to wash them. It wasn't like she had time, working with his father, and she believed exposing him to the things that bothered him would be "good exposure therapy." She wasn't wrong, but that hadn't made it any less uncomfortable. Sam didn't usually mind that his family and friends were attuned to his sensory issues; for his last birthday, Edward had given him noise-cancelling headphones which were now part of his essential equipment. They understood how overstimulating it felt to look someone in the eye...at least, they understood in theory.

"What's the best part of being married?" Edward grinned and opened his mouth to answer when Sam cut him off. "Besides finally getting a leg over."

He feigned offense. "Is that any way to talk about my delicate grand duchess?"

Sam snorted. "I've heard her say worse."

"So have I. Just this morning, in fact, she rolled over and asked me to..."

Sam held up a hand. "Stop. It's bad enough I have to hear it through the door."

Edward turned them back toward Bluffton, on the path along the sea cliffs. "In all seriousness, the best part is living with my best friend. She knows it all; the good and the bad. She's always there for me. I love that."

Sam nodded. He would, too. But at this point in his life, it seemed about as possible as crossing the Orangersian ocean in a bathtub.

Acknowledgments

- To my family: thank you for patience when Mama was on a roll and just couldn't stop typing, even though you needed my help. And thank you for believing in me, cheering me on, every step of the way!
- To my editors, Sylvia Cottrell and Jessica Gardner: your insights are invaluable. Thanks for helping me polish my work and put out the best book we can!
- To my beta readers, Angela, Liz, Rebecca, Melissa and Christine: you give such wonderful feedback! I can't imagine doing this without your help.
- To my writing group, Ruth, Magalie and Ashley: thank you for your steady presence in my life; you are a source of joy to me. I love our deep talks, our obscure musings. Your kindness in handling my first drafts makes it easy to share with you.
- To my cover artist, Steven Novak: Thanks for your persistence in getting our favorite couple just right! You rock.

Connect with Fiona!

THANKS SO MUCH FOR taking the time and spending the money to sample my work. I hope you enjoyed reading it even more than I enjoyed writing it, though I doubt that's possible. Being an author is a dream come true, and getting to share my books with delightful, thoughtful readers like you just adds to the sweetness. Drop me a line and let me know what you thought or leave a review on Goodreads!

Sign up for my monthly newsletter[4], The West Wind, for exclusive stories, deleted scenes, book reviews, and insight into my writing process.

On Twitter as @FionaWestAuthor[5]

On Facebook as @authorfionawest[6]

On Instagram as fionawestauthor[7]

On Goodreads as Fiona West[8]

Or email me at fiona@fionawest.net. I love talking to fans!

---

4.   https://wordpress.us12.list-manage.com/sub-
   scribe?u=3a2e64902a6f932607cd9da1a&id=ac0f3bc5d8

5.   https://twitter.com/FionaWestAuthor

6.   https://web.facebook.com/authorfionawest/

7.   https://www.instagram.com/fionawestauthor/

8.   https://www.goodreads.com/author/show/18433825.Fiona_West

RFIC WEST #2
West, Fiona (Fantasy romance author
The un-queen /
WB   1268677

02/10/20   **Ramsey County Library**
              Shoreview, MN 55126

CPSIA information can be obtained
at www.ICGtesting.com
Printed in the USA
LVHW020413301119
638996LV00003B/102

9 781732 877450